GIVEN
THE
CRIME

ALSO BY CHARLES DENNIS

Novels

Shar-li
The Dealmakers
Bonfire
A Divine Case of Murder
The Periwinkle Assault
This War Is Closed Until Spring
Somebody Just Grabbed Annie!
The Next-to-Last Train Ride
Stoned Cold Soldier

Plays

Soho Duo
Going On
Significant Others
Altman's Last Stand
Everyone Except Mr. Fontana

GIVEN THE CRIME

MARGARET BARRETT
AND
CHARLES DENNIS

POCKET BOOKS
New York   London   Toronto   Sydney   Tokyo   Singapore

POCKET BOOKS, a division of Simon & Schuster Inc.
1230 Avenue of the Americas, New York, NY 10020

Copyright © 1998 by Rangeloff-Century, Inc.

Library of Congress Cataloging-in-Publication Data

Dennis, Charles, 1946–
  Given the crime / Charles Dennis.
    p. cm.
  ISBN: 0-671-00151-5
  I. Title
PR9199.3.D44G58   1998
813'.54—dc21   97-24075
                                                         CIP

First Pocket Books hardcover printing January 1998

10 9 8 7 6 5 4 3 2 1

Printed in the U.S.A.

"Commit a crime and the earth
is made of glass."
—Ralph Waldo Emerson

GIVEN THE CRIME

LORETTA TESLA WONDERED why God was punishing her so after forty years of marriage. On the proudest night of her husband's life and hers as well, why was she suffering from gas?

Sitting on the dais in the Grand Ballroom of New York's Waldorf-Astoria Hotel, staring out at a sea of family, friends, and political big shots all gathered to pay tribute to Nicolo Tesla. But was Loretta basking in the reflected glory of the speeches that the Deputy Mayor, the Lieutenant Governor, and His Eminence George, Cardinal Corcoran, were making in praise of her husband? No, she was running through her mental directory of saints, praying to whomever that her body would not betray her and humiliate her family by emitting any embarrassing sounds from some unfriendly orifice. Why tonight?

A devout Catholic, Loretta prayed on a minute-to-minute basis for protection. That morning when the workmen had erected the scaffolding to repair the kitchen ceiling of her luxurious Glen Cove home, she had prayed to Bartholomew, the patron saint of plasterers, that no harm would befall these men or her kitchen. She lit a candle every day in tribute to St. Nicholas of Myra, the guardian of children, to watch over her beloved daughters and their little ones. And, whenever there was an unpleasant article about her husband on TV or the radio, Loretta would light candles to both the Archangel Gabriel and St. Raymund Nonnatus. The former being the patron saint of broadcast-

1

ers, Loretta would ask forgiveness for these misguided people who spread such falsehoods about her beloved Nick; the latter being the guardian of the falsely accused, she would pray to this saint to clear up the misunderstandings that constantly plagued her husband simply because he was an Italian who had made good in America.

But what about her gas? Should she pray to St. Martha, who watched over the cooks, to rescue her from the afteraffects of the hotel's bill of fare? Or did her dilemma fall into the bailiwick of St. Jude, who protected the faithful from all desperate situations? Ohhh! What pain, what discomfort. Perhaps the Cardinal might know to whom she should turn. She would ask him when he stopped speaking.

"When they asked me to say a few words this evening," said Cardinal Corcoran, standing in front of the microphone, staring out at the well-heeled crowd through steelrimmed glasses and clasping his hands behind his back, looking all the world like the fullback he had been at Notre Dame forty years earlier, "I refused at first. Yes, I did. How could I possibly limit myself to 'a few words' about a man who has been a pillar of both his community and the church? Volumes! That would be more like it. Ask me to speak volumes. Hopefully, a compromise was reached and I won't keep you here all night." The Cardinal licked his lips playfully and the audience roared with laughter. His Eminence raised his arms to silence them.

"But seriously, folks, as a former generation of comics was wont to say, we're here to honor Nicolo Tesla. Loretta's beloved Nicco. Mr. Nick, as the waiters all refer to him at his restaurant. Ah! that restaurant. I don't eat there as often as I'd like. I've had more luck battling for souls than battling my waistline after a hearty lunch at your place, Nick."

"Order half portions," chirped Nick Tesla, patting his

2

ample but hard stomach under his tuxedo jacket. "That's what I do, Your Eminence."

"Would it were that easy. But we're not here to talk about your food or your wonderful family, who are gathered here to pay tribute this evening. Your daughters Beatrice and Lucy, with their husbands and their beautiful children. Your daughter Antonia—little Toni—when are you going to stop breaking all the boys' hearts and settle down? And finally, little Nick Tesla . . . Junior . . . the apple of your father's eye."

The Cardinal had stared down at the ringside table where the Tesla children were seated and his acknowledgment was greeted by a warm smile from each child—except Junior, who was nowhere to be seen.

"We're heeeere," said George Corcoran, dragging out the word and sounding remarkably like Pat O'Brien impersonating Notre Dame's most famous coach, Knute Rockne, "to pay tribute to Nick Tesla, the environmentalist. Nick Tesla, who keeps our streets clean. Nick Tesla, who made the word 'garbage' beautiful for this generation of New Yorkers."

The Cardinal's speech was interrupted by a dreadful hacking cough from a table near the kitchen. He pulled his wire glasses down the length of his nose, peered out at the crowd, and spoke: "I'd know that cough anywhere. Ray Murphy, give up those dreadful cigarettes. I'm not ready to officiate at your wake yet, Ray." Polite laughter from the audience, then the Cardinal continued with his tribute.

The other reporters at Ray Murphy's table stared in terror at the veteran tabloid columnist who was, indeed, going through monumental paroxysms. At first this sixtyish, stocky, gray, buzz-cut alcoholic old wreck seemed an anachronism in the world of laptops and sound bites, a character more suited to a Warner Brothers city room playing cards with the likes of Barton MacLane, Frank McHugh, and Roscoe Karns. But "the Murph" had a nose for news, knew everybody in the city, and still came up with one good scoop a month.

Christ on a crutch! thought Murphy, even as his seared lungs were betraying his very existence. George Corcoran, God's most valuable player. Played too many games without a helmet, Georgie. Sitting on the wrong side of the bleachers tonight. But then Mother Church was always willing to forgive its bad boys, who donated their ill-gotten gains so generously to the collection plate. And the city fathers, too. Look at them all praising Caesar. Ask the widows and orphans of the men who dared stand up to Tesla and his ilk how they feel about the great man. Ask the honest garbage carters, who tried to make a living by charging a fair and lower tariff for their labor. If you can find one. Tesla and his pals chased them all out of town long ago. Mmmm. That'd make a good column for the weekend if those chicken-shit lawyers didn't talk the publisher out of it.

When the coughing had finally subsided, Murphy looked up at his breath-holding colleagues and asked in his vintage sandpaper voice: "Anybody got a smoke?"

"You had us worried there, Murph," laughed Draycott Simms III, a young hotshot from the *Times.*

"That's who you should really be worried about, kid," replied Murphy, nodding toward the dais, where Cardinal Corcoran was shaking hands warmly with Nick Tesla.

The man of the hour rose a moment later to speak, sniffed something, clasped his hand over the microphone, and asked his wife: "What's that smell?"

Loretta stared at her husband blankly and said a silent prayer to John of God, the patron saint of heart patients, to deliver her from a stroke.

Then the robust, silver-haired Tesla cleared his throat and began to speak into the microphone: "My parents came to this country for refuge. But when I was little I didn't understand the words and thought they came for 'refuse.' Little did I know sixty years later, a man could build a life on this refuse."

Tesla's speech was interrupted by thunderous applause. He'd used that refuge/refuse story a thousand times and it always worked. Broke the ice. Warmed the crowds. And this was some crowd. Everybody was here. . . . Except Junior. Where the hell was Junior?

WALTER GERHARDT WALKED away from the darkened dispatch office of Osborne Paper Fiber in the shadow of the Manhattan Bridge. Gerhardt was pleased with the assignment he had pulled for later that evening. Night pickups paid extra and, with his wife expecting another kid in the new year, the money would come in handy. A car horn tooted at him; it was the dispatcher waving good night.

Gerhardt climbed up into the cab of the disposal truck and waited for his partner to arrive. Goddamn Teddy! He was always late. Probably chasing some tail up in the Bronx. Let him get married and see what punctuality is all about. Gerhardt's wife, Nancy, always teased Walt for being "a real German" about efficiency. Let her tease. He was proud of being efficient and of being from good German stock.

Headlights flashed in his eyes. Was this Teddy? Stupid bastard has his brights on.

The car's motor stopped but the lights stayed on. Gerhardt squinted. No, it wasn't Teddy. No way he drove a Ferrari.

"There's one of the stupid fucks now," said the handsome, muscular thirty-something man seated behind the steering wheel of the Ferrari wearing a black tie and dinner jacket.

"Wha' you said?" The muscular man's companion spoke in a thick Cuban accent. He was long and lean and was distracted by the tiny spoon from whose bowl he was attempting to snort cocaine up his aquiline nose.

"Gimme a toot."

"Just a second, man. I ain't finished."

"You got a fuckin' nose like an anteater, Manny. There'll be nothin' left by the time you're finished."

"What the hell we doin' here anyhow, Junior? Ain' you supposed to be at your father's birthday party?"

"It's not his birthday, you goddamn iggie. He's getting an award from God."

"No shit!"

"All shit, Manny. All shit. Now, you see that truck there?"

"I don't see nothin', man. I'm so fuckin' wrecked."

"This is a job, Manny. Get it together, okay?"

"Gimme a break, Junior. I'm off duty now."

"What is this bullshit? Whaddaya belong to the Legbreakers Union or somethin'? You fuckin' go to work when I tell ya, Sanchez."

"Wha' you wan' me to do?"

"The guy in the truck. See the guy? See the truck? Go warn him."

"About what?"

"He's a fuckin' outlaw. He's stealin' our spots. Lean on him a little. Get goin'."

"I don' wanna get dirty, man. I gotta date tonight."

"A date? You mean some hoor up in Washington Heights. All you know is store-bought pussy, Sanchez."

"I got a wife, man."

"She ain't much. I had her twice. The second time was to make sure she was as bad as I remembered."

6

"Don' you make jokes about my wife," said Sanchez seizing Junior by the lapels of his tux.

"You don't even live with her."

"That don't mean I don't love her. You stay away from my women, Junior. I kill you, you touch one of my women."

"I just shit in my pants, Manny. Now, do you wanna put some of that macho bullshit to work or do we ship you back to Castro with my old Ricky Ricardo records?"

The Cuban spat something out in Spanish, then swung his long legs out of the sports car.

Junior Tesla watched as his hired gun strode unsteadily across the parking lot. He saw the driver step down from his cab to see what Sanchez wanted. The two exchanged words, becoming more vocal and aggressive with each retort. Then Sanchez pushed the driver back against the truck. Junior nodded approvingly. Attaboy, Manny. Give him a little pain now. Give him something to remember you by. Maybe he won't go bowling for a year. What the—? The Cuban was walking back toward the Ferrari and the driver was opening his door. What was that in his hand? A tire iron? Fuck you, Mighty Mouse. Junior reached behind his seat and pulled out his Club.

"Yer a fuckin' moron, Manny," said Junior, maneuvering his overdeveloped body out of the sports car.

"What I did?"

"Done. And you ain't done shit. Get outta the way!"

Junior hefted the antitheft device known as the Club in his right arm as he advanced toward Gerhardt.

"I'm warning you," said Gerhardt as Junior drew closer to him.

"You're warning me?" laughed Junior. "Who the hell are you to warn me? You're the fuckin' interloper." And Junior swung the Club powerfully, causing the tire iron in Gerhardt's hand to vibrate. "You people were warned—"

"It's a free country," said Gerhardt, trying to disguise the fear in his voice. Where the hell was Teddy?

Junior began to laugh hysterically, then took the Club

7

and smashed the window on the driver's side of the cab. "That's the funniest thing I ever heard," said Junior, and continued to whack away at the window until it finally cracked.

Gerhardt raised the tire iron and brought it down on the back of Junior's right shoulder. Anyone else might have writhed in pain instantly but Junior merely turned around in annoyance and growled: "That was stupid."

Junior raised the Club and brought it down ferociously on Gerhardt's skull. The last thing the trucker saw before he lost consciousness was the image of his wife, Nancy, six months pregnant. Junior continued pounding away mercilessly at Gerhardt's body.

Sanchez watched in horror as his employer reduced the blond truckdriver to a heap of bloody pulp. Finally Junior called out: "Hey, Manny! Come help me get rid of this garbage."

The Cuban walked mechanically toward the crumpled, bleeding body. Then some instinct for self-preservation—the same one that got him safely out of Cuba as a teenager—told him to get the hell out of there now. He might be a legbreaker but he wasn't a murderer. Sanchez turned on his heels and began running away from the parking lot.

"Manny! Get back here! Manny, you goddamn wetback. I'll find you. Get your ass back here or . . ."

The Cuban had vanished into the darkness. Junior Tesla was furious. He picked up the Club and began to pound away at Gerhardt's skull until pieces of bone and flesh tore loose and flew up into his face. Junior stopped. The rage had vanished and was now replaced by a familiar sense of betrayal and abandonment. He'd have to talk to his shrink about it in the morning.

ONE WEEK LATER and several miles north on the Upper East Side, the Patterson family (formerly of Tulsa, Oklahoma) was starting to rise in their furnished Sixty-eighth Street sublet between Park and Lexington. MarSue Patterson found the rented antique furnishings a bit oppressive and missed her own Southwest bed and decor from back home but her husband, Tom, was superstitious. He wasn't prepared to take the stuff out of storage until they knew for certain that his company was really going to have a chance in Manhattan against the ancient fiefdoms that controlled the business.

Ancient fiefdoms? Who was he kidding. The mob. Okay? The garbage business was in the hands of organized crime and had been for over forty years. And what chance did a bunch of yahoos from Oklahoma think they had in breaking that stranglehold? Even if these yahoos did run the second-biggest national carting company in the country. New York City was out of bounds. Hell, everyone except the police seemed to know that the poor Osborne trucker who was beaten to death the previous week had dared to cross the mob.

But Tom Patterson's boss was fifth-generation Oklahoman and he just didn't like taking no for an answer. And Tom was as stubborn as the old man. So here he was in New York with his wife and daughter, determined to give it a shot. Speaking of which, he rolled his long, gangly body over and wrapped an arm around his short, plump wife.

9

"What time is it?" groaned MarSue Patterson, her Oklahoma twang out of place on the Upper East Side.

"It's that time," growled Tom playfully, taking marching orders from his morning erection.

"Oh, it's always that time for you. The question is: have we *got* time?"

"Y'all know what Einstein said about time."

"What about Nellie?" asked MarSue, pulling her nightgown over her head.

"She's too young to have sex."

MarSue groaned and whacked her husband's arm, then said: "I'm worried about her."

"What now?" Tom felt his erection beginning to shrink.

"You make that sound as if I had an endless list, Tommy." Then MarSue pulled her nightgown back on.

"I guess we don't have time," said Tom, whose erection had now vanished with the reappearance of his wife's nightgown. He rolled over and contemplated getting into the bathroom before MarSue did.

"Come back here, Tom Patterson. It isn't funny. This Chester business is very disturbing to her."

"What can we do about it, MarSue? The dog ran away."

"How can you just dismiss Chester as 'the dog'? He's a part of this family. He's been with Nellie all her life."

"I've done everything I can to find him, honey. Short of hiring a private detective. A hundred-and-fifty-pound sheep dog just doesn't vanish. I don't know what more you can expect me to—"

"This isn't about you, Tom. It's Nellie's problem. This move to New York has been very traumatic for her and having Chester around was the one positive—"

"She loves it here!"

"She doesn't have any friends."

"What about that Mexican kid?"

"She's not Mexican. She's Salvadoran. And she's adopted."

"What does that mean?" Miracle of miracles: his erection had returned once more.

"Her parents aren't Hispanic. They're divorced."

"What country is that?" asked Tom as he slid his hand up underneath his wife's nightgown.

"This is *not* the time even if there was time."

The front door bell rang.

"Jesus!" groaned Tom. "It's ten to seven. Who the hell can that be?"

"I'll get it." And MarSue bounded out of bed.

Seconds later Tom Patterson stood under the shower soaping his body and wondering whether it was moving to New York, twelve years of marriage, or encroaching middle age. Whatever it was, something had wreaked havoc on his sex life.

Then he heard the scream. Even with the water pouring down on his head, he could hear MarSue's piercing wail. Wrapping a towel around his waist, Tom dashed out into the front hallway.

"What—what happened?" He stared at his wife, who was standing in the formal dining room, pointing toward the antique Chippendale table.

A pink cake box lay open on the dining table. As Tom advanced toward it, MarSue gasped abruptly: "Nellie! My God! Nellie mustn't see it."

"See what?"

Before she could reply, her daughter's voice called out from her bedroom: "Mommy! Daddy! What's wrong?"

MarSue spun around and tried to intercept Nellie before the child wandered sleepily into the room.

Advancing toward the open pink cake box, Tom stared in disbelief at what he saw: Chester's severed head. The tongue was protruding from the decapitated sheepdog's mouth and stapled to the tongue was a piece of paper— a note—which read: "Welcome to New York."

Tom's instincts had been right. The dog had not run away. Someone had snatched it. And the six-foot Oklahoman knew exactly who the kidnappers were.

"Please, Nellie, don't go in there!"

But ten-year-old Nellie Patterson broke loose from her mother's restraint and ran into the dining room. She stared in horror at the atrocity in the pink cake box. Then she began to scream and scream. Her parents were powerless to comfort her.

SUSAN GIVEN OPENED her eyes and stared at her bedside table. The tall glass of water she had placed in front of her digital clock the night before was obscuring the numbers. She could make out the 0 and the 2. But what preceded those two numerals remained a mystery. She reached her hand out and moved the glass of water. Still no good. She'd taken her contacts out the night before. She groped behind the water to find her reading glasses.

Oh, no! It was a seven. Not a six. 7:02 A.M. How had she slept so late? It was those dreams again. She was back in Jerusalem with Michael. Forget Michael. He's gone. It was a brief interlude, a strange interlude, some enchanted evening. How many times must she wash that man right out of her hair and similar Oscar Hammerstein motivational lyrics? Still she found herself thinking about Michael Roth constantly.

Where had he disappeared to after they'd said their good-byes so tenderly in the Tel Aviv airport six months earlier? Had their romantic five days together in Israel been a mirage? The first man she had cared for since her husband Hugh's departure had vanished in a puff of smoke. Perhaps she had put a curse on the relationship when she said: "Thank God you don't live in New York."

Wake up, Susan! Michael might just as well live in New York, considering the monkey wrench his dream visit had thrown into her schedule that September morning.

She opened her blinds and stared out at her view of Manhattan south of Eightieth Street with a corner of Central Park peeking out in the west. Then she was rocked into annoyance by the sight of her grimy curtains. When, oh when, were the new curtains and matching bedspread going to be delivered? And what about the floor men? They had promised her two months ago that the hardwood floor in the bedroom would take no more than— Stop it! Stay focused. You're a crime fighter. Not Martha Stewart. What was that noise in the wall? Inside the wall of her bedroom. Listening devices? Which of her defendants had installed them and how had they gotten past Cordelia Brown, her stalwart St. Kitts housekeeper? And had she become completely paranoid?

"Hardly," said Susan aloud, stretching out the vowel in her best patented New England tones. A good run would restore her to reality. Whipping her Mickey Mouse nightshirt over her head, she began searching for her jogging clothes. Where was her sweatshirt? Had Polly "borrowed" it again without telling her? What was the use of fighting crime when your own daughter was constantly ripping off your clothes? So she wouldn't match that morning. When did she ever? Settling for a faded pair of blue sweatpants and a "You Don't Know Me" Federal Government Witness Relocation Program sweatshirt, Susan Given was ready for—Oh, no. This was Wednesday. She was doing that live TV show at 9:00 A.M. Which meant she wouldn't have time for her usual four-mile run around Central Park. Oh, well, a quick turn around the Reservoir was better than nothing.

Rushing out of her bedroom, Susan collided with her fourteen-year-old, Salvadoran-born, adopted daughter,

Polly, stumbling like a blind person toward the bathroom in her red plaid Gap pajamas.

"What on earth are you doing up at this hour?" asked Susan.

Polly muttered something inaudible.

"I can't hear you," replied Susan.

"I've got basketball tryouts at seven-thirty," said Polly, enunciating every syllable with barely disguised annoyance.

"Oh, great! You made the team."

"Tryouts, Mother. Tryouts. Don't get excited. They're not going to have a dwarf on the team." Polly was sensitive about her five-foot-one-inch height.

"Is Ivy up, too?" asked Susan switching subjects to avoid a confrontation with her daughter.

"As if!" snorted Polly gazing in the direction of the other bedroom, where her ten-year-old adopted sister was still fast asleep. Then it was the teenager's turn to shift gears: "Mom? Can I borrow forty dollars?"

"Nooo. What for?"

"Never mind." And Polly vanished into the bathroom.

Forty dollars, mused Susan as she waited for the elevator to pick her up from the twelfth floor of her Upper East Side duplex. What does she need forty dollars for? Victoria's Secret? More bizarre lingerie that she'll never wear and I'll have to take back. Or, perhaps, it's another of those midnight telephonic assignations that she keeps with one of "the trained operators standing by to take your call" at J. Crew's mail-order 800 number. "Many happy returns," was definitely Polly's motto.

"Morning, Mrs. Carver Given," muttered Rocco, the slightly deaf, septuagenarian elevator man.

"Given Carver." This was possibly the five hundredth time Susan had corrected Rocco. "Actually, I just use Given now. Since the separation."

"Nah. I don't think it's gonna rain," replied the elevator man out of left field. "How's the numbers racket?"

"I beg your pardon?"

"Yer daughter tells me you're closing in on the spic numbers guys. It's about time."

Susan stared at Rocco and wondered which of her daughters had said what—if anything—about her policy bank case to the elderly elevator operator.

"Thanks for the tip," said Susan as the door opened on the lobby level. She had hoped to give the elevator man a dose of his own incoherent medicine.

"Any time," said Rocco cheerfully.

There was a touch of Indian summer that morning as the blond, hazel-eyed assistant district attorney began jogging along Eightieth Street toward Fifth Avenue and the entrance to Central Park. She could just make out the southern corner of the Metropolitan Museum, which reminded her to mail in her membership renewal.

Moments later she had joined the early morning pack of Upper East Side joggers ascending the steps toward the Jacqueline Onassis Reservoir path.

"Hi, Susan!"

She turned her head around in time to see unctuous Walter Sussman from the District Attorney's Appeals Bureau zipping past her.

"Congratulations!" he called over his shoulder.

"What for?"

"Later."

What had she done to warrant Walt Sussman's sucking up to her? What *hadn't* she done? Now, now, Susan. Being the head of the Manhattan District Attorney's Asset Forfeiture Unit hardly qualified one for the throne to the right of Zeus. It was hard work and long hours of painstaking—Save all that for the TV interview. Who are we going after today? Davis Kumba this morning and—at long last—Vinh Ho Chi and the Evanston Hotel. Stay focused, Susan. Sort through the case load. Top priority: the Evanston Hotel. Vinh Ho Chi would not bamboozle her again.

Back in the 1920s and '30s, the Evanston had been a literary haven for the likes of Dashiell Hammett and John O'Hara. Now the Gramercy Park hostelry had fallen on hard and sordid times and was the jewel in Vinh Ho Chi's chain of narcotics supermarkets.

Vinh had been a panderer and drug dealer in South Vietnam. But he had also been a CIA informant, whose work for the agency had bought him his green card and a seemingly endless list of paybacks in Washington and Langley to bail him out of past problems. He certainly carried on his present illegal activities as though he were still operating in freewheeling Saigon, where government intervention could always be avoided by an envelope bulging with currency.

The Evanston was known on the street as "Drugs 'R' Us": an anything-goes operation where drugs and sex were available on every floor at any hour of the day. A locked door meant a business deal was going down; your patience was appreciated. Otherwise, the doors were wide open in every room depending on what your pleasure and/or perversion was.

Susan had played it by the book in her attempts to get the Vietnamese landlord to clean up his act. She had sent Vinh several letters outlining the problems with his hotel and what it would take to restore the establishment from its present state of decrepitude and banish the presence of felons to her office's satisfaction. All her letters had been ignored.

Finally she had convinced Vinh's lawyer that a show-down was inevitable and a meeting was arranged at the Evanston for that afternoon as a final attempt to settle matters in an amicable fashion. After that—if the terms could not be met—she would turn the matter over to Ned Jordan in the U.S. District Attorney's office. (Even though a 1990 amendment gave New York State long-needed teeth as to what Asset Forfeiture could or could not lay its hands on, the seizure of real property remained almost solely in the hands of the feds).

Fifteen minutes later a hot and perspiring Susan descended the stairs from the Reservoir and jogged along the outer perimeter of the park toward Cleopatra's Needle. What was that story Michael had told her about the filming of *Cleopatra*? Forget Michael. Stay focused. Crime never sleeps.

Returning to her building, she discovered Nolan Parnell, a reject from Dublin's Abbey Theatre, guarding the front door.

"Are youse in court today?" the Irish doorman asked conspiratorially.

"Actually, I am. Thanks for reminding me." What to wear? What to wear? "Where did Rocco go?"

"Waterworks. So? Is it a juicy one?" asked Parnell, as he closed the cage on the wood-paneled *trompe l'oeil* elevator.

"What?"

"Yer case. Murder?"

"I don't try murders, Nolan. I seize criminals' assets." And that morning Susan would be going after the $300,000 a shady operator named Davis Kumba had bilked out of 150 expatriate Ugandan football fans. Unless, of course, Judge Silverberg had managed to lose his remaining marbles during the night.

"I love a good murder."

"Sorry, I can't help you there, Nolan."

Susan entered her apartment and prayed that Ivy would be dressed and eating something in the kitchen. She peeked her head round the corner. No Ivy.

Then she heard the sound again. In the wall. The same sound as before. What the hell was that?

"Ivy! Ivy!"

She must be in the bathroom, thought Susan, as she climbed the stairs to the second floor. 7:40. How did it get to be 7:40? She recoiled in horror as she stuck her head inside Ivy's bedroom and saw that her raven-haired, Salvadoran-born younger daughter was still fast asleep.

"What on earth are you doing?" asked Susan as she shook her daughter into consciousness.

"What time is it?" asked Ivy. "I'm tired."

"Into the shower right now, Ivy Carver. Do you hear

me? And you are going to bed at nine o'clock tonight. This is an outrage. I thought I could trust you—"

"Okay, Mom, okay. I'm moving."

Maybe I should get a live-in housekeeper, thought Susan, as she blow-dried her hair following her own shower. Nope, can't afford it. Stop running in the morning? Hardly. What mental and physical well-being she possessed were wholly dependent on her ritual exercise. Maybe Cordelia could come in earlier. Like when? Dawn?

Susan arrived in the kitchen and discovered Ivy staring dreamily out the window.

"What did you have for breakfast?"

"I'm not hungry," replied Ivy, continuing to stare out into space.

"You are not going to school without breakfast," said Susan, as she swung the freezer compartment door open and murmured a minor hosanna that one waffle remained in the box of Aunt Jemima's Frozen Lifesavers for Single Moms. "I'm not facing charges in Family Court because you refuse to eat—"

"When are you getting divorced?"

"What?!"

"You and Dad. Aren't you two ever going to—"

"What, pray tell, inspired this topic of breakfast conversation?"

Ivy leaped up abruptly from her stool at the kitchen counter and ran toward the pantry.

"Angela! I forgot to feed Angela last night!"

Angela was the most recent acquisition in a series of doomed hamsters Ivy had fallen in love with at first sight, then neglected because of her incredibly jam-packed social and school schedule. As the child shot past her out of the kitchen, Susan prayed that no harm had befallen the latest in Ivy's series of star-crossed rodents.

"You are truly amazing, Ivy. You haven't the slightest concern for your own health or nutrition but heaven forfend we don't feed Angela—"

A pathetic wail emanated from the upstairs bedroom

and reverberated throughout the duplex. Susan closed her eyes and envisioned Ivy descending the stairs like Diana Rigg in *Medea* displaying the body of yet another of her slaughtered children.

"Is it . . . Angela?" asked Susan with both sets of fingers crossed behind the back of her Hanae Mori dress.

Ivy nodded and Susan clutched her daughter to her bosom. The child was taking it fairly well. Normally her skinny little body would be vibrating like a tuning fork.

"We've got to find her," said Ivy resolutely.

"She's not dead?"

"She's escaped. Someone left her cage door open."

Three guesses who that might be, thought Susan. Then, when she realized where the hamster had disappeared to, she heaved a deep sigh of relief, knowing that the mysterious noises in the wall were not linked to her more recalcitrant defendants.

"I know where she is," said Susan.

"Where?"

"In the air-conditioning system."

"Oh, noooo! Call Waldo."

"I am not calling the super to track down another one of your hamsters. Waldo has better things to do around the building than—Ivy!"

"Yes?"

"It's five minutes to eight. The bus!"

"Okay, okay. I'm ready."

They rang for the elevator. Rocco opened the cage and Susan was pleased that the septuagenarian's waterworks problem had been solved. They walked out to the corner of Eightieth and Madison to wait for the eight o'clock bus that would take Ivy across the park to Balmoral School.

By 8:15 the bus had not arrived, and Susan was forced to flag down a cab. She'd barely make it to the TV studio for the nine o'clock broadcast. Halfway across the park, Ivy went into a panic state.

"My bathing suit! I forgot my bathing suit!"

"Are you sure?" asked Susan.

"We've got to go back."

"We can't go back, honey. It's twenty after eight. Your first class is in five minutes and I'm already late for my—"

"We've got to go back!" shrieked Ivy. The taxi driver spun around in his seat to make sure the child was not being tortured.

"Everything okay back there?" asked the driver.

"Couldn't be better," replied Susan, wondering how her mother's steely Greenwich, Connecticut, "I'll-thank-you-to-keep-your-eyes-on-the-road" voice had managed to come out of her mouth at that moment. The driver continued to eye Susan suspiciously in the rearview mirror.

Ivy was tugging at her mother's sleeve now and whispered: "I can't turn up without my—"

"I'll write you a note," said Susan, struggling to remain calm while she fished around in her red leather briefcase for some personalized stationery.

"It's okay," chirped Ivy, sinking back into the seat with an immense sense of relief. "I just remembered: I don't have swim class today." Then she squeezed her mother's arm affectionately and flashed her shiny braces at her. "What time are you coming home?"

"The usual." The near operatic scenario had ended as abruptly as it had begun and Susan found herself gazing down at her youngest daughter with the same sense of adoration she had felt when she first set eyes on her ten years earlier in El Salvador. Stroking Ivy's ebony hair, she felt all her tension evaporate. "What do you want for dinner?"

"Whatever," said Ivy, snuggling into her mother's arm.

Susan held her daughter's hand as she climbed the stone steps leading into the rotunda of the centuries-old Manhattan private school. She marched over to the battered wooden desk where white-haired Gladys Maitland had handled cranky parents and pupils for as long as anyone could remember.

"Good morning, Mrs. Carver. Is there anything I can do for you?"

"The bus was late, Mrs. Maitland. Ivy and I waited on the corner of Madison and Eightieth from seven-fifty-five until eight-fifteen. Then I finally had to—"

Gladys consulted the various bus schedules on her desk, then announced: "The bus was not late. Ivy was late. Her new pickup time is seven-forty-five."

"As of when?"

"As of today. Ivy was given a notice to bring home last Friday."

Susan turned to her daughter and asked: "Did you get a notice?"

Ivy shrugged. Then the little girl turned her head toward the double doors just in time to see MarSue Patterson race inside the building with a tear-stained Nellie in tow.

"Poor Nellie," said Ivy. "She's still in mourning."

"Who is Nellie?"

"My new friend. From Oklahoma. I've been over to her place twice now. She has a sheepdog named Chester. He's so cute. Except he vanished. Can we get a dog, Mom? Can we? Can we?"

"You can't take care of a hamster, Ivy. What are you going to do with a sheepdog?"

"It doesn't have to be that big. A terrier would be cool. A Scotty. Or a Westy. Or a Cairn. Or a Jack Russell."

"You've been doing research," said Susan, staring across the rotunda as MarSue Patterson knelt down, dried her daughter's eyes, and spoke soothingly to her. "What's wrong with your friend?"

"Huh?"

"She's been crying."

"Maybe she has an allergy."

"I don't think that's the problem."

"You think her mother beats her?"

"I never said that."

"You're in your crime-fighting mode, Mom. I can tell."

"I would be, if I could get out of here. Let's go say hello."

Susan crossed the rotunda floor and introduced herself to MarSue and Nellie Patterson.

"It's a pleasure to finally meet you, Nellie. Ivy's been telling me all about your sheepdog. I'm sorry it ran away."

Nellie burst into tears again. Susan stared helplessly at MarSue, who murmured sotto voce: "It was killed."

"I'm so sorry. I had no idea."

Ivy, the little mother, went over to Nellie and hugged her. Then, looking up at Susan, she uttered the solemn pronouncement: "You'd better go, Mom."

Susan stared at her wristwatch and gasped. 8:30. She'd just make it to the TV station for nine. Then a ten o'clock with Mr. Archibald, court at eleven, two o'clock at the Evanston Hotel . . . She kissed Ivy on both cheeks and repeated her daily catch phrase. "Crime never sleeps."

"Crime?" asked MarSue.

"I'm the head of the Asset Forfeiture Unit of the Manhattan District Attorney's Office. Quite a mouthful, isn't it?"

Susan watched MarSue Patterson's pupils grow larger at this announcement and was certain the woman was on the verge of either confessing to a felony or reporting one. After fifteen years in the D.A.'s Office, certain behavioral patterns couldn't be missed. Plus Nellie had a pleading look in her eye as though she wanted her mother to own up to something.

"Well, good-bye, again," said Susan. "And don't worry, Nellie."

"They cut his head off!" wailed Nellie, unable to keep the secret she had held onto since dawn any longer. "It was just horrible." And Nellie recounted through intermittent sobs the Grand Guignol tale of the pink cake box and its contents.

"I know how you feel," said Ivy, stroking her little friend's hair sympathetically. "I just lost my hamster."

"I don't think it's quite the same thing," suggested Susan.

"Please, Mom," reproved Ivy. "Not now."

"Did this really happen?" Susan asked MarSue, who answered with a nod. "When? How? Who?"

"I don't feel comfortable talking about it, Mrs. Carver."

"Given. Susan Given. But please call me Susan. Is your family being threatened? Forgive my intruding. I'm an assistant district attorney. I work for William Archibald. This atrocity sounds like some sort of threat."

"Please, Susan, I don't want to—"

"What business are you or your husband in?"

"Garbage. My husband. He works for Campbell-McCafee. The second-largest national carting company in the United States. Y'all heard of them?"

"No. I mean I suppose I must have. I don't really pay much attention to my trash. Other than separating the recyclables from—"

"The Mafia takes your garbage away, Susan. They have for forty years. Tommy—that's my husband—he was sent here to try and open the market for C-M. He's real good at his job, Tommy. Real personable. He saw the kind of prices that these companies were charging here in New York and he just fainted. Then he realized that C-M—Campbell-McCafee—could make a killing here. He went around to hospitals, schools, and hotels making bids that were fifty to sixty percent less than the going rates. Real bargain prices. But none of the people he went to would sign up. Tommy got the feeling they were scared. Scared to death."

"Has he been to the Department of Consumer Affairs?"

"They turn a blind eye to the whole thing, Susan. All they do is ask the carters to register the names of the businesses whose trash they're hauling. Then these companies just swap customers with each other. This business does one and a half billion dollars a year and these people are overcharging at least forty percent a year."

"That's six hundred million dollars a year. My office should have a piece of that." And Susan quickly explained what forfeiture was all about.

"Do you think you can help us, Susan?"

"I don't know, MarSue. My plate is rather full. . . ."

"I'm terrified of what they might do next. The kind of people that would do this to a dog . . . My husband's real stubborn. He left for work this morning spoiling for a fight. I'm afraid for him—for all of us."

"There's nothing I can do this second, MarSue. But I'm meeting with Mr. Archibald later this morning and I'll certainly tell him what you've told me. He'll know how to handle this. Okay? Now, if you'll excuse me. I'm being interviewed on TV in—whoops—ten minutes. Got to run. See you tonight, Ivy."

SUSAN DASHED INSIDE the *Manhattan in the Morning* TV studio on Ninth Avenue and was whisked immediately into makeup.

"We thought you weren't coming," said the production assistant, a nervous little rabbit named Stuart, who hovered breathlessly over Susan's chair.

"I'm here, aren't I?" asked Susan, staring up at the monitor where Lisa Mercado, the show's dazzling hostess, was interviewing a sorrowful pregnant woman. "Who's that?"

"Nancy Gerhardt," replied the makeup lady. Then added: "Poor thing."

"Why do you say that?"

"Cuz her husband was that trucker who got murdered down near Canal Street last week."

"Could you turn the sound up, please?" asked Susan. Stuart stood on tiptoes and adjusted the volume on the monitor, then spoke in hushed tones: "We're very lucky to get Nancy. She refused to do the *Today Show*. Can you imagine! NBC? Network!"

"How did you guys do it then?" asked Susan.

"Lisa. She's very hot. She's got that people thing. She's going to be bigger than Kathie Lee. Latinos love her. She's one of them. But she's all-American at the same time. Crossover City."

Susan stared at the screen and watched the Latina hostess—wearing a dress more suited to a Vegas showroom then a morning talk show—fighting back tears as she listened to the young widow's story.

". . . and when Teddy finally turned up in the parking lot, he found poor Walt's body lying in a pool of blood. There was a tire iron lying nearby. They found Walt's prints on it. The police say he probably put up a fight."

"Good for him," said Lisa reaching out her hand and squeezing Nancy's. "You were married to a fighter. A real man. Your baby will be proud."

"I don't know what I'm going to do," sobbed Nancy. "We've got—*I've* got two kids already. It's not fair."

"What about the police?" asked Lisa. "Have they got any leads?"

"Nothing."

"Hey, police!" said Lisa, staring defiantly into the camera. "What's going on? Can't you catch the animals who do things like this? With all your sophisticated crime-fighting equipment, can't you find the guy who killed Nancy's husband? This station will give ten thousand dollars to any person with information leading to the arrest and conviction of Walter Gerhardt's killer."

"We will?" asked Stuart, fiddling nervously with the buttons on his black Calvin Klein suit. "Does Mr. Holland know that?" Vance Holland was the Channel 8 news director and the station owner's son-in-law.

"I grew up in a climate of violence," continued Lisa. "I survived and escaped. I made something of myself. But I remember too many women like Nancy—the daughters, wives, and mothers of murder victims, grieving for their loved ones who perished needlessly on the streets of our city."

By the end of the speech Lisa had her arms wrapped around a sobbing Nancy Gerhardt and the screen faded subtly to black, then went into a commercial for menstrual cramps.

Susan sat in shock, appalled by the five-handkerchief performance she had just witnessed and wondering how she could effect her escape from the building before it was her turn on camera. How had she ever agreed to appear on this show? Who had talked her into it?

"Ms. Given?" Susan turned around and stared up at the sort of face she'd seen every Sunday night in the dining room at the Cedarhurst Club growing up in Greenwich. "Yes?"

"I'm Vance Holland. The news director here at Channel Eight. I just want you to know how thrilled I am that you're going to be on our show this morning. I know your brother, Henry—"

"Are you from Greenwich?"

"New Canaan. But Hank and I belong to the Stuyvesant Club and he's spoken of you often—"

"Heyyy, Vance! Was that a killer or what? Not a dry fuckin' eye in the house. Hey, Margo, do me, sweetie."

Holland and Susan turned around to see Lisa Mercado plop herself down into a chair for a quick touch-up.

"Lisa I'd like you to meet Susan Given—"

"Hi," said Lisa, not bothering to look over.

"—your next guest this morning. Ms. Given is with the District Attorney's Office."

"Fabulous!" said Lisa, swinging about abruptly and thrusting her hand out to Susan. "This'll be great follow-up on Nancy. You know, what you guys are doing to track down the killer. We can talk about the death penalty and Susan Sarandon—you know, the nun picture with Sean Penn—"

"I don't handle homicides," said Susan.

"Oh." Lisa was momentarily deflated until the rabbit in the black Calvin Klein suit thrust a bio and press clippings on Susan in front of her, then bolted out of the makeup room.

"Does that ring a bell now?" asked Holland acidly.

"Sure, sure," said Lisa, perusing the paper quickly. "Don't dis me, Vance. There's no need for that."

"Sometimes you do tend to overreach, Lisa. Like the ten thousand–dollar reward nobody authorized you to make."

"We'll talk later, Vance," said Lisa, leaping up from the makeup chair. Then she winked at Susan: "See you out there." And she vanished from the room clutching Susan's bio and press clippings.

"Astronomers peer into the heavens for years trying to discover new stars," said Holland caustically. "They wander in and out of here every day."

Susan glanced at her watch and grimaced. "I'm really cutting it short this morning, Mr. Holland. . . ."

"Oh, you'll be out there in a second—"

"We need her now!" said Stuart, rushing into the makeup room breathlessly. "Please. This way, Ms. Given."

As Susan started out the door she collided with a red-eyed Nancy Gerhardt returning from the ladies' room.

"I'm so sorry," said Susan. "Are you all right?"

"Doorways." Nancy nodded and patted her growing belly. "I always forget how difficult they become. It was my fault."

"No, no. Don't be ridiculous. I'm . . . sorry about your husband. I'm with the District Attorney's Office. I don't know what I can do but—"

"Ms. Given, please!"

The stark set consisted of a raised oval platform with two chairs and a telephone perched on a pedestal between them. Lisa was staring intently into the camera as Stuart helped Susan up onto the set. He took his leave of the blond prosecutor, then, as she crossed her shapely legs, he whispered: "Watch your hemline on camera."

Mine? thought Susan. Between Lisa's hemline and cleavage there's little left to the imagination.

"We're back again. With a very special guest this morning. Susan Given is the head of the Manhattan District Attorney's Asset Forfeiture Division." Lisa swung around in her chair and stared warmly at her guest. "Tell us about Asset Forfeiture, Susan."

"Well, Lisa, as a taxpayer, I'm sure you often wonder where the money is to come from to fight crime without digging deeper into one's pocketbook." Susan was certain she looked and sounded like the head of the Junior League in her Hanae Mori dress, shoulder-length blond hair, hazel eyes, and string of white pearls. It was an outfit her mother would heartily approve of. *If* her mother was home watching. Which was highly doubtful on a glorious golf day like this one.

"I hear you, Susan," said Lisa, who didn't really. The curvaceous hostess was too distracted by Stuart's relaying a mimed message to her from the control room that her on-camera cleavage was far in excess of normal standards on a morning talk show.

"I think one can hardly argue that our society is threatened on a daily basis by drug-fueled criminal acts. And the ever-shrinking budgets of city and state governments prevent the local authorities from combating these criminals effectively."

"Uh-huh," replied Lisa as she reluctantly pulled down the back of her dress to haul the front of it up to a G-rated décolletage. Then she read from the notes in front of her: "So, you're like Robin Hood, is that it?"

"Not really," said Susan, struggling to stay focused on the matter at hand and not Lisa's preoccupation with her dress. "Asset Forfeiture doesn't rob from the rich to give to the poor. We don't rob at all. We use the law to deprive criminals of their ill-gotten gains and use the confiscated moneys—or physical properties—to combat crime."

"Can you be more explicit?"

"Of course. Let me see. . . . Suppose I raid a crack house in Washington Heights and there's a hundred thousand dollars in cash on the floor. I can seize the cash under New York's forfeiture laws."

"Why Washington Heights specifically?" asked Lisa with sufficient edge in her voice to convince Susan that the "climate of violence" Ms. Mercado had "survived and escaped" from had undoubtedly been north of One Hundred fifty-fifth Street.

"Because the Thirty-fourth Precinct—which encompasses the Heights—has an extremely high quotient of felony crimes. Over nine thousand three hundred last year."

"West and Central Harlem had sixteen thousand," replied Lisa.

Susan was momentarily thrown by Lisa's unexpected backhand return. Then she said: "Those are four separate precincts: Twenty-sixth, Twenty-eighth, Thirtieth, and Thirty-second. They have a larger population."

"Which didn't prevent the police from making twice as many arrests there as in the Heights. Fourteen thousand versus seven thousand." Lisa flashed a row of shiny teeth and tugged her cleavage down in tribute to her dazzling display of crime statistics.

"I don't know why we're going off into this question of what precinct has more crime. One can hardly—"

"I'm just tired of people giving the Heights a bad rap." Lisa again flashed Susan her most plastic smile.

"Washington Heights has a long and proud history in this city," said Susan, trying to dig her way out of the potential public relations morass the Latina TV hostess seemed determined to drag the WASP assistant district attorney into. "But at the same time—like so many other historical sites—Washington Heights has fallen on hard times. It is now the hub of the city's high-intensity drug trade. Dealers have easy access by various bridges and highways in and out of the Heights. The George Washington Bridge zips one in and out of New Jersey. The Major Deegan and Cross Bronx Expressways flow into upstate New York, Connecticut, and New England. And all the drug traffic naturally leads to violent crime and a disproportionate number of homicides. I'm truly sorry, Lisa. But the place is a zoo."

"Well, I'm sorry you feel that way, Susan. So why don't we just throw our phone lines open and see what some of the 'animals' out there think. Good morning, you're on the air with 'Ms. D.A.' Go ahead, caller."

For the next ten minutes Susan felt like an air force fighter pilot dodging incoming missiles as she attempted responses to the angry Washington Heights residents, who resented her labeling their neighborhood a zoo. Lisa certainly did nothing to deflect any of the criticism as she sat nodding her head in agreement at all the "dissing" Susan was absorbing.

When they finally broke for a commercial, Susan leaped up from her seat and announced that she was late for an appointment with District Attorney Archibald.

"Don't leave!" pleaded Lisa. "We're just starting to cook."

"Thank you for having me," said Susan, holding out her hand as if she were leaving a dowager's tea party in Greenwich.

Lisa rose as well and, to Susan's astonishment, grabbed her in a hug and kissed her cheek. "Stay in touch, Ms. D.A. You're doing good work downtown." Then, as an afterthought, she added: "We'll have you on again."

Not in this lifetime, thought Susan, as she strode purposefully toward the makeup room to retrieve her red leather briefcase.

Susan was surprised to discover Nancy Gerhardt still seated in a makeup chair and staring dully at the monitor. When the widow noticed Susan her face lit up.

"Did you really mean what you said?" asked Nancy.

"What did I say?" Susan smiled. "After what I just went through out there, I don't remember my own—"

"You said you'd help me. . . . I know who did it."

"You know who killed your husband?" asked Susan.

"I don't know who actually killed him but everyone knows it was the cartel."

"What cartel?"

"The garbage men. Carlucci and Tesla and the others. Walt knew he was taking a chance but . . ."

Susan's mind flashed onto Nellie Patterson and her own little Ivy comforting the sobbing girl. She thought of Chester's head in the cake box. And now this woman's husband beaten to a pulp.

"I have a friend," said Susan finally. "Her name is Janie Moore. She's an A.D.A. like myself but she handles homicide cases. Let me call her and see if—"

"Susan Given?" Margo, the makeup lady, was holding the telephone out to the blond prosecutor.

Susan looked at her watch—9:45. It was probably Mr. Archibald's office confirming her meeting. How was she going to get downtown to Hogan Place in fifteen minutes?

"Hello? This is Susan Given."

"What the hell was that all about . . . Ms. D.A.?"

Susan shut her eyes as soon as she recognized the voice. It was her boss, Lydia Culberg, the deputy district attorney. Oh, God! Heads were going to roll over the on-air politically incorrect "zoo" comment. Susan knew hers would undoubtedly be the first in the basket.

"Hello, Lydia. Did you watch the show?"

"*Everyone* watched the show, *Ms. D.A.*"

"Lydia, I am not responsible for that appellation. The Mercado woman dreamt it up on the spot. As far as the comment about Washington Heights being a zoo, it's not what I meant at all—"

"The place *is* a goddamn zoo," said Lydia. "That's not what I'm pissed off about."

"It isn't?"

"No. I want to know where you get the balls to go on television and use 'I' instead of 'we' in reference to the District Attorney's Office."

"I beg your pardon?"

"You're not running a one-woman band on Centre Street, you know. When you said: 'Suppose *I* raid a crack house?' *You* don't raid anything, Susan. This office raids. Got it? Not Miss Susan Given of Greenwich, Connecticut."

Here we go again, thought Susan, as Lydia continued her harangue on the other end.

Lydia Slaney had been born in Hell's Kitchen forty years earlier with a gut-burning determination to make it to the top. The nearly six-foot redhead had scorned her brothers, who all followed their father into the sanitation department, happily embracing the pension that would be theirs after twenty years of service to the city. Entering NYU law school, Lydia married a fellow student, an overweight but hardworking plodder from the Bronx named Bob Culberg. Her family was not thrilled ("You always said Jews made money," was her sole defense to her father.)

Married life with Culberg was a nightmare. A chronic worrier, he binged on anything greasy in the hopes of calming his nerves. The sexual act for him had become the Thirteenth Labor of Hercules. He dropped dead at twenty-eight, leaving a secretly thrilled Lydia the sole guardian of their three-year-old son, Ethan. Lydia was working for the District Attorney's Office by then and she lost no time working her way up through the system. Blessed with a showgirl's body more suited to a Vegas runway than a courtroom, she employed it and the capacity to outdrink any man she came in contact with to gain patronage both official and unofficial.

Lydia was determined to eventually become Manhattan's District Attorney. The only person who stood in her way was Susan Given Carver. Lydia had loathed the beautiful blonde from Greenwich on sight. She was everything Lydia wanted to be: private school, the right accent, impeccable taste in clothes, Episcopalian. Every time she looked at Susan she could hear the 'dese, dem, and dose' Hail Marys of Hell's Kitchen echoing in her ears. To make matters worse—no, impossible—Lydia was convinced that Susan coveted her job as the deputy district attorney. Nothing was further from the truth. Susan was very happy in Asset Forfeiture. She liked going after the bad guys and depriving them of their ill-gotten gains. But this did not deter Lydia in her ceaseless efforts either to discredit and sabotage Susan at every opportunity or to take credit for all of Susan's media-attracting victories.

What time or energy Lydia managed to have left in her undeclared war against the head of Asset Forfeiture went into maintaining a wedge between Susan and their legendary boss, William Archibald. (As a minor postscript, Lydia's son, Ethan, who had inherited his late father's tendency toward obesity, was in the same class as Polly Carver at the New Amsterdam School.)

"So, Susan, while I've got you on the phone could you, if you're not racing over to NBC to do an interview with Tom Brokaw next—do you think you might deign to tell me the present status of the Evanston Hotel?"

Susan heaved a sigh, then turned to Nancy Gerhardt and asked the widow if she could please pass her red leather briefcase. Nancy did so and Susan withdrew her most updated report on the status of the Evanston Hotel. Two years of investigation, millions of tax dollars, and the District Attorney's Office was no closer to an outcome than Susan was to her divorce. When was Neil Stern going to—? Whoa! How did she get off onto her divorce? Stay focused, Susan. Crime never sleeps.

Susan cleared her throat to read the report when Lydia interrupted her with: "You know, Mr. Archibald is very upset about the lack of progress regarding the Evanston. And, with salary advancements his next order of business, he said it behooves you—"

"Mr. Archibald said 'behooves'?" William Archibald, the Manhattan District Attorney, was descended from one of the oldest families in New York. He had attended Trinity and Harvard. But despite his patrician background, he had always prided himself on being one of the boys (his mother had dreamed of his being a concert pianist but "Archie" much preferred playing boogie-woogie for his friends). He often affected a Bogart (another Trinity boy) snarl when he got started on the subject of fighting crime, which made Susan certain he would never dream of using a word like "behooves."

"Words to that effect," answered Lydia hastily.

"When did he say that?"

"We spoke on the phone just a second ago."

In addition to her reputation as a man-eater and two-fisted drinker, Lydia Culberg was known up and down Centre Street as a compulsive liar, whose blatant ambition was matched only by her incompetence. But somehow the volcanic redhead always managed magically to cover her ass. Except when it was worth her while to uncover it. Janie Moore had once remarked that Lydia had no compunction about using her body horizontally when it would advance her career vertically. This was the major difference between Susan's New England work ethic and Lydia's street-smart Hell's Kitchen upbringing.

Susan suspected she had caught Lydia out in a lie once again.

"Well, I can confirm that in ten minutes."

"What do you mean?" asked Lydia.

"Mr. Archibald has sent for me this morning. If he's displeased with my performance, I want to hear it straight from the horse's mouth. I am presently closing the net on Mr. Vinh and I want Mr. Archibald to know—"

"Calm down, Susan. Calm down. There's no need to overreact. Mr. Archibald may not have said those exact— Sooo! You're finally closing in on Vinh. Excellent, Susan, excellent. I told Mr. Archibald not to worry. That you'd come through in the clinch. I've always had the utmost faith in you. How soon can we expect an arrest?"

"Not until we locate and seize all of Mr. Vinh's assets. His cars, yachts, homes in Florida, California, and Colorado. Everything. If he so much as sniffs a subpoena coming his way, Vinh can dispose of it all and we'll be left—"

"Yes, yes. I know the rules of forfeiture. I'm not a complete dunce."

How many more box tops does she need before they send her the cap? That's what Susan thought but she was far too much the lady to ever say it aloud. Instead she replied: "I never thought you were, Lydia. Now, I am meeting with Mr. Vinh and his lawyer at the Evanston this afternoon." Uh-oh. Susan could hear the tumblers clicking in Lydia's head. Incipient Media Madness. Damage control was the order of the day. "One other thing, Lydia . . ."

"Yes? Yes?" The lusty redhead was mentally en route to Bergdorf's in search of a new ensemble for her triumphant press conference following the arrest.

"I'd rather you didn't leak a word of this prematurely to the press." Lydia Culberg's one great passion after liquor and men was seeing her name in print or, better, her image on TV. Her obsession with leaking unfounded rumors to the media had earned her the sobriquet "the Human Faucet."

"Susan, I'm shocked! I am not by any means the vainglorious creature people make me out to be. Stop by when you get back to the office. And keep up the good work, honey."

Keep up the good work. A double validation coming from the likes of Lydia Culberg and Lisa Mercado. Pray God these two never meet!

Susan replaced the phone and stared into the dewy eyes of Nancy Gerhardt, who was hovering near her like a faithful puppy awaiting its next command.

"Where are you living now, Nancy?"

"Our old place."

"Did Roger leave you any—?"

"Walt. Walter. There's some pension money from the union and a little insurance. . . . It's just the baby is coming in the new year and he won't be . . ."

Nancy began to sob and Susan found herself wrapping her arms around the weeping widow. Just like Lisa. Just like Ivy. Some two-fisted prosecutor, she thought. Strictly a soft touch. Right down the line.

Susan took Nancy's phone number, then gave her her business card with the promise to call as soon as she learned anything about the murder.

"Thank you," said Nancy, wiping her eyes. Then she added: "Ms. D.A."

FORSAKING HER NEW England thrift, Susan hurried out onto Ninth Avenue and hailed a cab with instructions to zip South to Hogan Place. All the way downtown Susan cursed herself for having said anything to media-mad Lydia about the Evanston. The volcanic redhead would be sitting in Ray Murphy's lap over a very wet lunch that afternoon and the story would be splashed across page 3 of the *Daily News* for sure the next day. Two years of work down the drain in tribute to La Culberg's ego.

It was ten after ten when Susan dashed through William Archibald's outer office and gasped to his secretary: "Sorry, Audrey." The secretary smiled and waved her on through to the private sanctum.

"Well, well, well," said the Manhattan District Attorney, "here is Ms. D.A. at last."

"You watched the show, too?" groaned Susan. The District Attorney was something of an idol to her and she hated to have him think badly of her because of her zoo faux pas.

"I think you should have your own series." Archibald

grinned. " 'Ask Ms. D.A.' Perhaps I might come on once in a while and play the piano. I'm just teasing you, Susan. You looked wonderful and you did the office proud." Then he flashed her what had entered legend as his "El Mocambo smile."

When William "Archie" Archibald returned from the South Pacific at the end of World War II, it was rumored that MGM had offered him a motion picture contract. The patrician son of one of FDR's Brain Trust was certainly handsome and charismatic enough to have been a movie star. It was also rumored that Lana Turner and Ava Gardner had come close to blows over his attentions in the powder room of El Mocambo. Archie could have gone on to become an international tennis star, a renowned concert pianist, or, at least, a major rakehell and dilettante. Instead, he became a criminal lawyer and had been the Manhattan District Attorney for the past twenty years. Like Susan, he was devoted to public service and loved fighting crime.

"I'm sorry I was late, Mr. Archibald. I didn't know about the viewer phone calls and then there was a woman whose husband— Never mind. Oh, wait! Are you aware of this ongoing garbage cartel that has been gouging the city for over forty—?"

Archie threw his head back and laughed. Then he looked past Susan and asked: "Didn't I tell you gentlemen this was the person for the job? A lawyer *and* a mind reader. Thank God, you're one of the good guys, Susan."

Tell what gentlemen? That was when Susan realized she was not alone in the District Attorney's office. She turned around and saw two men sitting together on the sofa against the wall, looking all the world like Mutt and Jeff. The taller one had a familiar look about him. So did the short, stocky one with the thick eyebrows.

"Susan Given, I'd like you to meet Tom Patterson. He works for Campbell-McCafee."

The tall Oklahoman got up from the sofa and offered her his hand.

"Are you MarSue's husband?" asked Susan.

"Y'all know MarSue?"

"We just met this morning. My daughter Ivy and your daughter Nellie are classmates. I . . . heard about Chester. I'm very sorry."

"Yeah," nodded Patterson appreciatively. "I just got finished telling Mr. Archibald about that."

"Oh," said Susan. "Well, then, you know all about it." She glanced at her watch and groaned internally. Forty minutes till she had to be in court. "Was there something specific, Mr. Archibald?"

"Yes, Susan, there is. The office has been speaking with Tom and his boss for several months. It's fortuitous that you've become involved as well."

"Involved?" No, she prayed. Not another case. She was overloaded as it was.

"Did you know that New York City produces five percent of the country's commercial waste?" asked the D.A. "And that the privately owned companies that hold our garbage for ransom number twenty-three? That's a lot of money for your unit, Susan. And a lot of self-respect we could give back to the city."

"Tom's boss flew up from Tulsa a couple of weeks ago and asked how they could crack the cartel here. I told them that they either cooperate with our investigation or stay out of the market." Archie was definitely in his tough-guy Bogart mode this morning. "They agreed to come on board and I'm glad."

"It got real frustrating," said Patterson in his Oklahoma drawl. "I had the Hudson Bank signed up. Forty percent less than they'd been paying for years. Forty percent!"

"Who was their previous carter?" asked Susan.

"Nicolo Tesla." The question had been answered by the short, stocky man with the thick eyebrows, who had remained silent up until now. He got up and walked over to Susan. "Tony Fusco."

"Sergeant Anthony Fusco," said Archibald. "Another one of our scarlet pimpernels."

"We met a couple years ago," said Fusco. "That crack house in the East Village?"

"Of course." Susan smiled and shook his hand. "You and Paul Regan were working together then."

"Good old Nip. Nip and me went through the academy together. I beat him out as the force's most eligible bachelor three years running. Anyhow, these Hudson Bank people thought they'd scored real big with their new carting deal. They got twenty-eight branches, right. Then one of the execs mentioned the switch to a pal of his who knew someone in the D.A.'s office. This party advised the pal to tell the exec not to switch."

"*Our* office?" asked a shocked Susan. "What division?"

"Take it easy," said the District Attorney, removing his suit jacket and rolling up his cuffs.

"Who was it?" asked Susan. "Did they get a name? Who could have said such a thing?"

"Take it easy, Susan," repeated the D.A. "That's not the matter at hand. We must concentrate our efforts on the cartel. It's been in effect since nineteen fifty-six and it's not going to be that easy to dismantle."

"The carters own the 'stops,'" explained Fusco. "The locations are called stops. And with their own cockeyed logic, any competition is called 'stealing.' Competitors are called 'outlaws.' And any outlaw what gets caught has a couple of choices. He can say 'scusa' and give the stop back. Or he can swap stops. Or he can pay a one-time-only penalty that's like fifty times the monthly revenue or . . ."

"He can have his sheepdog's head cut off," said Susan. Then she turned hastily to Patterson. "Sorry."

"A few years back," continued Fusco, "a big real estate company thought they'd buy a small fleet of trucks and do their own carting. Five of the trucks were blown up one midnight in the warehouse. The real estate people went back to their original carters at double the previous rate."

"Is that what happened to Walter Gerhardt?"

"Who?" asked Archibald.

"The trucker from Osborne Paper who was bludgeoned to death last week."

"She's on top of things," said Fusco admiringly. "Nip told me you were a pisser, Ms. Given. He just didn't tell me how much. What do you know about Gerhardt?"

"I didn't know anything until this morning. His widow was on Lisa Mercado's program with me."

"We can assume," said the District Attorney, "that Mr. Gerhardt was a fatality of the war. How we can ever prove that I don't know."

Susan could still feel Nancy Gerhardt's wet tears on her dress and, momentarily forgetting that one more case would easily send her Leaning Tower of Forfeiture crashing to the ground, asked: "What do we do first?"

"We wait and see how quickly the sharks come after the Milano Trucking Company," said Archibald.

"Who are they?"

"Yours truly," grinned Tony Fusco. "I'm in the carting business now. With a little help from Tom here."

"We set Tony up as our transfer man," said Patterson. "He hauls refuse from Manhattan over to our stations in Brooklyn. Then our trucks move them on to landfill sites."

"And you were getting away with this?" asked Susan.

"For about a week." Fusco shrugged. "Then I became the new girl in town. And I thought they just loved me for my mind."

Archibald tossed a folder onto the desk and gestured for Susan to examine the contents. At first she thought Archie had mistakenly given her proposals for a retirement package or travel brochures as she stared at a series of glossy black-and-white photographs displaying luxurious waterfront homes somewhere in the Caribbean. But when she flipped the pictures over they were identified on the backs as the getaways in Boca Raton, Florida, for Nicolo Tesla, Joseph Carlucci, Philip DeFillipo, and other infamous members of the Gotham Waste Removal Association. All the photographs included yachts no shorter than thirty feet moored at private docks in the foreground of the properties. After she had inspected the tropical properties, Susan examined the more baronial trappings where these men lived in Long Island, Staten Island, and New Jersey. Real estate bought through fear and intimidation.

There was also a transcription of a wiretapped conversation between Joseph Carlucci, one of the biggest carters, and Ernie "Red Meat" Mazzoli, a well-known organized-crime figure. During this conversation, the two men discussed the necessity of making a Campbell-McCafee truck "disappear" and making it look like it was a holdup.

"So who are you saving the last dance for?" asked Susan.

"Nicolo Tesla," replied Fusco. "He wants to meet me on Friday."

"Didn't the city just give him an award?" asked an amazed Susan.

"That's politics." Archibald shrugged. "He's a favorite of Cardinal Corcoran's. Lavish in his generosity to the Church."

"His wife's a loony tune," said Fusco. "Talks to the saints all day. Makes deals with them."

"Who's this?" asked Susan pointing to a grinning, well-built man of thirty in an Armani suit.

"That's Junior," said Fusco. "Nick's only son. The heir apparent and as daffy as his mother. But not so benign. Physical fitness freak with a hair-trigger temper."

"Charles Atlas meets Charles Manson," commented Archibald. "Your future business colleagues, Tony."

"Good luck," said Susan grimly.

"Hey, you, too." Fusco grinned. "We're all in this together."

SUSAN RACED UP the stairs of the Lefkowitz Building on Centre Street, entered the rotunda, and hurried across the dimly lit, tiled floor toward the bank of ancient elevators.

Halfway across the floor she heard a familiar voice call out: "Greenwich! Yo, Greenwich!"

Susan turned around and saw Janie Moore, five feet two, brunette, violet eyes, and (in her own words) "built like the hood ornament on a sexy foreign car." She was descended from five generations of New York City cops, had the mouth of a stevedore, and mercilessly ragged Susan's sex life, upbringing, and ladylike manner.

"Keeping real banker's hours now, huh, Greenwich? San Francisco banking hours."

"I was 'round the corner with Mr. Archibald," replied Susan defensively.

"Did he finally show you where the horse bit him?"

"Janie, that's disgusting!"

"Why? He's a widower. Still gorgeous. You haven't had sex since the Carter Administration—"

"Stop it!"

"I don't really count Jerusalem."

"How did you know about Michael?"

"I didn't. But I do now. Michael, huh?" grinned Janie. "That's how I trap murderers. Never fails."

"Speaking of murderers—"

"No, Greenwich. I cannot recommend someone to bump off your husband. You'll just have to make your divorce work."

"Have you got a lead on Walter Gerhardt's murderer?"

"What, are you working for the Mayor's Office now?" asked Janie testily. "I got his deputy grinding me day and night. I got no leads, no supporting roles, no cameos. Ray Murphy is calling up all his Irish markers trying to guilt me into an exclusive for the *News*. Who put you up to this? Your girlfriend Lydia."

"She's no friend of mine."

"Would you stop being such an uptight Episcopalian? That's black Irish humor, Greenwich. Relax and smell the jokes. Maybe you and Michael should get it on more often than every six months. How's Ivy? How's her artwork coming? Still drawing those zoftig Amazons?"

"Day and night. Do you think there's something odd about a ten-year-old girl drawing half-naked women? Do you think I should be worried?"

"They're X-Men."

"No. They're women."

"It's a cartoon show, Greenwich. Men and women. Superheroes. I wouldn't worry about Ivy drawing them as much as her emulating them. Stella told me she kicked the shit out of two boys on the Balmoral turf last week. One has a black eye now and the other one still limps a little."

"Ivy did this?" asked a shocked Susan.

"Her action was not unprovoked. They pulled her hair. She warned them not to. You've got a woman warrior on your hands there, Greenwich. So what's with the Gerhardt case?"

"I did a TV show with his widow this morning."

"How's she doing?"

"Not well. The baby's due in January. Do you think it has anything to do with the garbage cartel?"

"It has everything to do with the garbage cartel. But that's like: Does the rain have anything to do with the clouds? Are you moving on them?"

Susan nodded: "Archie just dropped it in my lap."

"Rotsa ruck. Carlucci and Tesla and all that gang have been robbing the city blind since I was in diapers."

"What do you know about Junior Tesla?" asked Susan abruptly.

"Not anyone I'd want to date. Unless I discovered I had an incurable disease and Dr. Kevorkian was too busy to help me out."

"You think he's a killer?"

"Do I think he's *that* killer? I can't prove it. We're in the proof business, you know. Certainly would make my life easier if he was. What's wrong, Greenwich?"

"Do you know what time it is?" Susan stared in horror at her watch.

"No. But if you hum a few bars— Hey! Did you hear about the two dyslexic drunks who wandered into a bra? Come on, Greenwich, lighten up. It's only crime."

They entered the battered wooden elevator together and Delbert, the hare-lipped operator, greeted them effusively. He asked them an unintelligible question then killed himself laughing.

"What did he say?" whispered Susan.

"I think it was the same joke I told you." The elevator stopped and Janie got off on her floor.

"Give my love to Kevin and Stella," said Susan. "Maybe we'll all have brunch—"

"Sure, sure. When pigs have wings."

"I'm serious, Janie."

"Too serious. Send for Michael."

"I don't have time for—"

"A girl always has time."

"What girl? I just turned forty-five."

"I didn't get my engine revving properly till forty. I recommend a monthly tune-up for you. At least."

The elevator door closed and Delbert dropped Susan off next on the eighth floor. She turned left, then walked down a narrow corridor, stopping in front of a door marked Asset Forfeiture. She opened the door and encountered a hand-painted, multicolored sign reading "Congratulations, Ms. D.A."

Susan scowled, grabbed at the sign, then looked questioningly at Gretchen, her slender, Afro-American secretary, who besides being efficient and superorganized, was also a master of diplomacy.

"What do you know about this, Gretchen?"

"It wasn't my idea."

"Becker!" Susan called out for her assistant, Alan Becker. No response was forthcoming. She turned back to Gretchen. "It was Becker, wasn't it?"

"I was too busy to notice. Here." And her secretary presented her with an inch-thick collection of messages, memos, and faxes.

The bulk of the thickness was due to the faxes. Susan shut her eyes and asked: "They're from him, aren't they?"

"I try not to look."

Susan nodded gratefully at Gretchen's tactfulness, then entered her office and shut the door behind her. He was *not* supposed to do this. He had been ordered by the court *not* to do this. But Dr. Hugh Carver was a law unto himself, unbound by the restrictions mere mortals had to suffer.

· Sitting at her desk, Susan buried her face in her hands, then stared out the window at the Statue of Justice, hoping for something akin to moral support. Finally she picked up the messages and faxes and read them.

TO: SGC
FROM: HC

Once again you are thwarting my authority. I deplore 'Melrose Place' and the values it represents. I do not want Polly and Ivy watching it. Unfortunately this mental equivalent of tooth decay airs on nights they are with you. Surely there are programs on Disney and Discovery that are more suitable for children. They sit at the dinner table discussing the peccadilloes of Michael and Amanda as if they were real people. It is not healthy. Consider their future.

TO: SGC
FROM: HC

Ivy arrived here the other night in a torn T-shirt and scuffed shoes. She looked like a street urchin. I cannot be responsible for their habiliments under your roof but please have enough respect to send them to me in a state of proper attire.

TO: SGC
FROM: HC

I notice that Polly is grinding her teeth in her sleep. She maintains nothing is troubling her. I doubt that. However, you chose to remove her from therapy and so any future dental problems that may result will be paid for by you.

TO: SGC
FROM: HC

I cannot allow the girls to stay overnight in Greenwich this weekend. I appreciate the fact it is your mother's birthday but I must have them here Sunday morning as per our agreement. However, should you wish to swap for the two succeeding weekends I will relax the rules and allow them to stay.

TO: SGC
FROM: HC

I called your office several times yesterday but your secretary rudely informed me that you were not available. I have not received responses to any of my faxes. Once again your intransigence makes civilized behavior impossible.

TO: SGC
FROM: HC

A friend of mine was passing by your building last night around 10:30 P.M. and noticed that Ivy's bedroom light was on. Why is this allowed? Perhaps one of the reasons she is so tired in the morning is her lack of sleep the night before. Allowing her to stay up and draw (or whatever other nonsense you indulge her in) is not contributing to the child's health. Try and monitor her activities more closely.

Susan's first instinct was to tear the faxes into a million pieces. No. Her first instinct was to scream and *then* tear the faxes into a million pieces. The man was positively insane! He needed a psychiatrist. What was she talking about? He *was* a psychiatrist. How could anyone in trouble possibly go to Hugh Carver for help? Yet he was considered one of the best in Manhattan. Perfect. In a poll of the wealthiest loons in New York City, 99 percent said they'd rather spill their guts out to Dr. Carver than to any other witch doctor. Ting-tang walla-walla bing-bang.

She drew a deep breath, then dialed Neil Stern, her divorce lawyer. After staying on hold for almost five minutes, Stern finally came on the line.

"Susan! What a pleasure!"

"Pleasure isn't the precise word I would use, Neil."

"How's the war on crime, Ms. D.A.? Thought you were great this morning."

"For the sake of our friendship and your retainer, I'm kindly requesting you to never call me that again."

"Touchy, touchy. So, what can I do for you?"

He's as crazy as Hugh, thought Susan. What the hell does he think I'm phoning for? Sell him tickets to the

Balmoral School Autumn Carnival? But the lady in her won out again and, with all the charm she could muster, she asked: "Where do we stand regarding *Carver* versus *Carver*? Have I got a hope in hell of being divorced before the coming millennium?"

"We're moving forward," chuckled Stern.

"That's not quite the answer I was hoping for, Neil. 'Moving forward.' How far forward? Does that put us in the same arena as global warming? Something that is inevitable but will not occur in our lifetime?"

"I'm so glad you've kept a sense of humor about this, Susan. So many other women I represent don't—"

"I don't care about the other women, Neil. I want this matter resolved. I want this nut job off my back. He started faxing me again."

"He's not supposed to. There's a court order—"

"Oh, Neil, you wouldn't survive a day in my office. It's called recidivism. We bust 'em, we jail 'em, and then they're back out on the street again. Hugh's not going to change just because some judge slaps his wrists. I walked into my office this morning and Gretchen hit me with the Collected Quotations from Chairman Whacko." Susan read her lawyer the faxes. " 'Peccadilloes'? 'Habiliments'? I had to look that one up in the dictionary. And who is he kidding with that crap about a friend of his looking up at Ivy's window? He has no friends. He was lurking in the shadows again. This is harassment, Neil. He's stalking us."

"You have no proof—"

"The doormen have seen him! How many other Gregory Peck lookalike nut jobs are there?"

"What do you want me to do, Susan?"

"I want you to get me a divorce. I want to end this madness. Every time we get a court date, I turn up and Hugh's lawyer has moved for a continuance or pulled some other legal fast one. Two years, Neil. It's been nearly two years since we started investigating him and where has it all led?" Susan caught herself. She hadn't been investigating Hugh. That was the Evanston Hotel. Try to keep the private separate from the professional. "Look, Neil. It's wearing me down. Maybe that's Hugh's hidden agenda. I wouldn't put it past him. Just try—please!—try and get a court date the man will actually show up for. And call that slice-and-dice lawyer of his. What's-his-name? Ralph Kregar. I want an end to these poisonous epistles." Susan heaved a deep sigh. "Just do the best you can, Neil."

This was pathetic, she thought, after she had replaced the telephone. Here she was an assistant district attorney, a "legendary crime fighter" (to quote Ray Murphy, when the tabloid journalist was well in his cups), a woman whose very name reputedly sent drug lord Vinh Ho Chi into fits of apoplexy. All these things and Susan *still* couldn't get a divorce. Why? Because after all the bad guys and perps she had come up against in her career, her strange and estranged husband possessed, perhaps, the greatest criminal mind she had ever encountered. The man had no conscience, no morals, no guilt, no fear. Nothing Hugh said or did could possibly be wrong. Other people were in error; he was faultless. He was the master timepiece by which all lesser beings could set their moral clocks.

Had Hugh always been like that? Susan could no longer recall. What she did remember was the skiing trip to Vermont eighteen years earlier. With Peg and Robin and Daisy. They had all been together at Bennington and this was a sort of reunion. Two were married and the third engaged. Which left Susan. Susan, who had flopped in acting, publishing, and advertising. Susan, who did not have a boyfriend.

The pajama-clad quartet had sat snuggled up the night before in their chalet watching an old Hitchcock movie on the late show. *Spellbound.* Gregory Peck was so young and so handsome and so screwed up. The girls were thrilled when beautiful Ingrid Bergman rescued him and restored his mental health. And on the ski slopes of Vermont, no less.

Bright and early the next morning Susan took the ski lift up to a secluded peak she had kept as her own little secret. There she saw . . . him. Gregory Peck on skis. Had she taken complete leave of her senses? How had she become Dr. Constance Peterson? She must still be dreaming. That movie must have really affected her. All those doors and those kisses. Here she was on skis in the same Vermont mountains and there was poor, tormented Gregory Peck. He hadn't killed anyone; he wasn't a psychiatrist; and he wasn't crazy.

"Why are you staring at me?" The man's voice was nothing like Gregory Peck's. It was almost whiny and high-pitched.

"Dr. Edwardes?"

"You've got the wrong man." Years later Susan would realize how prophetic that line had been. But at the time his reply only meant that she wasn't dreaming.

"You reminded me of . . . someone." She didn't dare tell him who. He'd think she was crazy. Later on she did tell and he latched onto the Peck persona totally. Watching his old movies over and over again. Banishing forever his suburban Detroit whine and replacing it with a clipped baritone. And a monomaniacal ego that had been waiting in the wings for some unsuspecting good-hearted soul to unleash. Reassessing the situation years later, Susan realized that Hugh hadn't killed anyone. But he was a psychiatrist and he was crazy.

"That window is filthy," she said aloud, interrupting her own daydream. Susan had a thing about cleaning. She ascribed it simply to being a Virgo but when under extreme stress nothing put her more at ease than a good bottle of Windex or a can of Ajax. She likened the cleaning products to disinfectant Prozac—capable of banishing not only all dirt but all cares as well. Removing the Windex and a roll of paper towels from the bottom drawer of her desk, she whipped off her Arche shoes and climbed atop the radiator to clean the large picture window overlooking Centre Street.

This was when Nip and Tuck, two very unsavory-looking characters, burst into her office unannounced. Nip and Tuck were the nicknames of two young undercover cops, who had been accumulating evidence for her regarding the illegal activities at the Evanston Hotel. Nip was a handsome redhead in his late twenties whose real name was Paul Regan and Tuck was Tucker Maxwell, a whippet-thin black man in his early thirties. Both adored Susan to distraction and treated her like a big sister.

"We had a rough time last night, Ms. Gee." Nip made this announcement after flopping down in the chair opposite Susan's desk. "We had to interview over half a dozen bimbos in that joint."

"Interview?" asked Susan wryly as she stood on tiptoe to reach the extreme left corner of the window.

"Comparative pricing," corrected Tuck. "Much less expensive than midtown. We also scored some coke and some crystal meth. Y'all missed a spot over there, Ms. Gee."

"Where?" Susan stepped back to look at her handiwork and almost lost her balance. Nip and Tuck leaped forward as one but Susan righted herself. "Oh, I see it. Thanks, Tuck. That looks better, doesn't it?" She started to climb down on her own but Tuck insisted on helping her. She slipped back into her shoes, then asked: "Am I to gather that Mr. Vinh has *not* followed any of the guidelines I sent him for cleaning up his establishment?"

"My granddaddy kept pigs in Mississippi," replied Tuck, "and they lived better than that."

"What about the new hotel security we asked for?"

"Where'd they hire the guy from? Tiffany's?" asked Nip. "Security! This mook's so crooked he can't lie in bed straight. Strictly on the ake-tay from day one."

"What!"

"Aww, Ms. Gee. Do I have to tell you about Santy Claus, too? This mook cops a Hamilton from everyone who walks in the joint. It's like an 'E' Ticket to Disney World. Ten bucks and he gives you the guided tour. You should see him strolling around the premises like the head floorwalker at Bergdorf's. 'Third floor: hookers. Fourth floor: crack cocaine. Please, watch your step getting in and out of the elevator.' "

"When do we bust him?" asked Tuck.

"You gentlemen will be the first to know." And Susan steered them toward the door. "Thanks for the visit."

"How are the girls?" asked Nip, pausing to stare at the photos of Polly and Ivy adorning the walls. "They haven't been around lately."

"School. They had to go back to school."

"They're a couple of heartbreakers."

"I'll tell them you were asking about them. Oh, Nip. I met a colleague of yours this morning. Tony Fusco."

"Tony the Fuss! How's he doin'? I used to throw my old girlfriends his way."

"That's not what he says. He claims he beat you out as the most eligible bachelor at the academy. Three years running!"

"Jeese! Where does a guy like that get off? Lucky thing I'm just half a wop instead of a whole wop like him. See ya 'round, Ms. Gee."

The two undercover policemen left her office. Then Tuck popped his head round the door a moment later and in a low growl added the postscript: "Y'all need anything done . . . just ask." And he was gone.

What had he meant by that? What specific services had Tuck been hinting at? Sexual? Baby-sitting? Leg breaking? That was an idea. Maybe they could take Hugh for a ride to Jersey. Past the Meadowlands. Stop it, Susan. This isn't funny. Besides, how could one destroy a deity?

The telephone rang on her desk. She answered it brusquely: "Given."

"Praeger," replied the female voice, followed by a giggle. "Have you got people there?"

"I never have people here. Just felons, knaves, and varlets. So how are you, Cynthia?" Cynthia Praeger was an advertising executive and the mother of the bar mitzvah boy whose rite of passage had been the reason for Susan's trip to Jerusalem six months earlier.

"Crazed. Barry's in Beijing again."

"Think he's having an affair?" laughed Susan.

"What have you heard?" asked Cynthia with an angst one could slice and serve on a Kaiser roll.

"Cynthia, please! I was just kidding," replied Susan, finally understanding how Janie Moore felt when she didn't get her pal's little digs. "Is something going on?"

"Did you always know when Hugh was cheating on you?"

"Who was cheating on me?"

"Not who. Hugh. Hugh."

"Hugh Carver?"

"What other Hugh were you married to? Damn! My other line's ringing. I have to go." Dial tone.

What was that all about? Susan was very fond of Cynthia but the woman was just a trifle high-strung. Like something rescued from a burning stable. Susan had hoped to ask if her husband had heard from Michael Roth lately. Michael was Barry Praeger's best friend from childhood but this was obviously not the best time. Trouble in paradise.

Her second line rang and she answered it immediately.

"Given!"

"Daddy is such a jerk!"

"What's he done now, Polly?" sighed Susan, trying to muster the facade of impartiality but secretly pleased with her daughter's assessment of Hugh's personality.

"He has crossed my personal boundaries once too often. He just had me pulled out of history class so he could talk to me on the phone. Do you know how many notes I have to take in history? And Mr. Griffin's the only teacher I like. Oh! I was so humiliated."

"What did your father want?"

"He wanted to know where I'm going after school

today. Plus who I'm going with. I'm surprised he didn't want their addresses and year of birth. I'm fourteen and he's still trying to run my life. And now he's forbidden me to ride on the subway."

"You ride the subways with me all the time."

"Good one, Mom. He says it's double jeopardy riding with you."

"Why?"

"Cuz he's convinced there's a bullet out there with your name on it."

"What has your father been reading? And when does he get the time? I thought he spent all his days lurking outside our apartment."

"So that *was* him last night!"

"You saw him?"

"No. But Callie Sheridan and her mother were coming home from the theater and they saw a man they thought was Dad hiding in a doorway across the street. What a nut job! Dr. Carver, the famous shrink. He's the one who needs a psychiatrist."

"Which is why he still sees Otto Schellenberg three times a week."

"I hate him!"

"Polly, please. We'll talk about this tonight."

"I don't have any friends."

"What?"

"Nobody likes me."

"Is that why you were elected class president?"

"That was political, Mom." Then she changed gears abruptly. "You're never in any real danger, are you, Mom?"

"Like what?"

"You know. From the people you send to prison. I mean they're not going to break out and kill you or anything."

"Of course not. It's a game. I try to take their money; they try to keep it. Nothing personal. No matter what

54

your father thinks. 'A bullet with my name on it.' He's the one who convinced me to become a lawyer."

"I think he meant lawsuits and stuff. Not fighting crime and getting your picture in the paper all the time. I think he's jealous of you."

"Something else he can talk to Otto about."

"Can we order pizza tonight?"

"No. Cordelia's making chicken."

"Mom, no! Not that voodoo chicken. Ivy'll have nightmares again."

"What are you talking about?"

"Don't you remember the last time? There was still blood on the chicken from some voodoo ceremony Cordelia had been to—"

"It was just normal chicken blood, Polly."

"Unh-unh!"

"Polly, I love you but I've got to go back and fight crime."

"Fine. I'm going to move to Ireland, shave my head, and become a rock-and-roll nun."

"Interesting. Good-bye, Polly."

Susan hung up the phone and stared out the window at the Statue of Justice just as a short, stocky, thirty-something man with a drastically receding hairline entered her office clutching a battered brown briefcase to his chest like Linus's blanket. He stood rocking back and forth in front of her desk and asked: "Are you ready?"

Susan spun around in her chair and glared at Alan Becker, her hyper but brilliant assistant. Becker's Bensonhurst accent was so thick that Susan used to think his name was spelled B-e-k-k-a-h until she read his interoffice memos.

"I did *not* appreciate the banner."

"What banner?" Becker nervously ran a hand through his receding hair.

"Ms. D.A.? I hate nicknames."

"Won't happen again. So, shall we go?"

"Where?"

"Davis Kumba. We're due in court in ten minutes."

"What time is it, Alan?"

"Ten-fifty."

"You're joking!" Susan leaped up from her chair and began cramming papers into her red leather briefcase. "How is this possible?" A second later she was buzzing through the outer office with Becker struggling to keep up with her.

"The rotation of the earth. Haven't you noticed it gets brighter as you move towards noon?"

"Very funny, Alan. You're wasting your time in Forfeiture."

"That's what my mother thinks. She wants me to be a comedian."

"Seriously?"

"No. But it's a good idea for a routine. 'My Son the Stand-up'. Just in case the law doesn't work out."

"Who says it works out? Come on, Alan. I can't wait all day for you. Gretchen, I'll be back for lunch."

"Shall I open your can of tuna for you?"

"No. I don't like taking advantage of the staff."

"Oh. This just came in for you."

Gretchen would not make eye contact with Susan as she handed her the latest fax.

TO: SGC
FROM: HC

> I will not have Polly riding the subways whether it is on your watch or not. I needn't tell you how the quality of life above ground has deteriorated in this city. Conditions below are positively at a third world level. The child's welfare is at stake and I don't think you have enough pluses in the ledger book to give way on this one.

"I fucking need this!" shouted Susan, crumpling up the fax and tossing it in the wastebasket. Then she hastily retrieved it, pressed it out for Neil Stern's file, and looked up to see Gretchen and Becker staring nervously at her. "Was I loud?"

"Like an old-fashioned Dodger fan," said Becker.

"I don't like being threatened." Then she muttered: " 'On your watch.' Does he think he's George Bush now?"

"Is it from Atticus Finch?" asked Becker, doing a half-assed impersonation of Gregory Peck.

"You don't have any relatives in Murder Incorporated, do you, Alan?"

"If I did, would I tell you?"

"What if I made it worth your while?"

"Is this like a loyalty test?"

"Forget it. The girls would never forgive me."

"My mother's cousin Flossie dated a guy who was Albert Anastasia's barber's third cous—"

"I don't want to hear."

"It was a long time ago." Susan and Becker were now facing the bank of elevators and waiting in silence for one to arrive. Becker resumed rocking back and forth.

"Do you think my hair's worse?"

"Worse than what?" asked Susan without thinking.

"Do you think it's receding more?" Becker was rocking twice as fast now. "It's getting like a corona around the edges of my head. What if I end up like Dr. Zorba?"

The elevator door opened and Elaine Morton emerged. Referred to behind her back as 'Miss Piggy,' Morton was another A.D.A. and a protégée of Lydia Culberg's. She now blocked Susan's path as the head of Asset Forfeiture attempted to enter the elevator.

"Morning, Elaine." Susan tried to sidestep Morton but the other A.D.A. took a lateral step and blocked her once more.

"We need to speak."

"I'd be delighted, Elaine, but I'm on my way into court and I'm really—"

"Your staff is monopolizing my storage space."

"What?!" Susan turned to Becker, who shrugged his shoulders helplessly.

"The cupboards in the conference room," said Morton. "We were supposed to have equal space for storing our files. Your people are eighteen inches over."

"Over what?"

"The line of demarcation."

"Are you serious, Elaine? Push the files back, if you want."

"It's not that easy. Come and see—"

"Elaine, it's ten to eleven. I've got to get over to Thomas Street."

"I told Lydia you wouldn't cooperate with me on this."

"Why did you have to go to Lydia about it? This is not a matter for the Deputy District Attorney."

"Allow me to decide what warrants my going to Lydia or not."

"What is the problem, Elaine? What is the *real* problem? It can't be the eighteen inches."

"You think it's petty, don't you? You think everything I do is insignificant."

"I never said that." Susan turned to Becker. "Did I say that?"

"Are we going down or what?" asked Delbert, the hare-lipped elevator operator.

"Elaine—" Susan turned in supplication to her colleague as she stood inside the elevator.

"Go ahead." And Morton sighed the sigh of martyrdom.

"Can't we handle this like—?" The elevator door closed before "adults" could leave Susan's mouth.

"What is her problem?" asked an exasperated Susan.

"Besides her face, her body, and her personality?" countered Becker. "Actually she's the perfect woman . . . if you want to marry your mother."

"I'm glad you're in such a buoyant mood, Alan. Dating anyone these days?"

"Not really," said Becker warily as Susan fished around inside her red leather briefcase.

"Good. There won't be much time for romance with our new case." She passed him the file she had brought back with her from Hogan Place.

"Nick Tesla?" asked Becker.

"And others. Joseph Carlucci, Philip DeFillipo—"

"My mother won't like this. I told her I don't do homicide."

"And you haven't lied, Alan. We've never had a murder in Asset Forfeiture."

"Yeah, but we never dealt with the Teslas before."

Junior Tesla was furious. He planned to get laid that morning before going to see his shrink. A good orgasm always gave him a rosier outlook on the world and made baring his soul to Dr. Rosenthal a lot easier than blabbing cold turkey. And Cashmere was purring in her high-rise like a prize-winning pussy waiting for her bowl of cream. Junior had even pulled another sweater from last month's hijacked shipment as a bonus for the hooker if she'd make him come three times in an hour (as she'd done the previous week).

But that plan was scrapped as soon as the old man had found him on the car phone. He wanted Junior to come to the restaurant right away.

"Stop-running-my-goddamn-life!" shouted Junior as he pounded out each word on the Ferrari's horn.

The driver in the Mustang in front of him thrust his arm out the window and gave Junior the finger.

Unfortunately the man was waiting on a red light at Fifty-seventh and Madison as an enraged Junior leaped out of his car, raced forward, grabbed the man's finger in his vicelike grip, and began crushing it backward. The man cried out in agony.

"Haven't you got any fuckin' manners?" rasped Junior.

"Please, please," whimpered the man, who thought he was going to lose consciousness from the pain.

"What the hell's happening to the quality of life in this city?" asked Junior. "Do I know you? Was I bothering you? What provocation did you have to give me the finger? I coulda had my little nieces in the car with me. How the fuck do I explain what the finger means to them?"

Numerous horns were now honking behind the two cars stalled inexplicably at a green light.

"You're breaking my finger," gasped the driver of the Mustang.

"Relax. You'd know if I'd broken it. A simple apology and I'm outta here."

"I'm sorry. I'm sorry."

"Okay." Junior grinned, released the man's finger, then gave him a playful slap on the cheek. "Behave yourself now."

Junior dashed back to his car, leaped in, and made it through the light before it turned red again. The Mustang's driver was incapable of using his left hand so he sat in agony, enduring the abuse of his fellow motorists.

As he sped his sports car west on Fifty-seventh Street, Junior mused on why the little altercation at the stoplight had relieved the tension he'd been feeling. It didn't seem so important now to get laid. Where the hell was that chanting CD? He groped around on the floor and found the compact disc that Cardinal Corcoran had sent him on his birthday. Good old Uncle George. Hard to believe that the man who had taught him to toss a football in his backyard twenty years earlier was now a prince of the church. Junior chanted along with the monks as he executed a death-defying three-wheeled left onto Ninth Avenue.

There was no parking spot available by the time he swung onto Forty-sixth Street, so Junior glided his car to a halt in front of a hydrant and climbed the stone steps leading to the private entrance of the celebrated eatery that bore his family's name.

Tesla's Restaurant was located in a hundred-year-old brownstone on Restaurant Row between Eighth and Ninth avenues in the theater district. Nick Tesla had acquired the property twenty years earlier and, while continuing to operate his carting business successfully, fulfilled a lifelong ambition of running a classy restaurant like the one his father had slaved in as a singing waiter when Nick was a child in the thirties.

The ground floor was sumptuously decorated in Italian antiques from the eighteenth and nineteenth centuries. The ceilings were a forest of breathtaking crystal chandeliers. French doors led out to a garden terrace that people booked throughout the winter in the vain hope of enjoying during the brief summer months it was open. There were several rooms available for parties on the second floor. The third floor was where Nicolo Tesla had his private office. It was up this third set of stairs that Junior was now trudging like a dray horse.

"Hey, Pop! It's like a goddamn Stairmaster comin' up here," puffed Junior as he invaded his father's sanctum. "When you gonna break down and put in an elevator? Or one of those sliding chair things? I mean I'm in shape but that's still a helluva— Hiya, Louie!" The last greeting was to Louie "The Patch" Torino, who had been his father's bodyguard and right-hand man as long as Junior could remember. The bodyguard and Nick Tesla had been watching a horse race on ESPN when Junior had burst in.

"Louie, go have a snack," said Nick Tesla, seated behind his rococo desk.

"I ain't hungry," replied Torino.

"Then go eat for me. I wanna talk to the kid."

Junior could feel the beginning of a migraine coming on. Why couldn't he call him Nick or Junior or "my son"? How come it was always "the kid"? He was thirty-four years old. He was too old to be the kid.

"Whad about the race?" asked Torino.

"It's the same fuckin' race we saw yesterday, Louie. You want a different horse to win? G'wan. And bring me back a sandwich. Open face."

Torino left the office and Tesla continued to stare in silence at the horses on the television.

"The Patch didn't know it was a rerun?" laughed Junior. "You shoulda bet him, Pop. You coulda made some money."

"Why would I want to fool The Patch? Louie's been with me from before you were born. From before I was stupid enough not to let my seed run down my leg instead of lettin' your mother be infected with you." Tesla switched off the TV set and rose from behind his desk to where his son was standing in stunned silence.

"Where the hell did I go wrong with you? Joe Carlucci's an animal but he's got a son who's a goddamn priest. Phil DeFillipo's so stupid he fucked goats in the old country but his son's a doctor and his daughter's a lawyer. Just me! I'm the only one's got a goon for a kid."

"Pop! What did I do? Why are you—"

'Don't play the iggie with me, Junior. I didn't fuckin' get where I am by lettin' some military school dropout hand me a line of shit—"

"You bringin' the academy up again?"

"Shut yer mouth! I don't wanna see that mouth open again till I tell you. Now, who the fuck told you to lean on that driver last week?"

"I don't know what—"

Tesla slapped his son furiously across the face. Junior went scarlet, balled his fist, and began to lift it in retaliation. Tesla stared at him in contemptuous disbelief and asked: "To a father? You raise a hand to a father?" Tesla slapped his son again and Junior dropped into a chair sobbing. "With your big muscles and your little brain this is how you thank me?"

"I'm sorry, Pop."

"You fuckin' better be sorry. I'm just sorry your mother don't know who the patron saint of morons is to pray to for you. What is your problem? Who made you a soldier all of a sudden? I sent you to the best goddamn schools. You got thrown out of them all. I built up a business so you could take it over. Not be a goddamn legbreaker." Tesla whacked his son across the top of his head with the palm of his hand for emphasis.

"I'm sorry, Pop," whimpered Junior, "I'm sorry."

" 'I'm sorry. I'm sorry.' Always like a little girl. Big muscles but no balls and no brains. I been shittin' a brick for a week now that some witness might turn up—"

"There was nobody there that night, Pop. I swear. Nobody but . . ."

"Yeah?"

"Sanchez. The Cuban."

"Oh, yeah. Yer cokehead protégé. And where the hell is he? Back in Havana, I hope. . . . Where is he, Junior?"

"I'm lookin' for him."

"You better be lookin' for him. Cuz if the cops know about him, they're gonna be flashin' a light up every asshole in this town trying to find him. He's the kinda witness they dream about. So you better find him first. But don't you touch him. Just phone me. Understand? No De Niro shit like in the movies. We know professionals who can take care of it this time. Y'understand? We're talkin' a conga drum filled with cement and a dead Cuban at the bottom of Long Island Sound."

9

SUSAN SET THE pace and Becker had trouble keeping up with her as they zigzagged through traffic en route to the courthouse on Thomas Street. Inside they took the elevator up to the third floor and made their way down a corridor littered with blasé and/or nervous lawyers whose cacophonous babbling echoed up and down the hallway as they waited for their cases to be called.

Walking into the courtroom, Susan spotted Davis Kumba, a huge, sixtyish, bald-headed West African seated at the defense table. He was engaged in heated conversation with Bart Sugarman, his bearded Armani-clad lawyer, who rocked back and forth with greater rapidity than Becker. Susan wondered aloud if they had attended the same law school.

Becker shook his head and whispered: "Yeshiva Tech."

Kumba turned his head, saw Susan, and flashed her a huge smile.

"I love your outfit," purred Kumba in his thick West African accent. "It goes with your hair."

"He certainly has hutzpah," whispered Susan.

"Chutzpah." Becker corrected her pronunciation. "Did you ever meet a con artist who didn't?"

"Did we find the girlfriend yet?"

"No."

"What!?"

"We don't *need* the girlfriend," hissed Becker.

"She's got the money, Alan!"

"Less than half. We still have the other assets."

Davis Kumba was facing charges of grand larceny. Using a phony tour guide company, Kumba Safaris, he had bilked 150 football-mad expatriate Ugandans, who had paid him two thousand dollars each for a World Cup package tour. When the Ugandans had turned up at JFK there was no plane, no Kumba Safari rep, and no office on Twenty-eighth Street. Susan's meticulous investigations had uncovered Kumba's bachelor apartment in the Waldorf Towers, a Lexus, a Cadillac, a Bentley, a house in Amagansett, a nineteen-year-old mistress (who had been a *Penthouse* centerfold), and a rundown apartment in Queens where his welfare checks for $176 were delivered every two weeks. The six-foot-six-inch confidence trickster also had a rap sheet that had criss-crossed the country for over thirty years.

The case would have been a slam dunk for Susan—if it hadn't ended up in Leo Silverberg's court. In his day, Judge Leo Silverberg had been a titan of jurisprudence. A veritable Solomon. But that day was long past and, like the old vaudeville comic who wouldn't quit while he was ahead, the judge would not relinquish the stage.

"There's no such thing as Alzheimer's," ruled Leo Silverberg. "It's just a cop-out." And, despite a few tragicomic episodes where the judge could neither remember where he was (the courtroom) nor how he had arrived there, his general lucidity and credibility made it difficult (if not impossible) to force Silverberg off the bench.

Had anyone from the Office of Court Administration popped into the court room the day before, it might have been a different story. Susan had spent close to an hour arguing a motion with Silverberg during which time he not only referred to her repeatedly as "Mrs. Logan" but finally admitted that the case he was referring to involved arson and had occurred during John Lindsay's tenure as Mayor of New York.

"When you've heard as many cases as I have, Mrs. Logan, you're entitled to have them overlap once in a while. I will grant your motion." Silverberg then tapped his fingers on the bench like a telegraph operator sending out an urgent SOS and moved to adjourn until the next morning.

Mario DeStefano, the roly-poly court officer whom everyone referred to affectionately as "Mr. Five-by-Five," entered the courtroom and drifted down toward Susan's table.

"Howarya?" asked DeStefano.

"Just fine thanks, Mario. How are you?"

"Can't complain."

"Have you seen His Honor this morning?"

"Uh-huh."

"And how was his mood?"

"We talked about baseball."

"Did he ask if Ty Cobb was playing?" asked Becker under his breath.

"Whadhesay?" asked DeStefano, compressing another sentence into one word.

"Nothing," smiled Susan, managing to kick sharply the wisecracking Becker simultaneously under the table. "Ah! Here he is now."

DeStefano whipped around and saw Leo Silverberg enter the courtroom: a once tall man now bent over; a full head of hair dwindled to long black wisps; a Gable mustache reduced to a cartoon smudge on his upper lip. The judge licked his lips, wiped his mouth, and mopped his brow frequently when he spoke.

"Order in the court. All people having business before this court, please rise."

"Sit, sit," boomed Silverberg as if everyone present had been invited for dinner. "So, Mario, what have we got today?"

"*Archibald* versus *Kumba*, Your Honor."

"Good!" Then the judge ran his hands through his remaining wisps of hair, rubbed his eyes, put his glasses on, and stared out at the courtroom. "Ms. Given! Good morning."

Susan smiled. "Good morning, Your Honor." The judge was in good shape today.

"Been a long time."

Susan's heart sank. What was she going to do about this wacky old jurist? She looked over at the defense table and saw Sugarman beaming at Kumba as though his client were already home free. Then he whispered something to the huge West African and rose to his feet.

"Your Honor, I move for dismissal at the present time."

"On what grounds?" asked Susan, shooting to her feet.

"The prosecution has failed to present sufficient evidence to show cause why—"

"We interviewed over a hundred witnesses—"

"None of whom was an American citizen."

"You tried that one two days ago, Mr. Sugarman. The judge ruled against you."

"What did I do?" asked Silverberg.

"Don't you remember, Your Honor? You said—" Susan realized she had made a grave error by asking the judge if he remembered.

"I remember perfectly, Ms. Given. I made no such ruling."

Becker groaned audibly at the prosecution table.

"On the contrary, Your Honor," smiled Susan, trying desperately to keep her exasperation under control. "If you check the transcript—"

"I don't need to check the transcript, Ms. Given. I know what I remember."

"I'm sure you do. But I don't remember what I forgot."

"Don't get smart with me, Ms. Given. I had a woman in here the other day thought she could put one over on me. What the hell was her name?"

"Logan," whispered Becker, rolling his eyes to the ceiling.

"Doesn't matter," said Silverberg. "This is my court. I say what goes down or not. Are we in agreement about that?"

"Absolutely. I just thought if the court reporter could read back the ruling from yesterday—"

"Logan! That was the woman's name. She tried to give me a hard time, too. I'm not a pushover, you know." The judge began tapping out another telegraph message with his fingers.

"Permission to approach the bench?" asked Susan.

"What for?"

"I have no desire to embarrass this court. I would like to speak to you out of earshot—"

Sugarman shot to his feet: "I object, your Honor."

"To what?" growled Silverberg. "Sit down before I find you in contempt. You may approach the bench, Ms. Given."

"Be careful," muttered Becker. "He's serving matzoh ball soup with no matzoh balls."

Susan began fiddling with the strand of pearls around her neck, then caught herself halfway across the courtroom and stopped. She was now close enough to Silverberg to see that the judge had missed a large portion of his face while shaving that morning.

"What is it, Ms. Given?"

"I'm . . . concerned." Susan spoke in a very low voice.

"Speak up."

"I said I was concerned."

"About what?"

"To put it delicately . . . about you, Your Honor. I have the greatest respect for you—"

"Yeah, yeah, yeah. Don't schmooze me, Ms. Given. I'm above all that and so should you be."

"Do I really have to read the transcript to you?"

"I don't give a shit about the transcript. Court reporters make mistakes, too."

"Please, Judge—"

"If you haven't got anything to say to me, sit down."

She dropped her voice to a near whisper: "Leo, don't do this."

"What!"

"I'm speaking to you as a friend, Leo. You're a little shaky this morning. You know me. You know my reputation. I'm not trying to pull a fast one. If we read the transcript, you're going to find something completely different from what you think."

Silverberg looked genuinely confused and began licking his lips and mopping his brow. Finally he asked: "What happened to Mrs. Logan?"

"She's . . . not here today."

"Just as well. She was a pain in the ass." The judge stared at his gavel for the longest time, as if he expected it to levitate. Then he turned his attention to the defense table and Davis Kumba in particular. Finally he asked: "Is that Robeson?"

"No," sighed Susan. "That's the defendant, Davis Kumba."

Judge Silverberg nodded, then rose to his feet abruptly and announced: "I have a previous engagement. Court is adjourned until tomorrow."

"What time?" asked a stunned Bart Sugarman.

The judge turned to Mario DeStefano and with a majestic wave of his hand said: "Tell him." Then Leo Silverberg left the courtroom to keep his previous engagement (real or imagined).

"What did you say to him?" asked Becker when she returned to the prosecution table.

"Somebody should phone his wife," said Susan. "He shouldn't be . . ."

"On the bench."

"Knock it off, Becker," snapped Susan. "You should only be half the lawyer this man was in his prime. He's seventy-eight years old. Okay? And he's heard the chimes at midnight."

"I'm sorry," murmured Becker. "Sometimes I think it's all about winning and I forget—"

"It *is* about winning, Alan. Don't kid yourself. But it's also how one plays the game. That bearded scumbag over there went in for the kill the moment he thought Judge Silverberg was *non compos.* That's despicable."

Susan had turned toward the defense table and her peripheral vision took in two spectators she had not anticipated seeing that day. She brought her head round again and stared blankly at her brother and her mother sitting together. What were they doing in court?

"Hello, dear," mouthed Marian Given, wriggling the fingers of her right hand in greeting to her daughter. Henry Given arched his eyebrows in salute. Except for his blond hair and her snowy white, the two looked exactly alike and could easily have been mistaken for siblings instead of mother and son.

"They must be related to you," said Becker, packing up his battered briefcase.

"Is it that obvious?"

"These are not people who work on a kibbutz."

"Come and meet them."

Marian Given was turning seventy that Sunday but looked a full ten years younger. If the U.S. Customs wanted to know if she had anything to declare, it would certainly not be excess weight. How had she given birth to Henry, Linda, and me without any hips, wondered Susan? Not fair. I have to run four miles every morning just to keep the status quo and my mother walks—walks! rides in a golf cart—around the grounds of her country club and never gains a pound.

"Is this the intermission, dear?" asked Marian.

"This isn't a Broadway show, Mother. We don't know when the second-act curtain will rise. Or if."

But Marian continued on in her proud stagemother mode as she turned to the newly introduced Becker and pronounced: "I thought she was awfully good. Didn't you?"

"Me, I prefer a musical."

"But what is there to see these days?" asked Marian, not getting Becker's sarcasm. "I ask you. I went with my

70

cancer ladies to see *M. Butterfly*. That is *not* a musical. I want something I can hum on the way home in the car."

"Did you see *Nixon in China?*" asked Becker.

"He sent us a postcard," answered Marian without blinking an eye. "Actually it was Pat."

"Why are you guys here?" asked Susan abruptly. "You know I hate surprises."

"Spur of the moment," said Henry. "Mother had to come into town to see her lawyer—"

"Is something wrong?" asked Susan.

"Your father's estate, dear. Do you remember that silver mine Digby wanted him to go partners in?"

"Digby who?"

"Clyde Digby. He and your father were at Cornell together. He was in the OSS—"

"CIA," corrected Henry. "He was in the OSS in the last days of the war. But his real career, or fake career, depending on how one—"

"He told everyone he was in the oil business," said Marian, "but your father got a bit tipsy one night and told me the whole story of Digby's secret—"

"What about the silver mine?" asked Susan.

"Taxes. Your father's been dead for two years and they still want taxes. I thought he'd relinquished his interest in the mine years ago."

"Is it a lot of money?" asked Susan.

"She can actually write it off," her brother answered reassuringly. "That's what Sheila said anyhow."

"Where is Sheila?"

"Beijing."

"So's Barry Praeger."

"I know. They're bidding on the same hotel."

"Is that your friend's husband?" asked Marian. "The ones who had the bas mitzvah in Israel?"

"Bar mitzvah."

"Isn't it the same thing? That's what they told me at the card store."

"One's for a girl and one's for a boy," said Susan.

71

"Oh, dear. Babs Chadwick's daughter married a Jewish boy. Years ago. And her grandson Randy had a bas mitzvah the other week."

"Bar, Mother. Bar."

"That's the point. I went into Townsend's to buy Randy a card—I enclosed a check as well—and there wasn't much of a selection. Frankly, I was surprised they had any. But one card said 'bar' and the other said 'bas' and when I asked Mr. Townsend what the difference was he said one was Hallmark and the other was recycled. The Hallmark was much prettier so I bought it. I hope Randy wasn't offended."

"I'm going back to the office," said Becker, certain he had wandered into the second act of a Philip Barry comedy. "Nice to have met you all."

"Wait, wait!" Susan called after him. "I'll go back with you."

"But we've come to take you to lunch," protested a crestfallen Henry Given, fiddling nervously with his bow tie. Henry was older than his sister by two years and lived directly across the park from her on Central Park West. His wife, Sheila, was in the hotel business and traveled round the world constantly, leaving their two sons in Henry's care the better part of each month. Henry rather enjoyed this setup and, being a homebody, it didn't interfere with his career as an historian (his specialty being the City of New York).

"Not today, Henry, please. I have my apple and a can of tuna back at the office and a very important meeting in Gramercy Park at two—"

"Where?" asked her brother.

"The Evanston Hotel."

"Perfect!" beamed Henry. "I made a reservation for us at the Stuyvesant Club. It's right around the corner." Then he nodded politely at Becker. "She'll be going with us."

"I didn't think she wouldn't," replied Becker. Then he moved to Susan and whispered in her ear: "You never told me your family was Jewish."

"I'll see you later." Susan smiled.

"Can I eat your tuna?"

"No. I'll save it for tomorrow."

"You *are* Jewish," mouthed Becker, then crushed his briefcase to his chest and left the courtroom.

Definitely not Jewish but certainly thrifty, the three Givens took advantage of Indian summer to walk up Broadway with Henry the historian pointing out the less familiar landmarks along the way while Marian questioned her daughter about the Kumba case.

"But if he lived in the Waldorf Towers, dear, why did he need to be on welfare?"

"He didn't, Mother. He's a compulsive crook. He'll rip off people with money or people without. It's the Kumbas of this world who fill my calendar."

"Well, it's all very fascinating but I do wish you'd get a juicy murder case once in a while. Something I can talk about at the club."

"I don't handle murder cases, Mother."

"Which is fortunate for Hugh Carver," piped up Henry. "Oh, look! There's the Sievewright. Or what's left of it." Henry waxed melodic about a fin de siècle building where Evelyn Nesbit had dallied with John Barrymore while her demented husband, Harry Thaw, prowled maniacally through lower Manhattan plotting the demise of architect Sanford White, whom he was certain had cuckolded him. Throughout her brother's fascinating impromptu lecture, Susan mused on the peculiarity of the world: On the one hand there was Alan Becker's mother, who was terrified her son might get mixed up in a murder investigation; then there was Marian Given, who was disappointed that her daughter wasn't.

"What's your next case, dear?"

"Waste removal."

"Don't be rude, dear."

"Garbage, Mother. Trash. It's controlled by organized crime."

"Wonderful. Perhaps there'll be a murder involved."

"I doubt it."

"And how *is* the divorce coming along?" asked Marian, in the same tones she might have used to inquire about the state of her Greenwich neighbor's rhododendrons.

"It took less time to build the pyramids."

"Is he being difficult?"

"Is the Pope Catholic? We're talking about Hugh, Mother. When was he ever not difficult? If it was pouring cats and dogs, Hugh would declare it wasn't raining just to make a point. And whatever that point *was*, he would undoubtedly carry it to his grave. Which hopefully will be sooner than later."

"Susan! You don't mean that. He is the father of your children."

"Thank God, they don't have any of his genes.'

"And how are the girls handling it all?"

"Better than I am. I don't know. Polly complains more about his behavior. Ivy just hangs up on him when he becomes too demanding."

"That's the telephone. How do they get on in person?"

"Hugh and Ivy? They scream at each other constantly. Polly says they're an absolute hoot. Like an old married couple.'

"Is he seeing anyone?"

"I'm sure I don't know." The last report Susan had received from Polly was that her father had resumed his on-again, off-again affair with an anorexic Barney's sales-girl named Sigrid, whose profile could have graced the prow of a Viking ship. Hugh and Sigrid were totally wrong for each other, which doubtless put the lanky six-foot Swede high on the neurotic shrink's list of unattainables to be attained. But Susan wasn't prepared to discuss any of this with her mother.

"I understand he's seeing that Swedish girl again," said Marian matter-of-factly.

"Does someone e-mail you in Greenwich, Mother? How could you possibly know that?"

"Ivy phoned me the other day. Wanted to know what

I'd like for my birthday. Isn't she the dearest child? Just tell her not to bring her hamsters on Sunday. We don't want to tempt Tony and Cleo again." Tony and Cleo were actually Antony and Cleopatra, Marian's beloved Siamese cats. Ivy had brought one of her hamsters for a visit the year before and had placed the cage on the kitchen table while she went off to the Cedarhurst Club to play tennis with Polly. When she returned an hour later, the cage was empty. She was forced to play her *Medea* scene *sine corpore*. No hard evidence ever pointed directly to the cats but Tony and Cleo did skip dinner that evening. "I don't know what he sees in that shopgirl."

"She was a psych major in Stockholm. I'm sure they have a complex relationship. . . . That was a joke, Mother."

"Hmmm. Let's talk about the weekend. I've got my golf tournament all day Saturday so the earliest I could pick
 • you girls up at the station would be—"

"It might just be me."

"Whatever are you talking about, Susan? It's my birthday. The girls have always spent—"

"Hugh has them on Sunday morning. He's holding them for ransom."

"That miserable son-of-a—"

"Mother! You don't mean that. He *is* the father of your grandchildren."

"What does he want? Hmm? The paintings? The jewels?" Marian's voice took on a hardness that Susan had rarely heard her mother use.

"He'll settle for two subsequent weekends with the girls."

"No!"

"But it's your birthday."

"I'll come into town and we'll have my birthday dinner at Petaluma. I won't have you bowing to blackmail."

There were moments when Susan's seemingly predictable mother could amaze her. This was one of them. "Mother, can I give you a hug?"

"On the street? Certainly not. But I appreciate the thought, dear."

10

AB ROSENTHAL ALWAYS felt a slight sense of superiority in the presence of his patients. He knew it was wrong. He knew it was egotistical. He blamed it on the sheer sense of power he experienced in having other humans tell him their deepest, darkest secrets and expecting him to be able to solve all their problems. Sometimes it made him feel like a god. (His colleague, Hugh Carver, had admitted to the same feelings one brandy-soaked evening.)

But the patient now seated in his office unnerved him. Rosenthal was physically afraid of this man and wondered why he had ever taken him on. There was no doubt in the doctor's mind that the man was violent and, possibly, homicidal. He had broken the law on numerous occasions and boasted about it in his sessions. But there was something fascinating about the man as well and Rosenthal's ego was seduced by the fact that such a brute could be as equally in his power as his other less dangerous patients.

"I got a fuckin' migraine," moaned Junior Tesla, as he sat on the edge of his chair, muscles clenched in tension.

"You've just seen your father, haven't you?"

"Yeah."

"You've disappointed him again."

Junior got up from his chair and began to prowl the perimeter of Rosenthal's office. He paused in front of a bookshelf that displayed a silver-framed photograph of a short, plump woman with close-cropped hair.

"This your mother?" asked Junior.

"That's my wife," replied the pudgy, bald, gray-bearded Rosenthal.

"No kiddin'! She's kinda cute. Know who she looks a little like? What's-her-name Bates. The one who played the cop in that Sharon Stone movie *Diabolicue*."

"It's pronounced *Diabolique*."

"No shit. Didja see it?"

"I saw the original," replied Rosenthal loftily. "With Simone Signoret."

"Original what?"

"It was a French film in the fifties. The one you saw was a remake."

"In the fifties!? Two broads eatin' at the Y and bumpin' off a guy, in the fifties? Far out!"

"We're straying, Nick. What about your father?"

"Fuck him."

"Hmmm. Still have that migraine?"

"I wouldn't come to see you if I didn't," said Junior, resuming his seat once more.

"What was it this time, Nick? What did your father do to you?"

"Same old shit. He won't give me any responsibility. Says he built the business for me to take over but then he never lets me show any initiative. . . ."

"The restaurant or the carting company?"

"Everything. I'm the only boy—man. I'm a man and he treats me like a kid. That's what he always calls me. 'The kid.' No respect. My two big sisters are perfect. They gave him grandchildren. My kid sister Toni is a goddamn hoor. She fucks anything. But my father treats her like Princess Di. Just me. I'm the one he says can't do anything right."

Junior pounded on the arm of his chair for emphasis and Rosenthal was convinced the antique was one good wallop away from destruction.

"Do you make notes after I leave?" asked Junior, finally coming out of a lengthy reverie. "You never write nothing down when I'm here."

"Occasionally."

"Occasionally what?"

"I keep a record," nodded Rosenthal, tapping his upper lip with his index finger.

"How safe are your records?"

"Aren't we straying off the subject?"

"This *is* the subject. I can't go to a fuckin' priest with my problems. They all work for my Uncle George."

"I don't understand. . . ."

"I need someone to talk to. Get all this shit off my chest."

"Isn't that what we've been doing, Nick?"

"I've been holding back. There's things I haven't told you."

"You'll feel better if you do. And it will make my helping you a great deal—"

Junior nodded, then dragged his chair closer to where Rosenthal was sitting and asked: "Did I tell you about the sheepdog?"

"I don't think so."

"You can't blab, right?"

"Of course not."

"And the cops can't make you talk."

"Not at all."

Junior Tesla heaved a deep sigh of relief, then got up from his chair and began to pace around the room again. Finally he spoke: "I killed a guy last week. I didn't mean to. It was on TV and in the newspapers. I did it for my father. Right? And he ends up humiliating me for it. What is his problem, Doc? He's the one should be in fuckin' therapy. Know what I mean?"

Junior continued on in the same vein for the rest of the session and, by the time he left Ab Rosenthal's office, the psychiatrist was no longer frightened of his patient. He was terrified.

SUSAN ARRIVED AT the Evanston at the stroke of two. Vinh Ho Chi did not. The notorious security man sidled over to Susan ready to extract his ten dollars in tribute. Susan whipped out her badge and the security man wilted in front of her eyes.

"Make yerself at home, lady." The security man waved grandly toward the lobby and its furniture, which might have qualified as antique if it hadn't worn so badly. All it looked like now was junk.

Removing a copy of the *Law Journal* from her briefcase, Susan sat down on a dilapidated sofa to wait for Vinh. By 2:30 the devious Vietnamese landlord had failed to appear and Susan was royally miffed as she sat crossing and uncrossing her shapely legs repeatedly.

This bit of choreography did not go unappreciated by a greasy-haired man in a Ban-Lon sweater slouched down in a seat opposite her. Wiping the drool from his mouth, the man staggered toward Susan. She could see take-out Chinese food stains on his shirtfront and smelled Thunderbird on his breath.

"Hello, girlie." He swayed back and forth over Susan, who was now seeking refuge behind the pages of the *Law Journal*. "Didn't we have a good time here once?"

"I don't think so." Susan fingered her pearls and wondered what there was about her dress that might lead the wino to think her a hooker.

It was now 2:40. Vinh had left no message for Susan at the front desk. The man wasn't late. He was rude. He was giving the District Attorney's Office the finger yet again. That was the last straw. Susan would return to Centre Street, phone Vinh's lawyer, and notify him that she had no other course to follow but— No! She would check out this "den of iniquity" for herself. Floor by floor.

"Would you like me to escort you?" asked the security man, hoping to ingratiate himself with Susan in case some sort of bust *did* go down that afternoon.

"No, thank you. I prefer the element of surprise."

Susan rode up to the twentieth floor in the rickety old elevator and worked her way down, giving each corridor a cursory inspection. By the time she reached the fifth floor, she was mentally awarding Nip and Tuck citations for their surviving the combined smells of filth, urine, and decay.

Stepping off on the fifth floor, Susan spotted a prostitute wandering aimlessly down the hallway. The hooker made eye contact with Susan for a moment, then smiled and continued down the hall humming the latest Hootie and the Blowfish hit. Susan leaped back as a pair of mice danced insolently past her on the threadbare carpet.

Nip and Tuck had explained to her that unoccupied rooms were always left ajar so that drug transactions could be handled speedily and informally. Susan decided to see for herself, not wanting to read from a police transcript in the courtroom. She would eyeball Vinh on the stand and say: "I was in your hotel, Mr. Vinh. I visited every floor and I saw what was going on—"

"What the fuck do you want?"

Susan had been going from room to room trying the doorknobs without any luck. This time she'd hit the jackpot and walked in on a naked black prostitute astride an elderly customer in a similar state of undress.

"What is it?" gasped the old man.

"Shh. Shh. Don't you worry 'bout nothin', sweetie. Hey, blondie! They sells postcards in the lobby. Git my drift?"

"Sorry. The door was supposed to be locked."

"Then wha'd you try it for? Y'all dress pretty fancy for a burglar."

"I said I was sorry."

The next two rooms were locked. Then she found another one open a crack. She knocked. No reply. She eased the door open and found a nude woman lying facedown on the ragged candlewick bedspread. Susan was about to apologize yet again when she realized the woman was not moving.

Every instinct told Susan to leave the room immediately and summon help. This was not exactly her area of expertise. She was no Janie Moore, who dealt with corpses on a regular basis. Asset Forfeiture. Seizing ill-gotten gains. That was her stock and trade. Yet all signs that day had pointed toward foul play. Marian's premonition at lunch. *Perhaps there'll be a murder involved.* Was that what drew Susan toward the body now? An inexorable sense of the inevitable? The body was now on her watch. Poor kid. She was only seventeen. Eighteen at most. A bracelet on her wrist read "Brittany." Was she really dead? Susan reached her hand out to take the girl's pulse.

The bathroom door burst open and a lean, muscular Hispanic man in his late thirties emerged unshaven and clad in his underwear. His eyes were ablaze with crack cocaine.

"Wha' you want?" growled the man in a thick accent.

"I'm frightfully sorry." Susan struggled to keep any sense of panic from her voice as she edged toward the door. "I seem to have the wrong room."

With athletic grace, the man vaulted across the bed and locked the door. Grabbing his trousers from the back of a rickety chair, he pulled them on, removed a gun from the right pocket, and aimed it at Susan.

"Y'ain' goin' nowhere. Siddown."

"I have an appointment—"

"You got an appointment with this, *puta.* Now, siddown."

He kicked the rickety chair toward Susan and she sat down reluctantly.

"Where do we go from here?" asked Susan, hearing Marian's voice coming out of her mouth for the second time that day.

"Shut up."

"What happened to her?"

"Shut up. I'm tryin' to think."

"And I'm trying to help you. If you didn't kill this girl, I don't see what the problem is. And if you did, there must be mitigating circumstances. I'm certain if—"

"What is your fuckin' problem, lady? Talk, talk, talk, talk. Can' you shut up?"

Susan could. Easily. But she was merely obeying a long-ago voice from a self-defense seminar urging her to keep talking. Establish a rapport with this man. Very important, Susan. Keep him from thinking and panicking. Lull him into a sense of surrender. Hopefully, you can both leave this room alive. As opposed to poor little Brittany.

"I'm Susan Given."

"Good for you."

"What's your name?"

"Manolo. Manny . . . Sanchez."

"That's a start. Would you like to tell me what happened, Manny?"

"Noooo!" Perspiration dripped heavily down Sanchez's face. He started to shake as he leaned back against the wall, staring up at the ceiling and muttering to himself in Spanish.

Susan glanced at her watch. Three o'clock. Ivy would be out of school in fifteen minutes and taking the bus home. Polly would be finished by four. Would she ever see them again? Stop it, Susan. Don't even put that thought out into the universe. The man is a junkie and probably more scared than you are.

"Where are you from, Manny?"

"What are you? A social worker?"

"No." Susan decided it wouldn't be a smart move to tell him she worked for the district attorney. William Archibald. Archie. The man Lana and Ava had quarreled over. Now, who had told her that story? Michael? No, Michael didn't even know Mr. Archibald. It must have been Becker. Alan knew all the dish on everyone. If Alan only knew where Susan was now. Perhaps he'd wonder why she hadn't returned by three? Three-thirty? Maybe he'd phone the hotel looking for her. No. Becker just thinks the meeting's going well. Would Gretchen wonder where her boss was? No. Susan operated autonomously. "See you later." No one questioned her comings and goings. Except Lydia. Maybe Lydia would want to see Susan that afternoon. Put out an APB. Send out the bloodhounds. Find that blond bitch! Nope. Susan was on her own. Held at gunpoint in this awful room in the Evanston Hotel with Manny Sanchez and poor dead Brittany.

"I'm from Miami."

"Hmm?"

"I come from Miami," snapped Sanchez. "You asked where I come from."

"What brought you to New York?"

"None of yer business. You ask a lot of questions."

"Sorry." The silence in the room made Susan acutely aware of the dead female lying on the bed. "Do you mind if I cover her up?"

"What?"

"Brittany."

"How'd you know her name?"

"Her bracelet."

"I don't know what the hell happened. I was bangin' her and then she moaned and then she just stop breathin'."

"That's okay, Manny."

"How you know my name?"

"You told me."

"When?"

"Before."

"You thirsty?" Manny's lips were cracked and he was licking them. Drug withdrawal.

"No. Yes. Why don't I call room service?"

"Don' touch that phone."

"I'd kill for a Diet Coke right now, Manny. Wouldn't you? My treat."

"They don' got no fuckin' room service in this joint. . . . What's your name again?"

"Susan. May I, please, cover her up?"

"Sure."

Susan got up from the chair, lifted the corner of the candlewick bedspread, and draped it across Brittany's body. Then she moved toward the window.

"Wha' you doin'?"

"Just checking the traffic. My kids will be coming home from school soon. Are you married?"

"I was."

"Divorced?"

"No. We just don' live together no more."

"Like me. But I'm working on it. Children? . . . Do you have any children, Manny?"

"Hey, Susan?"

"Yes?"

"Go back in the chair."

"Of course, Manny. But I *am* thirsty. And a bit hungry. I know a fabulous Chinese take-out place near here. Do you like Chinese food?"

"No."

"How 'bout Mexican? Beans and rice. Salsa. Tacquitos. Quesadillas. Guacamole. A bottle of ice-cold Tecate."

"Now you talkin', Susan. Maybe a six-pack."

"Two six-packs. I'm very thirsty, Manny. And remember: it's my treat."

"Go ahead. Phone 'em up. Tell 'em to make it quick."

"Want anything else?" she asked while dialing. "Cigarettes?"

"Nah. I'm tryin' to quit."

"Me, too. I mean I smoke about two a day now. . . . Hello? Is that El Sombrero? This is Susan Given. Yes, La Señorita Given. . . . Fine, thank you. How are you? I'd like to place an order. . . . I'm at the Evanston Hotel. . . . Room Five eleven. Do you still make that nip and tuck? Sounds like nip and tuck. Manny, what am I trying to say?"

Sanchez moved across the room like a wounded panther, seized the phone from Susan's hand, and barked into it in Spanish: "Did you ever fuck your grandmother?"

The voice on the other end asked: "Susan? Is that you? What's wrong?"

Sanchez cursed in Spanish, then slammed the phone down and turned menacingly to Susan. "You done a real stupid thing, Susan!"

ALAN BECKER WAS seated at his computer plugging into any and all information on the garbage cartel that he could download from the Internet.

The telephone rang and he grabbed it, emulating his boss's style: "Becker."

"What kind of way is that to answer a phone?" asked his mother, Rose Becker. "You can't be a mensch and say hello?"

"Hi, Ma. What's up?"

"So I watched your boss on TV this morning. Very impressive. Nice-looking. Gorgeous legs."

"She's a marathon runner."

"Just don't fall into her trap, Alan."

"What trap, Ma?"

"I know you idolize her. The two of you work very close. She's getting a divorce. She's an older woman. I know how these things work. But you don't marry her, Alan. Do you hear me? She'll use you."

"Ma, she's my boss. There's no romance."

"I hear how you talk about her. I know how impressed

you are by these blond New Englanders. There's nothing wrong with being Jewish from Bensonhurst. Stick with your own. Call Gert's niece Rusty. Very sexy. Also a runner."

"Ma, I've got to go. We've got a new case."

"What kind of case?"

"Nothing special," said Becker with just enough evasion to be picked up on his mother's sonar screen.

"Something dangerous?" asked Mrs. Becker.

"Nooo. It's just . . . garbage." Becker mumbled the last word.

"What did you say? Sounded like garbage."

"Yeah. You know, trash, refuse, carting."

"The Mafia! You swore you wouldn't get mixed up with the Mafia."

"Ma, it's not like that. This is Asset Forfeiture. It's like Citibank here. I swear. I'll call you later, Ma. There's nothing to worry about. Honest."

Gretchen walked into his office at that moment with a frown on her face.

"What's wrong?"

"I just had a weird phone call from Susan."

"Where was she?"

"At the Evanston."

Becker glanced at his watch. It was half past three. That was some meeting. Susan and Vinh must have really gotten down to the nitty-gritty. "Did she say how it went? Is she on her way back?"

"She asked if this was the El Sombrero."

"What!?"

"She wanted to place an order."

"Was she drunk?"

"Alan!"

"Did she say anything else?"

"No. This Spanish guy got on the phone and he was . . . well, very rude."

"What did he say?"

"He asked if I'd ever had sex with my grandmother."

"You're putting me on."

"Alan, I am telling you what just happened. Do you think anything's wrong."

"Did she say anything else?"

"No. Yes. She wanted to know if we still made nip and tuck. Something that sounded like nip and tuck. Then the Spanish guy got on the phone—"

Becker bolted forward and grabbed the phone. "Detective Regan, please? . . . What about Tucker? . . . What time are they expected back? . . . This is Alan Becker in Forfeiture. We have a situation. . . . The Evanston Hotel. . . . Susan Given Carver—" Becker turned back to Gretchen. "Where in the hotel?"

"Room Five eleven."

"She's in Room Five eleven. . . . No! For God's sake, don't send in the SWAT team. Get a hostage negotiator. Find Regan and Tucker. She asked for them specifically."

Becker replaced the receiver and stared mournfully at Gretchen. "My mother will never believe this."

13

VANCE HOLLAND SAT in his office at Channel 8 wondering how to deal with the latest development with the woman he had come to think of as "Evita." Why had he ever slept with Lisa Mercado? Probably because she had pulled her dress over her head in this very same office two years earlier (when she was working as a temp in payroll) and revealed the sort of body he had not seen since he and his frat brothers wandered into an old-style burlesque house years before in Boston. And she did a dance worthy of Salome with that same dress, pulling it between her legs, across her breasts, and, finally, around Holland's neck.

Fortunately no one else was around at that late hour as the ambitious girl from Washington Heights straddled the news director and extracted a promise from him to let her have a chance on-camera. At first it was just the weather, but people wrote in asking to see her do more. So they let her do a few remotes in Spanish Harlem and the Heights. She was a smash and Holland awarded her with the black hole spot at nine in the morning. No one could seriously compete with Regis and Kathie Lee. But Lisa did. Channel 8 came in second behind the ABC juggernaut.

Then the other networks came sniffing around. Wondering what this Latina bombshell was all about. William Morris signed her but didn't do anything with her. Lisa became antsy and more demanding. She wanted to do the nightly news but Holland was not ready to bounce Eve Lindsay, the present anchor (and his wife's sister, which also made her the station owner's daughter).

What to do? Not that Lisa was ready to take over from Barbara Walters or Diane Sawyer. But one of the big networks could groom her and make her a new Daisy Fuentes. No, Holland needed to keep her for the ratings she brought in and the possibility that she might be his private dancer again (something she hadn't been in over a year). What to do? What to do?

Then the phone rang. It was Holland's mole inside the District Attorney's Office. What a story! But was it true? Holland rolled through his Rolodex and found the number he wanted.

"Henry, old boy! Where have you been hiding? Haven't seen you at the Stuyvesant lately."

"Just had lunch there," replied Henry Given. "With my sister. She told me she was on your morning show today. I wish someone would let me know these things. . . ."

"She was sensational, Hank. Like all you Givens."

"That's very kind of you, Vance. How's Dierdre?"

"Great, great. And Sheila?"

"Beijing."

"We must get together when she gets back and Dierdre dries out. Say, Hank, you don't happen to know where your sister is *now*, do you?"

"I believe she went to the Evanston Hotel. Why?"

"Can I call you back, Hank? Somebody just walked in." Holland hung up the phone and improvised a flamenco dance around his office. Fate! That's who just walked in.

Holland walked down the hall and took the elevator downstairs to Lisa Mercado's dressing room. "Evita" was on the telephone rapping away to someone in Spanish when Holland walked in and held his arms out to her.

"I'm going to make you a star all over again, Señorita Mercado."

Lisa hung up the phone and stared quizzically at the news director. "What is it?"

"A scoop. An exclusive. Every network will pick it up. And you will be messenger to the world."

"What is it? What is it?" Lisa was absorbing Holland's excitement.

"Uh-uh-uh. Ground rules first." And Holland locked Lisa's dressing room door. "Dance for me, Evita."

14

By FOUR-THIRTY the Evanston lobby was a scene of pandemonium. NYPD patrolmen were struggling vainly to keep the media from entering the premises. All the occupants of the fifth-floor rooms had been rousted and assembled in the lobby for questioning. Alan Becker was hovering nervously with no real duty to perform. The hotel security man had opportunely gone to lunch and never returned. Nip and Tuck were jabbering away on cellular phones to headquarters.

Ned Jordan arrived on the scene and Becker rushed forward to greet him. Jordan was a handsome black man in his late thirties, who was one of the top federal prosecutors in the city. He had also been carrying a futile torch for Susan for a number of years.

"What the hell are the feds doing here?" asked Nip.

"Ned's a friend of Ms. Gee's," replied Tuck.

"How the hell did everybody find out about this? Where did the TV bozos come from? Orders were to keep a lid on it."

Jordan and Becker walked over to Tuck and the two black men shook hands.

"What the hell's going on here, Tucker?"

"Ms. Given's up in Room Five eleven with some crackhead."

"*Oi vey,*" groaned Becker.

"How did he grab her?" asked Jordan.

"He didn't," answered Tuck. "It was bad timing. She was supposed to meet with Vinny—Vinh Ho Chi—but he

90

never showed and she sort of started her own investigation—"

"Oh, Jesus!"

"*Oi vey*," echoed Becker.

"Far as we can tell, she walked into the wrong room. Some Cuban dude. And a dead body. Just bad timing."

"She said it wasn't a murder," whined Becker.

"What the hell are you talking about, Alan?" asked Jordan. Then he turned back to the two undercover cops and asked: "Anybody we know?"

"A baby hooker," said Nip. "She went up to the Cuban's room around one."

"Got a tag on the Cuban?"

"Manolo Sanchez. He was one of those Mariel boat people Castro turned loose. A real nut job. Came up from Miami a few years ago. Leg breaking mostly. Was working for the Teslas till he dropped out of sight a week ago."

"She lied to me!" wailed Becker.

"What are you talking about?" asked Jordan.

"She said there was no homicide on the Tesla case."

"What Tesla case?" asked Tuck.

"Mr. Archibald dropped it in her lap this morning."

"How'd you know so much about this guy Sanchez?" Jordan asked Nip.

"One of my snitches told me. Nobody knows exactly what happened but this guy Sanchez pissed off Junior Tesla. He's been hidin' out here in the Evanston hopin' Junior and his old man won't find him."

"All they got to do is turn on the TV," said Tuck, as his cellular phone rang. Then he answered the phone. "Yes, sir? . . . No, sir. She's still up there. The lobby's swarming with TV people. . . . Don't ask me, sir. . . . Uh-huh. . . . Well, there's a fire escape outside the room but I wouldn't want to guarantee its safety. The whole hotel is falling apart, sir. The damned thing might rip right out of the bricks if we put any kind of weight on it. . . . We're workin' on a backup plan right now, sir. . . . Uh-huh. . . . Uh-huh. . . . Uh-huh. . . . You'll be the first." Tuck hung up and needlessly informed the others. "Lieutenant Abrams. Wants to know what our backup plan is. Says he's in direct contact with Mr. Archibald. Doesn't want us to make a move without consulting him."

"Right. So's he can do his fly up before the TV cameras start rollin'. Good old Abrams," grinned Nip. "One of our finest military leaders. You must be proud of him, Becker. Didn't you serve under him in the Israeli army?"

"Very funny, I'm sure."

"Oh, Becker! You aren't gonna go all sensitive on us, are ya?"

"What does this Sanchez want?" asked Jordan, getting back to the matter at hand. "Has he made any kind of demands?"

"Nothing yet," answered Tuck. "The guy's nervous; he needs a fix; he's flippin' out. But he won't talk to us."

"Then how do you know all this?"

"We've got two guys monitoring their conversation in the next room with headphones."

"Does Ms. Given know that?" asked Becker. "She's a real stickler about her privacy."

"How's Susan handling it?" asked Jordan, ignoring Becker's last remark.

"Ms. Gee?" asked Nip. "Like a real pro. She's tellin' him the story of her fuckin' life."

15

"HAVE YOU EVER been to Israel, Manny?" asked Susan, lighting up another Salem Light, then holding the pack out to Sanchez. They had both given up any pretense of not smoking an hour earlier.

"Thanks." Sanchez lit up, wolfed the smoke hungrily down into his lungs, then exhaled it slowly. "No. I ain't been no place but Havana, Miami, and New York."

"Oh, you must visit Israel. It's the birthplace of all modern religions, you know." Susan's eyes darted quickly toward her watch. It was now five o'clock. Did anyone know she was up there? Did Gretchen contact Nip and Tuck? Had she understood that Susan was in desperate need of help?

Manny had freaked out following Susan's deception on the telephone. He had roared for a good twenty minutes like a wounded bear and Susan had feared the Cuban might actually strike her. When she remembered that Hugh had carried on similarly for years, the fear in her subsided. Let him shout. Let them all shout. The emotionally insatiable inner children of the world.

"What are you smilin' at?" asked Sanchez when his rage had subsided.

"Life. Just a big roller coaster, isn't it? I have a friend Michael Roth—more than a friend, actually. We met in Jerusalem six months ago. I washed the mud off his body at the Dead Sea—but that's an entirely different story. The point is that Michael's a writer. Books, plays, movies. And he said a really fascinating thing to me on the bus to

Jericho. He said that life is this big movie and we're all starring in it. And we all want to read the script. But God is the ultimate auteur—doesn't want anyone to know the ending—so the best we get are pink pages. . . . You don't get it, do you? Neither did I. You see, movie scripts always change from day to day. And the new pages are printed on pink paper. So the actors never know what's going to happen. It's actually a very clever analogy. Michael's very clever and funny and sexy. And he's just as good a listener as a talker.''

"Then he must be some kind of listener," said Sanchez wryly, "cuz you sure talk the shit out of a guy."

"I don't think that's—"

"Susan, you ain' shut up for an hour."

"Only because you're such a good listener, Manny."

"Is that why your husband left?"

"Do you really want to hear about it?"

Before Sanchez could reply, Susan was telling the Cuban legbreaker her entire history. From her gentrified childhood in Greenwich right up to the fateful *Spellbound* encounter with Hugh Carver on the ski slopes in Vermont. How Hugh had wanted her to quit her job and become a full-time wife and mother. How they had quarreled incessantly over everything. How the years had dragged/flown by until the morning Hugh finally announced that he was leaving.

"I can't tell you how happy I was, Manny. It meant I could ask God for real things again. Worthy things. I never felt right praying every day for Hugh to die." Susan paused, then sniffed an unfamiliar odor.

"What's that smell?" she asked.

"Her." Sanchez gestured toward Brittany's body lying on the bed.

"Jeepers!"

THE FIRE DEPARTMENT had sent its representatives along to the hotel to discuss the potential hazards of what CNN was now describing to its global audience as "The Evanston Siege."

"The place is just a fuckin' conflagration waiting to happen," said Deputy Fire Marshal Cornelius Monahan.

"What is that in English?" asked Nip.

"Now then," continued Monahan, ignoring Nip, "fire escapes are completely out of the question. We've sent Vinh a letter every month telling him to replace the existing fire escapes or else. He opted for 'or else.'"

"I'm going up there," said Jordan.

"And do what?" asked Nip.

"Talk to the guy. Talk to Susan. See if we can't work something out."

"The guy's a crackhead," said Nip.

"Yeah," said Jordan. "A crackhead, who's going to need a fix." And he turned toward Becker and added for emphasis: "Soon."

"What are you looking at me for, Ned? I don't even take Tylenol."

A uniformed cop shouted over to Tucker: "Yo! Detective Tucker!"

"What is it?"

"We just got a make on the dead girl." The cop led a reluctant dyed-blond eighteen-year-old girl over to the huddled conferees.

"Who's this?" asked Nip, giving the baby hooker in hot pants and fake leather bomber jacket the once-over.

"Her name's Terry Taylor," replied the cop.

"Nice ring to it. You know the dead girl upstairs?"

"Yeah."

"This isn't an IRS form, Terry. What the hell's her name?"

"Brittany. Brittany Bouvier."

"Bouvier?"

"She thought it was classy."

"Was Sanchez a regular john?"

"Regular? Like bran muffins? Or prunes?"

"Cute kid. You hook for Vinny?"

"I beg your pardon?"

"Is that all you beg for, Terry? I want to know who your employer is. And don't tell me Lenox Hill Hospital. My sister Kathleen works there and I'd hate to think you're a colleague."

"I want to talk to my lawyer."

"You have a lawyer?"

"Yeah. Surprised?"

"Bowled over. Let's go, Terry."

"Where?"

Before Nip could offer Terry her options, a murmur went up from the assembled policemen. Lieutenant Haskell Abrams had arrived on the scene.

"Now we'll really get somewhere," muttered Nip in tones of mock reverence. "The marines have landed."

With a head of fluffy golden curls and the glassy blue eyes of a plush toy, forty-five-year-old Haskell Abrams resembled a Wheaton terrier wearing a blue police uniform on display in FAO Schwarz's window. As ambitious as he was mendacious, Abrams was rumored to have exchanged some X-rated memos with Lydia Culberg on more than one occasion. (Becker swore he'd actually seen copies of these pornographic epistles.) If there were a twelve-step program for liars, the police lieutenant and the deputy district attorney would certainly have been charter members.

"Has he surrendered yet?" asked Abrams, staring at a nonthreatening spot somewhere over Nip and Tuck's head.

"No, sir," replied Tuck.

"Who are all these people?" asked Abrams, staring at the sea of reporters as if they were uninvited guests at his son's bar mitzvah.

"Media," said Ned Jordan.

Abrams examined the federal prosecutor dubiously until Becker stepped forward and introduced the two men.

"Of course!" Abrams grinned. "How foolish of me, Jordan. We've spoken many times." In fact, the lieutenant had never spoken to the federal prosecutor in his life. "Media. What the hell do they have to report everything for? Just makes our job all the harder. The British have the right idea, you know. Muzzle the press. Clap journalistic chastity belts on them and throw away the key. We could clean crime up in a week. Anyone spoken to Ms. Given? I cannot tell you how I admire that woman. She's like a sister to me." In fact, Abrams and Susan could not bear to be in the same room together. He thought she was pushy (i.e., a woman); she thought he was a nitwit (i.e., a nitwit). "The District Attorney's Office has been a better and more progressive crime-fighting force since Susan Given Carver joined it. I don't think there's a man or woman—"

"Who the hell's he making this speech for?" Jordan whispered into Becker's ear.

"I got to pee," said Terry, who was now standing on one foot.

"Who is this woman?" asked Abrams, miffed that his valediction should be marred by so coarse a coda.

"Drew Barrymore. Didn't you recognize me?"

"She's a friend of the dead girl," said Tuck.

"Dead girl?" Abrams's face assumed the blank stare of

a Wheaton waiting in suspended animation for his master's next command.

"Upstairs."

"No one told me there was a homicide." Then a look of total confusion, as if his guidebook had failed to reveal the proper phrase. "Not . . . Ms. Given?"

"No, sir. Brittany Bouvier."

"Bouvier?" Abrams was hopelessly starstruck. Dead or alive. "Was she related to . . . ?"

"We don't think so," said Nip. "That was just her *nom de poke.*"

"Well?" asked Terry, switching legs. "Is someone going to take me to the powder room or do I just squat down and—?"

"Get her out of here!" snapped Abrams. The uniformed cop quickly hustled the baby hooker away and the lieutenant turned back to his undercover force. "I want some action and I want it PDQ."

A microphone popped abruptly in front of Abrams's face.

"How is Susan doing?" asked Lisa Mercado with all the familial concern of some next of kin demanding answers at the hospital emergency ward.

"She's fine," lied Abrams, transfixed by the outthrust microphone as if he were Dracula confronted by the holy cross. "I've just spoken with her."

"What is going on up there? Is she being held hostage?"

Abrams said the first syllable of "hostage"—ha-ha-ha-ha—repeatedly until he sounded like Macy's Santa Claus atop the Thanksgiving Day Parade float.

"Where do you people dream up these stories?" asked Abrams when he was finally able to speak. "I realize you're ratings conscious. But to take a simple . . ."

"Yes?" Lisa Mercado was positively ravenous. She wanted the next word and every bit of meat that was on it. "A simple . . . ?"

"Deposition." Abrams had managed to say the word without blinking.

Mercado turned to her camera man and gave him the signal to stop rolling film. Then she looked back at Abrams and asked: "Who are you shitting, Lieutenant?"

Nip burst out laughing until Abrams turned on him with a withering "I'll remember this" glance.

"I'll ignore that comment, Ms. Mercado."

"Well, I can't ignore the fire trucks outside, the police barricades, the people being questioned over there, and the second-biggest media presence since the World Trade Center Bombing. All this for a deposition?"

"I think you've all been the victims of . . . a hoax." Abrams was in his Wheaton terrier mode again. No one could budge him.

"Can I quote you on the hoax?" Mercado had her arm raised to give her camera man the "roll film" signal.

"You cannot."

Mercado gave the signal to roll film anyhow and held her microphone up once again. "I spoke to my friend Susan Given—Ms. D.A.—a few brief hours ago. She was in excellent spirits. Vital, alive—"

"She's still alive!" blurted Abrams.

"Then why can't I see her?"

"Because she's not here."

"What?!" Mercado gave the signal to stop film again.

"Can I take you into my confidence?" asked Abrams in hushed tones. "Deep, deep background."

"Of course."

"All this"—Abrams gestured toward the sea of reporters—"is subterfuge." Then he held a finger to his lips, squeezed Lisa Mercado's hand conspiratorially, and led his colleagues toward an uncluttered corner of the lobby.

"If that bitch comes near me again, Regan, arrest her for soliciting. Now then, Tucker. What's the story? How do we know Ms. Given *is* still alive?"

"Cuz no one phoned downstairs to tell me otherwise." Tucker explained about the officers upstairs monitoring the conversation next door.

"Regan, gimme that phone. It's painfully clear there's

been a lot of Indians running around this lobby and no chief," Abrams announced pompously as he dialed the hotel's phone number. "I intend to put an end to the chaos. I am in charge now and there's no cause for alarm—How the hell do you work this thing?" Abrams looked close to tears as he desperately waved the cellular phone in the faces of his subordinates.

Nip snatched the cellular back, pressed Send, and asked for Room 511. Then he returned the phone to Abrams with mock obsequiousness: "There you go . . . Chief."

Susan's feet were killing her. It was close to six o'clock and she would normally be soaking them in the bathtub as soon as she got home. The price one pays for too many marathons.

"What happened then?" asked Sanchez.

"Sorry? Do you mind if I take my shoes off, Manny?"

"Go ahead."

Susan slipped off her shoes, crossed her left foot over her right knee, and began to massage it.

"Ain't you gonna finish?"

"I'm getting very tired, Manny. Aren't you tired?"

"You and Michael in the cemetery. I like that story. Finish it."

"I was jogging through an Arab cemetery in shorts and a tank top—not exactly the correct dress code—when these *mullahs* appeared and surrounded me. Accused me of desecrating holy ground. They probably would have stoned me to death on the spot if Michael hadn't arrived and—"

The telephone rang, startling Susan and Sanchez. They both stared at it as if awakened from a deep trance. It continued to ring incessantly.

Susan finally asked: "Do you want me to answer it?"

"No."

"It's just going to keep ringing."

Sanchez stared at the telephone resentfully, then picked it up. "Yeah? . . . Yeah . . . Just a minute." Sanchez covered the mouthpiece and turned back to Susan. "It's for you."

"Who is it?" Susan shook her head in disbelief at her instinctive bureaucratic response.

"Who is this? . . . Just a second." He turned back to Susan and mangled the name. "Housecall Abrams."

"Who?"

Sanchez shrugged and held the phone out to Susan. "Given."

"Susan? Haskell Abrams here."

Susan rolled her eyes toward the ceiling. What was that asshole phoning her for? Oh, no! Abrams knew. Which meant Lydia knew. Which meant the situation was completely out of control.

"Yes?" asked Susan warily.

"Can you speak?"

"Yes."

"Is he listening?"

"Yes."

"Susan, are you all right?"

"Yes."

"Then say something else besides 'yes.' "

"What do you want me to say?"

"Who is that guy?" asked Sanchez.

"It's all right, Manny. It's just someone from work."

"Susan, I want you to know that you are in absolutely no danger."

"I know that, Haskell."

"You're being very brave."

"Thank you." Then she yawned audibly into the phone. "Sorry."

"We have the building surrounded."

"Why?"

"To effect your rescue. I have informed Mr. Archibald of every—"

"Does Mr. Archibald know about this?"

"Of course. I have been in constant communication with him."

He's lying, thought Susan. Then she asked: "When did you speak with him?"

"We had lunch together."

"Where?" Susan had run into Mr. Archibald having lunch at the Stuyvesant.

"I beg your pardon?"

"Where did you have lunch with Mr. Archibald?"

"What does that matter, Susan? All that matters is getting you safely out of the clutches of this maniac."

"I am not in any clutches, Haskell. . . . Haskell, are you there? . . . Lieutenant Abrams? Hello?" Susan couldn't hear what Abrams was murmuring to the others on his end but she was certain she heard the phrase "Stockholm syndrome."

Then: "Susan?"

"Yes?"

"Is there someplace safe for you to hide?"

"Why?"

"We're going to make a preemptive strike."

"The hell you are!"

"We have no other choice."

"This is my choice, Haskell! Not yours."

"I'd suggest under the bed. I'm going to hang up now, Susan. Give us two minutes . . . then make your move. God bless you!"

Leave it to Haskell Abrams to screw up a situation that was just about handled, Susan thought as she hung up the phone. Then she made a snap decision and turned to Sanchez.

"Manny," she said. "We've got to go."

"But I like it here."

"I understand. It's been very pleasant. I've enjoyed our conversation immensely. But in two minutes some rather unpleasant people are going to break that door down and start shooting."

"Let 'em try it."

"No, no, no. Unacceptable, Manny. Someone is going to die needlessly. Pointlessly. This can all be avoided."

"They're gonna book me for murder."

"No, they won't. I believe you, Manny. I don't think you killed Brittany. Certainly not intentionally. I will do my best to help you."

"How can you help me with the cops, Susan?"

"I work in the District Attorney's Office."

"What are you, like a secretary?"

"I am the head of the Asset Forfeitures Unit. I'm an assistant district attorney."

"No shit! Why you don' tell me this before?"

"I didn't think you'd appreciate it. When we first met. Under the circumstances."

"I don' believe this. The whole afternoon I been shootin' the shit with the D.A." The wheels were spinning inside Sanchez's head. Maybe he could get this pretty *gringa* to help him.

"Just an assistant."

"Heyyy, Susan. Don't be so modest. You the head of the watchamacallit unit. I'm impressed. Son-of-a-bitch!"

"Manny, we've got less than a minute. I want you to give yourself up to me."

"I can' do that, Susan."

"Manny, you're facing a possible abduction charge un-less—"

"I don't give a shit about that. I know is not true. You know is not true—"

"Then what is the—?"

"I'm hidin' out, man. Somebody's after me. Somebody big. If I surrender to you, they gonna know where I—"

"Who? Who is it?"

"I can't tell you."

"Manny, please. We're friends, aren't we? You know all about me. Let me make a deal for you. I'll go straight to Mr. Archibald himself. Do you know who William Archibald is?"

"Do you know who Nicolo Tesla is?" countered Sanchez bitterly.

"Senior or Junior?"

"You know them both?" Sanchez's amazement matched Susan's.

"What do you have to do with the Teslas?"

"I used to work for them."

A tingling sensation started at the base of Susan's spine and worked its way all the way up to her brain. Finally she asked: "Were you there when Walter Gerhardt was killed?"

"I can' talk about that, Susan. Don' ask me that, man."

Susan realized she had inadvertently struck gold. A witness. Someone on the inside. Nobody was going to shoot this man!

"Manny, listen to me. How would you like to go on a vacation? Somewhere quiet. Far, far away from New York and the Teslas. All expenses paid."

"What I got to do?"

"Talk. Talk for hours into a tape recorder."

"Squeal?"

"I prefer 'cooperate.' Look, we both know the kind of man Mr. Tesla is. Father and son. They've been laughing at decent people for years. Now, it's our chance to laugh at them. What do you say, Manny?"

"Could we go to Las Vegas?"

"I don't think so. But it will be somewhere pretty and clean."

Susan could hear the sound of heavy boots clunking down the hallway. It was the SWAT team.

"Manny, I don't want to die. I can't believe you do either. Give me your gun."

"Will you visit me?"

"I beg your pardon?"

"Where I go. Will you come and—?"

"Of course, I will. I'll eventually have a great many questions to ask you."

"Okay. Let's do it."

Manny handed her his gun and Susan opened the hotel room door. She stared in mock amazement at the ominous presence of the SWAT team breathing heavily with their pump guns poised for attack. Down at the far end of the corridor, Susan recognized Hopeless Haskell Abrams hiding behind a fire hose, out of harm's way, looking very macho in his flak jacket and bullet-proof vest.

"Are you sure you gentlemen have the right room?"

LORETTA TESLA STARED at the calamari sautéing in the pan. She hoped that Nick would like them this time. She prayed to St. Monica, the guardian of mothers, that the meal would be a happy one. Toni had stopped by for dinner and, as usual, she and her father were fighting over the men she was seeing.

"What is your problem?" bellowed Tesla from the other room. "Are you nuts or somethin'?"

Loretta crossed herself and prayed to St. Dympna that her youngest child was not—God forbid!—mentally ill.

"I'm in love with him, Papa," replied his daughter.

"You're always in love with them," countered her father. "Why don't you try *liking* them for once? It might help. You can't keep jumpin' from guy to guy. Yer not a kid anymore, Toni."

"She's not?" asked her mother aloud as she poked at the squid in the pan. Had she made a mistake praying to Aloysius Gonnzaga, the patron saint of youth, the past few years? But then who would look after her precious Antonia?

Inside the family study Nick Tesla and his daughter were rehashing the same old argument while the TV screen revealed Lisa Mercado broadcasting live in front of the Evanston Hotel.

". . . now beginning the fourth hour of this dramatic siege inside this legendary Gramercy Park Hotel. I'm told that Dashiell Hammett once stayed here and—wait! Just a minute, folks. Here is Lieutenant Haskell Abrams. Oh, Lieutenant! Please, Lieutenant."

Lisa had removed the raincoat she was wearing inside the hotel lobby and Abrams did a double take when he saw the TV personality's fabulous legs.

"Hello, there," beamed Abrams as if he'd just run into an old college chum.

"Have you got a minute?" asked Lisa.

"I think I can squeeze you in." Abrams beamed.

"What is the situation right now?"

"I led my men in," lied Abrams, "and we got the job done. No loss of life. That's the NYPD at its best."

"I can't believe this," said Nick Tesla, oblivious to the unfolding drama on the television. "You're in love with a street singer?"

"He's a performance artist," said his daughter Toni, a reed-thin but striking-looking woman, who looked a decade younger than her twenty-eight years. "And very gifted."

"He sings in the street for quarters!"

"And Grandpa sang in a saloon for nickels. I've come full circle."

"What the hell's his name? This 'gifted performance artist'?"

"Torrid."

"First or last?"

"Both."

"What's the name on his rap sheet?"

"Just Torrid."

"Toni Torrid. What the hell kinda name will that be? Sounds like a stripper."

"I didn't say I wanna marry him, Papa."

"Oh, I know! You never wanna marry none of them. Tell you what. Send this Torrid 'round to see me. Maybe he can sing at the restaurant one night. Who knows? Maybe he could be my big discovery." Tesla stared across the library where signed pictures of Dean Martin, Tony Bennett, and Vic Damone, all embracing the restaurateur, dotted the walls.

"He's not that kind of bullshit singer, Papa. He doesn't do words."

Before Tesla could react to "bullshit" and inquire into the sort of sound Torrid *did* make, Ray Murphy's face popped up on the screen.

Looking like a feisty union leader in Santa's Workshop, the veteran tabloid reporter stared into the camera and rasped: "If it was anybody else, Lisa, I'd have put my black armband on. But Suzy Given's one tough tomato."

"Isn't that a bit sexist, Ray?"

"Whaddaya mean 'sexist'? That little broad can dish it out and take it. I'd like to see you held hostage for three hours by some mob gunsel, honey."

At the mention of "mob gunsel," Tesla turned his attention away from his daughter and stared at the TV screen. He was just in time to see a manacled Manny Sanchez being led out of the hotel by members of the NYPD SWAT team.

"There's the kidnapper now," said Lisa breathlessly. "We don't have an official ID on him but my sources say that his name is Manolo Sanchez, a Cuban refugee—"

"Holy shit!" roared Tesla.

"What is it?" asked Loretta, racing in from the kitchen, praying all the while to Claire of Assisi nothing bad had happened on the television, an invention the saint was supposed to guard over.

"What's wrong, Papa?"

Tesla ignored both women as he grabbed the phone from the side table and speed-dialed his son on his cell phone.

"Just once! Just once I'd like to find that fuckin' brother of yours when I need him."

Toni's attention turned to the TV for the first time and her eyes lit up affectionately: "Hey, it's Manny! I haven't seen him in ages. Still got the same great bod."

"You know him?" asked Loretta.

"We had drinks a couple of times. He's a sweet guy. But I could never understand what he was saying."

Tesla stared at his daughter in a mix of bewilderment and disgust. Then he called The Patch and told him to find Junior. Immediately. Then he phoned his lawyer, Alvin Gasmer.

"Hey, Alvin. Did I interrupt yer dinner? Tough shit. Quick question. You know a lieutenant named Abrams? Haskell Abrams. C'mon, Gasmer. I know you Jews are all related. . . . Hmmm. Well, who we got inside the jail? . . . What the hell do you think I'm talkin' about? We got to whack Manny Sanchez before he sings."

Tesla slammed the phone down and his wife said a silent prayer to Cecilia, the patron saint of music.

19

Cordelia Brown stared at the clock on the stove and wondered why Susan wasn't home yet. It was 6:30 and Susan would have phoned by now if she was going to be late. And soon Cordelia's family would phone from Harlem wondering why *she* wasn't home yet.

Polly shrieked from the second-floor library: "Cor-de-lia!"

"You gon' give me a hat attack, chile." The St. Kitts housekeeper had actually said "heart attack" but in her thick dialect it always came out more chapeau than organ. "What you gotta shout at Cordelia like dat for?"

"Come quickly!"

"Is de house on fire?" asked the short, sturdy, housekeeper as she pulled herself up the banister. "Call Waldo. Him get de fire department."

"Look! Look!" Polly was hopping up and down with excitement, pointing to the television as Cordelia entered the library. "It's Mom!"

Indeed, it was Susan Given being interviewed live in front of the Evanston Hotel by Lisa Mercado.

"Really, Lisa, I wouldn't call what happened an abduction." Strands of blond hair were obscuring Susan's face and she was struggling to push them back up onto her head. "I was involved in a routine investigation, that's all. It's a very old hotel, as you can see. The door got stuck and poor Mr. Sanchez and I could not get out of the room."

"Oh, my Lord!" shrieked Cordelia. "What dey done to you mama now?"

As Susan continued to talk to Lisa Mercado, "poor Mr. Sanchez" could be seen at the rear of the screen being led handcuffed into the back of a patrol car. The police were attempting to shove his head down into the car when he let loose a plaintive: "Susan!!"

"Hey, Ivy!" bellowed Polly. "Mom's on TV!" Her younger sister abandoned her drawing and raced across the hall from her bedroom and into the library.

"Cooool!" gasped Ivy staring at her mother's image flickering on the screen. Then she added: "Why didn't she brush her hair?"

"Shh! Shh! Listen."

"What case is this?" asked Ivy.

"It's not a case, moron."

"Don't call me that . . . butt-breath."

"She was a hostage!"

"So?"

"So?!? Do you know what a hostage is, Ivy?"

"No."

"She was being held prisoner. By him."

The camera now panned to Sanchez trying to break loose from the police and make contact with Susan. Nip and Tuck leaped in front of her.

"Who is that guy?" asked Polly. "He's kinda cute. Looks a little like Antonio Banderas."

"There's Nip!" squealed Ivy. "He's really cute. They look like they're having fun."

"Like I don't think so, Ivy."

"Is Mom okay? Why is she on TV?"

"If you'd shut up and listen for once maybe . . ."

Ivy stuck her tongue out at her sister, picked up the phone, and dialed Nellie Patterson's number: "Nellie? Hi, it's Ivy. Turn on Channel Eight. My mom's on TV."

The phone rang on the second line and Polly grabbed it, said hello, and was almost deafened by the sound of

"Hiii!" was being shouted at her long distance from Chattanooga.

"Hi, Aunt Linda."

"How are you, pumpkin?" Susan's younger sister had moved to the South twenty years earlier and had adopted something resembling the accent of that region. However, there was no explanation for the unseen, omnipresent hurricane that Linda Given felt compelled to constantly shout over. "Is your mom there?"

"No."

"Where is she?"

"On TV."

"Doing what?"

"She was abducted."

"You're kidding!"

"Nope."

"Phil! Phil, turn on the television! It's Susan. She's been abducted. Oh God, Phil! The dogs are loose again. Tell your mom I phoned. Y'all be brave. I'll fly up if y'all need me."

No sooner had Polly replaced the receiver and massaged her ear when the phone rang again. She gestured for Cordelia to answer it while staring in pride at her mother nattering away on screen.

"Given Carver residence . . . Yes, she is. One moment, please." Cordelia turned to Polly, sighed wearily, and announced: "It's you Daddy. Don' get into de fight wit' him. I don't need no hat attack."

"I just heard about your mother," intoned Hugh Carver in his best clipped Gregory Peck tones. "Are you girls all right?"

"We're fine, Dad," replied Polly coolly. "Why don't you ask about Mom? She's the one who was held hostage."

"She denied being a hostage, Polly."

"Of course, she did. It's Mom. She's from Greenwich, for crying out loud. If she was a corpse, she'd deny being dead."

"What are you having for dinner this evening?"

"I don't know."

"What are you having for dinner?" repeated Hugh.

"Voodoo chicken."

"I want you to eat vegetables, Polly."

"Dad—"

"You're not consuming enough greens—"

"Dad—"

"You'll thank me some day."

"I don't want to talk about food until Mom gets home safely. Okay?"

"Let me speak with Ivy."

"Ivy? It's Dad."

Ivy shook her head to indicate she didn't want to speak to her father as she continued chatting with Nellie.

"She doesn't want to talk to you, Dad."

"Why?"

"She's on the other line with her friend Nellie."

"Is she eating Sour Power?"

"No."

"I want to speak to her, Polly. Do you understand? Tell her she can call her friend back."

Polly carried the telephone over to her younger sister and hissed: "Say something. I don't care what."

"Hello," said Ivy with all the energy of a hundred-year-old woman.

"Why didn't you want to speak to me, Ivy?"

"Dunno."

"How was school?"

"Okay. I'm talking to my friend right now." And Ivy gave the phone back to Polly.

"Why did she do that to me?" asked Hugh.

"Dad, I want to watch the rest of the news—"

"Who is this friend of hers, Polly? Do I know her?"

"I don't think so, Dad. She's from Oklahoma."

"When was Ivy in Oklahoma?"

"Never. The kid moved here from Oklahoma."

"I'm going to the theater tonight with Sigrid."

"I hope it's in English." Polly was not a great fan of the anorexic Swedish *vendeuse*.

"Sigrid has an excellent command of the language."

"You don't have to get defensive, Dad."

"This is your mother's influence. She's poisoned you against Sigrid."

"I don't think Mom knows she exists."

"Tell Ivy I want her light off by nine. Or else."

"How will you know if it isn't?"

"I have my friends. Good night." And Hugh Carver hung up abruptly.

"What a nut job!" sighed Polly, replacing the phone. "Hey! What happened to Mom?" The picture on the TV screen showed a liquor store in Brooklyn that had been firebombed the previous night. "Where's Mom?" Polly surfed through the other channels but caught no sight of Susan. "Damn! I should have taped it."

The telephone rang again. It was Henry Given checking to see if his little sister was safe at home yet. Then Marian Given phoned from Greenwich. Then Cynthia Praeger phoned. Then Mr. Archibald's secretary. Then the floor man phoned to say he would finally be turning up the next morning.

At last the elevator could be heard making its way up the shaft and the girls raced to greet it. When the door opened, Susan stepped out, followed by Nip, Tuck, Ned Jordan, and Ray Murphy.

"I'm fine, Ned," insisted Susan. "How many times do I have to tell you—?"

"Yer in shock, Suzy," rasped Ray Murphy. "You need a drink. God knows I do."

"You girls look familiar," said Susan smiling at her beloved daughters staring expectantly at her.

Polly and Ivy flew into their mother's arms and all the girls' fears for her safety that they had been hiding even from each other bubbled up to the surface as they cried and showered her with adoring kisses.

"This is a nice reception," said Susan, fighting back

tears at the unabashed display of affection. "But nothing happened. Come on. Let's all have a drink. Cordelia, you go on home now. I'll take care of—"

"You ain't takin' care of no ting," said Cordelia, ushering Susan's guests into the living room. "I get de drinks. And what do you handsome boys want?" The last remark was aimed at Tuck and Ned Jordan, whom the St. Kitts housekeeper had a particularly warm spot for and loved to flirt with whenever they turned up.

Murphy managed to grab Susan before she reached the living room and rasped: "I want the lowdown, Suzy."

"Whatever do you mean, Ray?"

Before the reporter could reply, Susan had to endure one of his two-minute nicotine-induced coughing attacks. Finally: "Maybe some of those yippy-yuppy p.c. kids from the *Times* believe nothing happened this afternoon. But this is Ray Murphy. I'm no journalist. I'm a newspaperman. I want the dirt. I tried to talk to that flapjack Abrams but he's stonewalling. Says it was a false alarm."

"Well, Lieutenant Abrams does have the final say on what—"

"Hopeless Haskell isn't an authority on anything except how far he can stick his head up the chief's ass without getting lost. Christ on a crutch! C'mon, Suzy. Tell me what really went down."

Susan loathed being called Suzy but she did have a soft spot for Ray Murphy. Despite the fact he had helped her with several of her cases in the past, Susan was not in the mood to feed him the kind of melodrama his paper served up as a morning meal to the city's straphangers.

"Nothing happened, Ray. There was never any hostage situation."

"Then what the hell was Sanchez doing there?"

"Off the record?"

"Sure."

"I mean it, Ray. I'll give you the exclusive when it breaks."

"Is it good?"

"It's mother's milk for you, Ray."

"Suzy, I love ya. What's the story?"

"He's a material witness."

"Yeah? For what?"

"I can't tell you yet."

"That's it, Suzy? That's off the record? Can't you do any better than that? What the hell was Hopeless Haskell doing there in a flak jacket and a bullet-proof vest?"

"He and Lydia Culberg like to sneak off and get dressed up in the afternoons. Somebody at Foley Square blew the whistle on their little tryst and we had to stage the hostage thing as a smokescreen to sneak them out of the hotel." (In fact, it was Brittany Bouvier's body that was removed through a rear entrance to avoid the sort of three-ring circus "the Murph" loved to ballyhoo.)

Murphy's laughter plunged him into another coughing attack. This one lasted almost three minutes.

"Ray, you've got to stop smoking."

"Yeah, yeah, yeah. Okay, Suzy. I can see I'm not going to get anything out of you tonight. But don't forget, doll, I'm holding your marker."

"And it has the name Manny Sanchez on it. Now, come and have a drink."

An hour later the visitors departed after having devoured every morsel of Cordelia's voodoo chicken. Ned Jordan had gallantly offered to drive the housekeeper home to Harlem. Susan finally took the shower she had been dreaming about for hours while her daughters ordered take-out from the Viand Restaurant on Madison Avenue.

When Susan finally emerged from the bathroom with her hair in a turban and wearing a robe, Polly looked up from her mother's bed where she and her little sister were sprawled out like kittens and asked: "Does Lieutenant Abrams really get dressed up with Lydia Culberg?"

"You weren't supposed to have heard that."

"One could hardly have avoided it," said Polly in an

expert impersonation of her mother. "You do tend to project your voice."

"For the courtroom, dear. I learned to speak up the hard way. I used to vocalize every morning before I went into court."

"Can you teach me?"

"Why?"

"We're doing *The Sound of Music* at school. Miss Hutchins announced the cast today. You'll never guess who's playing Captain Von Trapp."

"Christopher Plummer?"

"Nooo. Ethan Culberg."

"You're joking! Isn't he a little . . . large?"

"A little large? He has to get permission from the Port Authority to go swimming. But he's got a pretty good voice and he plays the guitar." Then Polly dropped her voice to an almost inaudible whisper: "I'm playing Liesl."

"Lethal?"

"Liesl. His daughter. You know, 'I am Sixteen Going on Seventeen.' "

"How did you get the part?" asked an amazed Susan.

"Why? Cuz I'm Salvadoran."

"No, of course not. It's just that you're tone deaf."

"I am not!!" Polly's anger lasted for thirty seconds, then she burst out laughing. "But Miss Hutchins is!"

Susan joined her daughter in the joke and the two were soon rolling around on the bed laughing uproariously.

Ivy stared at them in confusion: "I don't get it." Then the doorbell rang. "Food!" Ivy leaped off the bed to greet the doorman and their take-out dinner. Polly went chasing after her little sister to try to intercept the food first.

The telephone rang again. Polly wasn't there to act her favorite role of secretary and intercept the calls, so Susan answered it herself. Mistake. Big mistake.

"How could you have done it?" The clipped Gregory Peck tones were unmistakable.

"Done what, Hugh?"

"I was appalled."

"Hugh, why are you phoning me?"

"How could you have left the children alone in a traumatic situation like the one this afternoon?"

"Hugh, have you finally, totally, completely gone crazy? How could I be with the children during that 'trauma' when I was in the trauma? The eye of the hurricane, Hugh."

"Precisely. Your favorite spot. The eye of the hurricane. Stage center. Look at me."

"Screw you."

"Is the truth that painful, Susan?"

"I don't know, Hershie. You tell me."

"I asked you never to call me that."

"Why? Are you so ashamed of having been Herschel Carverman? Must have been. It took three years of marriage until you told me you had changed your name."

"You have a great need to hurt me, don't you?"

"No, I don't. I just want to end this, Hugh." Then she shifted gears abruptly. "Didn't Sigrid like the play? You're home early."

"It's intermission. I couldn't concentrate in the first act. All I kept thinking of were those poor little girls home alone—"

"Cordelia was with them."

"—watching their mother in needless jeopardy—"

"I was doing my job, Hugh."

"You are *not* a policewoman, Susan. You had no right to put yourself in the line of fire. We have discussed ad infinitum your constant need for a melodramatic fantasy life to overcompensate for your safe, picket-fence childhood."

"*We* have never discussed anything, Dr. Carver. When did you ever want feedback? I was forced to listen to your diatribes for twenty years. But I don't have to anymore. So get off the fucking phone and stop faxing me at work!"

Susan slammed the phone down and prayed for the day—when? when? when?—she would finally be divorced.

Distant wailing grew louder and closer in her ears. Was it a siren? No, it was her daughters crying in unison. Had they heard? Were they reacting to her conversation? Had she been too harsh on Hugh? How was that possible? Seconds later the two girls rushed back into the bedroom, Polly clutching her nose and Ivy clapping a hand to the side of her head.

"What happened?" asked Susan.

"She broke my nose," sobbed Polly.

"I think I have a tumor," wailed Ivy.

"What did you do?"

"She did it!" wailed Polly and Ivy, each pointing at the other. The incident had centered around the struggle for a bottle of ketchup. Lots of pulling and pushing and heads bashing together. Having examined both her daughters' nonexistent wounds, Susan ate dinner with them, then put them both to bed.

By ten o'clock the head of the Asset Forfeiture Unit was tucked into bed as well, having browsed through that week's issues of *The Economist* and *The New York Observer*. She had switched off her light and was just drifting off to sleep when the phone rang. Please, don't let it be Hugh.

Susan picked up the phone and recognized the noisy chatter peculiar to New York bars in the background. Then a slurred female voice asked: "Wha' happened?"

It was Lydia Culberg. Definitely well oiled. "What the hell did you think you were doing?"

"Lydia? Are you okay?"

"I'm fine, sweetie. What the hell were you up to at the Evanston Hotel this afternoon?"

"I went to meet Vinh and he never showed—"

"So you thought you'd capture yourself some hot TV time, didn't you?"

"That was hardly my intent, Lydia. Oh! Congratulations on Ethan getting the lead in—"

"Don't give me that phony New England politeness. I know what you really think of me."

"We'll talk in the morning."

"We're talking now, sweetie. I'm your boss. Got it? There's a chain of command here, Little Miss Greenwich, Connecticut. Don't you ever forget that. Everything goes through me. Everything! And I don't want to see your face on TV again. Got it?"

Lydia slammed the phone down on her end and Susan lay there in the darkness listening to the distant wailing of sirens blending with the car horns honking twelve floors below. Crime does not sleep, she thought, and neither does this crime fighter. It had been one helluva day.

You had no right to put yourself in the line of fire. Shut up, Hugh. It was fate. I wanted to see what was going on. I do not lead a fantasy life. What I see every day is real. *You are the one who sits around all day listening to people's fantasies. Wealthy people's fantasies. People who have nothing really wrong with their lives except for the fact they don't have one.* Sleep. Come on, sleep. I'm waiting for you. Where are you?

And then the phone rang. Susan cursed and reached out for it.

"Hello? . . . Hello? . . . Hugh? . . . Lydia? . . . Hello?"

There was no reply person at the other end. Junior Tesla had merely wanted to hear Susan's voice. For future reference.

"Hello? . . . Hello?"

Finally the dial tone. Susan replaced the receiver on its cradle and lay unnerved in the darkness for several minutes before she finally fell asleep.

"WHERE THE HELL was this? . . . Whaddaya tellin' me? That's our spot, Dino. We been pickin' up from that spot for over twenty years. . . . He did what? . . . A pig farmer where? You gotta be kiddin'!" Nicolo Tesla roared with laughter as he sat in his third-floor office atop his restaurant. "Just have a little word with him. . . . Yeah. Double." Tesla replaced the phone and cursed under his breath: *"Figlio de puttana."*

Louie Torino walked into the office and caught his boss muttering away to himself.

"What's wrong, Nick?"

"What the hell's wit' people? They can't live up to a bargain? We got a deal. We got an arrangement. Goin' on twenty years and, behind my back, they sneak off and make a deal wit' some pig farmer from Jersey to pick up their trash for nothin'."

"Who? Who?"

"Whaddaya? A fuckin' owl, Louie? The coffee shop on Forty-eighth Street. Fuck those Greeks with double. I'll triple their rate."

"Wha's wrong? You didn't sleep good?"

Tesla stared at his bodyguard, then slapped his face affectionately: "Y'always know, don'tcha? We been through a lot, Louie. . . . I'm worried about Junior."

"What now? Knocked up another broad?"

"I'd walk him to the altar with an Uzi for that one. Nah. It's that Cuban. Sanchez. They moved him."

"Who?"

"The feds. They pulled him outta jail two days ago. He could be singin' the whole third act of *Rigoletto* in Alaska for all we know. This'll kill Loretta."

"Why don' you just send Junior away for a while?"

"Where? NASA don't want him for the space shuttle. What the hell am I gonna do, Patch?"

"You'll think of somethin', Nick. Y'always do."

"Yeah. So?"

"That guy from Milano Trucking's waiting downstairs. The transfer guy."

"Oh, yeah. Another goddamn mooch. Send him up."

Seconds later Tony Fusco aka Pete Palazzolo entered the office in a brown leather jacket and tweed cap. Tesla did a double take: the short, stocky undercover cop with the thick eyebrows was a double for his beloved, long-dead grandfather. Fusco swallowed hard, thinking for a moment that his cover had been blown.

"You wanted to see me?" asked Fusco.

"Yeah," said Tesla, blinking his eyes and recovering his composure. "What's yer name?"

"Palazzolo. Pete Palazzolo."

"Where ya from?"

"Jersey City."

"Nah, nah. Yer people. Where'd they come from?"

"Ragusa."

Amazing. Tesla's grandfather had also come from Ragusa. The guy could be related.

"You know why you're here?"

"Yeah."

"So?"

"So how much, Signor Tesla?"

"Yer a ballsy guy, Pete."

"I gotta feelin' that's all I'm left with when I leave here."

"Hey, hey," chuckled Tesla. "It's just business, kid. If it wasn't me, you'd have to deal with Carlucci or Phil DeFillipo. How come you didn't go to Phil?"

"Cuz I heard he fucked goats in the old country. With

you, I might be able to get a reservation here on a Saturday night."

"Take yer wife out to dinner?"

"I ain't got a wife."

Tesla looked appraisingly at Fusco. *We must be related. The kid's balls clang and he runs a good business. Nice-looking, too. He'd make a good husband for Toni. Wouldn't take any shit from her. Hey, hey, hey! Business first.*

"Y'owe the organization six hundred thousand dollars. Past dues and penalties for cutting into our action. . . . So?"

"Did you see me fall over dead from shock?"

Tesla roared with laughter: "I like you, Palazzolo."

"Good. Does that get me a discount?"

"No. But it gets you an invitation to dinner. *After* you pay what you owe."

Fusco examined a silver-framed photograph atop Tesla's desk. Taken the night of the Waldorf-Astoria testimonial, it revealed the entire clan surrounding Cardinal Corcoran.

"This your family?" asked Fusco.

"My wife, my children and my grandchildren," said Tesla proudly. "And our good friend Cardinal Corcoran."

"I guess you don't worry about Heaven much with a friend like that."

"He worries enough for all of us."

"That's some watch on his wrist," whistled Fusco, staring at the large gold Rolex on the churchman's powerful wrist.

"I gave him that watch for his sixtieth birthday. His Eminence and I go back a long way." Tesla slapped Fusco's back in farewell and added: "Maybe you'll get to meet him someday."

Fusco turned to leave and collided with what he thought, at first, to be a brick wall.

"Pete, I want you to meet my son. Junior, this is Pete Palazzolo."

"Milano Trucking?" asked Junior, staring down contemptuously at the undercover cop.

"Hey, Junior! You be nice to Pete. He's comin' out to the house for dinner."

SUSAN WAS EXHAUSTED. She simply could not find the energy to run around the circumference of Central Park that morning. The case against the garbage cartel was proving monumental. None of their customers was willing to discuss, let alone testify against, the extortionary carters. Susan was barely getting home before seven (much to the girls' annoyance) and by the time she was ready to fall asleep the phone would ring. The phantom caller. Who was it and what did they want from her? They never spoke; barely breathed. Why? Why? Crime never sleeps? It was suffering from terminal insomnia and threatening to take Susan along for the ride.

Maybe she'd just nip up the stairs at Ninetieth Street and do an abbreviated spin around the Jackie O. No, it would have to be the full circuit or hang up her Nikes forever.

By 7:40 A.M. Susan had stopped off at D'Agostino's on Lexington, ordered her groceries, and was heading back home for a shower.

Walking into her bedroom and whipping off 'her clothes, Susan was startled to discover Polly rummaging through the drawers in the walk-in closet. Mother and daughter both shrieked at the same time.

"You scared me!"

"You scared *me!* What are you doing here, Polly?" The girls had stayed at their father's Riverside Drive apartment the previous night under the terms of their parents' separation agreement.

"Trying to find something to wear."

"My clothes don't fit you."

"Some of them do."

"Did you walk Ivy to the bus stop this morning?"

"No. Sigrid walked her."

"Is she always so helpful?"

"Don't talk to me about her."

"Ivy or Sigrid?"

"Both of them. Ivy got into a screaming match with Dad at five o'clock this morning."

"What was that all about?"

"He was on his way to Grand Central to catch the train to Otto's."

"Otto Schellenberg? Otto lives on Riverside Drive."

"Not anymore. He moved to Long Island and Dad has to catch the five-thirty in order to be there by seven for his daily session."

"Why is Otto doing that to him?"

"Why is Dad letting him? They're both crazy. And Ab Rosenthal, too."

"Why Ab?" Rosenthal had gone through grad school with Hugh and they had both become shrinks at the same time.

"We went to dinner at his place last night. You know how Ab never stops talking. He's even more pompous than Dad. Well, he doesn't talk anymore. Sits staring into space like the Sphinx. It's so-o-o weird. Dad thinks it's his portfolio. He's in too deep and he's afraid to talk about it."

"So what happened with Ivy?"

"Dad woke her up at five. It's her debate today."

"Jeepers! I forgot to phone and wish her—"

"It's okay, Mom. She was completely freaked about it anyhow."

"Poor Ivy. What happened?"

"Ivy freaked cuz Dad woke her at five. 'What are you waking me for? Don't you know I have a debate?' 'I was only doing it to wish you luck.' 'What good is luck if I haven't slept, you moron?' "

"She called him a moron?"

"Well, he *can* be difficult. So, they're screaming away at each other and I'm lying in my bed begging them both to shut up so I can get a little sleep. And Sigrid comes racing into the room like the apartment's on fire—God! how I hate her!"

"Why?"

"Cuz she's sucking real hard to be the next Mrs. Hugh Carver."

"Let her! Let her! With my blessing."

"No way, Mom. She's an idiot! Plus Dad insists on her helping me with my homework. She can't speak English, let alone teach it. It took me twenty minutes last night to figure out who Yames Yoyce was." Polly whipped off the T-shirt she was wearing and held one of her mother's cashmere sweaters out admiringly at arm's length. Then a snapshot floated down from the sweater onto the floor.

"Who's this?" asked Polly studying the photograph of her mother with her arm wrapped around a man's shoulder and his arm around her waist. Both were wearing bathing suits and were covered in mud from head to toe.

"Oh, that was in Israel," said Susan, exuding fake insouciance while wondering how the photo came to be in her sweater drawer. "The Dead Sea."

"Uh-huh. Who's the guy?"

"A friend of Barry Praeger's." Then Susan shifted gears abruptly. "Your father maintains Sigrid has an excellent command of English."

"As if!"

"Don't you think you should put some clothes on?"

"Hey, Mom!"

"Yes, my angel?"

"What's with the phone calls?"

125

"Phone calls?"

"Late at night. They never speak. I know it's not Dad."

"Just some crank. Everyone gets them. It's just our turn. Don't let it bother you. Doesn't bother me."

"Then why are you smoking again?"

"I'm under a lot of pressure at work."

"I know. I know. I can live with the smoking but I couldn't handle it if anything happened to you. You know?"

"Yes, I do know." Susan fought back a tear as she hugged her daughter to her chest. "But thanks for telling me."

"Can I borrow the cashmere sweater?"

"Yes. But don't spill anything on it."

"I promise not to spill anything . . . except Ethan Culberg's blood."

"How are the rehearsals going?" asked Susan as she stepped into the bathroom and turned on the shower faucets.

"Okay. Except they always skip my song. Ethan says they're probably going to cut my number. Why does he say things like that? He's so twisted. He brings these little jars of creamed herring to rehearsal and eats them with a Swiss Army knife while he talks about his mother's lovers. Yeccch . . . I'm worried."

"I can't hear you," said Susan, who had stepped under the water by then.

"I'm worried about high school next year!" shouted Polly. "What if I don't get into a good one? Callie's going to Dalton and Trish wants to go to Nightingale."

"I can't hear you!"

"Maybe I'll just drop out and work as a waitress. Or become an artist's model for someone like Van Picasso. Can I borrow twenty dollars?"

"What did you—?"

"It's okay. I'll just take it from your pocketbook and pay you back later. 'Bye, Mom! Go fight crime."

By the time Susan emerged from the shower, Polly had

left for school. The blond prosecutor wrapped her hair in a towel and hobbled slightly toward her closet. What to wear? What to wear? The telephone rang. Eight o'clock. Who? Who?

"I've got to see you," said a breathless Cynthia Praeger without any salutation.

"I'm dripping wet, Cynthia. Can I phone you later?"

"It's an emergency, Susan. You must have lunch with me. Today."

"I'm really pressed for time. I've got an appointment on Sixty-third Street at 10:30—"

"Sixty-third Street. Perfect. A hop, skip, and a jump to Tesla's at noon. I just love Tesla's. Don't you? See ya."

Do I love Tesla's? Susan asked herself as she blow-dried her hair. Like the stalker loves its prey. But who's the stalker and who's the prey?

RACING UP THE steps outside the Lefkowitz Building, Susan heard a familiar voice call out: "Oh, Ms. Given! Ms. Given!"

Susan spun around and saw Ned Jordan flashing his teeth at her. "Oh, Ms. Given, I've seen you on television but I never dreamt I might actually meet you in person."

"Ned, stop it!"

"No, no, no. I know how fortunate I am to be allowed these few brief moments when men all over the country are pining away for you. Left virtually speechless."

"Oh, no!"

"Oh, yes, Ms. D.A. Our guest is not cooperating at all."

"I'm sorry."

"You should be. You're the one persuaded us to put Manolo Sanchez into the Witness Protection Program and that bird ain't singin' at all."

"What are you going to do?"

"Got any cowboy boots? Cowgirl boots? Cowperson boots?"

"You expect me to go to Wyoming?"

"No one said he was in Wyoming. But wherever he is, you may be called upon to make sexy purring noises for your country."

"I have never made sexy purring noises in my life."

"Not even in Jerusalem?"

How the hell did Ned know about Michael? Janie Moore. The Mouth of the Western World.

"I'm late, Ned."

"Uh-huh." And the federal prosecutor walked down the steps to Centre Street singing "Don't Fence Me In."

Emerging from the elevator on the eighth floor, Susan discovered Becker waiting for her on crutches—the result of an ill-advised roller skating date the previous week with a Gen-X physical fitness freak named Rusty Rubenstein (whom his mother had set him up with).

"I'll never get used to you on those crutches, Alan."

"I feel like Fred MacMurray in *Double Indemnity*. Except he was faking it."

"I thought only women faked it."

"You mean I broke my ankle for nothing?"

"Don't let Rusty hear you. What's up?"

Becker leaned forward perilously on his crutches and asked in hushed tones: "Is the Evanston still on?"

"What do you mean?"

"Rumor has it that Lydia is dropping all action against Vinh."

"The hell she is!"

"Vinh's lawyer is now claiming harassment. Maintains we engineered the entire Sanchez bust to sensationalize a legitimate operation."

"Are you quoting Brent Yacoubian to me? The man sleeps with pythons and cobras. We're not discussing a borderline case here. Vinh Ho Chi is an amoral, psychotic criminal, whose rap sheet in *this* country alone would make Oliver Stone think twice about filming it. I am personally embarrassed that our government was ever in business with this weasel. The Evanston Hotel is the second-largest single-room-occupancy building in the city. Before Vinny bought it, it was a haven for the elderly and infirm on public assistance. There was no drug activity. In the last three years it has become a blot on the moral landscape. Need I remind you of the teenage corpse who kept me company for four hours? Don't worry, Alan. I'm not done with the Evanston yet."

"Susan!"

"Yes, Gretchen?"

"It's you-know-who on the phone."

"Hugh?"

"Me?"

"No," laughed Susan. "My please-God-soon-to-be-ex."

"No. It's the person whose name we can't mention anymore."

"Oh, no!" groaned Susan. "Not again."

Susan closed the door to her office, sat down beside her desk, and picked up the phone: "Hello?"

"Susan? How ya doin'?"

"Manny, you mustn't phone here anymore. I thought I explained that to you the last time."

"Why you don' come out here? It's so pretty with the lake and the mountains and Hey, George! What you call those birds with the stripes? I never seen birds like that before."

"Manny, don't tell me where you are. I'm not supposed to know."

"Don' you wanna see me?"

"It would be grand to see you again, Manny. But I'm up to my ears in work here. I took on a new case the day after we met and it's been consuming—"

129

"You ain' goin' after the Teslas no more?"

"Manny, please, I can't discuss my cases with you."

"You tricked me, Susan!"

"I don't think that's true."

"I would never have give myself up except you said you'd come out here."

"What choice did you have, Manny? The Teslas would have shot you. I saved your life."

"I saved yours! Ah, shit! Man, I been straight for a month now. I ain' used to it. I look good, Susan."

"You're a very attractive man."

"You think so? You like dancin'? I'm a helluva dancer, Susan. Not the square dance shit they got out here, you know what I mean."

"I don't know and I don't want to know. Now I've been told by a very reliable source that you are *not* cooperating with the authorities where you are. Is that true, Manny?"

"Heyyy! I feed 'em a line of bullshit every day and they eat it up. But I'm savin' the real good stuff for you, Susan. Why you don' write me a letter or somethin'? Is so lonely here. Can' you just come for a weekend?"

Susan clapped a hand over the receiver and counted to ten. She'd never known a witness to have a crush on her before. Her second phone line lit up. She put Sanchez on hold and gratefully grabbed the second line.

"Given!"

"It's Elaine Morton. We really need to talk about this storage—"

"Not now, Elaine."

Susan hung up the phone and noticed that the light was still glowing on line one. Romeo Sanchez had not given up his ardent pursuit.

"Listen, Manny, please! I can't encourage you in this fantasy any longer."

"Who's Manny?"

"Who's this?" asked a startled Susan.

"Michael Roth."

"Very funny. Who is this?"

"It's Michael Roth. I'm phoning from Los Angeles. How are you? I've called your apartment a couple of times but this West Indian woman always answered. Didn't she give you any of my messages? I've been trying to reach you for the past month. Ever since I saw you on CNN."

"Ohhh! So that's what Cordelia's messages about 'me cold roast' meant. Any fool should have known she meant Michael Roth."

"What *was* going on in that hotel, Susan? I was glued to my set for four hours. I tried calling Barry to get news but he was away in Bora Bora or Boston or—"

"Michael? Is it really you?"

"Do you want my Social Security number?"

"Why?"

"As proof. What else can I tell you? I was born in Toronto. I've been married three times. Your daughters' names are Polly and Ivy. You abducted them from El Salvador at birth or some other fabulous tale. And you have the cutest little birthmark just inside your left—"

"Shh! Shh! I believe who you are. But where have you been all this time?"

"It's a long story."

"I always liked your stories."

That was true. From the first night in Jerusalem. She'd arrived late for cocktails in the Praegers' suite in the King David Hotel. Cynthia Praeger was prattling away to her Indiana relatives and pointing out the window below to the terrace where Paul Newman and Eva Marie Saint had sat during the shooting of *Exodus* years before. Barry was downstairs schmoozing with the hotel manager and talking shop. Daniel Praeger—the bar mitzvah boy—was bored out of his mind and was allowing his kid sister Emma to practice her nonexistent hairdressing skills on him.

Susan walked around the suite greeting everyone and asking about their respective flights from America. All the while she was aware of the dark, shaggy-haired man gazing at her with Pacinoesque intensity. This was Michael Roth, Barry Praeger's best friend since kindergarten.

Seated opposite her at dinner that evening, he never took his twinkly eyes off her as he regaled her with his humorous accounts of his life in London and Los Angeles. He had acted and directed in theater and films, had several plays produced and novels published, and—most fascinating to Susan—had been married and divorced several times.

"I'm having trouble doing it once," said Susan. "The divorce part. We were married for eighteen years."

"I was married for ten years . . . to three different women. Ironically, I have two older brothers, who have never married. I was the designated husband in the family. Not that I have anything against marriage; I just wouldn't do it again. I wasn't really equipped for the job. Hadn't studied up for it. On-the-job training isn't sufficient after you say 'I do.' It's like I'd been driving for a decade without a license."

Susan liked this unexpected guest (strange that Cynthia had given her a blow-by-blow description of everyone flying over for the bar mitzvah except Michael). He was funny; he was sexy; he didn't have to be in charge. He was the exact opposite of Hugh.

The next morning they sat beside each other on a private bus Barry had hired to take everyone sightseeing. Their first destination was Masada, the Alamo of Israel, a legendary mountain fortress where the Jews had held off the Romans for months until they were eventually massacred. Tourists usually took a ten-minute aerial tram to the top of the mountain to escape the crippling desert heat; Susan chose to run up the winding path to the summit. Half an hour later, she reached the top, only to discover an awestruck Michael waiting for her.

Later that day the group traveled to the Dead Sea, where they all bathed in the ancient biblical waters, then caked themselves in the restorative mud baths. Afterward, as Susan and Michael stood in their bathing suits under an outdoor shower, she guilelessly came up behind him and helped wash the curative mud from his body.

They chattered all the way back to Jerusalem on the bus: books, movies, plays, politics. They dined again together that evening. (Actually they were, as always, with Cynthia's Hoosier contingent and Barry's parents but they might as well have been tucked away *à deux* in some little hideaway; they only had eyes for each other.)

Drifting off from the others after dinner, they found themselves in a secluded park behind the hotel. Michael kissed her and she realized she had never really been kissed before. Accompanied incongruously by the cry of a muezzin atop a nearby minaret summoning the faithful to prayer, they made love the next evening—Friday—as the sun was setting. Michael explained to her that it was a mitzvah, a good deed, to make love on the Sabbath.

". . . so I finally persuaded her once and for all to move out of the house." Michael's explanation had failed to shatter Susan's reverie and she hadn't heard a word of it.

"Sounds fascinating."

"Fascinating! Were you listening to what I said?"

"Actually not."

"Serves me right."

"No, no, no. I was thinking about Jerusalem. We had a marvelous time, didn't we?"

"I had the best time with you, Susan. Ever. I just had unfinished business in L.A. and I didn't want to—"

"You don't have to explain to me, Michael."

"I just *did*, Susan. You didn't listen to any of it. Besides, I kept remembering your saying: 'Thank God you don't live in New York.' "

"Oooh, those darned *mullahs* should have ripped my tongue out in the cemetery. I wish you did live in New York. Or at least visit."

"Your wish has come true. I'm going to be there next month. I'm researching a TV movie about Cornell Woolrich."

"Wasn't he in Roosevelt's cabinet?"

"That was Cordell Hull."

"Do I get points for trying?"

"Absolutely."

"Where are you staying?"

"Not sure yet. Maybe the Essex House. The thing is, I'd love to see you. That is, if you have time."

"Why don't you stay here?"

"Where?"

"My apartment. There's a guest room. I'm sure the girls would find you fascinating."

"Are you sure?"

"Positive. Jeepers, Michael! It's a quarter to eleven."

"That's okay. It's only seven forty-five here. I've got fifteen more minutes till the rates change."

"No, no, no! I have to dash. I can't miss this appointment. See you next month. 'Bye!"

Susan forced herself to stop thinking about Michael Roth and being in his arms again as she stuffed some files into her briefcase, and dashed out of the office muttering to herself about the time. Waiting for the elevator proved interminable and when it finally did arrive, Miss Piggy—Elaine Morton—stood inside. Susan tried to enter the car but the other A.D.A. barred her way.

"We still haven't spoken about the storage space."

"Not now, Elaine. It's ten to eleven—"

"It's always ten to eleven, Ms. Given. Every time I want to address the problem—"

"Elaine, please get out of the way!"

"I will not be ignored!"

"Take the goddamn eighteen inches, Elaine! Just get out of my way!" And Susan grabbed her belligerent colleague's arm and whipped her out of the elevator.

23

It was 11:20 a.m. when a breathless and frazzled Susan finally stood outside the townhouse on East Sixty-third double-checking the address she had written on a piece of paper. It was the same building. This was too much of a coincidence.

Rehearsing the apology for her tardiness as she entered the third-floor reception area, Susan was surprised to discover her lawyer, Neil Stern, engrossed in a telephone conversation.

"What are you doing out here?" asked Susan.

"Ah! She just walked in. I'll get back to you." Stern, a small, compact man in a three-piece suit, hung up the phone and informed his client, "They're not ready for us yet."

"Oh, come off it! I'm leaving."

"Don't!"

"Neil, do you know who else works at this address? Do you? Hugh Carver! The ultimate anal. Never wastes a minute. He must have combed the Internet to find a lawyer in the same building."

"Susan, it's just a ploy to unnerve you. You've waited six months for this meeting. Don't blow it."

"How did he find a lawyer as big an asshole as he is? And in the same building! Do you think they have to fill it in on the application? Would it be 'Distinguishing Features' or just 'Hobbies'?"

"Shh!"

The door to reception opened and a large, rather florid

man with blond hair, a bulbous nose, and beady eyes emerged from the inner office wearing a blue blazer with an embossed gold crest over the left breast pocket.

"You must be Susan!" announced the man in a ripe, plummy voice. "You're exactly as I imagined you'd be. I'm Ralph Kregar."

"Good morning," said Susan professionally.

Kregar beamed at her, then recited: "The lark's on the wing;/ The snail's on the horn:/ God's in his heaven,/ All's right with the world!"

Then the lawyer drew a deep breath and sighed. "I just love October! Don't you? I suppose it's because I'm a Libra. Teetering toward the cusp of Scorpio."

"How nice for you." Susan smiled. Where had Hugh found this nut job?

"Hello, Neil. Nice to see you again. Come in. Come in."

Susan followed Kregar into his overly decorated office and discovered her portly, estranged husband striking a pensive Peck pose with his back to the room, hands clasped tightly against his buttocks, staring down at Sixty-third Street.

"Well, here we are!" Kregar's plummy pronouncements had the irritating quality of a cruise director trying to find a quorum for Bingo.

Hugh turned around from the window and Susan was startled to see he was wearing the same blazer and crest as Kregar. Had the two just returned from a fraternity meeting?

"Take a pew." Kregar beamed, lowering himself into the chair behind his desk.

Hugh made no move to sit. Susan wasn't prepared to have him tower over her through the proceedings so she wandered around the room examining Kregar's degrees on the wall and silver-framed photographs of his family on an antique table.

"Hepplewhite or Chippendale?" asked Susan.

"Repro," replied Kregar with a mock grimace. "Joyce—

my wife—saves the real stuff for her clients. She's a decorator."

Susan nodded, then paused an extra beat to examine a photograph of Kregar, a honey blonde she assumed to be wife Joyce, and a distinguished older gentleman with a liver-spotted bald pate, goatee, and mustache.

"Isn't this Otto Schellenberg?" she asked.

"Why, yes," replied Kregar. "He's Joyce's uncle."

"How convenient." Susan smiled in Hugh's direction.

Emitting an audible puff of carbon dioxide to convey that enough of his precious time had been wasted on social niceties, Hugh lowered his bulk down onto a faux antique wing-back chair and muttered, "Let's get on with it."

Susan settled herself in the chair's twin and crossed her legs. Neil Stern sat between the estranged couple.

"The first order of business," Kregar began, "is the common property of Hugh and Susan Carver." He then read the Eightieth Street address aloud. "My client, Mr. Carver, is offering Mrs. Carver three months to vacate the premises and find another place to live—"

"What!?"

"He's buying you out, Susan." Kregar beamed. "Quite generously, I might add." And he quoted a price.

"That sum is outrageous. The apartment is worth twice that amount."

"Not in today's market," asserted Hugh in his clipped tones.

Susan turned to Stern and asked: "Did you know about this?"

"I had no idea." Stern shrugged. "I thought we were getting together to bat around a few— This is not what we discussed, Ralph."

"I don't want to be bought out," said Susan firmly. "I love that apartment. I found that apartment. I helped decorate that apartment."

"With my money," said Hugh. "You did everything with my money, Susan."

"Where did the down payment come from on our first apartment, Hugh? The fifty thousand dollars that got us started."

"Didn't I tell you?" Hugh was beaming at Kregar. "This is the same delusion over and over again."

"What delusion, Dr. Carver? My grandfather died and left me fifty thousand dollars. You didn't have a pot to pee-pee in back then. I'm the one who put the money down."

"But I'm the one who made the monthly payments."

"We split the mortgage those first few years," said Susan.

"I paid it all when we moved to the big apartment."

"And I'm the one who sent you all your patients, Doctor."

"A few. A few."

"What about all those dinner parties where you steered the poor suckers off into the library to ask them 'what was really wrong'? My God! I felt like a psychiatric pimp all those years."

"Another delusion," murmured Hugh.

"The original fifty thousand dollars is applied toward your end of the settlement," said Kregar, trying to steer the conversation back toward an area of negotiation.

"We sold that apartment for six hundred thousand dollars, Ralph. I don't think that original figure is equitable. You can step in at any time you want, Neil."

"Let's put aside the matter of the apartment right now," said Stern. "What about support?"

"For the children . . . only."

"Do we leave now, Neil?" asked Susan.

"And custody?" asked Stern ignoring his client's question.

"Joint. Fifty-fifty."

"No way!" said Susan. "The man is a nut job." She fished in her red leather briefcase and withdrew a fistful of faxes she had brought with her in anticipation of such a moment. "Read these, Ralph. These are the diatribes he bombards me with daily. In violation of specific court orders. He could be charged with—"

"I think you should leave legal matters to your lawyer, Susan."

"I'm a lawyer, too, Ralph. Or didn't your client tell you that?"

"See what I mean?" asked Hugh.

"What did you mean . . . Hershie?"

"Who's Hershie?" asked Kregar.

Hugh bolted to his feet and examined his wristwatch: "I knew nothing would come of this. She is an insecure egomaniac. I was willing to settle this morning—"

"On your terms, Hugh. Always on your terms."

"Anything that isn't what you want, Susan, always becomes 'my terms.' This isn't about the two of us alone. There are the girls' interests to bear in mind—"

"I know. Believe me, I know. Someone has to protect them from a homophobic, vego-fascist, oral-obsessed, anti-Semitic—"

"I'm Jewish!"

"When it serves your purposes. You certainly haven't passed any traditions on to the girls. Polly wanted a bar mitzvah and you wouldn't let her."

"Bas mitzvah. And she only wanted it for the gifts. At least I'm consistent in my atheism. I'm sorry, Ralph. I tried. But, frankly, I'm not surprised. Now, I have to get back to my office. I have patients."

"That's news to me," said Susan.

"Always the last word," growled Hugh.

"It was a joke, Hugh. Patience and patients? Come on, Neil. I've got to go fight crime . . . real crime."

Stern caught up with Susan in reception and found the prosecutor searching feverishly through her briefcase.

"What's wrong?"

"Trying to find my cigarettes."

"We need to speak, Susan."

"I'll say. What was going on in there? You let them walk all over us."

Stern steered Susan over to a corner of the reception area then spoke softly and patiently: "This is a different area of the law than you're used to. They're playing dumb games. Trying to throw us off guard. I thought the matching blazers was a bit much, didn't you?"

"That was a tactic? I just thought it was a sale."

The front door opened at that moment and a white-haired woman in a sweater and pearls stuck her head in the office. Her face lit up when she saw Susan.

"Mrs. Carver! How nice to see you again."

"Hello, Nora. How are you?" Nora was the communal receptionist in Hugh's medical suite.

"Just fine, thank you. Wait a sec." And Nora walked over to the receptionist and handed a man's wallet to her. "Could you see that Mr. Kregar gets this? I found it lodged between the chair cushions after his session this morning. I don't want him to worry." Then she came back to Susan and squeezed her hands. "Give my love to the girls. They must be so big now."

Susan watched Nora leave the office in disbelief. Then she turned back to the receptionist and asked innocently: "Is Mr. Kregar a patient of Dr. Carver's?"

When the receptionist nodded, Susan took her lawyer by the elbow and steered him out of the office. Once in the hallway, she shook her head in disbelief.

"We are dealing with a cabal of cuckoos, Neil. Are you aware of that? Hugh's lawyer, Ralph Kregar, is in therapy. His shrink is his client, Hugh Carver. Hugh Carver is also in therapy. His shrink is Otto Schellenberg, Ralph Kregar's wife's uncle. It's ludicrous."

"What about the offer?"

"I would like the apartment and we will share the girls."

"He'll never go for that."

"We've got to start somewhere. All over again. Maybe if I hire Joyce Kregar to redecorate my place—Oh, no!"

"What's wrong?"

"What time is it?"

"Ten to twelve."

"I've got a noon lunch date at Tesla's."

"Is that safe?" asked Stern, then added hastily: "Just kidding. Rumor has it, it's a real Mafia hangout."

"Believe me, Neil. I'm a lot safer there than here. A lot safer."

SOUNDS OF SILVERWARE tinkling on glass and hungry diners devouring their food flooded into Tony Fusco's ears as he poked at the linguine pesto on his plate. He could feel Nicolo Tesla's eyes boring into him, and staring at the green pasta was the only escape the cop had from the gaze of his "new best friend." In the three weeks Fusco had been in business with Tesla, the carter had stuck closer to him than a bag of warm jelly beans.

At first Fusco thought Tesla was wise to him and waited in dread for the ax to fall. But the first visit to the house in Glen Cove revealed the answer: Tesla thought Fusco was the reincarnation of his grandfather. The carter showed him faded tintypes and Fusco had to admit there was a distinct resemblance.

Then there was the daughter. Definitely the type who slept with her finger in the light socket. She glared at Fusco all through dinner with blatant hostility but, by the end of the evening, she asked him for his phone number.

"Toni likes you."

"Huh?" Fusco looked up from his linguine and stared into Tesla's almond-colored eyes. Louie Torino and Dino

Marazonni, the manager of Tesla Waste Disposal, flanked him on either side.

"My daughter. She likes you." Tesla's eyes darted away from Fusco for a moment and he nodded at someone passing his table.

"You could do worse," advised The Patch.

It was lunchtime at Tesla's and the restaurant was packed as always. The staff was buzzing back and forth and occasionally pausing at "Mr. Nick's" table to inform him who their special customers were that day. Occasionally, Tesla would grab a waiter's sleeves and send a glass of wine over to a preferred diner's table with his compliments.

"She has a boyfriend," said Fusco.

"Whaddaya talkin'?"

"That guy. Torrid."

"He's not her boyfriend. I checked him out. He's like a hobby with her. Know what I mean? They don't do nothin'. They can't. The guy's got a big mouth and a little gherkin. You should take her out. She'd like that. Her mother would like it, too."

"Maybe I should just take your wife out."

"Take my wife out, I'll take you out. Just kiddin'. You got a helluva future in this business, Pete. Play yer cards right."

"All I gotta do is marry the boss's daughter?" asked Fusco, twirling the linguine round his fork.

"Hey, hey, smart guy. You should be so lucky to marry Antonia. How do I know you ain't got a gherkin, too?"

"I got a big dill pickle, Nick. But it stays in the barrel. *Capisce?*"

Tesla roared with laughter and shoved his plate of osso buco towards Fusco. "Here! Eat something substantial. Yer like Junior eatin' his carbs all the time."

The maître d' approached the table, bowed, then leaned into Tesla's ear and whispered something.

"Which one is she?" asked the restaurateur.

The maître d' nodded across the room where Susan

Given had just sat down opposite Cynthia Praeger, an attractive, strong-jawed, streaky blonde of pioneer stock.

"Send her over a bottle of Brunello."

"A *bottle?*" asked the maître d', shocked by his employer's largesse.

"Yeah. The eighty-two."

Susan was twenty minutes late by the time she finally got across town to Tesla's and Cynthia Praeger, who was on her second martini. Double martini.

"You'll never guess who phoned me this morning," Susan said, after politely turning down the waiter's offer to take her drink order.

"Oh, have a drink," said Cynthia.

"Can't. I'm in court this afternoon. . . . Michael Roth."

"What about him?"

"He phoned me. From L.A. He's coming for a visit next month. Actually, he's working but—"

"Did he finally break up with his girlfriend?"

"I think so. Yes. Yes, I'm sure he did."

"Barry met her in L.A. He had dinner with her and Michael. Said she was skinny. Sure you won't have a drink? Skinny but nice."

"How skinny?"

"What the hell does Barry know about nice? *I* know what nice is. Didn't I let him have his son's bar mitzvah in Israel? That was nice."

"*Your* son, too."

"What?" Cynthia was hyper at the best of times but two double martinis cast her into the dark zone where logic was not part of the lingua franca. "You were lucky. Doctor Carver didn't care about being Jewish."

"That isn't necessarily a good—"

"I didn't think Barry cared either. Until Danny turned twelve. Then Barry started in with this bar mitzvah shit. Okay, okay. So the kids didn't go to church either. But we have Christmas and Hanukkah and matzo and chocolate bunnies. Barry didn't like the New Testament tour we did. You know. When we went to Bethlehem. Couldn't wait to get out of there. Michael didn't mind, did he? That's because two of *his* wives were *shiksas.*"

"Why don't we order some food?"

Before Cynthia could respond to Susan's suggestion, the sommelier arrived at the table and ceremoniously presented them with the bottle of Brunello.

"Compliments of Signor Tesla," said the sommelier in a thick Italian accent.

"Send it back," replied Susan immediately, "with *my* compliments."

"Wait, wait, wait," said Cynthia. "That happens to be an excellent wine. We should switch to wine now anyhow before I get loaded."

"Please, signorina!" said the sommelier. "What will I tell Signor Tesla? Take the wine. He will be offended." The sommelier nodded nervously toward a table at the far side of the restaurant where Nicolo Tesla was having lunch with his cronies.

"I can't take this man's wine, Cynthia."

"Why not?"

Susan waited until the sommelier had reluctantly departed with the wine, then she pointed out Tesla's table. "He's under investigation."

"Is he a gangster? Which one? Ooh, he's awful! Are all those men gangsters over there?"

All except the undercover cop, thought Susan, when she recognized Tony Fusco shaking his head as Tesla roared with laughter at one of his own jokes. Did Fusco know about the bottle of wine? Had he blinked when Tesla proposed it?

"How is Linda?" asked Cynthia, not noticing she had spilled some of her martini down the front of her silk blouse. "Does she *really* like it in Chattanooga? And her twins? What are their names? Isabelle and Ferdinand?"

"Those are their dogs," murmured Susan. "The kids' names are—"

"How is that darling Cordelia of yours? She's an absolute jewel, do you know that? What I wouldn't give to swap her for Inez. Do you know what Inez did yesterday? She had the nerve to . . ."

Susan found herself zoning out. What was she doing at lunch with Cynthia Praeger? With her terminal caseload, the never-ending battle with Hugh, the Evanston hanging over her head, Tesla and the carters to do battle with, and a court date in an hour, why had Susan agreed to join her for this meandering meal?

"Cynthia?"

"Hmm?"

"Why did you want to see me?"

"When?"

"Now. This morning. You phoned and said it was an emergency. Where and/or what is the emergency that I had to meet with you to discuss?"

"Not so loud."

"I am not being—"

"Yes, you are. You have a very loud voice, Susan. You're not in court now, you know."

"I need to order some food." Susan shook her head in exasperation while signaling for a waiter. "Cynthia—"

"This isn't easy for me. . . ."

"Perhaps another time?"

"No, no, no. I was going to say let's nip it in the bud. But it's a flower, a bush, a fucking tree. It's a virulent virus that must be—"

"What are you talking about?"

Cynthia took hold of Susan's hand and squeezed it tightly. "I'm very fond of your brother."

"Henry?" Susan could not imagine where this wacky conversation was going next. Was Cynthia in love with her brother? Was that what this whole thing was about? "Oh, no, Cynthia, please! I don't know what you're thinking but Hank is very happily married and—"

"No, he's not!"

"How do you know?"

"Because his wife has been having an affair with my husband!"

"What!? Sheila and Barry?"

"They thought they could fool me but—"

"You're—you're—You've gone too far this time. I cannot sit here and—"

"Truth hurts, doesn't it?"

"Cynthia, you've got to get into therapy."

"With whom? Hugh? Maybe I'll have an affair with him. Wouldn't that be cozy? Barry and Sheila, Hugh and I. But that would only leave you with your brother. Oh, well, don't knock it till you try it, right?" Cynthia lifted her empty martini glass up and waved it at a passing waiter.

"You've had enough to drink," said Susan, grabbing Cynthia's arm and wrenching it back down to the table.

"Don't tell me what—"

"I want to know what—if any—proof you have to support so outrageous an accusation? What evidence?"

"He was in Beijing; she was in Beijing. He was in Bangkok; she was in Bangkok. He was in Sydney; she was in Sydney. Must I go on?"

"They're in the same business, Cynthia. They are competitors. They are bidding on the same—"

"They stay in the same hotels!"

"Not good enough! Circumstantial. I couldn't go into court with this." Court. Susan checked her watch. It was 1:30. She'd have to leave in fifteen minutes. No later. "Sheila is crazy about my brother. They have two sons whom they adore to distraction. She would never do anything to jeopardize the stability of her family. Even with someone as attractive as Barry."

"Do you think he's attractive?"

"I think he's very handsome. I always have."

"Have *you* been having an affair with him?"

"Please, Cynthia! Get a grip on yourself."

"Well, somebody's fucking him!" exploded Cynthia. "God knows I'm not." Uninhibited sobbing followed this confession.

Susan wrapped an arm around Cynthia to comfort her

146

but the drunken ad exec pulled away instantly from her embrace. "Don't! They'll think we're dikes."

"Why don't you take a trip? Go home to Indiana and visit your parents."

"That's your best suggestion?"

"Well, you could always put your head in the oven."

"That's not funny, Susan!"

"I don't know what you want me to say."

"I'm not happy," sobbed Cynthia.

"No, I can see that."

"Oh, don't be so patronizing."

"I'm not."

"Yes, you are. You're being oh, so superior and oh, so aloof. Nothing bad ever happens to you."

Across the room, Tesla and his cronies were discussing serious business—garbage business.

"You gotta be tough with these guys, Pete," said Tesla, teaching Fusco the basics of carting.

"Fuckin' A," echoed Dino.

"There's some real hard noses out there," continued Tesla, "who just never get it. Think they can get a better deal somewhere else. I take care of my customers, Pete. They're like family. Somebody comes in, tries to mess wit' my family—I kill 'em till they're dead."

The sommelier arrived at Tesla's table but dared not look his employer in the eye.

"Wassamatter, Pasquale? You look like an altar boy that peed in his pants."

"She wouldn't take the bottle," whispered Pasquale.

"Who? What?"

"The Ms. D.A. I took her the Brunello but she said 'no, thanks.' "

"Oh, she did?" said Tesla, staring across the floor toward Susan and Cynthia's table.

"Who's dat?" asked Dino.

"The little broad from the D.A.'s office who's investigating us. Gasmer says she's a real hard nose. C'mon, Pete.

Lemme show you how I operate. No, no. Louie. Relax. It's my joint. Nobody's gonna pull nothing in here."

Tesla and Fusco walked across the floor to the table where Cynthia was continuing her tale of woe. She halted abruptly as the two men loomed above her.

"Ms. Given? How are you? I'm Nicolo Tesla. Welcome to my restaurant."

"Mr. Tesla." Susan nodded primly.

"You don't drink wine?"

"On occasion."

"And this wasn't one of those occasions?"

"I have to appear in court this afternoon," said Susan diplomatically.

"Who's the judge?" asked Tesla.

"Minetti."

"Renata? No shit—pardon my French. She grew up on the same block as me. Give her my regards. Y'know I heard she parachuted behind enemy lines for the OSS."

"So the story goes."

"She's a feisty little broad. All you lawyer ladies are. Maybe you can come have a drink some time when you're not due in court?"

Cynthia rose from the table unsteadily and interrupted: "I think I'm going to be sick."

"Oh, dear," murmured Susan.

"I'm going to be violently sick."

"Do you know where the ladies' room is?" asked Tesla, estimating Cynthia's chances of making it safely across the dining room before she whoopsed. "Pete, go help the lady."

Cynthia opened her mouth to protest but succeeded only in vomiting on Fusco's shoes.

"Please, excuse us. . . ." And Susan hustled Cynthia into the ladies' room.

"Wasn't that exciting?" asked Cynthia. "Real-live gangsters—" She spun around abruptly and dropped to her knees.

"Oopsie. I'll wait for you outside," said Susan. Then

148

she thought twice about it and asked: "Are you okay? I've got to get to court."

"Go ahead," replied Cynthia, her voice echoing off the porcelain. "I'll be fine. Sorry we didn't eat anything. I'll call you later."

Maybe I can get a pretzel on the street, thought a very hungry Susan as she headed toward the front door.

"Ms. Given?"

She turned around and was surprised to see a mournful Haskell Abrams seated alone at the bar near the entrance.

"Lieutenant Abrams?"

"Can I buy you a drink?"

"Thanks very much but no. I'm due in court."

"Got a minute?"

"Not really."

Abrams gave her that abandoned Wheaton terrior look of his, then patted the stool next to him. Susan sat down and made a mental note to check her English phrase book and find out why the words "not really" were not working for her that day. At least there were peanuts on the bar. She grabbed a fistful and went to work on them while the mendacious police lieutenant stared mournfully into space.

"I feel a bond with you," said Abrams, breaking the silence at last. "Particularly after the hotel."

"Ah, yes. The hotel."

"You handled yourself like a pro. I was in awe of you that afternoon. Not just that afternoon, if the truth be known. I'd love you to give some of my people a seminar."

"Well," said Susan, rising from her stool and deciding that the truth would never be known to Haskell Abrams even if it jumped up and shouted 'Pinocchio' at him. "Pick a date and let me know."

Abrams patted her vacated stool emphatically. He wasn't done with her yet. Susan resumed her seat.

"When a man loves a woman . . ."

"Yes?" She wondered if he meant the song or the movie. She hadn't seen the movie.

"This is very difficult, Mrs. Carver. Given. Susan. Do you mind if I call you Susan?"

"Not at all. . . . Haskell." Oh, no. *When a man loves a woman.* What was going on today? First Cynthia and now—

"It's over."

"Is it?" What was over?

"She doesn't love me anymore."

"Who? . . . Oh!" Lydia. Of course. "Oh, I'm so sorry. Forgive my slowness. It's just that one never knew for real. I mean there were rumors but— You do mean Lydia?" Abrams nodded his head pathetically. "You two were very discreet about it."

"We had to. My job. Her job. My wife."

"Well, she must be glad. Your wife."

"She never knew."

"Still. It must be for the best, Haskell. Extramarital affairs never—"

"I loved her. I—I never met a woman like her before, Susan. So passionate."

"Is there . . . someone else?"

"For me?"

"No. Is she involved with someone else? Lydia."

"She says not but . . . I think she's lying. She lies a lot. I know that now. Doesn't change how I feel about her, though. Time'll take care of that, I suppose. I hope. I'd kill the guy if I knew who he was. No, I wouldn't."

"Of course not." Susan looked at her watch. She was going to be late. "Haskell, I'm due in court."

"You're a very attractive woman, Susan. I've always thought so. Even when I was with Lydia, I thought you were very attractive. You're separated, right?"

"Yes. But I'm seeing someone." He's got me lying, too. Not really. I *do* see Michael . . . in my dreams.

"That's okay. Forget what I said. My wife and I are working it out anyhow. Lydia was nothing to me. You were great at the hotel. Just great."

Susan grabbed a cab outside the restaurant and had it zip her over to the courthouse on Thomas Street.

JUNIOR TESLA STARED across the room at Ab Rosenthal. A patina of perspiration had spread across the surface of the psychiatrist's bald pate. He prayed that young Tesla had not been suspicious about his canceling their last three sessions.

"I get the feeling like you been avoiding me," said Junior. "Like you don't wanna see me no more."

"Why do you say that?"

"Cuz you canceled the last three sessions."

"I explained that I had—"

"I needed to talk to you, doc. My head was splittin' wide open."

"I'm sorry, Nick." Rosenthal swallowed hard. He couldn't believe he was actually apologizing to a patient. But then Junior was no ordinary patient. The doctor wished he could terminate their relationship. But this was no longer possible. Feeling professionally akin to the trapped mongoose staring in fascination at the cobra he knows will eventually kill him, Rosenthal asked: "How have things been the last few weeks?"

"Like you fuckin' care."

"Nick, please. We can't proceed if you have a hostile attitude toward me."

"Right, right. That transference shit again. Did I tell you about Palazzolo?"

"I don't re—"

"My old man's got a real hard-on for him. Thinks he can fuckin' walk on water. The guy waltzes in outta nowhere and the old man's practically puttin' clean sheets on the bed for this mook and my sister."

"Are you jealous?"

"I'm pissed off. He's a runt. I could squash him like a bug. All the time I hear: 'Pete says this. Pete says that.' The Gospel according to Pete. Lemme tell ya, doc. Something ain't kosher about him. I can't put my finger on it right now but when I do . . ."

"Yes? . . . Nick? What will you do?"

"So where'd you go all those times?" Junior switched gears abruptly. "What was so important you couldn't see me?"

"Private matter," said Rosenthal trying to assert some authority over his patient. "I'd rather you don't—"

"There's this woman," said Junior, veering off into yet another mental direction. "Works for the D.A. She's givin' us trouble. Real pain in the ass. Nice-lookin' though. Great legs."

"What about her?"

"I phone her up. Late at night. At first it was to scare her. You know. So she'd lay off. But now it's so I can hear her. I like her voice. Real preppy, New England kinda voice. Her name is Susan Given. Maybe you seen her on TV. They call her 'Ms. D.A.' "

Rosenthal was no longer certain if he was breathing or not. The ethics line had been crossed. With anyone else, he would have terminated therapy immediately or recommended them to a colleague. But who could he send Junior to? Hugh Carver?

"She's got these little daughters," continued Junior with increasing fascination. "I guess they're adopted. Mexican or something. Really cute."

"You've seen them?" asked Rosenthal. He flashed on the previous evening when Hugh had brought the girls over to dinner with that Swedish bombshell of his.

"I watch her apartment sometimes," shrugged Junior. "I seen them comin' home from school."

"Why?" Rosenthal wondered if he had been able to

disguise the mixture of horror and bewilderment he was certain he'd heard in his voice. "What do you want with Polly and Ivy?"

"Who?"

"Nothing."

"No, no. You said their names. How the hell did you know their names?" Junior got up from his chair and moved menacingly toward Rosenthal. "I'm talkin to you, doc. Answer me."

A FEW DAYS later Susan Given sat in her office on Centre Street listening to the tapes of Tony Fusco's secretly recorded conversations with Nick Tesla. She laughed out loud when she got up to the part about Torrid's private parts. *The guy's got a big mouth and a little gherkin.* No one in Greenwich had ever spoken that way. No one in Greenwich had ever discussed sex.

The telephone rang and Susan answered it: "Given."

"Susan? Hi, this is Nancy Gerhardt. You said I could call you."

"Yes, of course, Nancy. How are you?"

"Getting bigger. I was just wondering . . . you know, if you guys were any further along . . . about Walt."

"I can't really discuss it right now, Nancy. But there are several developments."

"Uh-huh." A child started crying in the background and Nancy could be heard trying to silence it. Then: "I don't mean to bother you, Susan. It's just—I don't know, with this other baby coming, I keep thinking I'll wake up and it will all have been a dream. Walt'll come through the door and everything will be fine." She began sobbing quietly.

"Have you got any family?" asked Susan quietly. "Someone who could—"

"Not really. I've got a sister in Oregon. We never really got along. Walt didn't have anyone except me."

"What are you doing Thanksgiving?"

"Gee. That's a long way off. . . ."

"It's next month," replied Susan. "How would you and your kids like to come over to my place? I always have a big crowd—"

"Oh, no, no. Gee, thanks a lot but . . ."

"Think about it. Okay?"

"Okay. Thanks, Susan."

Susan replaced the receiver sadly and put on an earlier tape in which Dino Marazonni explained to Fusco how the cartel cheated on the volume of garbage they charged their customers.

"We charge the highest buck here in New York," said Dino, "compared to Chicago, Philly, or L.A. But that don't really matter. We don't make money on the higher rate. If there's four hundred cubic yards, we can charge 'em for eight hundred. Nobody's gonna say our thumb is on the scale. *Capisce?*"

Susan switched the tape recorder off. She couldn't get Nancy out of her mind. What was the latest development in the Gerhardt murder case? She reached for her telephone just as Janie Moore walked into her office.

"You must be psychic," said Susan. "I was about to phone you. Nancy Gerhardt just called me—"

"There are no coincidences, Greenwich. That's why I'm here. What have you heard from Fusco lately?"

"My girlfriend threw up on his shoes a few days ago. In Tesla's. And we've got about fourteen hours of raw— and I do mean raw—transcribed tapes," replied Susan pointing to the machine on her desk.

"Does he mention the Gerhardt murder?"

"Not so far. Why?"

"Cuz I got a homeless guy, who's a car freak. Okay? Says he heard a Ferrari roaring out of the Osborne Paper parking lot. Junior Tesla drives a Ferrari."

"We can't do anything with that."

"What do you mean? I'm thinking of making a stuffed bunny out of it and giving it to Stella next Easter. Our former friend Ned Jordan sure ain't helping us."

"What's wrong?"

"Oh, nothing. You inadvertently had the case wrapped up when you walked into the Evanston last month. We had an eyewitness to the murder. Then the feds whisked Sanchez off to Neverland and they won't even acknowledge his existence, let alone allow this humble A.D.A. to talk to him."

"He keeps phoning me," sighed Susan.

"Who?"

"Manny . . . Sanchez."

"What do you mean he keeps phoning you?"

"He's got a . . . crush on me. It's my fault in a way. Oh! This is so unprofessional. I don't know what to—"

"Wait! Wait! Wait! The feds let him phone you?"

"I think so. There was someone named Fred—no, George—in his room when he called. He wants me to visit him. Have you ever heard such—"

"Do it! Visit him. Go down on him. Whatever. Just get his testimony for me and we can lock Junior Tesla up. The Governor will fry him. It's good for business."

"I can't go to Montana, Janie. Who'll take care of the girls?"

"Who said he was in Montana?"

The telephone rang and Susan grabbed it: "Given."

"Susan? It's Ab Rosenthal."

"Yes, Ab?" There was no reply and all Susan heard was the sound of car horns and the deafening sound of a jet either taking off or landing. "Ab, are you there? Ab?"

"Be careful."

The dial tone was all that followed and a baffled Susan stared at the phone.

"Who was that?" asked Janie.

"Ab Rosenthal. A friend of Hugh's. I haven't seen him for three years. Not since Hugh and I split up. He warned me to be careful."

"Of what?"

"He didn't say. But he sounded really scared." Susan shivered. "Eerie."

SUSAN ARRIVED HOME from the office at six and was pleasantly surprised to find her nephews chasing her mock-terrorized daughters up and down the staircase.

"Hi, Aunt Susan!"

"Hello, Donald."

Susan walked into the kitchen, where she found her brother, Henry, hacking away at a red cabbage with a cleaver.

"What a nice surprise," she said, kissing her brother's cheek.

"Hardly a surprise," replied Henry. "We made this date last week. Where's your little red book? You're getting as bad as Mother."

"Oh-oh. What's she done now?"

"She had a dinner party last night. Set the table for ten. Eight showed up. She finally phoned Babs Chadwick and asked her why she and Deke weren't there. Babs had no idea what Mother was talking about. She'd never been invited. They'll be talking about that one at Cedarhurst for years." Henry took another deadly whack at the cabbage.

"If beheadings ever come back, Hank, I want to be your agent."

"I do have a certain flair, don't I? Perhaps I could get a job as a freelance executioner. An outlet for all my more violent urges."

"Not too violent, I hope." Susan stared curiously at her big brother. Maybe it *was* true. About Sheila and Barry. "How's Sheila?"

"Great."

"Really?"

"Would you prefer wonderful? Splendid? Effulgent? Pretty good? So-so? Stop me when I hit a word that might be appropriate to your expectations."

"I was just asking."

"Your brow is furrowed, Sis."

"Not enough sleep."

"How goes the fight against crime?"

"As ever. Uphill . . . Hank, you'd tell me if there was anything wrong between you and Sheila, wouldn't you?"

"No."

"Why?" Susan was surprised and hurt by her brother's unhesitating, monosyllabic reply. "I have no secrets from you. I tell you everything."

"I appreciate your candor, Sis. But there are areas of my life where I simply can't reciprocate. My marriage is one of them. Husbands and wives are like fireflies. They switch on and off with alarming frequency. A slip of the lip that might cause a divorce at breakfast could end up the catalyst for great passion by lights out. So, if I tell you what a pain in the ass Sheila is now, by the time I get home I probably couldn't live without her. I certainly can't imagine being married to anyone else."

"You are the biggest onion in the world, Henry Given. Are you aware of that?"

"Spanish or Bermuda?"

"Layers and layers and layers. You're as enigmatic as

Mother. Have you ever thought of writing a how-to book on marriage?''

"Heaven forfend! Men don't want to read any of this. They're waiting for the Time-Life video hosted by the macho messiah who'll tell them it's okay to give the little woman a good smack on the backside once in a while. It's like the time I told Barry Praeger my O.J. joke. 'What two things does O.J. have that every man wants? . . . The Heisman Trophy and a dead wife.' Barry looked at me without blinking and said, 'I never wanted the Heisman Trophy.' "

Susan was now totally confused. Her brother's marriage was the one constant in her life. The thought of its being ruptured, even slightly, would be too much to bear. Finally: "Why did you mention Barry Praeger?"

"Because Cynthia phoned me this morning."

"Oh."

"Are you planning to litter the aural landscape with that one tiny vowel? Or will you dispose of it in the proper receptacle?"

"What did she want?"

"Probably for me to suffer as she suffers. I can't help her though. I've always been a great believer in the concept that neurosis is subject to the amount of time one is willing or able to lend to it. Frankly, I think her business is in trouble and that's why she spends so much time obsessing on her husband."

"What's wrong with her business?"

"There isn't any. The poor thing is no longer hot."

"Jeepers. I still can't believe she told you about Barry."

"Why? She tells everyone about Barry. The Korean grocer knows about Barry. The vegetable man at Fairway knows about Barry. John Gotti in his cell knows about—"

"But what do they know?"

"Ahhh! To quote the late, great King of Siam: 'Is a puzzlement.' I wouldn't want to go to the wall on this but I suspect that Mr. Praeger is a man more sinned against than sinning. One thing for certain: Mrs. Henry Given has no connection with this story."

"So the correct answer to the crossword puzzle is either Caesar's wife or Sheila."

"My dear little sister, I am the luckiest of men. I see my wife two weeks out of every month and honeymoon with her every time we are reunited. Can't recommend it enough."

An anguished Donald Given stumbled into the kitchen at that moment and groaned: "Ivy just kneed me in the balls."

"Testicles, son," corrected Henry. "And I'm sure you deserved it."

"How soon do we eat?" asked Henry Given Jr. with a pronounced lisp as he entered the kitchen. "What's wrong with Don?"

"Testicles," gasped his big brother.

The telephone rang. It was the doorman announcing that Janie Moore was in the lobby.

"Send her up, please," said Susan, wondering what could possibly be bringing her colleague by unannounced.

When Susan answered the door, she was surprised to discover Janie and Ned Jordan standing there together.

"And I thought *I* was the only woman in your life," said Susan to the handsome federal prosecutor. "You guys hungry? My brother is cooking dinner and he's a fabulous—"

"This isn't social, Greenwich. Something happened."

Ivy raced down the stairs when she heard Janie's voice and asked: "Is Stella here?"

Janie gave Ivy a big hug and stroked her hair: "No, darlin', she's home with her dad. How have you been?"

"Okay."

"She apparently just gelded her cousin," said Susan. "I want you to apologize to Donald, Ivy."

"No way! He crossed my boundaries. Hi, Ned."

"Hi, Ivy. I hope you start giving out maps soon," replied Jordan. "So that other boys don't make the same mistake."

"Ha-ha. Very funny."

"Ivy, why don't you go help Uncle Henry with dinner?"

"Okay."

Ivy danced off into the kitchen and Susan steered her visitors into the living room.

"What's all the mystery?" asked Susan once they were alone.

"We just got a call from Montana. Manny Sanchez has escaped."

"How? When?"

Before Jordan could reply, Polly dashed into the living room dressed in a Swiss dirndl and wearing a blond, braided wig. She clutched her hands in front of her chest and piped, "I am sixteen going on seventeen."

"What is that?" asked Susan, pointing in mock horror at her eldest daughter's head.

"You're freaked, aren't you?" asked Polly. "Is it the dress or the wig? Or my voice?"

"How many can I choose?"

"Thanks a lot, Mom. Wait till I'm a star!" said Polly, flouncing out of the room and back up the stairs.

"Now then," said Susan, following her daughter's cameo appearance, "What's all this about Manny?"

"He slipped out the bathroom window of his motel," said Jordan. "Then he hot-wired a car in the parking lot and was last seen driving in an easterly direction."

"But I just spoke to him this morning."

"So I gather," said Jordan. "What exactly did he say to you?"

Susan turned to Janie in embarrassment and her fellow A.D.A. gestured for her to speak.

"He said he missed me. Not in those exact words. He . . . he wanted me to come out and visit him."

"Did you say yes?"

"No. I mean I didn't get a chance. My other line was ringing and— Why are you staring at me like that, Ned?"

"What else did he say?" pressed Jordan. "Think."

"He said that I tricked him into giving himself up. Why did the feds let him call me?"

"Because he wouldn't talk to them. He said you promised—"

"I never did!"

"Relax, Susan," said Jordan. "It's not your fault. We just wanted you to be aware of the situation. There's nothing to worry about. He's a long way from here and he won't get far."

"Who else knows?" asked Susan.

"Just the three of us."

The telephone rang. Susan answered it and was greeted by a monumental coughing fit. Then: "Suzy? I'm callin' up my marker."

"What are you talking about?" Susan turned to the others and mouthed 'Ray Murphy.'

"I heard the coughing," murmured Janie.

"Christ on a crutch, Suzy! I know what I'm talkin' about. Manny Sanchez just broke out of federal custody and is on his way to see you. You wanna talk on the record or off?"

Susan clapped her hand over the receiver, turned to her colleagues, arched an eyebrow, and asked: "Just the three of us?"

28

IT WAS IMPOSSIBLE to hear another person speak in the depths of Cavity, a retro seventies nightclub in TriBeCa.

Tony Fusco, in his Pete Palazzolo identity, with his hair slicked back and fingers bejeweled, was dancing up a storm with an adoring Toni Tesla. Men of various shades would sidle up to the carting princess on the floor and whisper in her ear. Depending on Ms. Tesla's mood, these would-be courtiers received a grimace, a bawdy laugh, or the finger in response.

"Who are all those guys?" Fusco shouted finally.

"Jealous, Pete?" Toni ran her tongue around her painted lips. Then she leaned forward as she continued to gyrate and her left breast all but fell out of her sprayed-on, spaghetti-strap dress.

"What have I got to be jealous for? You don't mean nothin' to me."

"Don't you like me just a little, Petey?" asked Toni, pressing her body against his and grabbing his crotch. "Heyyy! That *is* a dill pickle!"

"Who you been talkin' to?"

" 'Bout what?" asked Toni, shoving a wad of chewing gum into her mouth and chomping on it feverishly.

"Where do you live?"

"Why?"

"Cuz I wanna see where you live."

Fusco lived in Brooklyn but didn't think it a good idea to take Toni back there. His apartment walls were covered with framed photographs, citations, and awards from the NYPD for his bravery and valor.

"I can't."

"Why not? You got a girlfriend? Huh? That it? You just stringin' me along, Mr. Palazzolo. My Daddy wouldn't like that. And when Nick Tesla don't like things it ends up like a bad Stallone movie."

"Isn't that a bit redundant?"

"Know any other five-dollar words?"

"I'm goin' to night school. Gimme a break."

"Why can't I go to your place? Y'ashamed?"

"No."

"So what's the big secret?"

"I can't tell ya."

"C'mon!"

"Okay. I live with my mother."

"You're kidding!" Toni stared at Fusco in disbelief. "You honest to God live with your mother?"

"Yeah. You got a problem with that?"

"No. Have you?"

"No. I love my mother."

Toni grabbed Fusco's face between her long slender fingers and kissed him full on the mouth.

"Wha'd you do that for?" asked Fusco after he pushed her away.

"I just fell in love with you all over again, Pete. A guy that ain't ashamed to say he loves his mother is a guy who loves women. I don't meet a lot of those."

"You got a screw loose. You know that?"

"No. My mother, *she's* got a screw loose."

"She seems a very devout woman."

"Even Cardinal Corcoran thinks she overdoes it. And he's got a direct pipeline to God. Wanna go to a hotel?"

"No." He disengaged her hand from his crotch and clapped it firmly on his back.

"You make me so horny, Pete."

"Drop it."

"What is yer problem? You like guys? Huh? That's what Junior thinks."

"You discuss me with your brother?"

"Why not? He hates your guts, you know."

"Geez! What did I ever do to him?"

"He has enough trouble with Daddy as it is. You've just made things worse. Wanna do some smack?"

"What!?"

"I know where to get some Red Rum. Didja see that black guy I gave the finger to? He just brought it back from Colombia."

"I don't think so, Toni." Then he lied hastily: "I got a record. If I get caught with any shit . . ."

"Sure, sure. I can dig it. Wow! Did you do time?"

"I don't wanna talk about it."

"Wait'll I tell Junior. He thinks you're a wuss."

"Let's just keep it our little secret."

"Sure, Pete. I really like you, you know."

"I'm glad. Cuz I gotta go home now. It's time for my mom's medicine."

"Want me to drive you to Brooklyn?"

"No, no. I got my truck."

"You're real different, Pete. I like that. I never thought I could have a relationship without fucking the guy's brains out first."

"You live and learn."

Fusco walked her to her car, kissed her quickly on the lips, then watched her roar away down the cobbled street. Once she was gone, the undercover cop took a deep breath and shook his head in disbelief. This would make one helluva chapter in his book some day.

He had walked about two blocks from Cavity when a tall, cocky redhead came towards him, froze in his tracks, and asked: "Tony the Fuss?"

"Nip! How the hell are you, you half-wop?"

"Yer just jealous of the Irish part," grinned Nip, grabbing his fellow policeman in a warm embrace. Then he dropped his voice to a low growl: "You on the job?"

"Nah. I just went off-duty. Buy you a drink?"

"No, I'll buy you a drink. And what's all this shit you told Susan Given about tossin' me your old broads?"

"Ahh! The truth hurts, Regan, doesn't it?"

The two old friends finally broke their embrace and went looking for the nearest bar.

Junior Tesla watched this scene in fascination from his vantage point across the street. He'd had his suspicions about Peter Palazzolo's virility for some time and now he had the proof. Wait till Antonia learned the truth about this *finocchio*. Junior laughed aloud. Yeah. That would be a good one. Too bad Dr. Rosenthal wasn't around anymore to discuss it with.

LYDIA CULBERG SAT behind her desk, pinning her flaming red hair up and letting it down repeatedly. This exercise in vanity was inducing motion sickness in Susan Given, sitting opposite her boss.

"Why are we still pursuing the Evanston?" asked Lydia while leafing through a brochure on BMWs.

"Why shouldn't we?" countered Susan. "It's our job. We are pursuing this case to its logical conclusion. We made all the necessary recommendations to help Vinh keep his hotel open legally. We told him to screen all hotel applicants. We advised him to install a buzzer system in the front door, surveillance cameras in the lobby, and uniformed security guards. We suggested that all guests carry photo ID. We told him to post and prominently display house rules in the lobby prohibiting controlled substances—"

"Okay, Susan. Okay. I'm sorry I asked." Lydia got up from behind her desk and walked over to the wall to wipe a smudge from the framed photograph of herself and His Eminence Cardinal Corcoran taken at a Gracie Mansion dinner the previous year. "So when are you going to seize it?"

"As soon as Ned Jordan gets the warrants together," answered Susan breezily. Actually, she knew the exact date but had no intention of giving The Human Faucet any advance warning.

"Well"—Lydia beamed—"do let me know when the balloon goes up. I'd love to pop by if my calendar permits."

Pop by? thought Susan. She'd pull up in a white stretch limo wearing a Thierry Mugler dress, flanked by Tom Brokaw and Peter Jennings. With Dan Rather lashed to the roof. But as she rose from her seat, Susan merely asked: "Is there anything else you wanted to discuss?"

"Actually there is."

"Yes?"

"You can tell me to mind my own business, if you want, but I think you're making a big mistake with Haskell."

"What?!"

"Susan, please. You don't have to pretend. I know you're having an affair with him."

"What on earth—!"

"He told me."

"He told you . . . what? I've never even—"

"Susan, you're an attractive woman. You're going through an ugly divorce. Haskell . . . has emotional problems. Believe me, honey. Frankly, the only reason he slept with you was to get back at me. I didn't want to say that, Susan. I'm sorry if it sounds cruel. But you can do a lot better than Haskell Abrams. You just have to have more confidence in yourself. Besides I hear he's fucking that hot tamale on Channel Eight. He's incapable of faithfulness. His poor wife. . . . Okay, honey. That's my pep talk. Go back to work and keep bringing that money in."

Susan drifted back to her office convinced she was wandering through Bellevue. Had Haskell really lied to Lydia about sleeping with Susan? Or had Lydia lied to Susan about Haskell? But how would Lydia have even thought of Susan and Haskell unless—And was Haskell now having it off with Lisa Mercado? And who was running the police force while all this was going on?

Gretchen looked up from her keyboard and told Susan: "Polly phoned while you were with Lydia. Wanted to remind you to pick up some pumpkins on the way home."

"Why?" asked Susan still in a trance.

"Halloween next week," said Gretchen.

"You're kidding! Where did October go?"

"Dunno. Oh. Mrs. Rosenthal phoned. Said it was urgent."

"Who?"

"Ruth Rosenthal. Says she knows you." Gretchen handed Susan the phone number.

Ruth Rosenthal? Ab's wife? Why were the Rosenthals communicating with her after all these years? What new tactic of Hugh's was this?

Susan closed her office door and dialed the number.

"Ruth? Susan Given."

"Susan, thank God you phoned me. I didn't know who else to turn to. The police have been of no use—"

"Slow down, Ruth. I don't know what you're talking about."

"Ab. He's vanished. Gone."

"Gone where?"

"If I knew, I wouldn't be phoning you. Not that I haven't wanted to, Susan. But Hugh made it clear that we were his friends and he'd consider it an act of treason if we spoke to you."

"You don't have to explain Hugh to me, Ruth. Now what about Ab? How long has he been missing?"

"Almost a week."

"Did you file a Missing Persons report?"

"It's a bit awkward when the missing person has taken his clothes. And half the savings account."

"Oh, Ruth, I'm so sorry. . . . Was there another woman?"

"Who on earth would find Ab attractive?" exploded Ruth Rosenthal. "I'm sorry. He just wasn't that way, Susan. The only person he'd think of having an affair with was himself."

"He didn't phone you at all? To say good-bye? From the airport or . . ." Susan froze in midsentence.

Susan, it's Ab Rosenthal.

Yes, Ab? Ab, are you there?

Be careful.

The cars honking and the sound of jets overhead. Ab *had* phoned someone. But why Susan? And what had he meant by "be careful"?

"I don't know what I can do for you," lied Susan. "I'm sorry, Ruth."

Susan replaced the receiver and wondered what the hell was going on.

SUSAN HAD FALLEN asleep with her clothes on, waiting for her visitor, when the night doorman called at eleven-thirty to inform her that "a Michael Roth" was down in the lobby.

"Send him up," she said impatiently. Then she bolted

into the bathroom, brushed her teeth, and quickly ran a brush through her hair. Too much static. Too bad. Seconds later she dashed down the stairs and greeted the elevator in what she hoped was a casual attitude. Michael stood there holding a laptop in one hand and his flight bag in the other. She had never seen him in an overcoat and fall wardrobe before. Her memories of him were in shorts and tropical shirts unbuttoned to the navel and exposing lots of tan. But autumn colors were flattering to him.

"Hello." She felt so darned awkward.

"Hi." He continued to stare at her.

She held her right hand out to shake, then changed her mind halfway and pecked him on the lips. He dropped his bag and wrapped his free arm around her waist, pulling her into him. It was a long, slow kiss.

"I remember you," she said when he finally released her from the embrace.

"Where are your kids?"

"Asleep. It's almost midnight. They were out late with Halloween and— Where have you been?"

"Up in the air."

"I meant the past eight months. Come in. Come in. I fixed up the guest room. There are towels and—"

"You look beautiful."

"Oh. Thank you."

"No, no. I wasn't commenting on a piece of furniture. I meant you. Your face. Your eyes. Your lips. I particularly remember your lips."

"Thank you. In a nonfurniture way. Jeepers, Michael. I'm not used to— Would you like to see the apartment? Besides the hallway?"

"Only if you promise to put some lights on."

Susan realized that she had run downstairs in the dark. "It is kind of dark, isn't it?"

"Not for Ray Charles."

"This is the living room. It has a beautiful view of the Carlyle dome and—" She could feel his breath on the back of her neck. She spun around and kissed him again.

Somehow they ended up stretched out on the couch. The lights still weren't on.

"Did you major in kissing at college?" she finally gasped.

"Kindergarten. I really like kissing." Michael's hand was underneath her cashmere sweater, caressing her breasts.

"I've—I've got a great idea," she said, wriggling underneath him.

"I welcome all submissions. Under the door or over the transom."

"Why don't we"—Susan managed to slide out from under him and rolled onto the carpet—"take your bags upstairs and then continue this . . . in a more comfortable venue?"

"Is that legal?" asked Michael, following her back into the hallway and picking up his laptop and flight bag.

"Going upstairs?" She froze on the third step.

Michael shook his head and explained: "Venue. Is that legalese or do you always . . . ?"

Susan cleared her throat and brushed her hair back from her face: "I'm sure I'll get used to this . . . next year."

"Why restrict yourself? The millennium's just around the corner."

"So's the Metropolitan. And the Frick."

"Will you be standing on the same step all night? I don't mind. So long as I can find a comfortable position for myself."

"Oh." She started climbing the stairs again. Michael tapped her on the shoulder; she turned around and he kissed her again. "We'll never get up the stairs at this rate."

Michael dropped his bag off in the guest room, then followed Susan back to her bedroom. She still hadn't turned the lights on.

"Are you at war with Con Edison?"

"I could turn the light on," said Susan, "but then we'd just have to switch it off again."

"Practical," said Michael approvingly as he pulled her sweater over her head.

She tried to undo the buttons on his shirt and popped one of them off. "I'll find it in the morning," she muttered as she continued to strip his upper body. "I wasn't sure about this."

"What part?" asked Michael as he eased her back onto the bed and removed her tights.

"The guest room or . . ."

"Here?" He kissed the inside of her thigh.

"Hear, hear," she moaned. "What city are we in?"

"Where would you like to be?" he asked as he stepped out of his trousers.

"Doesn't seem to matter as long as you . . . ooooh. Yes, yes. That's a nice city. That's my favorite city."

"Mine, too. Particularly the view from—"

"Shhh! Don't talk anymore."

They didn't speak for the next hour as they continued to touch and stroke and bite and kiss and reacquaint themselves with each other's bodies. Finally, when they were sated, she lay with her head on his chest, playing with his left nipple and whispering: "I never thought I'd see you again."

"You haven't seen me yet."

Susan giggled, then fell asleep.

It was close to two in the morning when the woman on the twenty-fifth floor screamed out in agony.

"Wha's wrong?" asked Junior Tesla.

"I think you just cracked my rib."

"Yer full o' shit."

"You don't know your own strength."

"C'mon, Cashmere. You can handle a little rough stuff."

"Not the way you like it, Junior. What the hell do you do to your legs to get them like that?"

"Strong, aren't they?"

"Too strong. This isn't fun anymore." Cashmere made a move to get out of the king-sized bed.

"Hey! I paid you for the night," growled Junior, who swung his legs like giant pincers and grabbed the prostitute around the waist with them. "You ain't goin' nowhere."

"Junior, please!" she gasped. "You're hurting me."

"You gonna come back to bed?"

"Yes. Yes."

"And you ain't gonna leave the bed without permission? Right?"

Cashmere could no longer speak but nodded her head up and down in dumb show.

"Okay then. I'll let you—"

He was interrupted by loud pounding at the door. Junior released his grip on Cashmere and rolled off the bed. How had they managed to get past security in the lobby? Unless they were cops. Where the hell was his gun? Where had he put his gun? Cashmere was coughing violently in her attempt to breathe again.

"Shut up, willya!" said Junior.

The pounding increased in intensity.

"Junior! Hey, Junior!"

"Who is it?" asked the younger Tesla, grabbing a robe from the back of a chair and advancing toward the living room.

"The Patch."

"Louie! What the hell are you doing here?" He called over his shoulder to Cashmere: "Put some clothes on." Then he shouted towards the front door: "Be right there, Louie. I was fast asleep when you—"

No sooner had he opened the front door when his father's powerful hand shoved him violently back into the room.

"I wanna talk to you," snarled Nick Tesla.

"Jesus, Pop. It's two in the morning. Can't you call first and—"

Tesla slapped his son across the face and asked: "You tellin' me when I can talk to you? Who the hell pays for this place?"

Cashmere emerged from the bedroom in time to witness the slap and asked: "What's going on here, Junior? Who are these guys?"

"And who pays for puttanas like that?" Tesla turned to Louie Torino and issued the order: "Get rid of her."

Torino grabbed hold of the prostitute and steered her toward the front door while she protested: "My bag! I need my bag!"

Once Cashmere was out the door, Tesla turned to his son and asked: "What's the story on that Cuban?"

"That's why you're here? That's why you broke in like a fuckin' torpedo—"

Tesla slapped his son again. "Don't talk to me like that. You haven't earned the respect to use language like that wit' me. I told you a month ago to find that Cuban."

"It's a dead end, Pop. The feds have him."

"How long have you known that?"

"Last week." Junior shrugged.

"And you didn't tell me?"

"I thought I could handle it myself."

"You? The only thing you can handle yerself is yer dick. I don't know why you waste good money on hookers. What the hell were you gonna do? Cross the Rockies with elephants and take on the whole FBI?"

"I had a plan."

"Well, get a new plan, kid. Cuz yer Cuban's gone. I just got a call tonight from some friends out West. The Feds are even stupider than you."

"Pop, please, I'm getting a headache."

"You *are* a headache! Yer mother fuckin' lied to me.

She must have bought you from Corsican peddlers. No way you can be my son!"

"Listen, Pop, we can't go on like this. You hittin' me all the time and not respecting me. You need help. I wish you'd go and see Dr. Rosenthal, too. He's helped me a lot."

"Who's Dr. Rosenthal?"

"My shrink. He's a brilliant man. One of the best in the city. He's really helped me with my headaches and shown me how so much of my—"

"WHAT SHRINK??" bellowed Nick Tesla.

"I've been seeing a psychiatrist for the past ten months. It's really been—"

"You were what? Are you completely nuts?"

"No, Pop. I just had these migraines and problems I couldn't work out for myself. Doctor—"

"What the hell did you tell him?"

"That's privileged information, Pop. Like seein' a priest."

"You blabbed? To a fuckin' civilian?"

"Try and understand, Pop. I'd reached a crisis point. You and I weren't—"

"I was wrong! No fuckin' Corsican palmed you off. You're a fuckin' Martian! Nobody on this planet could be so stupid—"

"STOP CALLING ME STUPID!!" Junior had now raised his father off the ground by his lapels.

"Put me down," whispered Tesla.

"Don't call me stupid," repeated his son stubbornly.

"Okay, okay. Put me down."

Junior lowered his father to the ground and released his hold.

"Where is this shrink?" asked Tesla, once he had sufficiently recovered his breath and dignity.

"I dunno. He's gone. I scared the shit out of him and he disappeared. Don't worry, Pop. He won't blab."

Sinking to the sofa, Tesla buried his face in his hands. Then he remembered: "The files. Did you get his files?"

"Whaddaya mean?"

"He's a doctor. You were his patient. He must have kept some kind of record on you."

"I think he did. Yeah. He said he made notes." Then Junior remembered the bald, bearded shrink's exact word: "Occasionally."

Tesla stared at Junior in silence and wondered if God could ever forgive him for having his only son bumped off. God might but Loretta wouldn't. Tesla sighed. There had to be another way to handle the problem.

Susan woke up and saw Michael Roth lying asleep next to her. It hadn't been a dream. He had arrived the night before and made wonderful love to her— Oh, no! It was six-thirty. She had to get up and run and he had to leave before—

"Michael! Michael!"

"What's wrong?"

"You've got to get up."

"Wha' time is it?" he groaned.

"Six-thirty."

"Are you crazy, Susan? That's like half past three in California. Come back to bed." He reached out to embrace her and she slipped away from him.

"No, no, no! The girls. They mustn't find you here. I don't do this sort of thing."

"You did last night. And beautifully."

"No, no, no. I don't even date. They mustn't suspect anything. We're just friends. Acquaintances. I'm doing

Barry Praeger a favor. Do you understand? If Hugh ever found out, he'd try and take the girls away from me."

"Are you serious?"

"Deadly. This is all he needs to prove me an unfit mother."

"But he can't do that."

"This isn't California, Michael. Things aren't laid back, with kids bringing their mother's boyfriends breakfast in bed."

"I don't want breakfast in bed. I just—Doesn't *he* date?"

"That's irrelevant in a New York courtroom. This is still the boys' club in matters legal and conjugal." Then she lowered her voice to a desperate whisper. "Please, please. Go to your room. Mess the bed. Sleep, if you want."

"Susan, calm down."

"I'll calm down when you're in your room."

Michael pulled his trousers on, gathered up the rest of his clothes, and left the bedroom humming "Getting to Know You."

"I must have been crazy," said Susan as she stepped into her closet and gathered up her running gear. Then she took a deep breath and remembered: It *was* wonderful. But too complicated right now.

Ten minutes later Polly screamed and rushed into her mother's bedroom, locking the door behind herself.

"Quick, Mom! Call Waldo! Call the police!"

"What's wrong?"

"There's a man in the apartment. I don't know how he got in here but—"

"That's Michael."

"Who's Michael?"

"Michael Roth. A friend of Barry Praeger's. He arrived late last night."

"Why's he staying here?"

"Because they don't have a guest room. I met Mr. Roth at the bar mitzvah. In Jerusalem. He's quite nice. Although I don't really know him. He's a writer. Books, movies, plays. He acted on *Star Trek*. Danced with Vivien Leigh. You know, Scarlett O'Hara."

"You okay?"

"Why do you ask that?"

"Because you're babbling."

"No, no, no. I'm just late. Slept in. Go wake your sister up. Make sure she has some breakfast. I'll see you guys tonight."

"Where?"

"Here, of course."

"Good one, Mom. Talk about staying focused. We're at Dad's tonight."

"Well, tomorrow then. Maybe Michael will cook for us. I love you."

"Hmmm." Polly left her mother's bedroom, crossed the hallway, and paused to stare curiously at the closed guest room door before slipping back into her own bed for a few extra minutes of sleep.

Susan left the apartment a minute later. The telephone rang and, when no one else bothered to answer, Michael picked up the receiver next to his bed.

"Hello?"

"Who's this?" asked a voice that sounded like a bad impersonation of Gregory Peck.

"Who's this?" asked Michael, returning the serve with his vintage Bogart.

"I asked you first," replied Hugh Carver tersely.

"S'posin I don't wanna tell ya," said Michael, deftly switching to Gary Cooper.

"Is this the Given Carver residence?"

"Now, come on, pal. Play fair," said Michael. "I already did Cooper and Bogart. You can't do Peck twice."

"This is Hugh Carver."

"Ohhh! You're Hugh. Hi. I'm Michael Roth. I've heard a lot about you."

"I've heard nothing about you. Where is Susan? Where are the children?"

"Probably sleeping."

"Where are you?"

"In bed."

"In *what* room, if I may ask."

"You may not. I'll tell them you called." Michael hung up the phone. But he couldn't get back to sleep. This guy Carver had rattled him. Susan had mentioned that her estranged husband was difficult. That was akin to leprosy being a minor skin disorder. What a pompous prick! And what a bad Gregory Peck impersonation.

Twenty minutes later, having showered and dressed, Michael wandered downstaris to the kitchen and discovered Polly pouring out some orange juice from a plastic carton.

"Hello. I'm Michael Roth."

"I know," replied Polly noncommittally.

"Polly?" She nodded. "Thought so. Going to school?" She nodded again. "Remedial speech therapy?"

"What?"

"Big thing in California now. Teaching kids to use words with more than one syllable."

"Did you ever take a mud bath in Israel?"

"Yes. How'd you know?"

"Just guessing. . . . Are you married?"

"I was."

"More than once?"

"What makes you ask that?"

"You're in show biz," shrugged Polly. "Aren't you an actor?"

"I'm a hyphenate."

"What does that mean?"

"I have various ways of being unemployed."

"So how many?" asked Polly. "Wives."

"Three."

"Would I know any of them?"

"Dunno," replied Michael, popping a piece of seven-grain bread into the toaster. "Have you ever served time in a women's prison?" Ivy entered the kitchen at that moment and stared suspiciously at Michael. "Hello there."

"Where's my mom?" asked Ivy defiantly.

"Nice to meet you, too," said Michael.

"Are you the floor guy?" asked Ivy, advancing toward Michael and giving him the once over. "My mom's been waiting months for—"

"Vat you vant?" asked Michael assuming an Eastern European dialect. "Ve got lots of customers. 'Vere is dis? Vere is dat? Vy you don't come?' Some pipple don't reallyize how busy is busyness."

"How'd you do that?" asked a spellbound Ivy.

"What?" asked Michael in his normal voice.

"That voice. How'd you do that voice?"

"He's a hyphenate," said Polly, sipping the last of her orange juice.

The telephone rang and Polly answered it: "Hello? . . . Oh, hi, Dad . . . What?!" She covered the receiver with her hand and hissed at Michael: "Did you talk to my father on the phone this morning?"

"Is that your dad?" asked Michael.

Polly rolled her eyes, then spoke into the phone again: "He's a friend of Barry Praeger's. . . . I don't know. . . . He slept in the guest room. . . . Dad, I am not conspiring against you. . . . Dad! Dad! Why aren't you at Dr. Schellenberg's this morning? . . . Please, not today. I've got rehearsal. Friday night. Remember? . . . No, Mom's coming Friday. You come on Saturday. . . . I don't know. Think Sigrid will understand it? . . . I was just joking, Dad. Wish me luck." Polly replaced the receiver and pulled at her long, thick hair in frustration.

"Never wish anyone luck," said Michael. "It's bad luck."

"It's bad luck to wish good luck?" asked Polly.

"In the theater. You *are* opening in a play?"

"*The Sound of Music.*"

"Break a leg. You playing Elsa Schraeder?"

"Nooo! She's a bitch. I'm playing Liesl. What made you think I was playing Elsa?"

"It's a more interesting part. Villains usually are."

Polly stared at Michael in a new light, then asked: "Are you coming?"

"No, I'm going to stay here and read the paper for a few minutes until—"

"Friday. Why don't you come with Mom and Ivy?"

"Thank you for the invitation."

The telephone rang again. Rocco the doorman reported Ivy's school bus was waiting. Seconds later both girls had vanished from the kitchen.

Their mother came back into the apartment a few minutes afterward, dripping with perspiration and calling out: "Helloo!"

"In here." Susan stuck her head inside the kitchen and smiled shyly at Michael. He looked up at her from the *Times* and asked: "You never miss a morning, do you?"

"Never. The girls get off all right?"

"I guess."

"Did you get a chance to talk with them?"

"Briefly. And their father even briefer."

"'You spoke to Hugh?"

"Sort of. Does he do that Gregory Peck thing all the time?" Susan nodded. "Why?"

"I don't know," sighed Susan. "What did he want?"

"Wanted to know what bedroom I was in."

"See what I mean? I wasn't being paranoid."

"No, you weren't." Michael held his arms out to her. "C'mere."

"I'm all wet."

"I like you all wet." Susan stepped into his arms and he hugged her. "Polly invited me to her show Friday."

"She did? She must have liked you."

"She has a strange way of showing it. The girl grilled me. Sautéed is more like it. Wanted to know if I'd ever taken a mud bath in Israel."

"She found the photograph of us. From the Dead Sea.

The girl's a born detective. We have to play it cool with her. Both of them."

"You mean I can't look at you adoringly, hungrily, lustfully? I can't leap up on the tabletop and tell the world that I—"

"Absolutely not. I'm from Greenwich. So what are you doing today?"

"Meeting Barry for breakfast. Then I'm going down to Gramercy Park. Research. Ever heard of the Evanston Hotel?"

"Is this a joke?"

"Why?"

"I'm planning to seize it. Tomorrow."

"Seize? Like epilepsy?"

"No, it's what I do. Asset Forfeiture."

"You never really explained what— Wow! I had no idea I was sleeping with Elliot Ness."

"Do you think I'm an untouchable?"

"I know you're not. Do you carry a gun?"

"No. What's your interest in the Evanston?"

"Cornell Woolrich. Remember?"

"I remember he wasn't in FDR's cabinet. But who *was* he?"

"The father of *noir* literature. One of the greatest pulp writers ever. They made zillions of movies out of his stories. *Phantom Lady. Black Angel. Rear Window* is probably the most famous. The Hitchcock picture."

"I loved that movie. Grace Kelly had a broken leg."

"Jimmy Stewart had the broken leg. Grace Kelly did other things. They had a great kissing scene but I think we outdid them last night."

"Stay focused."

"Thank you. Woolrich was a very weird guy. Lived with his mother in the Hotel Marseilles on the Upper West Side for thirty-five years. Never went anywhere— except in his head. Then when his mother died he lived in various hotels around town: the Franconia, the Gramercy Park, and the Evanston. The Marseilles is long gone but I thought I might check out the others. Unless you're seizing them as well."

Susan stared at Michael and asked: "Have I ever seen you in a tie?"

"The bar mitzvah."

"Of course. How could I forget? What are you doing this evening?"

"Footloose and fancy free."

"Think you could handle a roomful of lawyers?"

"Is this a trick question?"

"No, it's the Annual Bar Association Dinner. You'll get to meet a lot of my friends—"

The telephone rang and Susan answered it.

"Given."

"Heyyyy, Susan! How you doin'?"

"Manny, where are you?"

"Never mind. I'm gonna see you soon, Susan."

"Manny, listen to me. You have got to give yourself up before—"

A telephone operator came on the line at that moment and said: "Please deposit an additional seventy-five cents for—"

"Ohhh, shit!" groaned Manny. Then the dial tone.

"Oh, shit!" echoed Susan, hanging up the phone.

"Who is Manny?" asked Michael patiently.

Susan poured them both cups of coffee and told him the whole story.

FUSCO WALKED DOWN the stairs of the newly restored Hammerstein Theatre on Forty-second Street. It was truly a palace and celebrated the grandeur of show business at the turn of the last century. Once outside he walked west toward Eighth Avenue until he paused in front of a Chrysler parked beside the curb. He leaned against the car and lit up a cigarette.

The rear window zipped down electronically and Nicolo Tesla's head came into view as he asked: "How'd it go?"

"They've done a helluva job fixing that place up."

"Who you workin' for? The Chamber of Commerce or me? Wha' happened in there?"

"I made them an offer they could refuse," replied Fusco. "I told them I'd remove their trash for fifteen grand a month."

"Wha'd they say?"

"They went ape shit. They called it highway robbery. They own theaters in Chicago and St. Louis and nobody ever charged that kind of money. Yadda-yadda-yadda. I told 'em they weren't gonna find anyone cheaper in Manhattan."

"Yes, they are." Tesla grinned. "Me."

"I don't get it," said Fusco dumbly. In point of fact, the undercover cop got it perfectly but he was purposely playing the iggie so Tesla would spell everything out for the benefit of the hidden recording device Fusco was wearing.

"These guys are gonna be sittin' in their office moanin' and groanin' and wonderin' where they're gonna skim the money from to pay you. Cuz bottom line, they know they gotta pay. Then their Uncle Nick wanders in like an angel from heaven. 'Wassamatter, boys? Big Bad Pete wanted you to pay fifteen big ones a month? Shame on him! Dry yer eyes. Uncle Nick's only gonna charge you ten G's.' Much bowing, scraping, and kissing my ring and I have new best friends for life."

"You do that every time?" asked Fusco, praying his recorder was working.

"Nah. Just wit' the new kids on the block. Make 'em feel they're gettin' somethin' for nothin'. Plus they go home that night and give it to their old lady with a big dill instead of a little gherkin. So I'm doin' a little good for everybody. Wassamatter, Pete?"

Fusco was beginning to hear a faint humming sound from his recording device. He prayed Tesla didn't hear it as well.

"My stomach's botherin' me," said Fusco, forcing himself to burp.

"Who you been eatin'?" piped up Louie Torino, who'd been silent until now.

"Tha's a good one, Patch." Tesla laughed. Then added: "The first hundred times."

"I gotta get a bromo," said Fusco, who could feel a small rivulet of sweat dribbling down his spine.

Tesla clamped a viselike grip on Fusco's wrist: "Wait a second, Pete."

Christ! thought Fusco. He must hear the humming, too. It's almost deafening.

"What is it, Nick?"

"I want you to do me a favor." Tesla pressed a folded piece of paper into Fusco's palm. "Tonight. It's personal. I trust you to do this for me."

"What? What is it, Nick?"

"It's all written down on the paper. Make sure nobody sees you. Call me in the morning."

Two seconds after the Chrysler sped away from the curb, the tape recorder taped to Fusco's back made the most shrill sound imaginable.

Several pedestrians paused to watch the short, stocky man with thick eyebrows struggle to remove the device from his back. They merely shrugged off his behavior as another curious manifestation of life in the Big Apple.

But from his vantage point across the street, Junior Tesla watched in rapt fascination.

THEY SPED SOUTH by cab down Fifth Avenue with their knees pressed together. Occasionally he would bring his face over to hers and kiss her.

"I hope we'll be on time," said Susan, taking a deep breath and opening her eyes after the last kiss.

"We're only two blocks from the Plaza," said Michael.

"You're joking!" Susan began plowing through her bag looking for a brush. "I must look a wreck."

"No, I was very careful not to muss your hair."

"Michael, promise you won't kiss me in front of any lawyers."

"I promise."

Entering the Grand Ballroom of the Plaza Hotel, Susan was greeted by a trio of familiar faces: Janie Moore, her husband, Kevin, and Ned Jordan, who had arrived stag (which was not the handsome bachelor's usual style at all).

"No date tonight?" asked Susan.

"He's waiting to see if you go home with the same guy

you came with," smiled Janie, thrusting her hand out to Michael. "I know all about you. And I've saved a space for you on my dance card."

"Please excuse my wife," said Kevin Moore, a chiseled-featured commercial artist, who still dreamed of selling his own canvases someday. "She was struck on the head by a volume of *Peyton Place* as a child."

Janie made hissing noises at her husband and he mimed a chair and a whip to keep her under control.

"I'm amazed you're still hanging in there, Kev."

"Have to, Ned. I've insured her life for a small fortune."

"Are we everything she said we'd be?" Janie beamed.

Michael, having successfully run the gauntlet of these new acquaintances, was left behind to schmooze with Kevin and Ned while Janie steered Susan off to one side.

"I want all the details," said Janie. "This is the guy from Jerusalem, right? The one with the three wives—"

"Who told you?"

"He must be great in the sack. I've never seen you look like this before. You must have snuck in a quickie before you came here."

"Don't be disgusting!" Susan's face went scarlet. How could Janie tell?

"Hey, Greenwich. I'm not knocking it. He's a cute guy. So what's the story on his ex-wives? Know anything about them?"

"One was an actress, the other was a caterer, and the third was in retail."

"No obvious pattern."

"Are you looking for one? He hasn't been married for ten years."

"Sometimes they wait to start the cycle again."

"You've been working homicide too long, Janie. The man is not a serial murderer."

"He had three wives. Recidivism is recidivism."

"Are you equating marriage with crime? And wouldn't Cardinal Corcoran love to go on Charlie Rose with you and debate that?"

"Leave the Catholic Church out of this."

"When you declare a moratorium on Episcopalians. I'm sick of being the last politically incorrect target on the planet. How did we get off on this anyhow?"

"I merely pointed out that your Mr. Roth had three wives."

"He was married for ten years, to three different women," said Susan, using Michael's favorite line.

"Can you explain the subtle difference to a primitive Catholic like myself?"

"It's like the futures market. Okay? He bought long and sold short. An attitude I have come to appreciate, the longer my divorce drags on." Susan turned around and saw Michael chatting animatedly with Kevin and Ned. "What do you think they're talking about?"

Janie shrugged: "Baseball or tits. Hey! Is that Miss Piggy?"

"Where?"

"Over there. In the zebra dress. Am I seeing double or does she have a twin brother? Think he's her date? They look exactly like. Genetically engineered. Badeeba-deeba-deeba."

"Stop it."

"Ah, gimme a break, Greenwich. How are we supposed to get through an evening like this without dishing the guests?

"These are our colleagues, Janie, whether we like them or not. Our fellow lawyers."

"You'll never make me believe Elaine Morton knows anything about the law. Miss Piggy has the lowest conviction rate of any A.D.A. in the county. I don't know why Archie didn't can her years ago. But I figure she took a thorn out of Lydia's bra once and—"

"I thought it was a paw."

"I'm being polite—and our fearless leader has been grateful ever since. Ahhh! There's The Human Faucet now!" Janie's smile was a rictus as she stared at Lydia Culberg on the other side of the ballroom wearing a smashing Valentino number more appropriate for the Oscars than a solicitors' soiree and clutching the arm of a well-tanned, silver-haired Ralph Lauren lookalike.

"Who's her date?"

"Nathan Marshak. Big real estate lawyer. On the board of a zillion charities. Golfs with Archie. Lydia's really set the feminist movement back about two centuries, you know. This dame's determined to work her way through *Jew's Who* before she dies."

"Battle stations! Here comes Alvin Gasmer."

"Where?"

Susan nodded towards Nick Tesla's lawyer, who was marching aggressively in the women's direction.

"He doesn't look like a happy camper," said Janie. "Is it you or me?"

"Probably me. I've just subpoenaed all the carters' records for the past ten years."

"Hello, Ms. Given," said Gasmer, toucan-beaked, popeyed, with a wild shock of unmanageable hair. "I'm surprised you're here this evening."

"Why is that, Mr. Gasmer?"

"Well, with all the reading you have to do," replied Gasmer, whose attention had been diverted by Janie Moore's ample cleavage on display.

"You're not about to talk shop, are you, Mr. Gasmer? It simply isn't done, you know."

"My client says you were hostile to him the other week. All he did was offer you a bottle of wine with—"

"Have you been hostile again?" asked Janie, aware of Gasmer's pop eyes staring lustfully at her cleavage. "I've told you repeatedly not to— Hey, Gasmer! Are you some kind of collector?"

"Um . . . I, uh . . . Sorry?" asked Gasmer.

"They're not for sale or rent. Okay, Alvin?"

"I don't know what—"

"Busted. I caught you staring at my boobs. Now, be a good boy and take a walk before I report you to the ethics committee. Or your mother."

Having grown tired of the women's neglect, Michael Roth, Ned Jordan, and Kevin Moore came looking for them. The men's approach sent the humiliated Gasmer skittering off hastily in the opposite direction.

Shortly afterward Alan Becker arrived in the ballroom on his crutches accompanied by the notorious woman who had sponsored his accident, Rusty Rubenstein.

"I certainly hope you're going to marry Alan after all the pain you've caused him," said Susan gaily.

"Is she serious?" asked Rusty, a gung-ho, muscular aerobics instructress with an accent as thick as her date's.

Scarlet hues had engulfed Becker's face and were now seeping toward the borders of his corona.

"Of course, Alan made us swear to keep your engagement a secret," said Susan, mistakenly thinking she was on a roll with this routine.

"You told them we were engaged?" asked Rusty, in a tone that carried the double threat of a merciless tongue lashing and extended sexual deprivation.

"I—I—I—" Becker had lost the power of speech. Then he turned in pathetic entreaty to Susan and managed the word "Help."

"You mustn't mind Susan," said Janie, leaping to the rescue. "She's in a gay mood. Old-fashioned gay. This is how she grew up around the ancestral hearth in Connecticut. Girls in kilts, boys in blue blazers, drinking egg nogs, tossing the occasional Doberman on the fire, and engaging in the type of giddy conversation that combines the best of Jane Austen and Joan Collins."

"Is *she* kidding?" asked Rusty again.

"You guys are a very tough room," said Michael Roth, feeling a bit sorry for Rusty, who was clearly out of her depth with these cynical crime fighters.

"I must apologize for my distaff colleagues," said Ned Jordan. "An extensive but secret government survey has revealed that women crime fighters lose their minds more rapidly than men."

"Alan, why don't we get something to drink? Hmmm?"

asked Rusty, who pivoted her date around on his crutches and steered him toward the bar.

"We won't be going to that wedding," said Janie.

"No," concurred Jordan.

"I was trying to make light conversation," said Susan defensively. "Not incite a riot."

"Relax, Greenwich. You've probably spared Becker a needless trip down the aisle. So? Who else's life can we ruin this evening?"

"I feel terrible," said Susan. "We never gave Rinty a chance."

"Rusty."

"What?"

"His dog was called Rusty," said Janie. "Yours must have been Rinty."

"I didn't call her Rinty. Did I, Michael? I haven't even had a drink yet."

"Don't," murmured Jordan. "Not tonight. I need you clearheaded."

"What for?" asked a mystified Susan.

"Here you are at last!" The last line was delivered by Lydia Culberg, who had swooped down regally on the group with her Ralph Lauren lookalike in tow. "I've been looking everywhere for you, Susan. Not only the best damned lawyer in the office, Nat, but the best-dressed as well." And Lydia proceeded to kiss Susan on both cheeks. "Susan, I want you to meet Nathan Marshak. Nat, this woman is not only the best mother in the world—her girls are absolutely adorable, by the way—but she makes more money for the office than . . ."

Susan switched off the volume in her brain and merely watched as The Human Faucet's mouth continued to chatter a mile a minute. Lydia was the world's biggest liar. But for whose benefit was she fibbing so flagrantly? Ahhh! Nathan Marshak. Wants the well-tanned, high-rolling real estate whiz to see what a generous and loving soul she is. Or could pretend to be.

Or was it possible that Lydia really meant it? Why

couldn't Lydia have turned over a new leaf and finally realized that Susan wasn't her enemy? That they *could* work together.

"Where are you sitting, honey?"

"I'm sorry?" Susan's mind had drifted.

"What table are you at?" asked Lydia.

"I'm not—"

"You must come and sit with us. You, too, Janie. With your handsome husband. And Ned. Come on." Then Lydia leveled her eyes on Michael. "And you must be Susan's mystery man from Israel. We wondered when she'd finally trot you out."

"Actually I'm from Los Angeles," said Michael, as he introduced himself to Susan's boss. "And what exactly do *you* do?"

"He's got a sense of humor," gushed Lydia. "You need that, Suzy. Well, come on. You and Mike have got to sit with us. So much to talk about. Nat does all sorts of business in L.A."

And so it went throughout the dinner: Lydia lauding and applauding Susan ad nauseam to their fellow diners during the soup and main course. Citing the unit head's every victory hyperbolically even while the evening's guest of honor droned on at the head table. When Susan finally begged her boss to cease this endless and humiliating display of public adoration, she was roundly rebuffed and made to listen to even more exaggerated praise. Susan could do no wrong in Lydia's eyes. If only she, Lydia, could be more like her, Susan. If only the other A.D.A.s could follow Susan's sterling example, the entire legal system could be turned around for the better.

"Excuse me, please," said Susan, finally rising from the table to escape from her "new best friend" by seeking refuge in the ladies' room.

"Where you going, honey?" asked Lydia. "Oh! Good idea. Wait for me."

Susan turned her back on the table and quickly glanced at her watch. Ten to ten. When she returned, she'd use

Michael's jet lag as an excuse to escape from this cruel and unnatural punishment.

No sooner had they entered the powder room than Lydia grabbed Susan rudely by the shoulders and spun her around.

"Get one thing straight right now, Ms. Given! I am leading that raid on the Evanston Hotel tomorrow morning. Is that understood?"

"How did—?" So shocked was Susan by Lydia's knowing about the raid that she hadn't registered her boss's switch from Jekyll to Hyde.

"Do you think for a moment, Susan, that I don't know what is going on in every nook and cranny of my office? I didn't get this job by a fluke, you know. I clawed and scratched and fought every inch of the way to get where I am. I'm not letting go of it and I sure as hell am not going to surrender it to a string of cultured pearls. How dare you try and keep me out of the loop?" Lydia paused for breath and to check her makeup in the mirror.

"What have you done?" asked Susan. "Have you alerted the media? Did you tip off the press?"

"I will. At midnight."

"You'll blow the execution of the search warrants! Every drug dealer in the place will flush their stash down the toilet. We will look like the fools of the world. Oh, Lydia! Why would you want to screw up everything—?"

"—*you've* done? Have I stolen your glory, Susan? Is that what's troubling you?"

"Nooo! Not me. It has nothing to do with me. It's the job. It's the law. It's the money and the building we could have to fight crime and house the homeless—"

"You should be in politics, Susan. That little speech you do is highly effective. You actually make me believe that you care about what you do."

"I do care, Lydia. Why else would I do it? Why the hell do you do it?"

"Power. I like power. I'm addicted to it. The more I get, the more it gives me."

"You're very disturbed!"

"No, I'm a realist. Which makes me perfect for this job. You are an idealist. Which makes you a liability. You get your heart broken every day because you can't have the perfection you seek. There is no such thing as a world without crime, Susan. We can't eliminate crime. All we can do is control it. Tomorrow morning is an exercise in control. I will be leading the raid. I'll be delighted to have you there . . . a few steps behind me. I will acknowledge all the work of your unit in my speech but you are never—I repeat: never—to keep me out of the loop again. Do we understand each other? Good. Now, take that unbecoming scowl off your face and come back to the table smiling as sweetly as when you left."

Lydia swept out of the ladies' room and Susan began moaning. All those months of work. All the money that could have been dispersed. All down the drain because of this vainglorious creature's need for power. Why the hell did Susan bother? Why did she keep breaking her heart for some elusive myth called the law? She would hand her resignation to Mr. Archibald the next day. She hadn't the strength to fight any longer. Crime had won.

Wandering out to the lobby in search of a gift shop and some cigarettes, Susan was surprised to see Nip and Tuck seated in the Palm Court, wearing suits and browsing through the newspaper.

"You at some other function?" asked Susan.

"No," replied Tuck rising amiably. "We're just waitin' for someone."

"You been crying, Ms. Gee?" asked Nip.

"No. I got something in my eye at dinner and—"

"Let's go," said Ned Jordan, as he arrived accompanied by Michael Roth. Both men had their overcoats on and Michael had Susan's coat draped over his arm.

"Where are we going?" asked Susan suspiciously.

"Well, Mike here says he'd like to see the Evanston. For his research. So I figured we could kill two birds with one stone."

"What is the other bird?" asked Susan.

"Seizing the hotel."

"Tomorrow, Ned," whispered Susan. "Not till tomorrow."

"Yeah," nodded Jordan. "That's what Lydia thinks. That's what her spies think. That's what everybody else inside thinks. But it's actually happening"—Jordan checked his Rolex—"in twenty minutes."

"But the warrants! The overtime!"

"All made out for today. We'll swallow the overtime to get this right. Surprise is everything. Nobody flushes their stash or throws it out the window."

"When did you change them?" asked a bewildered Susan.

"The Human Faucet cannot exist without her Baby Drips. Some of them started leaking in my direction. I had to make a move."

"But why didn't you tell *me*? Don't you trust me?"

"Does it really matter, Susan? We're taking the hotel a few hours earlier, that's all."

"It does matter! I'd have brought along a change of clothes."

Jordan turned mischievously to Michael and said: "She cracks me up, you know."

"Yeah, yeah, yeah," said Susan, pinching a cigarette from Nip's pack. Then she stared at her male colleagues. "Well, what are we waiting for? Crime never sleeps."

35

NED JORDAN WAS at the wheel of the car as they pulled up outside the Evanston Hotel on East Twenty-seventh Street. He was also the first to spot the Channel 8 video truck double-parked in front and growled: "What the hell is she doing here?"

No sooner had Susan placed one shapely leg outside the car than Lisa Mercado was in her face greeting her with a big smile and a buoyant "Girlfriend! We got to stop meeting like this."

"What are you doing here, Lisa?" Susan's voice could have been used to pour martinis over.

"Working. Same as you. I'm here to cover the raid."

"This is not a raid," corrected Susan. "The federal government is seizing this property—"

"Whatever." Lisa lowered her voice and took Susan into her confidence: "Brush your hair this time before I interview you. It looks better."

"Thank you for that little fashion tip," replied Susan dryly.

Then she moved in Jordan's direction, mouthing the silent inquiry: "How did she find out?"

"I dunno." Jordan shrugged. "You ready?"

"Should I wait out here?" asked Michael.

"You got a bullet-proof vest?" asked Jordan.

"No."

"Stop it, Ned," said Susan. Then she took the federal prosecutor's cellular and handed it to Michael with her red address book. "Please do me a favor. Call Ray Murphy. Tell him where we are."

"Why'd you do that?" asked Jordan as they followed the U.S. marshals towards the hotel entrance.

"Because we owe Ray one from last month. When he didn't move on the Manny Sanchez story. I can't let Señorita Mercado have the exclusive on this."

The SWAT team and the marshals started on the top floor of the hotel and worked their way down room by room. They systematically ensured that only the legitimate tenants were occupying the rooms. Then they sealed all the unoccupied rooms and the ones where drug trafficking had occurred.

Four hours later it was déjà vu all over again in the lobby of the Evanston. Other TV stations had picked up the story of the seizure and microphones were thrust into the faces of Susan Given, Ned Jordan, and hotel owner Vinh Ho Chi, who was passionately playing the race card.

"This nothing but prejudice," shrieked Vinh, pointing across the lobby in Susan's direction. "This woman hate Asians. She make circus in my hotel two months ago. Try and drive guests from my hotel. She racist!"

"What do you have to say about that?" asked Lisa, waving her microphone in front of Susan's face.

"I'm sorry Mr. Vinh feels that way," replied Susan. "But it's not true. The District Attorney's Office gave him every opportunity to comply—"

Vinh broke away from his own media interrogator, planted himself between Susan and Lisa, and asked: "You call Vinh liar?"

"I really think you should wait until your lawyer arrives," said Susan, "before you make any further—"

"You no tell Vinh nothing. He know 'bout racist like you. Hate all Hispanics. I good friend Uncle Sam. Good friend CIA. You blond bigot. Hate all Third World!"

Susan sighed, opened her wallet, and removed a photo

of Polly and Ivy. "These are my daughters and that'll be quite enough of that talk, Mr. Vinh."

Lisa waved enthusiastically for her cameraman to get a shot of the Carver girls but Susan quickly folded her wallet and put it back in her bag.

Then a murmur spread through the lobby as the press corps was informed that District Attorney Archibald had arrived on the scene. They moved en masse across the lobby to greet the popular D.A. All except for Ray Murphy, who was chatting happily with Michael Roth.

"So how long you and Suzy been going steady?" asked the veteran reporter, lighting up one of his marathon cigarettes.

"We're not exactly—"

"She's a great little broad," said Murphy. "From the old school. Know what I mean? Ballsy but feminine. Yer a lucky guy, Mike. What kinda writing do you do?"

"Books, movies. I worked on a newspaper when I was a kid."

"No kidding. Her husband's a jerk, you know. Treated her like shit. Nice to know she's found a—"

"Ray," said Susan arriving on the scene and dreading what the reporter had been saying to Michael, "don't you want to hear what Mr. Archibald has to say?"

"Archie's gonna say what Archie always says," replied Murphy. "Federal and local crime fighters have done it once again. City's a safer place. Barump-bump. Nah, I want to hear more about you guys. When you two tyin' the knot? How come you been keepin' this guy such a secret, Suzy? He's not exactly the rubber man or a pinhead. Christ on a crutch! He's a fellow writer."

The District Attorney finished his speech to the media, then gestured for Susan to join him.

"Let's take a little walk," said Archibald, taking Susan's elbow and steering her out of the building.

"I'm frightfully sorry, Mr. Archibald."

"For what?"

"This spontaneous media event. We weren't supposed to seize the building until tomorrow but—"

"Good for you. I'm sure you and Jordan had your reasons for moving the date up. That's not what I want to talk about. We have a bigger problem."

"What's that?"

"There's been a terrible accident. A fire—"

"Not my kids?" gasped Susan. "Has something happened to—"

"No, no, no." Archibald squeezed Susan's hand reassuringly. "Nothing that personal. This was over on Fifth Avenue and Ninetieth. A fire broke out in a doctor's office around nine o'clock this evening." The D.A. glanced quickly at his watch. "Last night now. Fortunately the smoke alarms were working. Fire department got it under control before it could spread to other units."

The District Attorney paused in his story and Susan stared at him, wondering what it all had to do with her. Finally Archibald resumed his story:

"The firemen found a body inside the office. From the way he was dressed and the tools in his hand, it would seem he was a burglar. They found his ID and did a routine check with the police. It was an alias. All the appropriate alarm bells went off and, of course, they got in touch with me. . . . It was Tony Fusco."

THE FERRARI ROARED up the gravel driveway toward the antebellum mansion. Junior sat behind the wheel exuding cool and confidence. Why not? He knew his mother would cover for him. Not through a scintilla of criminality but because Loretta's nonexistent sense of time made her the perfect alibi. If Junior said he'd been visiting her all evening, it must be so.

The younger Tesla slammed on his brakes when he saw the limousine parked in front of the porticoed entrance. What the hell was Uncle George doing there? He wouldn't make the journey all the way from Manhattan unless something had happened to—

Junior leaped out of the car and raced toward the front door. The Patch opened the door and Junior grabbed him by the shoulders. "Louie! What happened? Is it Pop? Did something happen to Pop?"

Before the bodyguard could reply, Loretta Tesla descended the staircase, wiping her eyes with a handkerchief.

"Oh, Nicky," she wailed when she saw Junior. "It's so sad." Seconds later she was in the hallway clinging to her muscular son like a lost child. Something wasn't right about this. Where were his sisters? Why weren't their cars outside? If something had happened to their father, they would have been there.

"Where's Papa?"

"Upstairs with Uncle George."

"Is he okay?"

"Of course," replied his mother, as if her child had asked whether the sun had risen that morning or not. "Why shouldn't he be okay?"

"Then what's Uncle George doing here?"

"It's Toni." And Loretta began sobbing again.

"What happened to Toni?" Before his mother could even attempt to reply, Junior took the stairs two at a time to the second floor.

Bursting unannounced into his sister's bedroom, he discovered his father and Cardinal Corcoran sitting on either side of Antonia's bed, holding her hands.

"What the hell happened?"

Tesla gestured impatiently for his son to leave the room. Seconds later he joined him out on the landing.

"What happened to Toni? She OD?"

"What're ya talkin' about?"

"I told her to lay off that Red Rum."

"Your sister's takin' smack? I'll break her fuckin' neck."

"I dunno." Junior retreated quickly, realizing he'd said too much. "What's wrong with her then? What's Uncle George—?"

"We had some bad news. Pete Palazzolo. He was doin' some work for me. . . ."

Junior stared at his father in disbelief. Pete had broken into Rosenthal's office under the senior Tesla's orders? He *wasn't* a cop? Then what the hell was that thing strapped to his back on Forty-second Street? A pacemaker?

"What sorta work?"

"If you must know, I sent him to get that fuckin' file of yours back from the shrink."

"But what happened to him?" Junior was convinced the whole thing was a dream. Following Pete around for days. Then up to Rosenthal's office that night. Watching Pete steal the file, read it, and learn the truth. Then bashing Pete on the head with that antique paperweight. Again and again. Then setting the files on fire.

"Our friends with the police figure he walked into a heist by accident. Can y'imagine? Talk about bad luck! All Pete did was go up there to steal yer lousy medical. And some real crooks bust in and—"

"Pete! Pete!" Toni's cry was shrill, heartbreaking.

"I never seen yer sister like this before. She really loved him." There was a catch in Tesla's throat when he said the last sentence. "I gotta get a drink."

Five minutes later His Eminence, George Cardinal Corcoran, entered Nicolo Tesla's library and found his old friend sitting by the fire with a double whiskey in his hand.

"Would there be another one of those, Nick?"

"Sure, sure." Tesla walked over to the bar and poured the Cardinal a stiff one. "How's Toni?"

"Junior's with her. The sleeping pill should kick in anytime now. Thanks, Nick."

"Thank *you*," said Tesla, clinking glasses with the Cardinal. "It was a helluva thing your coming all the way out here for us. I didn't know who else to—"

"Nick, Nick." Corcoran squeezed Tesla's arm. "How far back do we go? How many favors have you done me?"

"There's just all this pressure lately, George. I try not to let it show. You know the way Loretta worries. Keeps the saints workin' overtime. But the D.A.'s after me."

"Why?"

"That's what I want to know. I been in the garbage trade forty years now. My clients are the biggest and most respected businesses in the city. Hotels, banks, hospitals, theaters. Do they ever complain? Have I ever given them less than perfect service? Forty years! Now the law's after me. They want to put me outta business and let some cowboys from Oklahoma walk in and take over. Why? Cuz the cowboys are gonna charge less. Of course, they are. They're a national fuckin' company. I'm a local businessman. I pay my taxes, George. I donate to the church."

"Generously," added Corcoran.

"What the hell am I doing wrong? Why are they after me?"

"Just you?"

"No. Of course not. DeFillipo, Carlucci. All of us. Same old story, George. It's the WASPs after the Catholics. A century later and they're still tryin' to keep us down."

"Perhaps I could speak to someone in the District Attorney's Office."

"Please, don't stick yer nose in, George. I appreciate it but—"

"I have someone I can speak to, Nick. A little word."

"Thank you." Tesla gulped his drink, then tilted his head toward the ceiling and the room where his distraught daughter lay.

"What was the boy's name?" asked Cardinal Corcoran.

"Palazzolo. Pete Palazzolo." Tesla fought back a tear as he added: "He looked just like my grandfather."

The Cardinal leaned forward and squeezed Tesla's knee affectionately. "I'll say a special prayer for the boy at this morning's Mass. And a novena for Toni's speedy recovery."

WILLIAM ARCHIBALD AND Susan Given leaned against opposite walls, staring at each other in silence. They were in the Intensive Care Unit at Mount Sinai Hospital and it was almost four in the morning as they awaited news of Tony Fusco's condition.

Susan had forced Michael to go home and get some sleep an hour earlier. She was grateful that the previous night had been Hugh's turn to have the girls. This was all too weird. Why on earth would Fusco have been involved in a burglary? It made no sense. Yet the firemen had found him with the tools in his possession. . . .

"This is all my fault!" blurted Paul "Nip" Regan as he strode down the corridor toward them, breaking the silence.

"What do you mean?" asked Archibald wearily.

"When I went out for a smoke just now," answered Nip, "I checked my machine at home. Just to break the monotony, you know. And there was a message from Fusco. He'd called my place around seven. But Tucker and I had already gone. Getting ready for the—"

"Yes, yes," said the D.A. impatiently. "Go on."

"The Fuss said it was the Delevan case all over again and he needed my help. That was an undercover gig about three years ago. We had to do a little B and E in a security building. I figured a way to disable the TV monitors in the lobby temporarily till The Fuss could get in and out without— Anyhow, he left the address on Fifth Avenue and asked me to meet him there. But I never made it."

"It's not your fault," said Susan.

"He needed backup, Ms. Gee. I wasn't there for him."

"He should have informed his superiors in any case," said Archibald. "Fusco had no business risking his safety or his cover— He *was* admitted in here as Palazzolo?" Susan nodded. "I just don't understand why he did it. And where does this Dr. Rosenthal fit into the picture?"

"Abner Rosenthal?" asked an amazed Susan. "That's whose office he broke into?"

"Yes," replied Archibald. "Do you know the man?"

"This is too peculiar," said Susan. "We used to be friends. Ab's a colleague of my husband's. I had a phone call from him the other week. He sounded extremely agitated, frightened. He warned me to be careful. I didn't know what to make of it. Then his wife phoned the other day. Wanted help. Ab was missing and the police weren't cooperating."

"Why not?"

"Because Dr. Rosenthal had taken all his clothes and half their bank account before he vanished."

"I'll get a list of his patients," said Nip, taking out a pad and writing the name down.

"All the records were destroyed by the fire," said the District Attorney. "I don't get it. Fusco had to have done it for the Teslas. What connection could there possibly be involving them and Rosenthal? It had to be something horrible and threatening enough for him to abandon his family and practice—"

The District Attorney was interrupted by the appearance of an earnest young resident from Bombay dressed in green scrubs, who emerged from the operating theater at that moment and approached the intense trio.

"Mr. Archibald? I'm Dr. Veda."

"Yes, doctor? How is he?"

"I've done all I could for now. I frankly do not know why Mr. Palazzolo is still alive. I don't wish to sound melodramatic but whoever did this was an animal, a monster. I'm so sorry. All that we can do now is pray."

Veda retired to the doctors' lounge and the trio looked at each other as if they were all wired to the same central computer.

"Junior Tesla?" asked Archibald.

"It's the same MO as the Gerhardt murder."

"I know this is really whacked," said Nip. He was about to speak, then changed his mind. "Forget it."

"What?" asked Susan.

"I'm out on a real limb with this. But what if Junior was in therapy with this Rosenthal? Wait, wait. And he had second thoughts. 'Whoa! I'm spillin' my guts to someone whose name doesn't even end in a vowel?' So he breaks into the shrink's office to retrieve his file."

"Where does Fusco come into this?" asked Archibald.

"Maybe he told The Fuss about the file and asked him to get it for him."

"Then why try and kill him?"

"I dunno, Mr. Archibald. I'm just spinnin' my wheels."

"Keep spinning, Regan. You're probably closer than you think. In the meantime, Fusco remains Palazzolo. If the Teslas find out he was one of ours, everything of theirs that isn't stashed away already in Switzerland or the Bahamas will be there by tomorrow night."

"And if they find out he's still alive," said Nip, "they'll have a hit man here before Joan Lunden says good morning, America."

"Then *we'll* kill Palazzolo," said Archibald, who when he saw the shock on Susan's face, hastily added: "And secretly move Fusco to the Kessler Institute in East Orange."

"That's a rehab hospital," said a bewildered Nip. "The doctor said he couldn't—"

"I'm not going to let that boy die," said the District Attorney. "And I'm not going to let the Teslas get away with this. Now, you two go home and get some sleep."

THE CARDINAL ROSE from behind his desk and walked to the middle of the room to greet the tall redhead, who had just been announced.

"Your Eminence."

"Ahhh, Lydia! How kind of you to come."

"I'm honored that you invited me."

"Please," chuckled Cardinal Corcoran. "Let's not bury each other under mutual admiration."

"I'm being entirely sincere, Your Eminence. I'm well aware that my marrying a Jew was not looked upon kindly by my family or the Church."

"That your *late* husband was Jewish was far from a mortal sin. His premature passing was tragic. But that *was* some time ago, if I'm not mistaken. And his bequest to you was more than—"

"Bob died without a penny."

"I meant Ethan. Your son."

"It's not my fault about the bar mitzvah. Bob's parents insisted."

"Lydia, Lydia. We aren't living in the Dark Ages. *You*

have remained a dutiful daughter of the Church. Perhaps someday Ethan will embrace his mother's faith as well. He's young. He'll do the right thing. But what a terrible host I'm being. Making you stand all this time. Please, sit down, Lydia. Would you like some tea?"

"No, no." Lydia drifted toward the oak-paneled wall where the Cardinal's numerous framed photographs with world leaders were on display. She gasped when she saw the same picture that adorned the wall of her office. She and the Cardinal the year before at Gracie Mansion.

"You have my picture on your wall," gushed Lydia.

"Don't spread it around." Corcoran winked. "I'm supposed to be celibate." Then the Cardinal roared with laughter at his own joke and the blush it had brought to Lydia's cheeks. "I hope I didn't shock you with that one. Now, I insist you sit down. Oh, how did this newspaper get here?"

The Cardinal had purposely planted that morning's *New York Times* on the chair before Lydia walked in. Scooping up the paper before the deputy D.A. sat down, His Eminence glanced at the front page and, with studied casualness, remarked: "That was quite a coup your office pulled off at the Evanston. Surprised you weren't there, Lydia."

He dangled the *Times* in front of Lydia's face so she might stare with smoldering rage at the photograph of William Archibald, Ned Jordan, and Susan Given standing in front of the seized hotel.

"I read the article this morning," replied Lydia noncommittally.

"Your Ms. Given is certainly zealous about her work. One might even say overzealous. Does the woman never sleep?"

"She brings in a lot of money for her unit."

"But at what cost, Lydia?"

The Cardinal turned the pages of the *Times* until he came to a full-page ad of a Brandoesque Mafia type sitting in a rocking chair, stroking a large tabby cat in his lap.

Underneath the photo was the caption: "Whaddaya mean you wanna change yer garbage man?" At the bottom of the page in bold letters was: "Campbell-McCafee . . . A safe, alternative way to remove waste."

"There's no excuse for this sort of thing," said His Eminence, walking over to the wall and removing the framed photograph of himself with the Teslas at Nick's testimonial at the Waldorf. "These are old and dear friends of mine." He flashed the gold Rolex on his wrist at her. "Nick Tesla gave me this watch when I turned sixty. Keeps perfect time. To the second. Nick takes care of his wife and children, he pays his taxes and he goes to church. He does not need to be unduly harassed. And now with this unfortunate death in the family—"

"Who died?"

"The youngest daughter's boyfriend. Very tragic. The funeral is tomorrow. They've all been shattered by it. I don't want them disturbed any further. So I'd appreciate it if you'd ask your Ms. Given to back off a little."

"Don't worry about Susan," said Lydia coldly. "I'll take care of her."

THE CASKET WAS lowered into the ground and the priest made the final blessing before the dirt was shoveled in on top.

Wearing black armbands, the deceased's two brothers stared stoically across the freshly dug grave at the Tesla family and their entourage, who had come to pay their last respects. There were no other mourners present.

How could there be? Pete Palazzolo had never existed. So who were the two brothers? And where had they come from?

When Susan had finally crawled home exhausted from Mt. Sinai a few mornings earlier, she told Michael about the D.A.'s decision to "bump off" Palazzolo. Of course, there would be no body in the coffin that was to be buried in the Queens cemetery, and finding "relatives" to mourn poor Pete might prove a bit of a problem.

With years of experience in theater and film combined with a flair for improvisation, Michael offered/insisted on representing Palazzolo's family at the interment.

"But you never knew him," said Susan when he first made the suggestion, adding: "He never existed."

"Of course, he did," countered Michael, "and, as far as the Teslas are concerned, he is a man to be mourned. And he's got to have had a family. Otherwise they'll be suspicious."

"But you're not Italian!"

"I've played Italians. I've spent half my life being mistaken for Italian. Tell Mr. Archibald not to worry."

When Susan *did* worry was when Michael drafted Barry Praeger into service to play Palazzolo's "other" brother.

"Why do there have to be two brothers?" asked Susan, after Michael dropped this bombshell.

"What kind of Italians have small families? I need Barry there. And not just for moral support. People have thought we were brothers for years. We pretended to be the Fellini Brothers in London in nineteen seventy—which is a whole other story. I can certainly act the distraught relative. But what if the Teslas say something to us? Barry speaks fluent Italian—all those hotels in Italy."

Not only did Archie go along with the idea but he commended Michael and Barry for their volunteerism.

So there they were mourning a man who never existed while somewhere, a hundred yards away, Nip and Tuck—disguised as groundskeepers—were photographing the mourners through telephoto lenses.

"Remember when we were the Fellini Brothers in London?" murmured Barry, who was thoroughly enjoying this little masquerade. "And we got thrown out of the Dorchester trying to capture that nympho's runaway chinchilla?"

"Shh. For Chrissake, Barry. Not now."

"*Scusi.* Oops, we got company."

Nicolo Tesla moved toward the two impersonators, his face lined with legitimate grief.

"I'm sorry for your trouble," said Tesla, crushing both their hands in his powerful grip. "He was a very special guy."

"*Grazi,*" said Barry, who then began an amazing tale of Pete's childhood accomplishments—all in fluent, high-toned Italian.

"Yer a college guy. I can tell." Then Tesla paused and stared at the two "brothers." "He didn't look nothing like you two."

"He looked like our mom," sobbed Michael.

"Funny." Tesla nodded. "I always thought he looked like my grandfather. Maybe cuz we're all from Ragusa."

"Ahhhh," sighed Barry. "Ragusa."

"If there's anything you guys need . . ." And Tesla left the rest of the offer blank as he moved away sadly.

Junior was the next one to come forward, looking like The Terminator in a black suit. He stared interminably at the two Palazzolo Brothers, then grabbed both their hands in bone-crunching grips and muttered: "Yer brother was a good guy. I didn't know him very well."

Bullshit, thought Michael, as he waited for the feeling to come back to his hand. Susan had warned him about Junior. He was the prime suspect and, for Michael's money, he was a shoo-in. The way he had stared at Michael and Barry—defying them to blurt out their suspicions.

"He spoke highly of you," said Michael.

"Oh, yeah?"

"All the Teslas," said Michael hastily. "The way you welcomed him into your family."

"He was the brother I never had," said Junior, staring into Michael's eyes with no emotion whatsoever.

This guy did it, thought Michael. You could just smell it on him. Suddenly the writer understood why Susan did what she did. Fighting crime. How she got off on it in her own New England way. Growing up in Toronto with the crooks and the cops walking in and out of his old man's place, Michael had always felt a stronger affinity for the cops (even though he had a soft spot for the crooks with their lingo and stories). What on earth was he doing trying to write a movie about Cornell Woolrich and his mother? To hell with them! He'd write about Susan and the Teslas and— Who the hell was this? Who shows cleavage at a funeral?

"I was crazy about your brother," sobbed Toni Tesla. "I don't know if he told you about me or not."

"Oh, yes," said Barry, twinkling his Tony Curtis eyes, then taking her hands in his and kissing them. "Many times."

"Really! What did he say? Please, please, tell me," begged Toni.

Barry Praeger stared soulfully into the heartbroken young woman's eyes and began a litany of praises for her hair, her eyes, her lips, her mouth—all in Italian.

Oh, my God! thought Michael. He's hitting on her. At the funeral. We're never getting out of this cemetery alive.

40

THE DISTRICT ATTORNEY was examining a series of glossy photographs on his desk when Susan entered his office.

"You wanted to see me, Mr. Archibald?"

"Susan! Where did you find this enterprising man you're keeping company with?"

"Michael? In Jerusalem. Why?"

"Look at these photographs. What a performer! Both of them. The droop of their shoulders. The sorrow on their faces. I wonder what Nick Tesla's saying to them. Goodness! Isn't that young woman dressed rather inappropriately for a funeral? Did she wander in by mistake? Michael's friend seems quite keen on her."

"That's Toni Tesla. And she was just as keen. Michael says she was ready to marry Barry on the spot. Or, at least, register at a motel."

"Wonderful. We've never been able to get a man that deep inside the mob before."

"He's already married. To a friend of mine."

"Well, it was a thought. I must compliment Tuck on the quality of his photographs. I remember a time when he'd forget to take the cap off the lens. Just look at these pictures of Junior Tesla. How do they cut suits for a body like that?"

"Any news on Tony?"

"Not really. He's in a private clinic. I was a little premature thinking we could move him to Kessler. But I do have some good news. I'd like you to meet Mr. Roselli."

Susan turned around and saw a tiny, dapper man in

his late sixties with plastered-down white hair and a pencil-thin mustache, perched expectantly on the edge of the leather sofa. He made an effort to rise as Susan approached him with her hand held out.

"Please, don't get up. I'm Susan Given."

"Gaetano Roselli." He held a manicured, liver-spotted hand out for Susan to shake.

"Mr. Roselli is the owner of Osborne Paper Fiber."

Susan paused for a moment, wondering why that name rang a bell until she remembered: "Walter Gerhardt worked for you."

"That's right," replied Roselli in a high-pitched voice. "A lovely guy. What a terrible thing to have happen. And his wife expecting another baby."

"Yes, I know." Susan felt a pang of guilt. She hadn't spoken to Nancy for weeks.

"Mr. Roselli has offered to work with us," said the District Attorney, flashing a grateful smile in the old man's direction.

"I should have come a long time ago," said Roselli. "But I was scared. Those scum. What they done to Walt. . . ." He shook his head. "For forty years I was in the recycling business. Made a nice buck. Then somebody said: 'Gaetano, you got the trucks. Why you don't haul trash?' So I looked around. I found a customer down near Wall Street. I asked what he paid to have his garbage removed. He said ten thousand a month. I told him I'd do it for four. So we had a deal and he recommended me to other people. Soon I was very busy."

"Who was the previous carter?" asked Susan.

"Nicolo Tesla. We'd been picking up the garbage maybe six months when some guys came around to my warehouse and set an empty truck on fire. I guess they thought I'd quit after that. But I didn't. I reported the incident to the Consumer Affairs Department. Two days later Walt Gerhardt was killed. I decided maybe I should stop hauling trash.

"But then a funny thing happened. I stopped sleeping

good at night. Something was bothering me. I couldn't figure out what. I had no trouble with Tesla no more. But I had trouble with myself.

"When my father brought us here in nineteen thirty-four it was to get away from Mussolini and the fascists. My father didn't speak English so good but he taught himself the Pledge of Allegiance and he made us say it with him every morning. 'With Liberty and justice for all.' Oh, how he loved those words. I have disgraced his memory. So, now, I say we get these bastards once and for all."

"You're willing to take on the Association?" asked Susan. "Knowing what they might do to you?"

"I'm an old man, Ms. Given. I had kids and my kids had kids. What they gonna do to me? There's got to be justice for Walt."

"I look forward to working with you, Mr. Roselli."

"Actually, Susan, you'll be working more closely with Mr. Roselli's nephew."

"Where is he?"

Archibald picked up the phone and buzzed his secretary. "Audrey? Has Dominic Roselli arrived yet? . . . Good. Would you send him in, please?"

The door opened from the outer office and Dominic Roselli bounced into the room. Early thirties. Jet black hair. Almost too black. There was something vaguely familiar about him.

Susan stared at the nephew in disbelief.

"So what do you think of my new look, Ms. Gee?" asked Nip with his arms held wide apart. "Half a wop is better than none."

41

THEY WERE ALL there. The members of the Gotham Waste Removal Association. Assembled in a private room on the second floor of Tesla's. Mumbling, grumbling, cursing in Italian, English, and Sicilian. Two waiters wandered gingerly through the smoke-filled room offering coffee, wine, and bruschetta to the disgruntled members of the cartel.

Fifteen minutes before noon Nicolo Tesla walked in from his upstairs office, followed by Junior and Louie Torino. He shook hands with his various colleagues and rivals, then he held up the full-page ad that had run in that day's *New York Times.*

"Anybody didn't see this shit today?"

"We saw it," snarled Joe Carlucci, wiping his thick bifocals with a handkerchief. "Why else would we be here? Your food gives me heartburn."

"You gotta have a heart to burn first." Tesla smiled. "And if you don't like the food so much, Joe, how come yer daughter had her engagement party here?"

"Just cuz I got taste, don't mean my kids do." Carlucci waved to a waiter at that point and had another piece of bruschetta. "This stuff ain't bad."

"Yer a funny guy, Joe. So what are we gonna do about this new campaign? Hmm?"

"These cowboys oughta be shoved up and done over," spat out Phil DeFillipo, readjusting his rhinolike frame on the antique chair. "Tell you one thing. If I was Brando, I'd sue for usin' my picture."

"That ain't Brando," said Carlucci scornfully. "It's a guy what looks like him."

"They done it with computers," explained Leo Gerussi, fast talking and whippet thin, the first of the carters to venture onto the Internet. "They take a little piece of different people and stick 'em together. That way they don't got to hire no actors."

"I'd sue those computer pricks if they used any part of me," said DeFillipo, still trying to find a comfortable position on his chair.

"The only part of you worth usin'," said Carlucci, "they couldn't print in a newspaper."

"Fuck you, Four Eyes," snarled DeFillipo.

"Hey! Hey! What are you, the Bowery Boys or somethin'?," asked Tesla. "I'll book you in downstairs on amateur night. Meanwhile we gotta form a united front to deal with this. Certain people are lookin' for us to make a reaction."

"I say we don't do nothin'," said Gerussi.

"What're you crazy, Leo?" asked DeFillipo. "Yer wife puttin' melatonin in yer minestrone? We can't just let these fuckin' cowboys walk in here and piss all over us."

"I say we hit 'em," said Junior Tesla. "Hard. Blow up maybe five, ten, twenty of their trucks. Like the Japs did to us at Pearl Harbor. Bing-bang-boom. They're gone."

The carters stared at the muscular young man in astonishment. Was he serious? There hadn't been that kind of war in the city since—

"Please, excuse my son," sighed Tesla. "He watches too many old movies."

"I'm not sayin' we do it ourselves," said Junior, refusing to be quiet. "Someone like Red Meat Mazzoli could take on—"

"Where the hell do you come from to throw names like Ernie Mazzoli around?" asked Tesla. "You keep yer mouth shut and listen. Maybe you'll learn something." A red-faced Junior rose to leave after this public chastising. "Siddown! We're not done here yet. Okay. Here's the way I look at it. The D.A.'s after us. Why after all these years,

I dunno. Maybe this Given broad's menopausal. But I ain't gonna give her no extra help. Gasmer says we can tie them up in court for years. And still keep business goin' on like usual. I know one thing: If we fight with one another, the only person's gonna win is the customer."

The veteran carters—all bottom-liners when the day was done—stared at each other either muttering or nodding agreement.

"These cowboys think they're pretty smart," continued Tesla, "buyin' fancy ads in the newspaper. Makin' fun of the wops. Real sophisticated, right? Except nobody reads the fuckin' paper any more. They watch the TV. My grandkids sing commercials like I used to sing Verdi."

Tesla paused to let the notion sink in until Carlucci peered through his thick glasses and broke the silence with: "Hey, Nick! Watcha doin'? 'This Is Your Life'?"

"I want you to meet somebody," said Tesla, nodding in Torino's direction at the same time. The Patch got up and left the room. "It's gonna cost us a couple two-three bucks but I figure it's worth it."

Torino returned to the room a moment later followed by a nervous Cynthia Praeger carrying a huge portfolio, a boom box, and a collapsible easel under her arm.

"This is Cynthia Praeger. She's one of the top ad people in town and she's come up with a very interesting idea for some commercials."

"I'm so happy to be back in your restaurant again," said Cynthia breathlessly. "I hope you've forgiven me for getting sick on your friend's shoes the last time I was here." Cynthia searched the faces of the dozen men staring at her for a glimpse of Fusco. "He's not here?"

"He died."

"Oh! Oh, I'm so sorry. I didn't mean to be disrespectful."

"S'okay. Go ahead, Cynthia."

She cleared her throat, set up her easel, and began to display her storyboards.

"Okay," began Cynthia. "This campaign will combine

the idea of your strengths and Campbell-McCafee's weaknesses in the New York market. On the plus side of the ledger, you gentlemen have been here for forty years and established a solid rapport with your customers. The C-M people are hayseeds at the World's Fair."

Unveiling her first board, Cynthia revealed a gleaming truck with a smiling uniformed driver waving to a jolly, aproned greengrocer, whose trash he has just removed. Then she pushed the Play button on her boom box and a friendly New York voice was heard to say: "Like old friends, we take care of each other. . . ."

Then Cynthia produced a second board revealing a beat-up truck with Oklahoma plates and a huge steer horn on the roof, driving around Columbus Circle. The third board showed two cowboys inside the cab of the truck staring hopelessly at a map of New York City. Then two redneck voices emerged from the boom box:

"I ain't got no idea where we are, Slim. How in the heck are we supposed to find the World Trade Center?"

"Beats me, Joe Bob. I think we're just drivin' 'round in circles here."

A fourth board revealed a fleet of gleaming white trucks with a squad of smiling uniformed drivers standing in front of it. Then the friendly New York voice once again: "We speak your language. And we never get lost. Old friends are often worth a little extra."

Cynthia switched off the tape and stared expectantly at her prospective clients. Finally, when she could stand the silence no longer, she asked: "What do you gentlemen think?"

"I think you nailed it," said Tesla.

"I think it's classy," said DeFillipo.

"It's subtle," said Carlucci. "That's what it is. Subtle."

"User friendly," added Gerussi. "I like that last line. What was it again?"

" 'Old friends are often worth a little extra,' " quoted Cynthia. "I'm rather proud of that one myself."

"You did good, Cynthia," said Tesla, wrapping an arm around her shoulder. "I think we're in business."

TOM PATTERSON STARED up at the gargantuan crystal chandelier hanging down from the thirty-foot-high ceiling and emitted a long, impressed whistle.

"That's nothing," said Susan Given, standing next to the tall Oklahoman in the main dining room of Molnar's, a gourmet palace on the site of a former robber baron's Fifth Avenue mansion, "wait till you see the menu."

"Prices are steep, huh?"

"They aren't listed, Tom. You order, eat, and go into shock when you get the bill at the end of the meal."

"Can I help you?" asked an exotic-looking young woman with a lilting Hungarian accent. "We don't serve again until six o'clock."

"I'm here to see Mr. Molnar," said Susan, showing the young woman her badge.

"Would you like a drink while you wait?"

"No, thank you. If we could just see Mr. Molnar."

Two minutes later a lean, intense, mustached man in his early sixties with a cigarette dangling from his lips descended the ornate staircase from the second floor and entered the dining room.

Nodding first at Patterson, then at Susan, the man introduced himself in a deep-voiced Hungarian accent: "Istvan Molnar."

"Susan Given," she said, ready to catch the two inches of ash hanging precariously from his cigarette before it dropped down to the expensive carpeting.

"Ah! Miss Given, I told you I would not see you."

"No, Mr. Molnar. You said you wouldn't *talk* to me. I said I would come and see you anyhow."

"You are the husband?" Molnar asked Patterson, in a tone that suggested the Oklahoman should take greater responsibility for his wife's behavior.

"This is Tom Patterson," said Susan. "He's with Campbell-McCafee."

"You are both wasting your time," said Molnar, who removed the cigarette delicately from his mouth and called out: "Ildiko!"

The pretty young girl, who had greeted Susan and Patterson, was hovering nearby. Molnar snapped an order at her in Hungarian and a second later she produced an ashtray for her boss's cigarette.

"Did Ildiko offer you a drink?" asked Molnar.

"Yes," said Susan, "but we didn't want anything."

"Then there is no reason for you to stay. Good afternoon."

"Mr. Molnar," said Susan, holding her ground. "How much do you pay a year to have your garbage removed?"

"I don't know."

"I do. Last year you paid one hundred thousand dollars. That's a lot of money."

"It's the price of doing business." The restaurateur shrugged.

"My company would only charge you forty thousand," said Patterson.

"No, thank you."

"That's sixty thousand you could be puttin' in your pocket," drawled Patterson.

"I'm not interested. Good morning."

"Are you afraid?" asked Susan.

"Of course, I am afraid," replied Molnar. "Only a fool would not be afraid. Do you see that chandelier? It once hung in the palace of the Emperor Franz Josef. How long do you think that chandelier would hang here if I used a carter who did not belong to the Association? I would come in one morning and find it lying on the floor smashed to pieces. With all my plates and crystal, as well."

"You've been threatened?" asked Susan.

"I have an imagination, Miss Given. As a child in Budapest, I watched what the Nazis did to my countrymen. I became acquainted with the face of fear. Then as a young man I watched what the Communists did. So I came to this country where they promised freedom, and got it— but for a price. I don't resent paying tribute. But the inflation!"

"Our records show you switched from Tesla Carting to Carlucci Brothers."

"They switched me," said Molnar, lighting up another cigarette. "I had no say in the matter. Tesla signed me for fifty thousand, then sold me to Carlucci. My rate doubled."

"Did they say why?"

"It was a mistake. My garbage weighed more than they thought. When they got it on the scales it was more. Much more. What am I to do, Ms. Given, weigh my garbage every night?"

"Have you really lost your taste for freedom, Mr. Molnar?" asked Susan. "I never experienced the Germans and the Russians. But I have seen the faces of fear far too much in my work. Wouldn't you like to beat them for once? One little snowball can start an avalanche."

"We can do a five-year, fixed-price contract," said Patterson. "Hell, I'll make it ten."

Molnar stared at his two guests, then up at the ceiling and asked: "What about the chandelier?"

"Can't we talk about that over a drink?" asked Susan.

"Ildiko!" Molnar snapped an order at the girl and she vanished from the dining room. Then he turned back to Susan and smiled at her for the first time since her visit. "Why do I suspect you are part Hungarian?"

43

By TWO O' CLOCK that afternoon Susan Given was utterly exhausted. The "friendly drink" at Molnar's had turned into two, then three. Before lunch! She followed the huge glasses of Bull's Blood with several double espressos, which left Susan totally wired. But it had all been for a good cause: the Hungarian had ultimately agreed to switch his garbage business to Campbell-McCafee.

Staring at the clock on the wall, Susan wished the hour hand might magically whiz around to five so she could go home and prepare for Polly's opening night. Maybe she'd even leave at four. What the hell! It was Friday afternoon. Everyone else was—

The telephone rang, jarring Susan's already jarred nerves. Forcing herself back into an operative mode, she answered: "Given."

"I want to see you in my office." It was Lydia and she was using her take-no-prisoners voice. "Now."

"I'll be right down."

What could it be now? wondered Susan, as she slipped her feet back into her shoes. Maybe it's the show tonight. Ethan *is* playing Polly's father. Does she want us to go together? As if! Lydia's behavior toward her had been a tribute to Nanook of the North since the Evanston raid.

The phone rang again and Susan debated whether to answer it or not.

"Given."

"Susan? Ruth Rosenthal."

"Ruth! I have been thinking about you for the past three days. Have you heard anything from Ab?"

"Of course not. I was calling to see if you knew anything. I'd hoped when his office caught on fire that maybe the police would—"

"Ruth, did he have duplicate files?"

"Of what?"

"His cases."

"Ab never discussed his patients with me."

"Oh, come on, Ruth! How long was I married to Hugh? He never stopped talking about his—"

"Ab wasn't like that. He believed in the sanctity of the doctor-patient relation—"

Susan's other line rang: "Hold on, Ruth. . . . Given!"

"Hi, it's Nancy Gerhardt."

"Nancy, I'm on the other line. I'm sorry I haven't phoned. Can I call you tonight? No, no. Not tonight. My daughter's school play. Um. I'll call you on the weekend. . . . Ruth?"

"Yes?"

"I wasn't casting any aspersions on Ab's professional integrity. I'm trying to help you. Did he ever discuss a patient whom he might have . . . been frightened of?"

"What are you saying, Susan? Do you think something happened to Ab? Why did he take his clothes? Why did he take my money?"

"His money, too, Ruth."

"Fine, fine. Take his side."

"Ruth, you're being paranoid. I'm not—"

"Ohh! So now you're a doctor *and* a lawyer. Good luck to you." The receiver slammed down on the other end.

Susan was about to dial Ruth back when the phone rang again. She grabbed it immediately. "Ruth, let me explain what I meant—"

"It's Michael."

"Ohhhh."

"That good a day, huh?" asked Michael picking up on her agonized moan.

"Ha!"

"Amazing," said Michael. "I've never heard anyone do such a brilliant Bette Davis in one syllable before. 'Ha!' Vintage. What's wrong?"

"All I want to do is go home."

"Then come home. Rescue me from Cordelia's passionate embraces." The St. Kitts housekeeper's cackling could be heard in the background.

"So you've made a hit with Cordelia as well?"

"Somebody here has to like me."

"Don't you think I do?" asked Susan.

"Your husband doesn't. I just had another run-in with him on the phone. He wants to know why I'm still here. I told him to go piss up a rope."

"You didn't."

"Well, there's no challenge in pissing down a rope. Do you know if he's had his shots this year?"

"Just ignore him."

"That's what Cordelia says. Actually she said: 'Please don't make trouble when trouble don't make you.' I think I can get her a book deal. Can't you just see her on Oprah?"

Susan began laughing just as her other line rang. She answered with a slight giggle: "Given."

"What the hell are you doing up there?" demanded Lydia. "I've been waiting for—"

"Coming." She hung up one line, then told Michael: "I'll be home by five . . . I hope."

Susan walked out of her office and discovered Gretchen in an agitated state. Without looking up from her computer screen, the slender woman asked: "Did Lydia get hold of you?"

"Yes, thank you."

"I kept telling her you were on two lines but that didn't matter. She just kept phoning every other minute. And reading me the riot act. Where the hell does she get off talking to people like that?"

"What did she say?"

"It's not what. It's how. She's got terminal attitude and one of these days—"

"Don't! Please, Gretchen. You might go through with it and I don't want to be responsible for not stopping you. Where is Alan? I haven't seen him all—"

"Getting his cast off. Oh, your daughter phoned, too."

"Which one?"

"Polly. She sounded nervous."

"It's her opening night. Poor kid. Wait till she grows up and discovers every day is an opening night." Susan took a deep breath, then: "If I'm not back in half an hour, tell my children that I loved them more than anything on this nutty planet."

"Can I have your pearls?" asked Gretchen.

"No! I want to be buried with these pearls. They were my grandmother's."

Susan entered Lydia's office and discovered the Deputy District Attorney in her most schizophrenic mode, alternately haranguing and cajoling the parties on two different phone lines.

"Listen, you dipshit, I want that car repaired for this evening. Do you understand me? Just a second . . . Fred, Fred, darling, is it such a favor to ask? So she's royalty. We're not talking Princess Di here, Fred. Bump her. She'll probably never get a visa again. I need you to do my hair at five. Just a second . . . So what's the story? Ohhh, now you *can* get a part for it. Isn't that amazing! I'll pick the car up at six-thirty. . . . What? Well, you'll just have to stay open a little later, won't you? . . . Freddy? . . . I knew you could do it. It's a special occasion. My kid is a star tonight. Ooh-ooh-ooh. Kisses."

Lydia hung up the phone, walked around from behind her desk, and without taking a breath began a verbal assault.

"Do you have any idea just how much trouble you're in? Hmm? Do you know how close you are to being fired?"

"What are you talking about?" asked Susan.

"You're just lucky I like you or your face would be buried in the want ads, as we speak."

"You're the one doing all the talking."

"There you go again, Susan, with your goddamn superior attitude."

"All I ask is a clue, Lydia. Is this because of the Evanston? I told you already I had no idea the feds were going to move up the—"

"Did you think that was cute having your boyfriend turn up at Palazzolo's funeral the other day?"

"He was authorized by—"

"What if Mr. Archibald found out?"

"—Mr. Archibald himself."

"What are you talking about?"

"He had Archie's complete approval. And, frankly, what does it have to do with you?"

"What is this vendetta of yours against Nicolo Tesla?"

"Vendetta? It's a forfeiture case. A huge one."

"You're making a big mistake going after Tesla."

"Would you care to read the transcripts of the wiretaps, Lydia?"

"That's what I'm talking about. Wiretaps. Undercover cops. I don't want to see this office paralyzed by a multi-million-dollar lawsuit because of your overzealous—"

"I am acting with the full knowledge and authority of the District Attorney."

"You're going over my head again, aren't you?"

"The Teslas are guilty as—"

"You don't have a case, Susan. Maybe you do against the others. But I don't see where—"

"Do I have to go to Mr. Archibald about this?"

"Try it, Ms. Given, and it will be the last thing you ever do in this office."

"Are you threatening me?"

"No. I'm pulling rank. Take my advice: back off from Tesla if you want to keep your job. There are powerful people involved, who could make your life miserable."

"Whose side are you on, Lydia? What's in this for you?
Winning this case makes us all look good—"

"I hear they cut your kid's number tonight."

"What?"

"Your daughter couldn't hit the high notes. They've cut
her number. Too bad. Ethan says she's a nice kid."

Blind rage propelled Susan back into the elevator. Why
were all these things happening at once? Poor Polly. That
was probably why she phoned. How could they cut her
number? This wasn't a Broadway production. What was
Lydia's interest in Nick Tesla? Who were these "powerful
people" she was referring to?

"The job's finally getting to you, huh?" asked Delbert,
as he watched Susan mutter away under her breath.

"What?" Susan was annoyed at having been caught
conversing with herself.

The elevator operator's harelip made his conversations
difficult to fathom at the best of times but this afternoon
he was positively unintelligible. "Sorry," he grumbled.

"No, no, Delbert. It's me. The planet is slightly askew
today, don't you think?"

"Win some, lose some." Delbert struggled painfully to
enunciate this little bit of philosophy.

"But who has the rule book, Del?"

"Ha-ha! That's a good one. See ya."

Gretchen handed her boss a fax as she walked back into
the forfeiture office. "This just came in."

TO: SGC
FROM: HC

I telephoned the apartment the other morning to
speak to my daughters and was shocked to hear
a man answer. He was rude and abusive and
hung up on me. I phoned again just now and he
was still there. Ruder than before. Frankly, I never
thought you the type to take up with gigolos but,
as your behavior has become progressively more

aberrant, I realize you are now capable of anything. I want that man out of your bed and out
of the apartment immediately or I will take aggressive action to remove Polly and Ivy to a
healthier environment.

Susan flew into her office, slammed the door shut, and
dialed Neil Stern. His secretary informed her that Stern
was in court.

"Oh, great! How did he manage to get some other
woman into court? Ask him to phone me as soon as he
comes in. No! Sooner."

Susan could hear herself breathing as she continued to
stare at the telephone. She knew she ought not to do it.
But she was human. She dialed the phone and Nora
answered.

"Dr. Carver's office."

"Nora? It's Susan Given."

"Hello, Ms. Given. How are—?"

"Is he there?"

"He's just finishing with a patient."

"I want to speak to him, Nora. Do you understand?"

"I really can't interrupt—"

"It's two minutes to three, Nora. He's got to come up
for air eventually. Shall I hold?"

"If you don't mind."

"He's kept me waiting this long." Susan stared at her
watch. How did it get to be three o'clock? Where do all
these days go? Her second line began to ring. "Could
you please get that, Gretchen? Gretchen! Where are you?"
Susan groaned and pressed the second line. "Given!"

"Mom?"

"Ivy! What a wonderful surprise. How did you know
you were the one person in the world I wanted to hear
from right now?"

"I'm in trouble."

"What sort of trouble?" She can't be pregnant. She's
only ten.

"We were playing up on the Turf." The Turf was an open-air, Astro Turf–covered surface located on the roof of Balmoral School. "And Dylan Chandler ran right past me and stepped on my foot. It really hurt. So I took my shoe off and whacked him hard. And now I'm in trouble."

"Are you under arrest?"

"Very funny, Mom."

"I'm sorry, angel. Are you in a detention room?"

"Huh?"

"Are you being punished?"

"Miss Slocum says that you have to decide on the punishment. She's sending me home with a letter. I'm sorry. But Dylan shouldn't have—"

"Ivy, we've talked about this before. You can't go around blithely— Oh, shit." Susan saw that the other light had gone off on her phone.

"What's wrong?"

"We'll talk about this after school." The telephone rang again. "I love you, Ivy." She hung up the second line and picked up the first. "Given."

"What do you want?" It was Hugh.

"You could say hello."

"What do you want?"

"Fine. We'll play it that way. How dare you send me a fax like that? How dare you send me any faxes? You are forbidden by law to harass—"

"Who is that man?"

"None of your goddamn business."

"Does he desport himself in the nude?"

"Are you sure you don't mean comport? Maybe display? Or are you just trying to sneak one past me? I trust you're more precise with your patients."

"Once again, Susan, your mockery is a smokescreen for your own insecurity."

"My insecurity? As opposed to yours?"

"I won't play word games, Susan, and I won't have my daughters—"

"My daughters, too."

228

"I won't have them exposed to your casual pickups strutting around the apartment with nothing on."

"Projection! Projection! Michael is a guest in my home. He has his own room. You are the one, Dr. Carver, who ought to have a turnstile installed with all that bimbo traffic you've got servicing you over there on Riverside Drive."

"That is slander."

"Really? What do you think a family court judge would make of Sigrid's role over there? Nanny or nooky? How 'healthy' an environment can it be when a father habitually seduces his daughters' piano and tennis tutors? Or maybe they didn't become tutors until *after* you seduced them? Frankly, I'm amazed how a man with a gherkin like yours manages to do it at all!" The dial tone was heard on the other end and Susan felt a sense of triumph. Cheap but triumphant. Where did she get that gherkin line from? Oh, yes. The Tesla transcripts. The telephone rang again and Susan pounced on it like a lioness: "What is it now?"

"Mom?"

"Polly?"

"You okay, Mom?"

"Yes. I just hung up on your father. Actually, he hung up on me."

"Oh, great. I'm the one he'll take it out on."

"Why?"

"Cuz that's his pattern. I'm not a shrink's daughter for nothing. It's okay. I'll be dead by the time he finds me. Or back in El Salvador. Only I can't speak a word of Spanish."

"Oh, Polly. I'm so sorry."

"About what?"

"That your number was cut."

"Says who?"

"It wasn't?" Susan had bought into another one of Lydia's lies. Maybe the "powerful friends" story was a line, too.

"I wish it was. I can't do this."

"It's just a song, darling."

"It's not just the song, Mom. It's the play! The play! We just had a dress rehearsal and I was awful. They couldn't hear me in the second row when I spoke and every note I sang was flat. I can't—I can't—I can't go on tonight."

"You have to."

"Why? The show'll be a lot shorter if I'm not in it."

"That's not the point. You wanted to be in this play. You auditioned for it. You must have beaten other girls out for the part. Doesn't that mean anything?"

"Be careful what you wish for; it may come true."

"What you're experiencing are opening-night nerves. They're a normal reaction. Adrenaline pumping overtime. I still get them before I go into court. You'll be fine."

"Really? I feel sick."

"Just relax." Susan's other line rang. "I've got to go, Polly. Will I see you before the show?"

"Oh, sure. You'll find me hanging in the shower when you get home."

"Very funny. Good luck, Polly."

"Don't say that. Michael says it's bad luck. You have to tell me to break something."

"Do you like Michael?"

"See you later."

Susan hung up and switched to the other line. "Given."

"Heyyyy, Susan. Long time, baby."

It took Susan a beat to recover from the shock of the greeting and to realize the caller was Manny Sanchez. On the run and out of his mind. "Hello, Manny."

"You recognize me?"

"You have a very distinctive voice." Susan stretched the phone as far as it would go, opened her office door, held her hand over the receiver, and called out hoarsely: "Gretchen! Alan! Somebody!" She wanted the call traced.

"Hey, Susan! Where you gone?"

"I'm right here, Manny. I've got someone on the other line. Why don't you let me get rid of them so we can have a nice long chat?"

"You think I'm stupid or somethin'? You just wanna trace the call. C'mon, Susan! Sometimes you get me so pissed off. Like the time in the hotel when you ordered the take-out. That was no goddamn restaurant. You called the cops."

"I was just doing my job, Manny. It was nothing personal."

"You such a bad liar, Susan. You lied to me about coming to visit in Montana."

"That's not true, Manny. I was hoping to visit. Then you escaped. That was not part of the bargain."

"I missed you, Susan."

"That's very sweet, Manny, but we didn't really know each other well enough for you to—"

"What you talkin'? We got real close that afternoon in the hotel. You told me all about your kids, your husband, and your boyfriend. Whassis name? Michael."

"Did I? I don't remember." Susan was now seated in front of her computer furiously tapping out an e-mail message to the Investigative Unit: "This is Susan Given in Asset Forfeiture. Have escaped fugitive on the telephone. Urgent that the call be traced. Don't know how much longer I can keep him on the—"

"You were jerking my chain that afternoon, weren't you?"

"I'm sorry, Manny. What did you say?" Susan's attention had been distracted by the e-mail message she was writing.

"I don't even know what I bother to phone you for."

"Where are you now?" Susan's heart was sinking. He was going to hang up before the call was traced. Doesn't anyone in the building read their e-mail? She stared towards her open door. Somebody please walk into the office and help me. "Would you like to have lunch, Manny? I'm positively famished."

"You just tryin' to trace the call. I know your tricks."

"Manny, I'm all alone here. I swear to you. I have no way to trace this call. Where are you?"

"Sometimes I lie in bed in Montana and think about you. I get real hard, Susan. I could see the veins bulging in my—"

"Manny, not on the phone."

"Do I disgust you?"

"No," lied Susan. "I've just never been one for phone sex. With me, it's the real thing or not at all."

"You are interested in the real thing?"

"Absolutely."

"If I come there—back to New York—would you—you know—the real thing?"

"I'd be waiting for you at the airport. Grand Central. The Port Authority. Wherever." Where the hell is everyone? I can't keep this routine up much longer. "I'd buy a new dress, Manny. Blue. I look good in blue. With a plunging neckline." Is this phone sex? Is this what I'm doing?

"Susan, I'm getting hard again."

"And I wouldn't wear any stockings. Well, maybe for you. But you'd have to take them off me, Manny. Slowly."

"Oh, I'd take them off real slow, Susan."

"I like it slow, Manny."

Sticking her head in the door at that moment, Elaine Morton managed to hear the last part of the conversation and muttered with embarrassment: "I'll come back later."

"No!" shouted Susan, as her colleague vanished from sight. "Don't leave!"

"What is it?" asked Manny. "You okay?"

"I'm sorry. I lost my concentration."

"Is somebody there?"

"No."

"You lying again."

"I'm all alone. I swear to you." Get the hell back here, Miss Piggy. Do something useful for once in your troublemaking life.

"Is Michael there?"

"Who?"

"You boyfriend. Is he with you?"

"Um . . . he's in the city. Why?"

"Everything was okay till he turned up again."

"I don't follow." What was he on? Sky-high. "Manny, you don't have to be concerned about Michael."

"Is that what you tell him about me?"

"I've never discussed you with him."

"Why not?"

"Because he only came here a few days ago. I've barely seen him."

"You lying again."

"I'm not. Please, Manny. Come to New York. We'll go dancing. You wanted to go dancing. Remember? You phoned me last time and talked about—"

"When I come to New York, Susan, I only do one thing. I'm gonna kill you boyfriend."

"Now, don't be immature, Manny. . . . Manny?" Dial tone.

Alan Becker walked into her office at that moment and held his arms up over his head like a triumphant toreador and announced: "Look, Ma. No crutches!"

"Where the hell have you been?" demanded Susan as she stormed out of her office, leaving a hopelessly confused Becker in her wake.

NIP STARED AT the huge blowups of the TV celebrities adorning the walls of the reception area on the twenty-third floor of the ultramodern United Cable Network Building on Avenue of the Americas.

"Who's that?" asked Nip, pointing at a photograph of an obese comedian shuffling a deck of cards.

The dour-faced receptionist looked up from her romance paperback and asked: "Were you addressing me?"

"No. I was just talkin' to you, sweetheart. You'll have to get somebody else to put a stamp on. Who's the fat boy?"

"Gordon Blake. He used to be on *Friday Frolic*. He has his own show now on UCN."

"Uh-huh. Do you watch it?"

"Not really."

"Wanna buzz Claypoole again?"

"Mr. Clayborne said he'd be out in a minute."

"Yeah, but I been waiting ten."

The double doors swung open five minutes later and a harassed Gen-Xer in short sleeves and horn-rimmed glasses searched the empty reception area as if he'd lost his date in Times Square on New Year's Eve. Finally his eyes fell on Nip.

"Mr. Roselli?"

"Mr. Clayborne?"

"No; I'm Glen Bailey, Mr. Clayborne's assistant. Would you follow me, please?"

The office Bailey led Nip into commanded a spectacular view of Central Park. Keith Clayborne, UCN's vice-president in charge of business affairs, bore an uncanny but unfortunate resemblance to the network's star comic Gordon Blake. Shoving a doughnut into his mouth while grunting repeated 'Uh-huhs' into the telephone, Clayborne held his palm up like a school crossing guard. Bailey and Nip froze in their tracks.

Finally Clayborne uttered something more than a grunt: "How much is MCA willing to cough up? . . . Uh-huh. And the BBC? . . . Uh-huh. So why should we do the deficit financing?" Clayborne's eyes darted back over in his visitors' direction and he pointed toward the sofa against the wall. "It won't fly. There's no way I can take those numbers upstairs. DOA. I promise you. Sorry."

The V.P. of business affairs put down the phone and stared blankly at Nip, now seated on the sofa. He turned to his assistant and asked: "Who?"

"Mr. Roselli," replied Bailey. "Osborne Paper Fiber."

"Gotcha," nodded Clayborne, licking the last bit of jelly from the corner of his mouth. "Glen? Phone Molnar's and see if I can get a table for tomorrow night. No. *Insist* on a table. For six."

"Isn't that early?"

"Six people, Glen. For eight."

"Gotcha," said Bailey, rushing away like the White Rabbit.

"So, Mr. Roselli, how can I help you?"

"I'm gonna help you," said Nip, getting up from the sofa and walking over to Clayborne's desk. "I'm gonna save you a shitload of money, Keith."

"How do you plan to do that?"

"Yer payin' three hundred fifty thousand dollars a year to have yer garbage removed."

"Who told you that?"

"I know things, Keith. I also know that the Teslas are bumping their rate up to four fifty and yer not happy about it."

"How do you know all this?" asked a mystified Keith Clayborne.

The information actually came from the last recordings Fusco had made before his savage beating. But Nip couldn't reveal this to the cable TV exec. Instead, he shrugged and said: "I got my ways. How'd you like to pay one fifty instead?"

"Did you say pay or weigh? I've got about as much chance to do either. What's your angle, Roselli?"

"No angle, Keith. We're a smaller operation lookin' for business and we can afford to make a lower bid. Not as many employees and—frankly—a helluva lot more honest than the people you've been dealin' with."

"But what happens to the Teslas? Won't they—?"

"What are they gonna do? Blow up yer building? Yer too big for them to take on. It's not like yer some Greek coffee shop or a chain of shoe stores. I'm talkin' three hundred G's, Keith. That's gotta look good in the ledger book. It's a cutthroat world we live in. Downsizing everywhere. Nobody's job is safe anymore. But a guy who can walk into a corporate meeting and say: 'Boys, I just saved us three hundred big ones.' He's gonna sleep great at night. Hell! He'll probably get a fat promotion. So whaddaya say, Keith? We in business or what?"

MICHAEL ROTH AND Ivy Carver were in a serious cooking frenzy in the kitchen.

"Are these pieces small enough?" asked Ivy, looking at the mound of green peppers on the chopping board.

"Perfect. Ready for the mushrooms?"

"Uh-huh. Can I stir them in the pan?"

"Absolutely. Where does your mom keep the cayenne?"

"Who?"

"Your mother."

"No, no. Did you say Cheyenne?"

"Cayenne. Red pepper. Don't you have any?"

"Let me see." In a second Ivy had scrambled up onto the kitchen counter with the lithe agility of Sabu climbing up the gigantic stone idol in *The Thief of Bagdad*. "Is this it?" asked the child as she waved a tin in Michael's face. At that moment Polly entered the kitchen like a somnambulist. Ivy stared at her with a long face and finally asked: "What's wrong with you?"

"Don't speak to me," said Polly slowly. "I am holding my center of gravity."

"You look like a zombie," said her little sister.

"Shh, Ivy. Shh. Leave her alone," said Michael. Then to Polly: "How do you feel?"

"Weird."

"But not scared?"

"No."

"Works, doesn't it?"

"What did you do to her?" asked a baffled Ivy. "Is she hypnotized?"

"No," said Michael. "She's just relaxed."

"Is my mom back yet?" asked Polly. "It's almost six. She promised she'd be home early and I'm going to have to leave for school."

The elevator could be heard coming up the shaft as the telephone rang. Ivy grabbed the phone as Polly rushed to meet the elevator.

"It's for you," said Ivy, holding the phone out to Michael.

"Hello?"

"Ikey-may," said Barry Praeger, using their second language, pig latin, in which he and Michael had communicated to each other since grade school.

"Arry-bay. What's up?"

"What smells so divine?" asked Susan, entering the

kitchen with her arm around Polly's waist. "Michael, what on earth have you—"

"He's teaching me to cook!" shouted Ivy, as if her entire family had just gone deaf. "With Cheyenne pepper."

Michael held a finger up to his lips to silence the child and listened intently to the information Barry was imparting to him on the other end of the line. Occasionally he would break the silence with comments like "You're kidding!" or "You're making this up." Susan watched him in rapt fascination.

Finally Michael said good-bye, hung up the receiver on the wall phone, and shook his head in disbelief.

"What happened?" asked Susan.

"The Praegers—"

"Are they getting divorced?"

"No. Nothing that simple. Cynthia has finally found a new client."

"How wonderful! This is just what she needs to turn her life around and—"

"Nick Tesla."

"You're kidding!"

"Not just Nick Tesla," said Michael, "but the entire cartel. She's going to revamp their image."

"You're making this up! How the hell did she land this account? Where did she—?"

"Wait, wait. We aren't up to the good part. They're having dinner tomorrow night. At the restaurant. Cynthia wants Nick to meet her husband."

"They've already met," said an edgy Susan, lighting up a cigarette.

"Tell me about it. There's no way Barry can set foot inside Tesla's. Particularly if the bereaved daughter is anywhere in the vicinity. She'll jump Barry on the spot. I've lived through this before. He's catnip to the ladies."

"So what's Barry going to do?" asked Susan.

"That's why he phoned me," replied Michael. "I got him into this mess. Now, he wants me to get him out of it."

"Sorry to interrupt," said Polly, "but I've got to go now. I need to be alone before the show. Concentrate. Find my center of gravity."

"Do you know what she's talking about?" Susan asked Michael.

"Absolutely."

"Aren't you going to eat anything first, Polly?"

"Can't," replied Polly. "Noives."

"Break your legs," said Ivy, walking her big sister to the elevator.

"This case is getting too close to home," said Susan, after the girls had gone downstairs in the elevator. Then she brought Michael up to date on the threat from Lydia and Manny's latest phone call. Finally she said: "I blame this all on Nancy Drew."

"I don't think I know the lady."

"Of course not," replied Susan. "You were too busy with the Hardy Boys to appreciate a female detective—"

"Ohhh! That Nancy Drew."

"I used to get one of her books for my birthday every year. I wanted to be her so badly."

"Be careful what you wish for—"

"It may come true. That's what Polly said on the phone before. I knew you two would hit it off."

"How soon are you moving on these garbage guys?"

"Not soon enough. Fusco's accident set the criminal end of the case back several—"

Ivy returned from her ride down to the lobby with Polly and solemnly reported: "I think someone's watching the building."

"Other than the Good Fairy?" asked Susan.

"I'm serious, Mom. Polly and I have both noticed him."

"What does he look like?" asked Michael.

"Please," said Susan, sotto voce, "don't encourage these little dramas."

"He's big!" said Ivy, holding her hands high and wide above her head. "Good-looking. With black curly hair. And huge muscles."

Susan and Michael's eyes locked together. They knew exactly who Ivy was talking about.

"When did you first see him?" asked Susan, kneeling down beside her daughter.

"Couple of weeks ago. When I got off the bus from school."

"Why didn't you tell me?"

Ivy shrugged. Then: "Is he the guy that calls at night? The one who doesn't speak?"

"Who's that?" asked Michael.

"Before you arrived," said Susan dismissively.

"Which means he knows I'm here. That's why he stopped phoning."

"Not necessarily," said Susan. "Was there anything at the cemetery that gave you the idea he knew you?"

"Who? Who?" asked Ivy.

"No one," replied Susan. "It's just business. Go on and change for Polly's show."

"Aren't we going to eat?" asked her youngest daughter.

"Change first. Hurry up."

Ivy dashed up the stairs. Susan walked into the living room and over to the window, where she stared out pensively at the city.

"What is it?" asked Michael.

"Walter Gerhardt. Tony Fusco. Ab Rosenthal. Now, me. Or, worse, my kids."

46

THEY WERE JUST getting up to his favorite part—an enraged Lee Marvin tosses the pot of scalding coffee into Gloria Grahame's face—when the telephone rang. He pressed the Pause button on the VCR and answered the phone.

"Hello?"

"Junior?"

"Oh, hi, Pop. Whassup?"

"We got a problem."

"Nothing you can't handle, Pop."

"Stop kissin' my ass. We just lost UCN. The business affairs guy just called Dino and said he's not renewing their contract."

"Who'd they go with? Carlucci? DeFillipo?"

"If they did, there'd be no problem. Nah, they made a deal with Osborne Paper."

"I thought we put 'em outta business."

"Apparently not. Roselli's been running around town the last two days tryin' to steal all our spots."

"That old man? He can hardly walk."

"Not Gaetano. His nephew Dominic."

"Where the hell did he come from?"

"Who the fuck cares? I want you to go have a talk with them, Junior."

"It'll be a pleasure."

"No, no, no. Yer not listening to me. I know all about yer pleasure. I really want you to *talk* to them. No rough stuff. Not with a grand jury downtown. All we need now are criminal charges and that pain-in-the-ass Given broad'll padlock the restaurant and grab everything else that ain't nailed down."

"Why don't you let me take care of her once and for all, Pop?"

"What are ya fuckin' deaf? I just said no more rough stuff. Don't they give you a good enough workout at that fancy gym of yours?"

"So whaddaya want me to do?" Junior was massaging his temples now and praying the dull ache wouldn't turn into a migraine.

"Go see the Rosellis. Be charming. Tell 'em they've neglected to join the Association. Probably an oversight. But we'll meet with 'em and get it all straightened out."

"What if they say no?"

"They've already lost a truck and a driver, kid. With the penalty they're gonna have to pay us, they can't afford to lose anything else. Now, get goin'."

Junior hung up the phone and lurched toward the bathroom to get a fistful of aspirins. This migraine was going to be a killer. Goddamn his father. Goddamn Rosenthal.

Where the hell had the shrink vanished to? How dared he disappear like that? Didn't he have a responsibility to his patients? Hadn't he sworn a fucking oath? Junior had been tempted to visit the doctor's wife and grill her as to her husband's whereabouts but figured it wasn't a case-ace move to make.

Junior's attention drifted over to the TV, where Gloria Grahame's horrified face was frozen on the screen. He liked Gloria Grahame. Great mouth. What had she said to Glenn Ford that cracked him up? "I've been rich and I've been poor. Believe me, rich is better." He'd have to finish the movie later. Walking over to the closet, he selected an Ermenegildo Zegna cashmere sports jacket from his rack of expensive oversized designer clothes.

Then the doorman buzzed him to say that the police were in the lobby and were on their way up to his apartment. A minute later two plainclothes detectives were knocking at his front door.

"You guys got a search warrant?" asked Junior, whose laconic Mitchum wannabe delivery was much closer to Stallone.

"You got something to hide?" asked the detective. "We just have a few questions. Can we come in?"

"I'm just goin' out."

"We won't be long," said the second detective, walking into the living room without asking permission to enter. "Nice view."

"Thanks."

The second detective stared at the crammed bookcases running up to the ceiling without a book on them—only videotapes.

"That's some video collection. How many you got?"

"Three, four hundred." Junior shrugged.

"Lotta gangster pictures," said the second detective, studying the titles printed on the spines of the boxes.

"I got war pictures, too," said Junior defensively.

"Heyy! I like gangster pictures," said the second detective. "Ever seen *White Heat*?"

"Lots of times."

" 'Top of the world, Ma. Top of the world.' Remember the part where Cagney kicks the chair out from under his wife? Always cracks me up. And what about *Kiss Tomorrow Goodbye*? That's even more violent. For an old movie. I mean, for *real* violent you got to watch Peckinpah."

"I got *The Getaway* and *Killer Elite* there," said Junior, pointing to the bottom shelf.

"Where were you nine o'clock on the night of September eighteenth?" asked the first detective abruptly, referring to the night Walter Gerhardt was murdered.

"Ask Cardinal Corcoran," said Junior cockily.

"Funny guy," grunted the first detective.

"Who's bein' funny?" asked Junior, walking over to the wall behind the big-screen TV and removing the framed photo of His Eminence surrounded by the entire Tesla clan the night of Nick's testimonial dinner.

"See?" asked Junior. "See that clock on the wall? Nine-fifteen. That's where I was. The Waldorf Astoria Hotel."

"Do you mind if we borrow this?"

"Heyy," replied a superaccommodating Junior, as he removed the photograph from the frame. "You can keep it. We got lots of copies."

The younger Tesla escorted the two policemen to the front door urging them to drop in anytime. Once they were gone, he removed a vial of cocaine from his pants pocket, shook the white powder out on the back of his hand, and snorted it deeply into his lungs.

Am I smart or am I smart? thought Junior. Didn't I tell Pop not to worry? He thought that fuckin' clock would do me in. That's cuz he doesn't know shit about computers. I coulda taken him outta the fuckin' picture and nobody woulda believed he'd ever been there.

Nick Tesla, Jr., took a deep breath of triumph and realized, a second later, that his migraine had magically vanished.

THE NEW AMSTERDAM School was located on Seventy-sixth Street between York and East End Avenues. By 7:45 that evening the foyer of the school was filled with well-heeled parents sharing the kind of excitement and expectation one usually associated with a Broadway opening. The auditorium doors were still locked because of last-minute production problems and this only added to the captive audience's heightened sense of anticipation.

Susan, Ivy, and Michael arrived at the school late and

in a minor state of panic following a fruitless attempt to locate Zoe, another of the youngest Carver girl's hamsters, that had vanished inside the apartment's heating ducts.

"I'm sure we'll find her," said Susan, repeating by rote for the hundredth time the phrase of futile reassurance as they entered the foyer. She was still agitated by the notion that Junior Tesla might be out there somewhere, lying in wait for her family.

"I can't even find Zoe to give her a proper burial," said Ivy tragically. Then: "A dog wouldn't get lost."

"Other things would happen," replied Susan. "There is no dog in our future."

Ivy turned to Michael and beamed. "Do you like dogs?"

"I'm just visiting," said Michael.

"I don't think so," said Ivy. Before anyone could ask the child what she meant by that cryptic remark, she pointed across the foyer and exclaimed; "There's Sigrid. And Dad."

"I thought he wasn't coming tonight," grumbled Susan.

Michael stared in disbelief in Hugh Carver's direction, then began moving toward him as if by enchantment.

"Where are you going?" asked Susan. "What—?" When Michael didn't answer, she followed after him reluctantly with Ivy in tow.

"Annabel? Is it really you?" Michael was staring at the rail-thin, black-swathed Swede, but she did not reply. "Annabel?"

"I think you've made a mistake," replied Hugh in his loftiest tones. Then he turned to Sigrid and asked: "Do you know this man?"

Sigrid seemed to be translating the question from English to Swedish then back again. Finally she shook her head from side to side.

"Three years ago," said Michael. "Los Angeles."

"Ja. You must have made mistake," said Sigrid, trying to end his persistence. Then she turned in bewilderment to Hugh and asked: "Is this is some sort of yoke?"

"What is with that accent?" asked Michael.

"You heard the lady," said Hugh, straightening up and pulling his shoulders back. "Now, would you please leave us alone?"

Susan arrived at Michael's side and was shocked to see Hugh had put on twenty pounds since their last encounter.

"Don't you know this man?" Hugh had misinterpreted Susan's reaction to his ever-increasing rotundity. Michael's glance went back and forth from him to Susan. Finally the light bulb went on.

"Hugh?"

Susan sighed and nodded. Michael held his hand out to the psychiatrist, who ignored the gesture and, instead, clamped a plump, proprietary hand on Sigrid's arm. "Shall we take our seats?"

"Hello, Dad." Ivy stared at her father with her arms folded across her chest. "Remember me?"

"Sorry, Ivy." Then he stared at her mother and intoned: "Rudeness is contagious."

"What does that mean?" asked Susan.

"My lawyer will contact your lawyer tomorrow."

Michael continued to stare at Sigrid in disbelief until the Swedish girl pried herself loose from Hugh's grasp and whined: "I just got one of my migraines, Hughie. I feel terrible. Can't we see the show another night?"

"Of course, darling. Good night, Ivy. Please explain to your sister." And, purposely ignoring Susan and Michael, Hugh Carver escorted the stricken Swede out of the school building.

"Talk about rudeness!" bristled Susan. "His behavior is beyond the pale. He didn't even introduce us to his mistress."

"You know Sigrid," said Ivy.

"Only from her police blotter," replied Susan.

"Annabel has a record here?"

"I was joking," said Susan. "Why do you call her Annabel? Her name is Sigrid."

"Not in L.A. I'm sure that's Annabel Dwyer."

"An old flame?"

"What's an old flame?" asked Ivy.

"An old flame is someone you'd like to forget," said Michael, "until some other woman forces you to remember."

"Your checkered past," purred Susan.

"You guys are talking funny," said Ivy. "Come on. Let's get seats before they're all gone."

"Where do I know Hugh from?" asked Michael, moments later as the trio sat together inside the auditorium waiting for the show to begin. "His face is so familiar. Was he ever an actor?"

"All his life."

"No, professionally. Did he ever live in England?"

"Not that I know of. Why?"

"Because I know this guy. I'm sure of it. Somewhere. Way, way back. It'll drive me nuts."

"Please, Michael. We can't allow Hugh to drive both of us crazy." Susan looked around the audience and smiled at several parents whom she knew. She was surprised that Lydia had not arrived yet for her son Ethan's big night. The lights started to dim as she whispered: "Was she really an old flame? Annabel?"

"I'll tell you later," replied Michael as the school orchestra struck up the familiar opening chords of Richard Rodgers's overture. "Are you thrilled?"

"I would be," sighed Susan, "if I could get Junior Tesla out of my mind. What if he really *is* stalking us?"

"Shh," said Michael, nodding toward Ivy, who was rocking back and forth in her seat with anticipation.

Susan snapped out of her despondency the minute Polly stepped out onto the stage. Ivy applauded her big sister rapturously until Susan finally grabbed hold of the kid's hands and pressed them together like the pages of a hymnal.

"But it's Polly!"

"Later," whispered her mother. "At the end."

Ivy made a face, then sat on her hands.

Miss Hutchins, the director, had wisely decided to do away with Polly's blond, braided wig, thus enabling the girl to be herself (which wasn't as ludicrous as it might have been, because the other Von Trapp children were African-American, Jewish, Japanese, and a token WASP). What amazed Susan most about her daughter's performance was Polly's heretofore unrevealed ability to hit every note miraculously on key.

"What did you do to her?" whispered Susan sotto voce into Michael's ear. "The girl is tone deaf." He held a finger up to her lips to silence her. Making sure Ivy's attention was glued to the stage, Susan popped his finger into her mouth and sucked on it.

It was following the 'Do, Re, Mi' number, however, that Susan became convinced she had cracked under the strain of her public and private life. The children had just finished trooping joyfully about the stage under Fräulein Maria's tutelage when they were interrupted by the presence of Captain Von Trapp.

Granted Ethan Culberg was huge for his age and his size was one of the reasons he was cast in the role of the martinet. But the imposing figure Susan stared at on the New Amsterdam School stage was a veritable titan. And he was staring directly at her. Ominously. Menacingly.

This was impossible. How had Junior Tesla managed to squeeze into Ethan Culberg's costume? Why hadn't any of the kids on stage noticed the switch in players? Polly, of all people, should have recognized—

"Are you okay, Mom?" whispered Ivy.

"Why do you ask?"

"Cuz you're sweating."

Susan raised a hand to her forehead and felt a patina of perspiration. "I've got to get some water." She rose in a crouching position and sneaked up the aisle while Junior Tesla continued to bellow out commands to his children.

There was no one in the lobby except a security guard, who was wearing a uniform one size too small and pinching a homemade chocolate chip cookie from the sweets table that had been set up for intermission.

"Where is the water fountain?" asked Susan.

"Want some lemonade?" asked the security guard in a thick Bronx accent, holding up a Dixie cup with a largesse out of proportion to his position. "It's pretty good."

"No, thanks. I just want some water."

"Over there. In the corner."

Susan nodded her thanks, walked over to the fountain, and turned the handle. I must be dehydrated, she thought. What other possible explanation could there be for that hallucination? Breathe deeply. Deeper. More water. Relax. What was that center of gravity thing Michael had taught Polly? Maybe it will work for me.

As she swallowed more water, she could hear the security guard ask someone else: "Can I help you, ma'am?"

Then an all-too-familiar, intoxicated voice replied: "I don't need help from any more fucking cops tonight."

"Have you got some kind of business here?"

"Yeah. I'm the school commissioner. Okay, asshole?"

"I can't let you inside."

"Try and stop me."

Susan looked up from the water fountain and saw the security guard holding up a hand in a vain attempt to restrain Lydia Culberg, drenched in mink, from entering the auditorium. Susan dashed across the tile floor and was at her boss's side a second later.

"Why aren't you inside?" demanded Lydia, her breath ablaze with Bell's whiskey. "Is it that bad?"

"No, it's delightful. I just needed a drink . . . of water."

"I've been in the bag myself tonight. Fucking car wasn't ready at six. So I went around the corner for a quick shooter. Six-thirty those fucking Arabs were still messing around under the hood. What kinda name is Farhi for an auto mechanic? So I went back for another. Goddamn thing wasn't ready till seven-thirty."

"Could y'ask her to keep her voice down?" asked the

security guard in a hushed voice, pointing toward the auditorium.

"Why don't youse go back to the Grand Concourse?" Lydia asked the guard. "I'm talkin' here. When they tore down the Berlin Wall, they should have stuck it back up outside the Bronx."

"Watch yer mouth, lady!"

"Yeah?"

"Yeah."

"Yeah?"

"Please," said Susan, steering Lydia away from the harassed security guard. "Let's all calm down."

"I'm calm!" said Lydia. "Now. You shoulda seen me when I hit the fuckin' car."

"Where was this?"

"About two blocks from the garage."

"Was anyone hurt?"

"Nah. The car was parked. Nobody was in it. But I couldn't start mine again. Goddamn Arabs. They see a redhead and all they wanna do is fuck with her and her car."

"Did you report it? The accident?"

"I didn't have to, Susan. The cops were all over me like baby oil on a horny nun. Try and find one when there's a fuckin' felony in process. No way! But have a little accident with your car—I let 'em have it. Threatened to have all their goddamn badges. I was gonna call Haskell but then I remembered . . . So they towed the car away, gave me a summons, and then the bastards wouldn't give me a lift to the fucking school."

"Did they charge you with drunk driving?"

"Let 'em fucking try!"

The auditorium doors opened at that moment and Michael slipped out, looked around, and spotted Susan. "You okay?"

"Who's that?" asked Lydia.

"Michael," answered Susan. Then too hastily. "You met him at the Plaza."

"And he makes you blush to talk about him. I guess you're human after all, Susan. Interesting."

"I've got to go back inside, Lydia."

"Me, too. Kid'll wonder what happened to me. How is he? Any good?"

"Ethan?" Susan didn't dare mention the boy had been replaced by Junior Tesla. No, no. That was just her mini breakdown. Ethan was definitely up there. "He has great presence."

"At close to two hundred pounds, I should hope so. Hope the poor kid doesn't croak like his old man." By this time the two women had arrived back at the sweets table and Lydia flashed her best Vegas showgirl smile at the security guard and asked: "Is that coffee?"

"Yeah," replied the guard warily.

"Be a doll and pour me one, willya?"

EARLY THAT EVENING Nip Regan sat in his office at Osborne Paper Fiber, poring over the company's ledgers and trying to absorb as much information as he could. Should anyone question him about the ins and outs of the carting business, he wanted to be the last word on the state of the industry.

The phone rang and a familiar voice asked, "Is this Dominic Roselli?"

"Becker, is that you?"

"Hey, Mr. Roselli, how did it go today?"

"I finally nailed an account, Becker. Big time. United Cable Network."

"Congratulations, Dominic. You might want to think about staying on there full-time."

"Very funny. It's only a matter of time before the goons come knocking at my door."

"Exactly, Nip—I mean Dominic. Hopefully the goon will be Junior Tesla himself."

"Yeah. I owe him one for The Fuss. Any news on him from the clinic?"

"Dr. Veda phoned yesterday. Tony's still in a coma. But I spent all afternoon listening to him—his tapes. Those are really nasty people you're involved with."

"Tell me about it, Becker."

"So far they're looking at enterprise corruption, grand larceny by extortion, coercion, falsifying business records, combination in restraint of trade, and conspiracy to commit all these crimes. Not to mention possible arson charges and first-degree murder for Junior. Of course, the irony of all this is we can't get them for violating the Donnelly Law."

"Antitrust?" asked Nip, lighting up an unfiltered Camel. "These guys? No way. The only law they obey is: Thou shalt not compete. If one of them steals a customer from another one, they pay. They'll do anything to cover their asses for fear of being charged with violating antitrust— Wait a second, Becker. I think somebody just came in. Lemme call you back."

Nip replaced the receiver and heard a voice calling out: "Roselli! Yo, Roselli!" He stepped out of his office and walked into the reception area, where Junior Tesla was about to drop-kick a wastepaper basket down the length of the building.

Christ! thought Nip, staring at the demented titan looming large in front of him. Look at the size of this guy. He's bulging right out of that cashmere sports jacket. What the hell! Y'only live once. The undercover cop hunched his shoulders, ran his hands through his greasy dyed black hair, and assumed his best "fuck you" attitude.

"You got a problem?" asked Nip, staring into Junior's eyes without blinking.

"Where's Roselli?" asked the younger Tesla, thrown by Nip's carefree reaction.

"It's after office hours, pal. You got business here, come back in the morning."

"I got business now. With Gaetano Roselli."

"My uncle's gone home. He don't feel so good. Any business you got, you can talk it over wit' me. I'm Dominic Roselli."

"Oh, you're the nephew! I heard about you. Busy boy. You did a dumb thing today, nephew."

"Oh, yeah? What did I do . . . sonny?"

"Wha'd you call me?"

"Yer Junior Tesla, aintcha?"

"I'm Nicolo Tesla Junior till I tell you otherwise."

"Got any smelling salts? I think I'm gonna faint."

"What have you got, Roselli? A death wish?"

"You gonna make me dead, Mr. Tesla? Just 'cause I stole a spot from you?"

"So you admit it?"

"Ever heard of free enterprise?"

"Not in the carting business, pal. Yer gonna pay for that spot. And yer gonna pay a penalty."

Nip was kicking himself. Every bone in his body told him that the egocentric younger Tesla was on the verge of spilling some very important dirt that Ms. Gee would love to have on tape. Only problem: the recorder was locked in a drawer in his office.

"Don't I know you from somewheres?" asked Junior, staring hard at Nip, certain he'd met him before.

"Why? You gay?"

"Want me to tear yer fuckin' head off?"

"That ain't no answer."

"No, I'm not," said Junior.

"Me neither. So I guess y'aren't tryin' to pick me up. Was y'ever an altar boy?"

"What the hell kinda question is that?"

"I never knew a Catholic who wasn't."

"Yer a weird motherfucker, Roselli. Anyone ever told you that?"

"All my life. How 'bout you, Junior? I'll bet you got a helluva story to tell. Wanna have a drink and tell me it? And maybe you'll tell me about my penalty. I owe the library a lotta money, too."

"I *do* know you, Roselli. Don't I?"

"Maybe it was the Mr. Universe Competition. You think about it while I go pee."

"Make it fast."

"Hey! I drink a lot of water. It takes time. I'll meet you in the parking lot."

Nip removed the recording device from his desk, popped inside the bathroom, removed his shirt, and proceeded to affix the device to his back.

Outside, Junior Tesla tapped his foot impatiently and gazed toward the spot where he had beaten Walter Gerhardt to death. Stupid jerk! Wha'd he have to go be a hero for? Junior turned his head in the other direction and, in his mind's eye, he could still see Sanchez running away into the darkness. Goddamn Ricky Ricardo retard! Sanchez would have to stop running one day and, when he did, Junior would be there to shut the squealer up once and for all.

Emerging from the building, Nip discovered a pensive Junior leaning his overdeveloped body against the side of the Ferrari.

"Nice wheels," said Nip admiringly as he zipped up his leather jacket and walked toward the car.

"Thanks," said Junior. "Hop in."

"After you."

"No, you first."

"You sure about that?" asked Nip. "Aintcha ever heard: First is first, second is nobody?"

"Hey! That's from *The Big Combo*," said an impressed Junior.

"Sure," replied Nip casually, happy that he had immersed himself in Junior's file with the same eye for detail as Osborne Paper's. The muscle-bound killer was a freak for old gangster movies. "Mr. Brown said that."

"Richard Conte, right? Didja ever see *New York Confidential?* He played Charlie Lupo—"

"No; he didn't. Broderick Crawford played Lupo. Conte played Nick Magellan."

"Right, right," said Junior, nodding appreciatively. "I knew that. My mind was goin' too quick. Remember the scene in the barber shop? When he rubbed the guy out?"

Junior revved up the motor and drove away from the scene of the murder he had committed a few months earlier. He couldn't believe Roselli liked these old pictures as much as he did. Maybe they could be friends. Watch movies together. The possibility of a relationship temporarily erased his concern about where the hell he knew this wacko from.

As the Ferrari roared out of the parking lot, a homeless man lying next to a dumpster stirred from slumber. The noise of the car's motor had awakened him. It was the same sound he had described to that woman from the District Attorney's Office a few weeks ago.

THE CURTAIN HAD come down to tumultuous applause at the New Amsterdam School. The parents waited impatiently in the foyer for their thespian offspring to appear. Polly emerged first, in full makeup and radiating a self-confidence Susan had never seen before as her fellow players congratulated her yet again on her performance.

"It worked!" bubbled Polly when she saw Michael. "I hit the notes."

"Brava." Michael grinned.

"Did you hear me, Mom? It was like magic."

"You were really good," said Ivy, who held a bag of Sour Power—the ultimate accolade—up to her sister. "Dad was here."

"Where?" asked Polly, spinning around a full 360 degrees in panic. "Where?"

"He didn't make it inside," replied her kid sister. "Michael scared him away."

"That's not true," said Michael. "It had nothing to do with me. It was Sigrid."

"What did she do now?" groaned Polly. "Not another migraine?"

"How did you know?" asked Susan.

"She always gets them when she doesn't want to deal with something. So they didn't see the show?"

"They're coming tomorrow."

"You hungry?" asked Michael.

"Starved!" answered Polly.

"That's what I figured. How 'bout I take you all to Petaluma?"

"Oh, Michael, you don't have to—"

"Yes, I do, Susan. It's your daughter's first first night. It's a great tradition. Come on."

The four of them left the building a second before the foyer was shattered by Ethan Culberg's bellowing: "Why do you have to put on a fucking show for everyone?"

A hush fell over the foyer as everyone turned to stare at Lydia Culberg with her arm wrapped around her son's beefy shoulder.

"I'm not putting on a show, sweetie," gushed Lydia, smiling at all the parents staring at her. "You were fabulous. The best thing on that stage."

Ethan wrenched loose from his mother's grip and wheeled around on her. "So where were you for the first act?"

"I was there," lied Lydia. "In the back. I moved down at intermission. . . ."

"You were in some bar, weren't you?"

"Of course not, sweetie."

"Bullshit! I can smell liquor on your breath. Who were you with this time? The Mayor? The Governor? Who was more important than me—besides everyone?"

"I had an accident, Ethan. It wasn't my fault."

"It's never your fault, is it? Why did you bother coming at all? I hate you." Ethan stormed away from his mother and rushed out of the foyer and onto Seventy-sixth Street toward the East River.

Having missed this little contretemps, Susan continued to lavish praise on Polly as they walked with Michael and Ivy toward First Avenue. She was surprised when someone tapped her on the shoulder and she turned around to stare at a breathless Lydia, asking, "Have you seen Ethan?"

"No. But he was just marvelous in the play. He has such a good voice, Lydia. I had no idea. You must be so proud."

When her boss did not reply, Susan foolishly thought her critical kudos might have paved the way to come in under Lydia's radar and get the Deputy District Attorney to rethink her position on the Teslas in light of the various Junior sightings.

"What, are you fucking nuts?" asked a wild-eyed Lydia, still reeling from her only child's punishing rebuke. "Don't you ever stop? My poor kid may have drowned himself by now and you're still rattling on about the Teslas? Didn't I tell you this afternoon to lay off them?"

"I just thought—"

"I don't want you thinking any more, Ms. D.A. Your thinking is proving counterproductive to the effectiveness of our office. I've got a mountain of complaints lodged against you—"

"From whom?"

"Stop questioning me, Susan! This is something your

poise and your pearls and your butter-wouldn't-melt-in-my mouth attitude won't get you out of. You're on suspension, sweetie. Okay? Pending an investigation."

"On what charges?" demanded Susan, her entire body vibrating with rage.

"How about gross incompetence and mismanagement of your unit for starters?"

"That is an outrageous—"

"Just don't show up tomorrow. Okay? And get yourself a good lawyer. You're gonna need one."

Lydia then draped her mink coat across her shoulders and marched toward the East River with the regal detachment of Catherine the Great having served the death notice on half a million peasants.

KEVIN MOORE ROLLED over in bed and reached an arm out to stroke his wife affectionately. All he got was a fistful of goosedown pillow.

"Janie? . . . Where are you, honey?"

No reply. Kevin raised his left eyelid warily and stared at the bedside clock: 11:15. She had crawled into bed with him at 10:30. He was certain of that. Where could she have gone to?

"Janie?"

He put on his bathrobe and instinctively went to check on Stella's safety. His daughter wasn't in her room. The chiseled-featured commercial artist took a deep breath, then heard whispers coming from the living room.

Seconds later he entered the room and found Stella

curled up in her mother's lap on the sofa, staring at a glossy eight-by-ten photograph.

"What's going on?" asked Kevin.

"Stella had a nightmare," said Janie.

Kevin walked over to the sofa and stroked the little girl's hair. "You okay, honey?" Stella nodded, then he said to his wife: "I didn't hear her."

"You didn't hear my heart pounding with ecstasy either, Tarzan. You're the only man in the world who takes double espressos to get to sleep."

"Was this my night to get lucky?"

"Every night's your night"—grinned Janie—"if you'd only stay awake."

"What are you guys talking about?" asked Stella.

"L'amour, my darling daughter. The stuff that dreams and babies are made of."

"Why don't you come back to bed?" asked Kevin, feeling familiar stirrings, as he stared at his violet-eyed, dark-haired wife. "I'm awake now."

"We haven't solved the puzzle yet," said Stella.

"What puzzle's that, honey?" asked Kevin.

"Junior Tesla's alibi," said Janie, holding up the eight by ten of the Tesla clan and Cardinal Corcoran. "I've been getting static from upstairs about the Gerhardt murder. Ray Murphy ran a piece the other day about Nancy Gerhardt's poor little baby coming into the world at the end of the year with its father's murder still unsolved. It's not unsolved; it's just unproved."

"You're sure Tesla did it?" asked Kevin, examining the photograph.

"As sure as I know what's under your bathrobe, Tarzan. I sent two homicide detectives around to his apartment to question Junior this afternoon. All they did was bring me back his alibi. The coroner said Gerhardt was murdered between nine and nine-thirty. There's the clock on the wall at the Waldorf, and it reads nine-fifteen."

"So why are they drinking brandy?" asked Kevin, pointing to the people in the photograph.

"What?!"

"There are brandy snifters on that table."

Janie snatched the photograph back from her husband. "Ahh! That brilliant artist's eye for detail. I knew there was a reason I married you, Moore, besides the obvious. Brandy snifters! Brilliant. A dead giveaway. I mean, who drinks brandy at nine-fifteen?"

"People who've been drinking it all evening," replied Kevin. "People who had dinner at six. What time did this affair begin?"

"Wait, wait, wait! You just solved the puzzle. You can't back away from—"

"You're not going to get a conviction because there are two brandy snifters on the table. You're trying to prove opportunity. Correct? How long was the window of opportunity for Junior Tesla to—?"

"Am I stupid!" said Janie, leaping up from the sofa and carrying the photograph over to the antique writing desk on the opposite side of the room.

"What is it, Mommy?" asked Stella. "Did you finally solve the puzzle?"

"Shh! Shh! Don't anybody speak," said Janie, rummaging through the desk. "Where the hell is it, Kevin?"

"What?"

"The magnifying glass that was in here. The big one."

"I haven't seen it."

"Relax! I found it." Janie let the magnifying glass glide across the photograph as if she were a rainmaker seeking water with a divining rod. Then: "Yesss!" She howled with triumphant laughter. "Remind me to go to St. Pat's and light a candle tomorrow."

"What is it?" asked Kevin.

"I was looking at the wrong timepiece."

51

ONCE SHE HAD finally put the children to bed, Susan Given went downstairs to the kitchen and poured herself a glass of chilled white wine.

Ten minutes later, Michael Roth entered the kitchen in bare feet and pajama bottoms, carrying a weather-beaten copy of Cornell Woolrich's *The Bride Wore Black*.

"Where is your top?" whispered a shocked Susan, putting down her glass as she sat at the kitchen counter and staring out at the darkened skyline. "What if the kids see you?"

"The kids are in bed. Where you should be, too. With me."

"I can't sleep."

"Lydia?"

Susan nodded her head. "She spoiled Polly's opening night, that's for sure. I wasn't much fun at Petaluma."

"I don't think the girls noticed. Ivy was too busy idolizing her sister at the restaurant and Polly was . . . Polly was a star."

Susan stared silently into her glass of wine. Then: "Lydia's never been that venomous before. She put me on suspension."

"She's a lush, Susan. I'll bet she doesn't remember a thing when she wakes up tomorrow. Come to bed."

"I'm too wired. I'd never be able to sleep."

"What can I do to help?"

"Tell me a story. No, no. Tell me about Sigrid. Who is she really, Michael?"

"When I first met Annabel, she was a stand-in for Co-lette Cooke."

"Who on earth is Colette Cooke?"

"You're kidding! Colette was Playmate of the Year in nineteen eighty-something. Then she hosted *Friday Frolic* a couple of times and was very funny. I did a movie with her in Canada and—"

"My god, Michael! She wasn't one of your wives?"

"No, no, no. Although she led me to believe it wouldn't be a bad idea down the road. Anyhow, she's married to a big Washington lawyer now. What the hell's his name? He's partners with Dwight Pelham."

"Mitchell Levenstein? OICB Bank?"

"Yeah. Do you know him?"

"The bank is under federal investigation. Money laundering. What does Sigrid—Annabel have to do with all this?"

"Nothing. She was Colette's stand-in on a couple of shows. Till she went to work for Sonja Carvell."

"Another name that means nothing—"

"Ever heard of Heidi Fleiss?"

"The madam? Yes."

"Sonja was in the same business. Annabel was one of her girls."

"You're joking!"

"One of Sonja's favorites, as a matter of fact. One of her *trusted* favorites. Until Sonja gave Annabel a hundred G's to deposit in the bank for her one afternoon. That was the last time anyone ever saw Annabel again. Until this evening."

"You're making all this up. It's from that Woolrich man's book, isn't it?" asked Susan pointing to the tattered copy of *The Bride Wore Black* lying on the counter. "Was Sigrid . . . Annabel ever formally charged with the theft in California?"

"How's a madam going to press charges against one of her top girls? Sonja told me she hired private dicks to track her down for a few months but—"

"You know this madam?"

"She was an actress, too."

"What kind of a life were you leading out there, Michael?"

"Eventful. That's how I write so much."

"If Hugh ever knew the truth . . ."

"That's your call, Susan. It might come in handy one of these days. But I'd like to know just one thing before we call it a night."

"What?"

"How did you ever hook up with Hugh Carver?"

"Please. We'll be up all night trying to solve that riddle. Don't think I haven't pondered the mystery for years. He's an enigma. When I first met him, he was a double for Gregory Peck. Now . . . he's just double."

Michael howled with laughter until Susan clapped a hand over his mouth and reminded him in hushed tones that the children were asleep upstairs.

The telephone rang.

"It's eleven-thirty," said Susan.

"Do you know where *your* children are?"

"Who could be phoning at—?"

"Hello?" Susan said.

A familiar female voice asked: "Were you doing it?"

"Very funny, Janie. What if this had been a wrong number?" asked Susan in mock outrage.

"C'mon, Greenwich. Fess up. You were doing it. That's why you're so pissed."

"I'm not even in bed, Janie. I'm in the kitchen."

"Where's Michael?"

"Sitting beside me. What's up?"

"I think I've cracked the Gerhardt murder! I just can't prove it. I've got a photograph of the whole Tesla family with Cardinal Corcoran at the Waldorf the night Gerhardt was bumped off. The clock on the wall reads nine-fifteen. That's Junior's alibi. But the Cardinal's Rolex—the one Nick Senior gave him for his birthday—reads eleven-fifteen. Don't you love it? Nick Tesla's gift is gonna put his own son in the gas chamber. Course, I'm not sure how we go into court with all this. But Kevin's got a friend does art direction for HBO. He might know how to prove the picture was doctored. Then—"

"Janie?"

"Yeah?"

"Why are you telling me all this?"

"Cuz I thought you'd fuckin' care. Okay? Didn't you promise Nancy Gerhardt you'd— "

"I've been suspended."

"What?! Is this a joke?"

After Susan finished recapping her Lydia story, Janie said: "There's something wrong with this story. It smells. Lydia's covering for something. You've got to go straight to Archie."

"I can't do that. I can't go over Lydia's head."

"She's standing on top of *yours,* Greenwich. And you're six feet under water. With sharks swimming all around you. You've stumbled onto something."

"What, Janie? What have I stumbled on? I can't go to Mr. Archibald with a conspiracy theory and no proof." The second line rang at that moment. "Hold on, Janie." Susan pressed the second line and, before she could even say hello, was greeted by: "Who *was* that man?"

"What are you talking about, Hugh? Have you any idea what time it is? Hold on a second." She pressed the first line: "Janie, I've got to call you in the morning. Sorry." Back to line two: "Where were we?"

"Is he some sort of blackmailer?" asked Hugh Carver. "Is that his game? What strange hold does he have over you and the children?"

"Are you drunk?"

"I am in mourning, Susan. A fine and wonderful woman has been chased away by your 'friend.' Banished from my life. I will never forgive him for this. Or you."

"What has happened?"

"Who is it?" whispered Michael

"Hugh."

"Who are you talking to?" demanded her husband. "I heard you talking to someone."

"You. I said Hugh. Then you interrupted me. Hugh." Susan held a finger up to her lips for a laughing Michael to be silent. "Now, what has occurred?"

"When we arrived home, Sigrid went straight into the bedroom and began packing her suitcase. Without a word of explanation. I begged her to speak. Pleaded on bended knee."

"You sweet old-fashioned thing. How did you manage to keep your balance?"

"Don't make fun of me, Susan. Not now. Sigrid's gone. I'm desolate."

"And what do you expect me to do, Hugh? Console you?"

"I want to know what that man knows about Sigrid."

" 'That man' has a name. Michael Roth."

"What did I do?" whispered Michael.

"Listen to me, Hugh. It's very late. You're better off without this Sigrid woman. Trust me on this one. She'd only have brought you grief in the long run. You'll meet someone else. You always do. Now, please go to sleep." Susan hung up the receiver, turned to Michael, and announced: "The man is a complete nut job."

"Annabel left him?"

"You must have put the fear of God in her."

"Your being an A.D.A. couldn't have helped either."

Then the telephone rang again.

"Should I tell him about Sigrid?" asked Susan. "No. I want to see his face when I do." She reached for the wall phone once more and asked: "What is it now, Hugh?"

But it wasn't her estranged husband.

"*Where* are you?" asked Susan in disbelief. "What? . . . Jeepers! . . . I don't know. It's awfully late. . . . My children are asleep. Besides, I don't really have an official position anymore. I'd like to help but . . ."

Michael stared curiously at Susan. Her words were those of consolation but the expression on her face was one of increasing delight. What was going on?

"All right. Try and stay calm. I'll be over there in fifteen minutes." Susan hung up the phone, then pirouetted across the kitchen floor and out into the hallway.

"Publishers Clearing House?" asked Michael in rapt fascination at this burst of energy so close to midnight.

He followed her out into the hallway and up the stairs to her bedroom, where Susan paused, spun around and, gazing deeply into his eyes, said: "Michael, I have to ask a great favor of you."

"I remain your obedient servant."

"Please, go back up to your room. In case the girls wake up looking for me, I don't want them to find you in my bed while I'm gone."

"Where are you going?"

"Twentieth Precinct. Just across the Park on Eighty-second Street. I won't be long. I've got to get someone out of jail."

"What? Who?"

"My boss."

"Lydia?"

"Mmm. Poor thing. Seems she went into a bar over on the West Side to drown her sorrows after her son refused to forgive her. Seems she got into a bit of trouble with a male patron and the bartender. I'm not sure which one she kicked in the private parts. Anyhow, a cop came in to the bar to break it up and she slugged the cop. Of course, she didn't dare give them her real name at the station house. Imagine the scandal! Deputy District Attorney Lydia Culberg arrested for assault scant hours after driving under the influence and smashing into a parked car. Ha! I know. I know. I sound like Bette Davis."

By this time Susan had slipped on a pair of black silk trousers, pulled a turtleneck sweater over her head, and was removing a blue Jean Pierre jacket from a hanger in her closet.

"Crime never sleeps," she pronounced as she headed for the bathroom to brush her hair and teeth.

"What are you going to do?" asked Michael as he stood mesmerized in the doorway of the bathroom watching the woman he adored prepare herself for battle.

"Get her out of jail, of course. The poor thing sounds positively terrified. Her entire career is in jeopardy, you know. Imagine if Ray Murphy ever picked up on this story. She'd be ruined. And I'm the only one who can save her . . . *for a price.*"

"EVER NOTICE IN a lot of those early Mitchum and Lancaster pictures they'd strip 'em down to the waist and whip 'em? Like in *Kiss the Blood off My Hands* or *His Kind of Woman*. Hell, they cuffed Mitchum to a steam pipe in that one before they beat him. Know why they did that? For the fags. They like stuff like that. Watchin' muscular guys get whipped and worked over. Sick, huh? Sure you don't wanna toot? I'll never forget the first time I went over to Italy and saw those Michelangelo sculptures. I said to myself I can be like that. I'm descended from these people. Sure as hell none of those old wops took steroids. Right? Sure you don't want any?"

Junior Tesla held a tiny silver spoon filled with cocaine out to Nip Regan.

"Can't," replied Nip, tapping the side of his nose. "Deviated septum. I gotta have surgery."

"No kiddin'. That's too bad. This is good blow. Primo. Probably wondering how I can go on and on about takin' care of my body and then take this stuff, right? Right? Well, Roselli . . . nobody's fuckin' perfect." Junior howled with laughter at what he had said and slammed his palm down on the top of the corner table he and the undercover cop were occupying inside the dimly lit bar in Little Italy.

"Wha' time is it?" asked Nip.

"Wassamatter? You got a wife waitin' for you?"

"No. I just don't like sitting around till one in the morning listening to you talk about old movies and yer gorgeous body. Know what I mean? We been to three bars in the last four hours. We haven't picked up any broads and we ain't talked about the penalty. All I've heard is how you wish you coulda fucked Gloria Grahame. The broad's been dead fifteen years. I wanna know what the deal is with the penalty. What kinda money are we talkin' about?"

"How can you fuck with a deviate whatsit?" replied Junior ignoring Nip's question completely. "Don't it hurt?"

"I don't fuck wit' my nose."

"Want another drink?" Junior signaled to the waiter to bring him another double scotch.

How the hell can he abuse himself like this, thought the undercover cop, and keep that body he's so goddamn proud of? Nip had stained the carpets of the previous three bars, spilling his drinks under the table every time Junior wasn't looking. And all the while the muscle-bound thug hadn't stopped snorting coke, doing bad impressions of Richard Widmark and Edward G. Robinson, and praising the benefits to the colon of wheat grass enemas. But not a word that would have been of any value to the District Attorney's Office. How the hell could he get the guy to open up and—?

"Now, c'mon. Quit jerkin' me around," said Junior for the umpteenth time. "Where the fuck do I know you from? I know you from somewhere. And don't gimme that Mr. Universe shit again."

"Y'ever in the merchant marine?"

"Get real!"

"Pro ball. Hmm? Didj'ever play pro ball?"

"Did you?"

"Nah. Didj'ever fuck a duck in a drawer?"

"Yer nuts, Roselli."

"*I* did! Great sex."

"I like my sex normal."

"Right! You wanna fuck dead movie stars and you call that normal? That's twisted. Weird. C'mon. Off the record. What's the weirdest thing you ever done?"

"You don' wanna know."

"I do. I love weird. Hey! I'm out wit' you, aren't I?"

"What the hell does that mean?"

"It means I like you for some sick reason. Means I can tell you things that I can't tell other—"

"I cut a dog's head off."

Nip's pulse began to race. Wasn't there a dog story Ms. Gee told him right from the beginning? A head in a pink cake box. "You mean a horse's head. You can do better than *The Godfather*, Junior. C'mon, tell me something weird you really did."

"I cut a fuckin' dog's head off. Okay? A sheepdog."

"Wha'd you use? A Black and Decker or a—?"

"You don' believe me?"

"You got this on videotape, Junior?"

"Don't call me Junior." The younger Tesla reached across the table and seized Nip by the collar. "I'm not anyone to fuck with."

"I like this shirt."

"You got iron balls, Roselli," said Junior, releasing his hold on the undercover cop. "I'll give you that. But don't ever push me too far. And don't ever cross me. There are guys out there who wished they'd never met me."

"Guys in heaven, too, I'll bet. Or maybe the other place."

"Maybe."

"So c'mon," grinned Nip. "Now that we're pals again. Tell me the truth. Didj'ever fuck a duck in a drawer?"

Junior threw his head back and howled: "You got iron balls, Roselli. But it's gonna drive me nuts till I figure out where I know you from."

53

ARRIVING AT THE Twentieth Precinct, Susan presented herself to the desk sergeant as Mamie Gallagher's lawyer and asked to see her client.

There was a distinct Susan Hayward seen-it-all-done-it-all aura about Lydia—face dirty, hair tangled, clothes disheveled, mink coat hanging limply from her shoulders—as the policewoman escorted the redhead into the interview room. Susan Given wondered if she wasn't back home in bed dreaming it all.

Lydia refused to make eye contact with Susan as she sat on her side of the table. When Susan finally spoke, her first question was: "Mamie?"

"It was my mother's name. That way it didn't seem so much like lying."

As if that ever bothered you before, thought Susan, surprised by the aura of vulnerability surrounding this trapped and exposed Lydia. Something that appealed to the compassionate side of Susan's nature. "The sucker in you," as Janie Moore would have put it. All Susan's bravado with Michael back in the apartment was ebbing away as she stared at Mamie Gallagher's wayward daughter.

"Are you gloating?" asked Lydia, still not looking up at the woman she thought of as her nemesis.

"No."

"Why not? I'll bet this makes your day, doesn't it? Seeing me stuck in here with all the scum of the city. My one fear as a kid was going to jail someday. Too many neighborhood dads had spent time there. And their kids always carried the mark of their fathers' shame. I'll bet you never thought about it once in Greenwich."

"Only when we played Monopoly."

"That's what I'm talking about. You're gloating."

"Not at all. I'm reminiscing. 'Go directly to jail. Do not pass Go. Do not collect two hundred dollars.' I was a ferocious Monopoly player."

"Remind me to call Barnes and Noble for a copy of your autobiography. Now, get me outta here, willya?"

"How do you propose I do that without revealing your true identity?"

"Call Haskell Abrams. He'll get me out of here in a flash."

"If it was that easy, why didn't you call him to begin with?"

"What are you, a moron? Don't you know anything about men? I broke the poor jerk's heart. I can't expect him to jump through hoops for me again that quickly."

Susan stared at Lydia in disbelief, then shook her head: "I actually felt sorry for you a moment ago. How, pray tell, did you just manage to switch from self-pity to arrogance without stopping off at contrition?"

"I do contrition with my priest. Okay?"

"Why didn't you send for him then?"

"Because I knew you'd come. For all of our petty differences and little tiffs, Susan, we're still on the same side."

"Petty differences? Little tiffs? Lucrezia Borgia never plotted against people the way you do against me."

"That's not true."

"You suspended me this evening, Lydia. Don't you remember? You were going to have my unit investigated."

"I was upset. My kid hurt my feelings. God! He's so much like his father."

"Don't change the subject. What about your charges against me of gross incompetence and mismanagement?"

"I'll drop them. I never planned to file them anyhow. I was drunk, Susan."

"And what about the Teslas?"

"What?"

"I've got a major forfeiture case and Janie Moore has a homicide. The Teslas—Senior and Junior—are smack in the middle of both of them. I want my hands untied."

"I can't do that."

"I'm out of here," said Susan rising abruptly.

"Wait, wait. It's not me. These orders come from higher up."

"The only person higher than you is Mr. Archibald. Are you telling me the District Attorney is protecting the Teslas?"

"Is that beyond the realm of possibility?"

"Yes. He's the one assigned me to the case originally. Who's pulling your strings, Lydia?"

"How dare you!"

"I dare! Okay? You got me here in the middle of the night to save your ass. I want to know what the deal is with the Teslas."

"I can't explain at the present time. It's bigger than the office. It involves— Oh, God! I could go to jail for this."

"You *are* in jail."

"Prison. Okay? Federal prison."

"I don't believe you."

"I have a special phone number at the White House." Lydia's voice had lowered to a whisper. "Call it."

"Do you have a publishing contract? You give great fiction."

"Look, I've gotta get out of here, Susan. I'm sure I got fleas from some old douche bag in that holding cell. I'll go crazy if I have to stay in there another— Okay. Okay, you've got a free hand with the Teslas. I won't come after you. I swear. Do what you want with them. What is it? What are you staring at me like that for?"

"Why should I trust you? How do I know ten minutes after you leave here, I won't be arrested on some trumped-up charge?"

"You've got my word."

"Ha!"

"What the hell does that mean?"

"I want it in writing."

"What?"

"I want a letter from you to me. Agreeing to all the things we discussed about the Teslas. And I want all threats against me to cease. Present and future. I want it all spelled out."

"No way! That's blackmail. What if *you* do something wrong? What if you commit a crime?"

"There's always compensation," said Susan. "One way or another."

"I don't get it," said Lydia. "You looking for a kickback? You want money from me?"

"Oh, Lydia. How did you ever get into a position of responsibility? I'm speaking of Emerson."

"Who?"

"Ralph Waldo Emerson. My dad was a great fan. When I was first offered a job in the D.A.'s office, I wasn't sure if I was up to it. Fighting crime. Going after the bad guys. Holding my own against high-priced lawyers. My dad read me a passage from an essay of Emerson's called 'Compensation.' Then he made me memorize it."

Susan paused for a moment to search her memory, then recited: " 'Commit a crime and the earth is made of glass. Commit a crime and it seems as if a coat of snow fell on the ground such as reveals in the woods the tracks of every partridge and fox and squirrel and mole. You cannot recall the spoken word; you cannot wipe out the foot track; you cannot draw up the ladder so as to leave no inlet or clue. Some damning circumstance always transpires.' . . . So? Do we have a deal?"

54

Becker, Gretchen, and Tina Gattuso, another A.D.A., sat in Susan's office waiting for their boss to get off the telephone. Finally Susan replaced the receiver, turned to her staff, and beamed. The news she had just received, coupled with the fact that she would be going into court the next day to finally obtain her divorce, made Susan Given a very happy woman, indeed.

"Judge McCintire has agreed we have sufficient cause to issue the search warrants against the carters."

Tina and Gretchen applauded; Becker stuck two fingers in his mouth and let loose an ear-piercing whistle.

"Now comes the drudgery," said Susan. "We need to determine the amount of proceeds—gross revenues—generated by the Gotham Waste Removal Association. In order to obtain these figures, the following documents should be seized by the police when the search warrants are executed. First: any and all tax returns for the indictment period. Second: any and all documents detailing the methods by which the carters calculate the fees that are charged to their customers for waste removal."

"Don't forget a list of customers, the number of stops, and the poundage of garbage collected," said Becker.

"That's next on my list, Alan. Just be patient. I'm going to get a sworn affidavit from Istvan Molnar and at least half a dozen more customers attesting to the inflated weights they are being charged for."

The telephone rang and Gretchen answered it: "Susan Given's office. . . . Just a second, please." Gretchen clapped a hand over the receiver and turned to Becker: "It's your mother."

"Tell her I can't talk to her now," said a red-faced Alan Becker.

"You tell her," said Gretchen.

"If I tell her, I'll be talking to her."

"I'm sorry, Mrs. Becker. He can't talk right now. He's in a—" Gretchen turned back to him once more. "She says it's urgent."

Becker turned beseechingly to Susan, who gestured for him to answer the phone.

"Hi, Mom. What's up?"

"You're too busy to talk to me now?" asked Rose Becker of Bensonhurst.

"Mom, I'm in a very important meeting," hissed her son. "What's wrong?"

"Uncle Label's sister had a heart attack. In Florida."

"Have I met his sister?"

"No. What does that matter?"

"Because I don't know why you're phoning me to tell me about a stranger's—"

"Thanksgiving is why I'm phoning you. I always go to Esther and Label's for Thanksgiving. But now they're going to Florida to be with the sister. What am I going to do?"

"Isn't there somewhere else you can go?"

"Where? You're not married. I don't have grandchildren to spend Thanksgiving with. Your father's been dead eight years. My sister Esther is the only—"

Becker clapped the phone to his chest and turned to Susan in embarrassment: "I'm sorry. My mother's flipping out. She has nowhere to go on Thanksgiving."

"Bring her to my place," said Susan matter-of-factly.

"Are you serious?"

"Absolutely. I always feed an army. She can talk to my mother."

"About what?" asked a mystified Becker, who couldn't

275

imagine a conversation between Rose of Bensonhurst and Marian of Greenwich.

"Just invite her and get off the phone."

Rose Becker couldn't understand why a stranger would invite her for Thanksgiving but her son was not prepared to go into any lengthy explanations. Once he hung up the phone, the meeting resumed.

"Where were we?" asked Susan.

"What the cops are looking for," said Tina Gattuso, a petite workaholic with a keen eye for detail. "You got up to the poundage—the overcharging."

"Thanks, Tina. We need any and all records detailing the fees paid by the carters' customers for waste removal. Ditto the documents detailing the fixed assets—property, waste plants, equipment—owned by the carters. Also any and all computerized hardware and software."

"What about safe deposit box keys?" asked Tina.

"Yes, absolutely. Would you add that to the list, please, Gretchen?"

"Got it."

"Great. Once we have all these documents, our next move will be a motion for an order of attachment, a preliminary injunction against the members of the Association, and the appointment of temporary receivers on notice with a temporary restraining order."

"What's the projected forfeiture amount?" asked Becker.

"About two hundred fifty million," replied Susan.

"Those garbagemen are going to let out one hell of an angry scream," said Tina.

"Yes"—Susan nodded—"but the city can finally let out a sigh of relief."

"And that's why they pay us the big bucks," said Becker ironically.

The telephone rang again and Gretchen answered it.

"If that's your mother . . ." teased Susan.

"It's for you," said Gretchen, staring at her boss. "Neil Stern."

276

"Tell him I'll call him back—No, no. I'll take it. . . . Neil, how *are* you? I'm glad you phoned. I can't decide on a dress for tomorrow. What *does* one wear to a divorce? . . . What? . . . Another continuance? But I thought—How can they keep doing this? They promised this time they wouldn't—Yes, yes . . . I will. I've got to get back to work, Neil."

Susan slammed the receiver down, then turned to her staff, who were all staring at imaginary stains on the office carpet. Anything but look their boss in the face.

"It's all right," said Susan. "Nothing we haven't dealt with before. I just don't understand a justice system that allows me to bring criminals to trial but won't let me have a divorce. I suppose the answer is to make marriage a crime." She took a deep breath, then: "Okay. Where were we?"

"WHY DON'T THEY go home?" hissed Polly Carver as she entered the kitchen. "They came for Thanksgiving lunch. It's ten o'clock now."

"They're having a good time," said Susan, standing on the countertop in her stocking feet, peering into the back of the kitchen cabinet.

"What are you doing, Mom?"

"We're out of coffee. I could have sworn I saw a tin of Medaglia d'Oro tucked away back here the other—"

"Good! Let them go home. I don't know who half these people are anyhow."

"You recognize your grandmother, don't you?"

"Very funny, Mom. But who's the tiny woman with the frizzy red hair she's talking to? She walked all over the apartment checking the bottoms of the porcelain and making faces."

"That's Becker's mother. Isn't she a hoot? What's she talking to Grandmother about?"

"Silver polish."

"Ahh! I knew they'd find common ground."

"Why did Becker bring his mother for Thanksgiving?"

"Because I invited them. Her sister's in Florida and he just broke up with Rusty."

"I thought he broke up with her months ago."

"That was a different Rusty."

"Becker went out with two different women named Rusty?" asked Polly in amazement. "That's bizarre."

"I believe it's a Biblical name."

"Like I don't think so, Mom. And who are those kids who keep spilling chocolate milk in the living room? The ones with the runny noses."

"Those are the Gerhardts," replied Susan, climbing down from the counter top. "And *where* exactly did they spill the chocolate milk?"

"In front of the fireplace. Who are the Gerhardts?"

"Their mother is the very pregnant woman—"

"The one who just went into labor?"

"You're joking!"

"Uh-huh," smiled Polly. "Just wanted to see if you were listening. Who is she?"

"Her husband was murdered a few months ago. Janie's been investigating—"

Right on cue, Janie Moore popped inside the kitchen with her hands on her hips and asked: "Do you have any idea where my husband is?"

"Kevin?"

"Do I have another husband? He's been missing for an hour. I thought maybe he'd run off with Marta, the Estonian bombshell Ned brought. Where does Ned find these women? This one has a 'carving' for chocolate. That's all she kept talking about. Her 'carving.' I thought she worked for Godiva. Turns out she means 'craving.' " Then as an afterthought, she added: "Your boyfriend's missing, too."

"Who?" asked Susan, turning red.

"Your boyfriend. You know? Michael."

"He's not my boyfriend," enunciated Susan, shaking her head and pointing a finger toward Polly, who was staring out the kitchen window dreamily. "He's just a friend."

Polly didn't seem to hear any of this, then asked abruptly: "Can I go over to Callie's?"

"No," said Susan, "it's after ten. And we have guests. Tell Uncle Henry I'm sorry but I'm out of coffee."

"I don't think he cares. He's watching the football game with that tall guy from Oklahoma."

"That's Tom Patterson. I thought they went home an hour ago."

"The wife left. But Nellie's still upstairs with Ivy and Stella."

"What are they doing?" asked Janie. "I was just up there and the bedroom door was locked."

"Devil worship," said Polly. "We all did it when we were ten."

Marta, Ned Jordan's Estonian bombshell, appeared in the kitchen, weaving back and forth unsteadily with her hair obscuring much of her face. She smiled vaguely, then asked: "Where is, please, the bathroom?"

"Polly, please show her."

"You are much kindness," replied Marta, shoving her hair off her face and taking Polly's hand. "And very pretty. Are you Mexican?"

Janie waited till Polly and Marta had left the kitchen, then asked: "Do you think there's a catalog he orders them from?"

"Who?"

"Ned! 'Date wanted: No hips, big breasts, no English.' There's definitely a pattern here."

"You and your patterns. And would you please not discuss Michael in front of the girls?"

"You think they don't know?"

"I don't want to give Hugh any ammo."

"For what? That sadist is never going to give you a divorce. Look at the stunt he pulled last week. He's just going to keep on—"

"Don't say that!"

"Don't say what?" asked Michael Roth, sauntering into the kitchen with Kevin Moore, both smiling like Cheshire cats in their overcoats with the chill of November still on their cheeks.

"Where have you two been?" asked Janie. "And what were the sluts' names who put those grins on your faces?"

"See what I mean, Michael?" asked Kevin, embracing his wife. "We sacrifice everything for them—our safety, our reputations—"

"You've been drinking," said Janie, shoving her husband away. "You left us here to go drinking?"

"We've been to the Waldorf," said Michael. "Drinking was our cover." And he withdrew a Nikon from under his cashmere overcoat. "But our purpose was scientific."

"What were you doing at the Waldorf?" asked Susan.

"Getting my darling wife her Christmas present," said Kevin. "What would you like more than anything, Janie?"

"Do you know what the hell they're talking about, Greenwich?"

"What would that poor woman in the living room like more than anything?" asked Kevin, pointing in Nancy Gerhardt's direction. "Look!"

Kevin removed a folded piece of Waldorf-Astoria stationery from his pocket and flattened it out on the counter. There were drawings of two clocks.

"We'll get the photos developed first thing in the morning," said Michael, "but Kevin drew these in the meantime."

"These new three-D imaging programs are so clever," said Kevin Moore. "They even create fake shadows. See?

Nine-fifteen. See where the shadows fall to the right of the nine and the three. Very, very subtle. Just like the real time. Here. Look." And the artist removed the photo of the Teslas and Cardinal Corcoran from his jacket. "We stopped off at home and picked it up. Just to make sure. See the shadows?"

Susan and Janie both nodded.

"Problem is," said Michael, "whoever doctored this photograph didn't take into account the real light source."

"I don't follow," said Janie.

"The shadows in the doctored photo are to the right of the nine and the three," said Kevin. "But the real light source in the ballroom is to the right of the clock, so the shadows should fall on the *left*." He pointed to his drawing of the clock face.

"So the clock on the wall is wrong?" asked Susan.

"Not just wrong," said Michael. "Intentionally altered to give Junior his alibi."

"I knew it," said Janie.

"And now you proved it," said her husband.

"I've got me a murderer. Thank you, Kev." She put her arms around her husband's neck and kissed him.

"And I can proceed with the forfeiture," said Susan, throwing her usual caution to the winds and kissing Michael.

NICK TESLA STORMED out of the Chrysler before Louie Torino had barely turned off the ignition. With The Patch and lawyer Alvin Gasmer hard on his heels, he moved like a man possessed toward the entrance of the Tesla Waste Disposal Company's headquarters.

Inside Tesla found Dino Marazzoni, the company manager, waiting nervously.

"What the hell happened, Dino?"

"They come in here wit' search warrants, Nick. I couldn't stop 'em. They took all the files, records, floppy discs, canceled checks, safety deposit keys, you name it."

"Jesus Christ!"

"You wanna drink?" asked Marazzoni.

"No, I don't want a fuckin' drink. It's ten o'clock in the morning. I wanna know what we're gonna do about this."

"Don't worry," said Alvin Gasmer soothingly.

"I'm worried, Gasmer. Okay? They been sniffin' around for months. Now they pounce. George Corcoran promised he'd put in a word for me. Must have been the wrong word. Where the hell's Junior?"

"On the phone," said Marazzoni, nodding toward an office at the back.

"Who the hell's he talkin' to? Fuckin' roof just caved in and he's probably lining up some pussy for tonight—"

"Take it easy, Nick," warned Torino. "Yer blood pressure."

"Don't worry 'bout me, Patch. I ain't got no fuckin' blood left. Goddamn D.A.'s sucked it all outta me. They took the key to my safety deposit box? These people are animals. I got private correspondence in there."

"Hey, Pop!" said an outraged Junior, emerging from the back office. "Can you believe this shit? I just spoke to the Carluccis. They got hit, too. Same with DeFillipo, Gerussi, and all the others."

"It's not as bad as you think," said Gasmer.

"Maybe not for you," said Tesla, wheeling around on his lawyer. "You and all the other bloodsuckers can retire on what we're gonna have to pay you to get us outta this mess. It's the goddamn Oklahomans! From the day they came to town, it's all turned to rat shit. And you—" Tesla turned around and confronted Junior. "What the hell did you think you were proving cutting that dog's head off?"

"It wasn't me!"

"Bullshit! Nobody else is nuts enough to do something like that. Mother of God! I had four customers phone me yesterday worried 'cause the D.A.'s office is leaning on them to testify against me. Against what? I'm servicing them. They never complained before. If they were unhappy, they could go to Carlucci or DeFillipo. They don't need to go to strangers. The D.A. doesn't get that. We're family."

"I met with Roselli's nephew," said Junior, hoping to give his father some good news. "They're gonna join the Association."

"If there's an Association left," replied his father bitterly. "Gasmer?"

"Yes, Nick."

"What happens next? Now that they got all the paperwork."

"They'll move to attach your property, freeze your assets—"

"The restaurant, too?"

"We'll fight that all the way, Nick. Relax. This will all take months to weave its way through the courts."

The telephone rang and Marazzoni answered it. Then he called out to Tesla: "Nick, it's for you."

"Who is it?"

"Cynthia Praeger."

"What the hell does she want?"

"She says she hasn't been paid for the work she did. Did we misplace her check by accident?"

"Tell her to phone her girlfriend Susan Given," replied Tesla. "She's got my checkbook."

NIP KNEW IT wasn't going to be a picnic the minute he and Gaetano Roselli entered Tesla's that first week in December.

Roselli had barely stepped inside the private dining room on the second floor when the rhinolike Phil DeFillipo stuck out his foot and sent the old man sprawling onto the carpet. Nip bent down to help his "uncle" to his feet but the feisty Roselli waved him away and struggled with great dignity to right himself.

"Well, we're off to a flyin' start," said Nip, angrily glaring into DeFillipo's eyes with undisguised hostility.

"He had it comin'," said DeFillipo without blinking. "Now, it's done."

"What if I wanna keep it goin'?" asked Nip, sticking his face into DeFillipo's. "How'd you like to try it with someone who don't fall down so easy?"

"I don't talk to no worms," sneered DeFillipo.

"Pretty picky for a guy what used to fuck goats. Which one of youse smelled worse?"

Lurching towards Nip, DeFillipo reached his prosciutto-sized hands out to strangle the undercover cop when Nicolo Tesla stepped between the two.

"Hey, hey," said Tesla. "We're here to straighten things out, not make 'em worse."

"Everything okay, Uncle Guy?" asked Nip, helping the elderly carter into a chair.

"Yeah, yeah," nodded Roselli with a wave of his hand. Nip hoped Roselli understood it wasn't just his health but the recording device strapped to the old man's body that he was referring to specifically.

"I'm okay, Dominic."

By this time DeFillipo, Carlucci, Gerussi, and the other members of the Gotham Waste Removal Association had taken their places at the banquet table that had been set up to accommodate them all.

"Okay," said Tesla, gazing at Nip and Roselli sitting alone at a small table, staring back at the members of the Association. "Let's call this meeting to order."

"Aren't you gonna introduce us?" asked Nip pointedly, hoping to get all the cartel members' names on tape.

"Hey, Roselli," said Joe Carlucci, "why don't you teach yer nephew some goddamn manners?"

"Who the hell are you?" asked Nip.

"Joe Carlucci. That okay wit' you, punk?"

"It's an honor, Mr. Carlucci." Nip smiled. "Just like to know who we're doin' business with. Y'know? What about Twinkletoes here who tripped my uncle?"

DeFillipo bristled and raised his huge hands again but Tesla calmed him down, then hastily introduced the other members of the Association. Then Nip asked: "So where's Junior?"

"Don't you know?" asked Tesla. "Isn't he out hoorin' and boozin' with you every night?"

"We give it a rest sometimes." The undercover cop grinned. In point of fact, Nip had purposely been avoiding the brutal bodybuilder the last few nights. He wouldn't be able to dump his drinks on the carpet forever without Junior catching on. Or sit up to the wee hours in

Junior's apartment watching him freeze-frame film noir goddesses like Jane Greer, Ida Lupino, and his beloved Gloria Grahame, then crawl drunkenly to the screen on his hands and knees to kiss their video images. That and the younger Tesla's cocaine-induced, buddy-buddy confessions were becoming all too alarming even for a veteran cop like Regan. He had been thrilled though two nights earlier when Junior all but admitted bashing Walter Gerhardt's brains in.

But when Junior switched his obsession from Gloria Grahame to Susan Given—rhapsodizing about her hair, her legs, her voice—it all became too surreal. Nip never thought of Ms. Gee that way and he sure as hell didn't want to hear about some psycho's perverted plans for her when he got her alone. Ms. Gee was in serious danger from this guy. Nip had to warn her. But the cop didn't dare make a move until they had an airtight case.

"Forget Junior," said Tesla contemptuously. "We're here this morning to welcome Osborne Paper as a new member to the Association."

"It's about time," muttered Carlucci, removing his thick bifocals and wiping them clean with a handkerchief.

"Tell me something," said Nip, "before my uncle and I accept your gracious invitation. What's the use of joining an organization that's goin' down the tubes?"

"What're you talkin' about?" asked Carlucci.

"I read the *Post*, the *News*. Didn't the cops raid all your headquarters last week? Seize all yer books?"

"That don't mean shit," said DeFillipo. "They're just lookin' for publicity. They got nothin' on us. We got good books. Nothin' to hide."

"Just askin'." Nip shrugged.

"No problem," said Tesla. "You don't ask, you don't learn. So, let's break out the champagne and welcome the new members. But before we do there are a few little items of bookkeeping we need to address. Like the four hundred twenty thousand dollars Osborne Paper Fiber owes the Association."

"For what?" demanded Roselli. The old man had already been prepped by the District Attorney's Office that this would happen and that the D.A.'s Office would advance the necessary moneys. The old man was merely playing his part well for the benefit of the tape recorder strapped to his body.

"For all the months you was stealin' from us," spat out DeFillipo.

"And the UCN account yer nephew stole from me last week," said Tesla. "It adds up, Gaetano."

"I didn't steal nothing," said Roselli. "Those are my customers. UCN didn't want to pay your new rates. We made them a cheaper offer."

"Didn't nobody tell this mook the rules?" asked Gerussi irritably. "Why are we wasting our time?"

"Shh, shh, Leo," said Tesla soothingly. "He's an old man. Those were our stops, Gaetano. *Capisce?* You're paying us back for the money we lost—with a little penalty. Unless you want to give them back to us."

Nip looked up from the tablecloth he was scribbling on and blurted: "Little penalty?! It's thirty times what we made."

"That's so you won't forget," said Carlucci. "We are the garbage business in New York City. Nobody's bigger than us."

"What about those Oklahomans?" asked Nip. "What the hell are they called? Campbell-McCafee?"

"They're scared shitless of us," snarled DeFillipo.

"Why?" asked Nip. "Cuz you cut a dog's head off?"

"What's he talkin' about?" asked Gerussi.

"Junior told me," said Nip.

"My son's got a big mouth," said Tesla quietly. "The Oklahomans are dead in this town. No one'll do business with them. People are loyal to us. Wait'll you see our new ads on television. The strong-arm days are over, Dominic. This is a multimillion-dollar business."

"So who killed our driver?" asked Nip, trying to push the conversation toward indictable information.

"What is this guy talking about?" demanded Carlucci. "What the hell are we wasting all this time for?"

"I just want to set the record straight," said Nip. "If we're gonna be in business together. Who killed Walter Gerhardt?"

"A Cuban," said Tesla without blinking. "Crazy guy used to work for us. Name of Sanchez. The feds had him under wraps. Till he flew the coop."

"That's not what Junior told me," countered Nip, praying, at the same time, he could push one of Tesla's buttons.

"What else did my son tell you?" demanded Tesla.

"Yeah," said Junior Tesla, standing in the doorway pounding the Club from his sports car into the palm of his hand. "What else did I tell you? Huh?"

MICHAEL HAD RETURNED to Los Angeles two days after Thanksgiving and Susan was miserable. She didn't realize how much a part of her day-to-day life Michael had become until he was gone. The girls missed him as well. Even Cordelia asked when he was coming back. The only person who didn't miss him was Hugh.

Susan threw herself into her work with a vengeance. The interminable case against Eduardo San Juan, aka The Matador (named thus because of his dazzling agility in avoiding all attempts to bring him to trial), had come back to haunt her again. Why had she ever offered to do Dick Rashley that "little favor" and take over his last case before he left the office? San Juan's dossier now filled two filing cabinets and the case was still continuing its snail-like progress toward a trial two years later.

Susan and Becker were sitting in her office that morning in December, staring in disbelief at the latest proposal from The Matador's lawyer.

"You know," said Susan, "if anyone had the audacity to suggest it, The Matador could probably solve the budget crisis in Washington and dig the country out of debt. He certainly could run the World Bank. But, because of his natural inclination to distrust anyone not born in Puerto Rico, he limits his great skills to the numbers racket. His policy banks around the city generate four hundred thousand dollars a week. Twenty million a year. Do you think we're in the wrong business? . . . Becker? . . . Becker?"

"I need to talk to you," said Becker, after a great silence.

"I thought that's what we were doing. Till you went into your trance," said Susan. "How do you want to respond to—?"

"Please, Susan. Not business.

"What else is there?"

"Love."

"Oh, no! Not another Rusty."

Becker shook his head. Then: "I don't know what to do about my mother."

"You're in love with your mother?"

"Please, Susan, don't kibbitz with me. I need your advice. You're responsible. I wouldn't have met her if it wasn't for you."

"Who?"

"Nancy."

"Nancy Gerhardt? You're in love with Nancy Gerhardt? How wonderful!"

"How horrible! My mother is not going to buy a daughter-in-law named Gerhardt."

"That's only her married name."

"She was Olafson before that. A widowed *shiksa* with

two kids and a third on the way! Am I completely and totally *meshugge?"*

"Are you?"

"Nooo! But that's what my mother will say."

"Honestly, Becker, in this day and age—"

"It isn't this day and age for my mother. Her calendar is permanently set to nineteen fifty-five. Maybe earlier. Nineteen thirty-five."

"Forget your mother! Tell me about you and Nancy. Have you seen her since Thanksgiving?"

"Once. But we talk on the phone all the time. We can't stop talking."

"How wonderful!"

"This isn't what I want you to say, Susan!"

"But it *is* wonderful. I'd never have dreamed of the two of you as a couple. But now that I think about it—"

Susan was interrupted by Janie Moore bursting into the office, followed by Tuck.

"We got a warrant," grinned Janie.

"Anyone special?" asked Susan.

"Junior."

"Have you got enough?"

"We know the picture from the Waldorf's a phony," said Janie. "We got the testimony from the homeless guy who heard the Ferrari. And now we've got Nip's latest tape from his date with Junior. I haven't heard it yet but Tuck did and he says Junior was boasting about the guy whose brains he bashed in with his Club."

"That ain't all that's on there, Ms. Gee," said Tuck, lowering his voice in confidence. "There's stuff about you."

"Me?"

Tuck nodded. "It ain't nice, Ms. Gee. We gotta lock that psycho up real fast. And Mr. Archibald better call Nip in even faster. I got a real bad feeling about this case. Real bad."

59

THE MEMBERS OF the Gotham Waste Removal Association turned to stare at Junior Tesla standing in the doorway of the private dining room hefting his Club like a Neanderthal hunting for dinner.

"Wassamatter?" asked Nip, keeping his eye glued on Junior as he advanced toward him with a fee-fi-fo-fum gait.

"You. You're the fuckin' matter."

"Hey! What's going on here, kid?" asked Nick Tesla. "We're talkin' business."

"I think you want to hear this, Pop. I think you'll be glad to hear this. Something about Dominic's been botherin' me. From the first night I met him."

"What are you talkin' about?" asked Nip, playing cool but praying his cover wasn't about to be blown.

"I thought I'd seen you before," said Junior, moving around the room like Perry Mason making his summation to the jury, "but I couldn't remember where. Then it came to me early this morning. In a dream. Down in TriBeCa. You was with Pete Palazzolo."

"Who?"

"At first I thought you were a couple o' fags, the way you were huggin' each other. Yer hair was different then. Red."

"Is this yer dream or what?" asked Nip.

"What the hell are these guys talkin' about, Nick?" demanded Joe Carlucci. "Who cares about their fuckin' dreams? We got a business to run here."

291

"I knew somethin' was fishy," said Junior, ignoring Carlucci. "I just guessed the wrong fish. Never dawned on me Pete was a cop till I heard him buzzing on Forty-second Street."

"Buzzing?" Nip made a face and laughed. "You better lay off the blow first thing in the morning."

"Stay with the program, Dominic. You know what I'm talkin' about. I started following Pete after that. Caught him breaking into Rosenthal's office—"

"That's enough!" snapped Nick Tesla.

"It's okay, Pop. I know what I'm doin'. Sorry about Pete. I know you had plans for him with Antonia. But I'm convinced now he *was* a cop. Just like this one here."

Junior's prowling about the room had brought him to a halt directly behind Nip. But instead of taking a seat, he grabbed the undercover cop's arms abruptly in a paralyzing grip and called out: "Somebody tear this guy's shirt off!" The veteran carters were stunned by the younger Tesla's melodramatic gesture. "Well, what the hell are you waiting for? The fuckin' cop's wearin' a wire!"

Sitting in the backseat of an unmarked police car, Susan Given gasped as she listened through headphones to the conversation across the street in Tesla's restaurant.

"Junior's going to search him," whispered Susan urgently, as if Tesla and the others might hear her.

"Relax, Greenwich," said Janie, sitting next to her. "Nip knows what he's doing."

"Does he, Tuck?" asked Susan, as she leaned forward and tapped the lean black man hunched intently behind the wheel of the car on the shoulder. "Where's the backup?"

"On their way, Ms. Gee."

"We've been here twenty minutes, Tuck. What are they doing? Taking the crosstown bus? What if Junior finds Nip's wire?"

"Nip ain't wearin' no wire, Ms. Gee."

"Then how are we managing to hear the conversation?"

"Cuz old Mr. Roselli's wearin' the wire."

"And what if they strip *him?*"

"Then we pray the backup gets here," said Tuck. "But I figure Junior's gonna look like such a fool nobody's gonna pay any more attention to him."

"Oh, no!" groaned Janie, staring into the rearview mirror. "How the hell did she find out?"

"Not Lydia?" asked Susan.

"Worse. Señorita Mercado. That goddamn Haskell's got a lot to answer for."

Susan turned around and saw the Channel 8 remote truck lumbering down Forty-sixth Street.

"Maybe she's doing a restaurant review," said Susan hopefully.

A few seconds later a miniskirted Lisa Mercado was tapping at the police car window and wiggling her fake red fingernails in Susan's direction.

"Hey, girlfriend! Long time."

Susan rolled down her window and gave the newscaster her most polite smile. "Lisa, how nice to see you!"

"Gonna make a big bust, huh?"

"Actually, we're just waiting for the restaurant to open for lunch. It's impossible to get a reservation—"

"C'mon, Susan. The skinny is you're finally going to bust Junior Tesla for the Gerhardt murder. Heyyy! This is our story, Susan. Remember? We met on this one. Nancy Gerhardt? My old morning show?"

"Really, Lisa, you have this entirely wrong—"

Three patrol cars pulled up at that moment and Lisa promptly abandoned Susan to make sure her cameraman captured their arrival on tape.

"You two have great chemistry," cracked Janie. "Maybe you could get a cable show together."

"Not funny," replied Susan, then with icy politeness: "Tuck, could you please get me Lieutenant Abrams on the phone?"

Tuck passed the phone back to Susan, who placed it to her ear and heard: "Abrams here."

"Lieutenant? Susan Given."

"Susan! I was just about to phone you."

He's such a liar, thought Susan. Then: "Where? Where were you going to phone me, Haskell?"

"Where are you now, Susan?"

"Trying to keep your girlfriend from screwing up an arrest."

"What girlfriend? Is this some sort of joke? I'm a happily married man, Ms. Given. I don't appreciate—"

"Where the hell is she going now?" asked Janie Moore, watching Lisa Mercado and her cameraman cross the street toward the restaurant.

"Tell him to let go," said Nip, staring into Nicolo Tesla's eyes and speaking with forced calm. "Me and my uncle have taken enough shit from you guys today. I don't need yer cokehead son leaving permanent blue marks on my biceps."

"Shut up!" snarled Junior.

"You talkin' to me, Junior? I can't hear so good with that stuff running out of yer nose. Hey, Mr. Tesla, you wanna call yer pit bull off? It's kind of embarrassing."

Nick Tesla's eyes darted back and forth between Junior and his "prisoner." Then over to Louie Torino, who nodded at his boss. Finally he said: "Okay, Roselli, if it ain't true, prove it."

"Whaddaya talkin' about?"

"Take off yer shirt."

"What for?"

"To prove my son's made a mistake."

"I'm not making a mistake, Pop!"

"And if he's made a mistake?" asked Nip. "Then what? What do I get? A goddamn apology? How 'bout a rebate?"

"The guy's stallin'," said Phil DeFillipo. "Frisk him."

"Who the hell asked you, you goat fucker?" said Nip. "We ain't finished with each other yet."

"Some reason you don't want to take yer shirt off?" asked Tesla.

"Yeah," nodded Nip, his eyes glued to the floor.

"I knew it!" crowed Junior. "He is a cop."

"I dye my hair."

"What!?"

"Your son was right about me bein' a redhead," said Nip. "Redheads weren't his type. Know what I mean? Said he preferred dark-haired guys. So I dyed it for him."

"He's full of shit!" exploded Junior.

"I don't know who this Palomino guy is," said Nip, continuing the outrageous riff he hoped would save his life. "The only two men makin' out on the street in Tri-BeCa were me and your son, Mr. Tesla. I love him and I don't care who knows. There! I said it, Nicky. And I feel so relieved. Why can't you say the same thing once and for all? Remember what Gloria Grahame said to Bogey? *In a Lonely Place?* 'I was born when you kissed me. I died when you left me. I lived a few weeks while you loved me'" Nip sighed and tore open his shirt, revealing a bare, pale-skinned, freckled torso with no trace of a hidden microphone.

Louie Torino did a quick search of Nip's inner and outer legs, then shook his head: "He's clean, Nick."

"See, Nicky?" asked Nip. "It's not so hard. All you had to do was tell your old man the truth. You didn't have to make up this whole bullshit story about me being a cop."

Junior Tesla's face was beet red and he looked as if he might explode with apoplexy.

"If there's no more business," said Tesla, unable to look his son or his associates in the face, "I think we should adjourn—"

"Wait a minute!" roared Junior. "Yer not gonna swallow this shit, are you?"

"Sounds like you were the one did the swallowing," chortled Joe Carlucci.

For a moment it appeared the younger Tesla might strangle Carlucci in front of the others. Then Junior shifted his gaze to Gaetano Roselli and, as if guided by divine inspiration, pointed a finger at the old man and whispered: "He's the one. He's wearin' the wire."

"I gotta go to the bathroom," murmured Roselli, as he struggled to his feet.

"You're not going anywhere," said Junior, shoving the frail septuagenarian back onto his chair. "Take off yer jacket."

"Okay, Junior," said Nip. "That's enough. Me and my uncle are leaving here now. And you should go back to seein' Dr. Rosenthal."

"How did you know about him?" asked Junior.

"Who?"

"Rosenthal. I never told you—"

"Sure you did."

"Bullshit!" Junior turned to The Patch and ordered: "Lock the doors, Louie. This guy's a cop for sure."

"Look, kid, haven't you caused enough—?"

"There's no way he'd know about Rosenthal, Pop, unless he was a cop. Strip the old man and you'll see."

Before Tesla could make a decision, the maître d' entered the room timidly and said: "I'm sorry to disturb you, Signor Tesla, but the police are downstairs. They want to see your son."

"Didn't I tell you?" asked Junior, pointing a finger at Nip and Roselli. "Cops!"

"Relax, relax," said Tesla. "It's probably about the parking. I go through this every week."

"There's three cop cars out front," said Leo Gerussi, peering out the window. "And a TV news truck."

"I knew it! I knew it!" shrieked Junior, pulling out an amber vial of cocaine from his pocket.

"Get rid of that shit!" roared Tesla, knocking the glass vial across the room. "Now, pull yerself together and come downstairs with me."

"No way! You're not givin' me over to the cops!"

"What the hell are you talkin' about?" hissed Tesla, steering his son over to a corner of the room. "Stop watchin' all those movies. You're my son. Relax. I been through this a million times, we all have. It's strictly routine."

"They're gonna arrest me, Pop!"

"So? I'll have you out on bail in an hour. That's what I pay that putz Gasmer for. Don't sweat it, kid."

Nicolo Tesla and his son descended the stairs to the bar area, where they discovered Susan Given, Janie Moore, and six uniformed policemen waiting for them.

"Ms. Given, how nice to see you again! You must have really liked the food to turn up this early. We aren't even open."

"I'm afraid this is business, Mr. Tesla."

"Should I phone my lawyer?"

"It's your son who needs a lawyer," said Janie, as she produced a warrant from her brief case. "Nicolo Tesla, Junior, you're under arrest for murder." Then she nodded toward the arresting officer, who stepped forward and proceeded to recite the younger Tesla his Miranda rights.

All the while Junior glared at Susan with undisguised hostility until he erupted with: "You did this! You set me up! You and Rosenthal were in on this together right from the beginning. It's fuckin' entrapment. The whole thing was a setup. I should have taken care of you long ago."

"Shut up!" warned Tesla. "Don't say another word."

"I'd suggest you cooperate with us," said Susan, meeting Junior's wild-eyed gaze. "There are more officers outside who—"

"Fuck you, Ms. D.A.!"

Then Junior abruptly grabbed an antique side table and shoved it toward the cops. They in turn pulled their guns from their holsters as Junior swung around and bolted in the direction of the kitchen. Just then Lisa Mercado and her cameraman came through the swinging doors, where they had been hiding in silence, waiting for an appropriate moment to make a dramatic appearance.

"This is an exclusive, New York," whispered Lisa breathlessly into her microphone. "Nicolo Tesla Junior is about to be—"

Junior crooked his powerful arm under Lisa's neck and cut off the oxygen in her windpipe. Then he dragged the blue-faced newswoman backward towards the kitchen, warning: "Anyone makes a move, she's dead."

THE SNOW WAS falling lightly outside the bar on Mercer Street, where Susan sat by a window with Ray Murphy. She was shaking her head vigorously.

"Why would I lie to you, Ray?"

"Wouldn't be the first time, Suzy."

"I have never lied to you. I have withheld information from you, which is totally different, but—"

"I need a scoop for Christmas," pleaded the veteran reporter as he chain-smoked another cigarette.

"And I need a new pair of ski boots. Maybe we should both write to Santa. There's still a week left."

"Christ on a crutch! You trying to tell me the police have no idea what happened to Junior Tesla?"

"You know exactly as much as I do, Ray. He dragged poor Lisa out into the garden, then disappeared through the little door in the wall."

"Poor Lisa!" Murphy laughed. "The Puerto Rican bombshell was unconscious through the whole thing. Missed her own exclusive."

"She had no business being there. The woman's lucky to be alive. I can't believe she's back on the air already."

"How's your boyfriend?" asked Murphy abruptly, lighting another cigarette.

"Who?"

"The writer from L.A."

"He's in L.A."

"You guys have a fight?"

"He lives in L.A. He was just visiting." Susan looked at her watch. It was almost seven. She rose from the table. "I really have to get home, Ray. I'm sorry I haven't been any help."

"One last question, Suzy."

"Go ahead."

"What happened to Manny Sanchez?"

"No comment."

"C'mon, Suzy. Did the feds ever recapture him?"

"I never knew he'd escaped. Correction: I never knew they had him. Merry Christmas, Ray."

Susan left Ray Murphy coughing his lungs up in the bar and walked east along Prince to Broadway, then across to Lafayette. She caught the packed number 6 subway uptown at Astor Place.

Memories of that bizarre morning two weeks earlier flashed through Susan's mind as the train rattled north. The look of horror on Janie's face. The cops, desperate to do something but not daring to make a move. Nick Tesla shouting at his son to give up while there was still time. Poor Lisa turning blue, losing consciousness, then disappearing through the secret wooden door in the wall at the bottom of the garden.

Nip and Gaetano Roselli had managed to slip away in the ensuing confusion. The secret recordings that the undercover cop delivered to the Lefkowitz Building the next day would give Archibald's office a solid case against the cartel. Susan felt good about that even though it wouldn't bring Walt Gerhardt back to life or rouse Tony Fusco from his coma. But she had followed the path of crime through the snow and trapped it in its lair.

Entering the apartment at 7:30, Susan instinctively

called out to the girls. Then she remembered it was their night at Hugh's. She was alone. Normally, Susan would have welcomed an evening like this. Soak in a hot bath, catch up with her reading. Go to sleep early. But tonight she didn't want to be alone. Why? Because the snow was falling outside? Because it was the day after Michael's birthday and they had been forced to spend it a continent apart?

Susan walked into the library and saw the red light flashing on the answering machine. Four messages. Maybe someone was inviting her to dinner. She pressed the Play button.

"Hello, dear. It's Mother. How are you? Just wondering if you and the girls want to come out to Greenwich this weekend. Oh, wait! I won't be here. I'm going to visit Linda in Chattanooga. What *can* I be thinking of? 'Bye." . . . *Beep.* "Hi, Sis! It's Linda. How y'all doing there? Mom's coming down for the weekend and the only reason I didn't invite you and the girls was because there was no room with the twins coming home from college as well. But Randy just phoned to say he was going to visit his girlfriend's family and Brandy is going skiing so if you and the girls— Oh, Jesus, Phil! The dog just ate the other remote. I'll call you later, Sue." . . . *Beep.* "Susan? This is Bill Archibald. I thought you'd like to know that Tony Fusco just spoke. One brief Anglo-Saxon expletive. But a word nonetheless. Isn't that wonderful? I'll see you at the office tomorrow." . . . *Beep.* "Hi. It's Michael. You're obviously not home yet. Oh, dear. I've recovered from my Not-Being-With-You-On-My-Bithday Blues and am looking forward to spending Christmas with you. I am looking forward to doing other things with you as well. But I'm not going to get into that now in case Ivy plays back these messages. I love you. Am I allowed to say that on your machine?" *Beep.*

Yes, you are, smiled Susan, as she reached for the phone to dial Michael's number in California. But instead of the dial tone she heard a familiar voice say:

"Hello."

"Polly? My firstborn. What a delightful surprise!"

"How come the phone didn't ring?"

"Probably because I was just about to dial—"

"Don't tell me. You were calling Michael. Why doesn't he just move here? It's got to be cheaper than your phone bills."

"You have a great sense of humor, Polly."

"Yeah, sure."

"I'm serious. Do you remember last year when I went out with that eighty-year-old man?"

"Vincent De Mumbles?"

"DeMunzel. He was very nice. He had a famous porcelain collection."

"Yeah, Mom. But he was eighty years old."

"I remember. And I remember what you said after you met him. You said you wanted me to get a life—not an *afterlife!*"

"What are you doing tonight, Mom?"

"Not much. I wish you guys were here."

"Sure, sure . . . Uh-oh. Dad's having a hissy fit. See you tomorrow."

"I love you, Polly."

"Love you, too."

Susan felt a great loneliness when she hung up the phone. She dialed Michael immediately but all she got was his answering machine. She thought of phoning Henry, then remembered he and the family were watching Donald play hockey that night. She switched on the TV, then switched it off immediately. She picked up a book from the shelf but couldn't focus on the words. What was wrong? Why was she feeling this way?

The telephone rang again. She prayed it was Michael. He could snap her out of this.

"Susan?"

"Yes?" The woman's voice sounded vaguely familiar but . . . strange.

"It's Ruth Rosenthal."

"Ruth! How are you? It's been ages."

"I've just heard from Abner."

"You're joking! Where is he? What happened to him?"

"I can't talk on the phone. Could you, please, come over? Have you eaten?"

"No. I'm starved. Would you like me to pick up some Chinese take-out?"

"No, no. I have lots of food. Please, come now."

"Oh, Ruth! You have no idea how timely your phone call is. You've rescued me from the doldrums. I've been walking around this apartment like—"

But Ruth had hung up and all Susan could hear was the dial tone.

The night had turned bitterly cold as Susan emerged from her building. The doorman had hailed a cab for her and she gave the driver the Rosenthals' address on Sutton Place. Actually, Sutton Square.

Hugh had always envied Abner and Ruth's townhouse at the end of the square off York Avenue with its private garden hanging over the East River. Susan never ceased to be amazed how her husband could sit entranced in the Rosenthal living room for hours, staring out at the boats on the river and the lights of the Brooklyn shore. Hugh would interrupt his own self-imposed silence with the occasional murmured phrase: "Promise me, Ab, I'll have first refusal when you sell. Promise me."

The vest pocket park at the end of the square was empty as Susan emerged from her taxi. Too cold for the dog walkers and lovers who normally sat on the benches overlooking the river.

Susan was about to ring the front doorbell when she noticed the door was slightly ajar. She stepped inside the vestibule and called out Ruth's name. Music was drifting down from the living room and Susan assumed her hostess was in the kitchen whipping up one of her legendary gourmet meals. But there were no exotic aromas wafting out to greet her. Just the music piping through the sound system. Ab was a jazz buff and the song was "This Time the Dream's on Me" from one of Tony Perkins's rare fifties albums. Did this mean the missing shrink was finally home? Was this why Ruth had acted so mysterious on the phone?

Susan climbed the stairs leading to the living room. Halfway up she spotted her hostess's heavyset legs crossed on the edge of the sofa. Reaching the top step, Susan discovered Ruth fast asleep.

Poor thing, thought Susan, as she stepped gingerly toward the sleeping woman on the sofa. These last few months can't have been easy for her. Susan reached a hand out to shake Rosenthal's wife gently into consciousness.

But instead of opening her eyes, Ruth Rosenthal tumbled off the sofa onto the floor. Susan gasped.

She was about to bend down and examine the woman's body when the front door slammed shut.

"Honey, I'm hooome!"

Who was that? It wasn't Ab's voice. Susan spun around in fright to see who else was there. There was no one. Just Tony Perkins singing.

"Didja miss me, honey?"

Susan could now hear footsteps coming up the stairs. The song continued to come through the speakers.

"Thank you ever so much for coming, Susan," said Junior Tesla, attempting what he thought was an upperclass accent as he stepped into the living room with a mischievous grin on his face.

"Is she dead?" asked Susan, nodding toward Ruth's body.

"Probably."

"Why? Why did you kill her?"

"I didn't kill her, Susan," said Junior, stepping menacingly toward the blond prosecutor all the while. "You did."

"What are you talking about?" Susan edged away from the grinning, musclebound killer.

"You and Ruth. You killed her husband. Just like in

303

that Sharon Stone movie. But Ruth's conscience bothered her. So she wrote out a confession. It's over there on the desk. You found out and you killed her."

Susan picked up the letter from the antique writing desk and read the demented, illogical confession Junior had obviously forced Ruth to write.

"I don't understand. . . ."

"Wassamatter? Don't you speak English?"

"Why did you do all this?"

"I had to get to you somehow, Susan. The cops were watching my apartment, the restaurant, my parents' place. It drove me nuts for a week. How could I get you alone without anyone following you? Then I remembered Dr. Rosenthal. Your old pal."

"Did you kill Ab, too?"

"No way," replied Junior indignantly. "He just asked too many questions and, when I freaked out, he vanished. I must have scared the shit out of him. Do I scare you, Susan?"

"No," she lied.

"Good. Cuz I think we can have some fun together before I have to . . . Ruth wasn't much fun. She had no flair for drama. I thought she was very stiff on the phone with you. She's even stiffer now. Take a look at her, willya? A hundred eighty pounds of boiled pasta. No wonder the doc took a powder so easily. I probably did him a favor. . . . Take your dress off, Susan."

"I beg your pardon?"

"Wassamatter, doll? You work out regular. You got a nice bod. Show it off."

"Listen to me, Nick. It's not too late for you to give yourself up. The District Attorney's Office can make a deal. It doesn't have to be the death penalty."

"I don't need to make a deal with you, Susan. I'm the one holdin' all the cards. Nobody knows where you are. Nobody's gonna rescue you. Now, take your clothes off before I hurt you."

Susan's eyes darted about the room, praying a little

wooden door would materialize for her as it had done for Junior in the garden of the restaurant.

Then a loud knocking was heard at the front door.

Susan cried out for help. Junior lunged at her and brought her down on the carpet next to the fireplace. He clapped a powerful hand over her mouth. She sank her teeth into his hand until she drew blood. He howled in pain. Struggling to get loose from under his muscular weight, Susan's hand reached out and touched the fire irons.

Clutching the poker in her hand, she whipped her arm back and delivered a solid blow to his head. Junior moaned in pain and Susan managed to wriggle loose from under him, leaving her shoes behind.

She scrambled to her feet and started toward the steps when Junior shot out his right hand and grabbed her ankle. Susan was still holding the poker and was about to bring it down on him once more when he twisted her foot in his viselike grip and brought her crashing down on the carpet once more.

The knocking continued at the front door. Now pounding. Then a voice crying out: "Susan! Susan!"

"Who the hell is that?" whispered Junior hoarsely.

"I don't know!" Then Susan called out: "Help! I'm in here!"

"Dumb!" rasped Junior, pounding her thigh with his fist. "Come on!"

He leaped pumalike to his feet and wrenched her up beside him a beat later.

"Where are we going?" asked Susan, in unbelievable pain from the blow to her leg.

"Just get moving!"

Junior shoved her toward the double-glazed French doors leading out to the garden. He whipped the door open and nodded for her to go outside into the winter cold.

"Let's go!"

"I want my shoes," said Susan.

"You won't need them."

"It's freezing out there."

"Get going, Susan, or—"

"What? You're going to kill me anyhow."

A boat on the river sounded its fog horn. Susan thought about Polly and Ivy. If she really was going to die, Hugh would end up with full custody. She couldn't do that to the girls.

"I'm not going to let you kill me," said Susan resolutely.

"You got no choice. You ruined my life and my whole family. You gotta pay. Yer gonna fall over the railing and have a very nasty accident."

"And that's going to solve your problems? Ha! You must really be stupid."

"Don't call me stupid," warned Junior.

"Why? You'll kill me twice? You must really be stupid to stand around with blood pouring down your head."

Junior paused to think about this, touched his scalp, and felt the wound Susan had inflicted. Then he stared at the blood on his palm in disbelief.

In the split second Junior took to look at his hand, Susan shoved him backward into the garden, slammed the French door shut, and locked it.

Then she dashed toward the steps leading to the front door even as she heard Junior's cry of anger and the sound of glass shattering. A beat later Susan could hear Junior reentering the living room in search of her.

Susan was at the front door now, fumbling with the double locks and dead bolts.

"Fuckin' bitch!" roared Junior.

Then he was flying down the stairs toward her. His hands were on her throat ready to choke the life out of her.

He had been waiting outside the building on Eightieth Street praying for her to appear. When she finally did, she had jumped into a cab before he could even speak to her. Then he grabbed a cab and followed her east past Park, Lex, and finally over to York and Fifty-ninth.

Her cab pulled into the square but he got off at the corner and followed her on foot.

So, he thought, this is where Michael lives.

He paced up and down in the freezing cold deciding what he would do, what he would say. Give her the chance to choose or just kill him.

He knocked fiercely at the front door. She cried out from inside. He called out to her. No response. He knocked at the door, then pounded it with his fists. He called out: "Susan! Susan!"

He walked down to the tiny park adjacent to the house. There was a high, spiked wrought-iron fence atop the cement wall separating the park from the private patio.

No sweat, he thought, as he climbed up the fence. His fingers were already numb from the cold but the promise of seeing her again drove him on. He cut his left hand on the spikes but managed to get over the fence and crash to the floor of the patio.

The French door was wide open and there was broken glass on the floor as he stepped inside the living room.

"Susan! Susan, where are you?"

He heard a muffled cry from the bottom of the stairs.

He leaned over the railing and saw a couple embracing in the shadows.

"I told you I'd come back, Susan, and I'd kill your boyfriend."

A voice in the shadows called out to him: "Sanchez? What the hell are you doing here?"

Manny Sanchez was taken aback. He knew that voice.

"Who the hell are you?" asked Sanchez.

"I'm your boss, you fuckin' wetback. Who the hell do you think I am? Now, get outta here!"

"Where is Susan?"

"I'm here, Manny!"

Junior clapped a hand over her mouth and hissed at her to shut up.

"I want to see you, Susan. I come a long way to see you. Wha' you doin' with Junior?"

Then Junior dragged Susan back up the stairs with him into the living room. Sanchez stared at the blood streaming down Junior's face as he clasped his hand over a struggling Susan's mouth.

"Why ain't you got your shoes on?" asked Sanchez, staring at Susan's bare feet.

"Listen, you fuckin' moron," said Junior. "I don't know what yer doin' back here but I want you gone. Every cop in the city must be lookin' for you."

Sanchez ignored Junior and stared at Susan in confusion. "Where is Michael?"

"Who the hell is Michael?" asked Junior.

Susan's eyes darted back and forth between the muscle-bound maniac whose fingers were leaving permanent dents in both her arm and her face and the long, lean Cuban shivering so pathetically and staring at her so slavishly. How many gamblers had she arrested in her career? Now she was about to take the biggest gamble of her life.

Susan opened her mouth and sank her teeth ferociously into Junior's hand. He cried out in pain and released his grasp.

"There is no Michael," blurted Susan. "There never was, Manny. It was Junior. It's always been Junior."

"What the hell are you talking about?" asked the younger Tesla, massaging his wounded hand. "Yer as nuts as he is."

"Junior knew how I felt about you, Manny. He laughed at you."

"Din I warn you, Junior?" shrieked Sanchez. "That night in the parking lot when you killed that poor guy."

"Who did he kill?" asked Susan. "Was it Walt Gerhardt?"

"Shut up, Sanchez!"

"I warned you then. Touch one of my women and I kill you." Sanchez abruptly pulled a gun out of his pocket.

"Manny, don't! Let me call the police and—"

"No, Susan! You ain't gonna trick me again."

"You're a material witness to a murder, Manny. You can send this man to—"

Junior slapped Susan across the face and sent her reeling against the wall.

"Now, put the fuckin' gun down, Sanchez!"

Junior advanced on the Cuban, who, to the younger Tesla's amazement, actually shot him.

"You need glasses," grunted Junior with subdued rage when he saw the blood pouring out of his right side. Clasping his left hand to his wound, Junior grabbed a stunned Sanchez's throat with his right hand and began choking him as he drove him backward toward the patio. The Cuban struck at the younger Tesla's hand with his gun until he lost consciousness and finally let the weapon fall to the carpet.

Then Junior dragged Sanchez's body out onto the patio. He stood at the railing and lifted the unconscious Cuban up over his head and was about to hurl him down onto FDR Drive.

"Put him down, Tesla!"

Junior turned around and saw Susan standing in the doorway holding Sanchez's gun.

"You haven't got your shoes on," laughed Junior.

"Put him down."

"You want him?" asked Junior. "Catch."

The younger Tesla hurled Sanchez's body at Susan at the same moment that she fired the gun. She went flying backward into the living room as Junior was propelled backward over the railing.

Just before Susan Given lost consciousness, she heard the distant sound of car horns blaring and brakes squealing to a halt below on Franklin Delano Roosevelt Drive where Nicolo Tesla Junior's lifeless body—a bullet through his left eye—had landed in the midst of traffic.